INITIATE

INITIATE

A GILDED WINGS NOVEL: BOOK THREE

AIMEE AGRESTI

SHALLOW BROOK PRESS

ISBN (Paperback edition) 978-0-692-05220-4
ISBN (E-book) 978-0-692-05221-1

Library of Congress Control Number: 2018902306

Printed in USA
First printing

Published by Shallow Brook Press
Washington, DC

Cover design by FionaJaydeMedia.com
Cover photograph by Bradley Meinz
Interior design by TheDeliberatePage.com

For Brian, Sawyer and Hardy

"Face this world. Learn its ways, watch it, be careful of too hasty guesses at its meaning. In the end you will find clues to it all."

The Time Machine by H.G. Wells

"The night was starless and very dark. Without any doubt, in the gloom, some mighty angel was standing, with outstretched wings, waiting for the soul."

Les Misérables by Victor Hugo

1

I Can't Believe
He Would Risk It

Lance. The sound of his name made me ache, my fury rising only to be just as swiftly snuffed out by the chokehold of failure. My failure. The others were talking now. Hypothesizing, planning, shouting to be heard over that angry howling wind and the relentless rush of rain pelting us with heavy drops. We all wore battle scars from the night's work, our tattered, soaked clothes adhering to our battered and bruised bodies; scrapes and slashes etched wildly across the canvas of our skin; burns branded upon us from our respective tangles with the denizens of the underworld. But at least we were here. We had made it.

Lance. I paid no attention to them all. I couldn't bear to listen. I felt Lucian's eyes on me. Water coursed around me, the downpour a static drowning out everything, everyone. I didn't even realize I was still kneeling on the pavement of New Orleans' Royal Street, my knees red and raw, until Lucian, still silent, reached for my hand, pulling me up. It didn't occur to me to look at him.

Lance. What were they doing to him right now? What were they doing to him, to the boy I loved who was captured to spite me?

"Here, see?" Dante shoved his glowing phone in my face, that mysterious cell phone that matched the ones Lance and I had and had dictated such cryptic riddles to us all. I didn't look, I gazed through it to the glowing embers just yards away: all that remained after the Prince seized Lance, imprisoning him in a ring of fire and vanishing with him. I could only imagine they had rematerialized in the underworld and that pain and suffering awaited him. A shudder swept over me, chilling me.

"I can't believe he would risk it," Lucian muttered in a pained voice, eyes fixed in that same glowing space the Prince had occupied.

I had done this. I had let Lance down. I had let this happen. He was gone because of me. I may never see him again. I kept turning it all over in my mind to let the sharp blade of under-standing wedge firmly in my heart, let the sting sharpen. This was a punishment for my complacency. For taking too long to appreciate what I had and for taking too much for granted. It's so rare to find people who understand you, who are going through what you're going through, who can let you make mis-takes and still love you. You need to hang on to them, tightly. Fiercely. We weren't like other people, Lance and I. Even before learning we were angels, we just weren't like other people. We were like each other, though. And we were better together than apart. I would get him back. I would find him. Now. There must be some way.

The anger trickled into my bloodstream, jolting me back to life, replacing the numbing shock with vitriol. A spark lit, and I took off without warning on swift, sure legs. My arm slipped from Lucian's grip as he tried to hold me back. Instead I darted into the LaLaurie mansion where the party that had beat on through both natural disaster and devil warfare still pulsed, the masked Mardi Gras revelers managing to perse-vere—relocating to the lower floors of the building now that a shattered skylight had left the top floor ballroom exposed to the elements of the hurricane swirling outside. The crowd as a whole seemed to have digested this violence, accepted it and decided to make the best of it all. They bobbed their heads to the music, sipping their drinks, yelling in each other's ears to be heard, and smiling in that slow, late-night way of people with few cares and many hours to fill in pleasurable ways. So long as they had electricity and refreshments, there was no need to change their plans.

I pushed through them all with more force than was necessary, knocking a glass from a hand here and there, causing a high-heeled guest or two to lean against the imposing banister and to stumble as I charged up the staircase to that familiar fleur-de-lis tapestry: the portal. Lucian had used this regularly since our arrival in New Orleans months earlier, a bridge from the dark side he longed to escape. Lance and I had found our way back from the underworld through this very passage not too long ago, during our night of horrors shadowing the Krewe, the devil enclave here. That night, we had ventured too far while studying their ways in an effort to learn how to defeat them. We had landed in the underworld and had been lucky to make it out alive. Tonight, though, we had come so close to passing the second of our three tests toward angelhood, so close to those wings we worked so hard to earn. Our small, strong cadre of angels-in-training—my childhood best friend Dante, his new love Max, sweet Drew, southern belle Emma and the unlikeliest of paramours, resident goth River and all-American jock Tom—had managed to make it through the evening's battle against those deadly creatures. It had been only in those final seconds that we had lost one of our own.

Reaching the mansion's second floor, I swept the tapestry aside, nearly shearing it from its anchors, prepared to hurl myself into that abyss, down, down to unknown terrors and to

Lance. But I stopped short. There was nowhere to leap. I patted at the wall, my hands not recognizing the smooth, hard surface that greeted them. Solid. It shouldn't have been a surprise: as I had been told so many times before, at midnight on this Metamorphosi Day, the demons were to return below with their new recruits and seal their various entry points behind them. But my wounded heart didn't want to accept it. It couldn't. I had to try.

"Haven!" Lucian called from the foyer, a defeated strain fraying his usually silky tone. The image of Lance being taken flared again in my mind, setting my blood on fire, desperation rising. I needed him *now*.

Once more my body sped off before my mind could fully reason with it, knocking past the same masked figures I had jostled on the way up. I blew past Lucian and Dante, clipping their shoulders and whipping past the whole group as I threw myself back out into the storm. Running against the deluge toward my only other hope, the only other portals we knew: the tombs of Saint Louis Number 1, the cemetery where Lance and I had spied the devils' dark rituals and even stolen away into a smooth marble crypt leading to the underworld below. Behind me, many footsteps, a small herd of them, splashed through ankle-deep water, dodging the airborne debris torn from the Mardi Gras floats now many streets away. The group pushed onward following me, shouting for me to stop, but I just tuned them out.

I sped up as I neared the gates, gathering momentum and launching myself up and over the wrought-iron barrier with the easy effort usually reserved for leaping over a puddle on a street corner. Something had happened tonight. The power available to me in every muscle and every cell had been cranked up to a new level, every movement felt like a match striking dry kindling.

I raced back to that crypt Lance had helped build, remembering how I had watched from afar as his firm shoulders and the rippled muscles of his back had hoisted slabs of marble like they were cardboard. As I ran, the saturated dirt and gravel swallowing my feet with each step, the memories piled up like snapshots scattered on the desktop of my mind: Lance chasing me into the mansion that night a while back when the devils' toxins had taken hold of me; his strong arms sweeping up my lifeless body after the levitation ritual had purged the poison from my soul; our walk in the garden when we set everything right again; that kiss as the parade had begun so many hours ago, when we had allowed ourselves a moment—one single moment—to revel in the thrill of being at the center of such excitement and life. And then finally, our first kiss, back at the Lexington Hotel, its opening night shrouded in so much mystery, and us fumbling so blissfully in the dark, tumbling into this new love.

Cutting through to the back of the cemetery, I veered off, taking sharp turns into dark alleys toward those other familiar tombs. I stopped to ram my shoulder against any of the openings from which I had once seen devils creeping out into the night. But nothing would budge. Finally I reached it, what was left of Lance's crypt. The police had torn it up days earlier acting on an anonymous tip—called in by our group, of course—reporting that the spot had factored in a recent crime spree in the city. They had found nothing, least of all an entry to the underworld, but the structure had been chiseled into pieces, which now lay in this muddy pit. The rain began to let up, no longer cascading in sheets. I waded through the muck, my combat boots sinking until I was in up to my shins. Ribbons of yellow crime scene tape shredded by the wind and stuck in the ground reflected up like eels in the deep sea. I scooped up a handful of mud and another and another; it poured through my fingers, dripping down my arms. There was nothing left here, though, nowhere else to look. This portal, too, was closed to us. The full weight of this loss settled onto my body, squeezing the air from my lungs. I couldn't breathe, move, think.

The others gathered around me, heads hung as though at a funeral, stealing quick pitying glances at me. Except for Lucian. Stepping into my line of vision, he fixed his deep, remorseful gray eyes on me. He took me gently by the wrist but I reflexively shook him off with a sharp swipe. He stepped back without a word. Beside me Dante draped his arms around my shoulders. The rain lessened to a light spitting drizzle, the storm quieting at last. "Listen," Dante whispered, in a firm tone he rarely used with me. "Enough now. We will get to him, but not like this."

With that he led us back to the house. The others fanned around us in a horseshoe as we walked, forming a silent, protective barrier between me and the world.

We returned home to our Royal Street sanctuary, the LaLaurie mansion next door now plunged into darkness, to find our windows blown out, our floors soaked, and our belongings scattered and studded with glass shards. And then the reminder of another loss: Connor's empty room. Our guide through this second stage in our quest for wings, he had led us through physical trials and prepared us for the psychological battle against these vicious demons. But, after taking us as far as he could, he had been forced to leave just before battle to let us fight on our own. Without Lance here, I felt Connor's absence even more, registering it like another stake to the heart, another lump in my throat. I could have used his comfort now. I needed someone, some kind of authority figure, to tell me it would be OK. Because it didn't feel that way.

We filed into the living room, trying the lights but finding all power out. We didn't need much light to see that the once-bold décor—the riot of Mardi Gras-themed gold, purple and emerald shades and sleek-lined furniture—had dulled and worn in these short, violent hours. The mammoth mask, the room's focal point encompassing one wall, had been knocked from its perch and lay face down, bent in sharp angles on the wet carpet, as though discarded by a giant at the end of a raucous party. We had arrived here back in January knowing that Metamorphosi Day would come, but not knowing what lay on the other side of it for us. Like our surroundings, we had been knocked around, beat up and nearly destroyed.

Without a word, the group set to work righting the furniture, dusting off the bits of glass, trying to bring some order to the space and to our lives. The air outside settled into such a perfect stillness, I forgot for a moment that the windows were gaping, jagged holes. Lucian took a seat beside me on the damp velvet couch, staring at me like he wanted to say something but just fidgeting instead. I could read the anguish in his face, in his dead eyes and furrowed brow, his spirit as dim as I had ever seen. I wondered how much of that had to do with his transformation. At midnight, after an extremely close call, he had escaped the underworld. He was no longer one of them, a demon, but he wasn't one of us either. He was mortal. Dante knelt before me on the damp carpet, saying something, holding out his phone as he had earlier. I forced myself to listen, though my thoughts were far away.

"See, I'll read it," he said. "'If you live past midnight, don't despair at those you've lost. Look to an old foe for answers. You will find him. As you proceed, a word of warning: you must complete the loop. *Allons-y.*' So I got that before…everything happened. Did you get anything?"

I didn't even know if I still *had* my phone. I had wedged it into my combat boot for safekeeping earlier in the night and had gotten so used to the feel of it there, making such a snug place for itself against the firm leather, that I had forgotten about it. I freed it from the side of my boot now, pulling it out of my dirty, torn sock. The phone was caked with mud, much like my arms and legs, and its screen was cracked. Still, it came to life with the push of a button. I read the waiting text silently, Lucian looking over my shoulder, and then flashed the screen at Dante. He read quietly and nodded. My message was identical to his except where Dante had the word "foe," I had the word "flame." I wasn't the only one who noticed this.

"I know. I'm here," Lucian said in a soft voice, his eyes darting and apologetic. "I'm here for everything I can do to help you. Even if it kills me." His heavy tone told me that it was a serious offer. And it was true, unfortunately; his freedom from the underworld made him an even greater target and his new-found mortality meant he could be easily destroyed.

"Good idea," Drew said, watching us from across the room. She urged the others to take out any devices they had and set them in a circle, switched on to provide a little light, like a low electric campfire.

"Can I see that again?" Dante asked, leaning toward my screen. Max appeared at Dante's side, cradling water bottles in his arms, distributing them, quietly caring for us all as was his way. The other four angels took seats across the room, murmuring to themselves, curling up as though any remaining adrenaline was draining out by the second.

"Maybe someday we'll find out who the hell is sending these," I said to Dante, aggravated. I chucked the phone onto the sofa. Just another of the mysteries we had failed to uncover.

"Hopefully it's not actually someone in hell," Dante offered, just light enough, as though trying to calm me. He stood now, stretching his limbs after the exertion of battle.

"I don't think it is, to be honest," Lucian offered. "It's not their style."

"They prefer leaving messages in blood and things," Dante said, flippantly. It was no hyperbole in this case: we'd once been greeted by a rendering of angel wings painted in blood on our front porch.

"They aspire to a certain level of…spectacle," Lucian agreed.

"What's the deal?" River, on her feet now, barked at us like someone not used to being kept in the dark. Tom, hands clasped behind his head, looked at her then returned his gaze to the ceiling.

"What are you guys talking about?" Emma asked quietly, confused, mascara running down her face, probably as much from the elements as from the emotional torment of the night. Her boyfriend, Jimmy, had been the first of our fellow angels-in-training to fall to the dark side. We had fought against him tonight and Lance had defeated him.

Dante and I traded glances, silently agreeing to share this last remaining secret we had guarded for so long. He nodded, pushing me to explain, probably since I had been receiving these odd directives longer than he had. "We've been getting these messages. For a while now. They used to be written out longhand, but since we got here they started coming electronically. Lance found these phones that had been left for us—" I grabbed mine and tossed it to River to have a look. She caught it in one hand.

"Left by who?" Emma asked. She pulled her long, auburn locks back, twisting them into a bun, as though signaling the need to bring order to the chaos.

"We don't know," Dante said. Max appeared at his side bearing a plate of assorted cookies, some broken, salvaged from the kitchen.

"Why are we just hearing about this for the first time now?" River asked, scrolling through the messages. "This is some crazy shit."

"Tell me about it," I said under my breath.

"I wanna see," Tom grabbed River's hand and pulled her next to him.

"No secrets. OK?" Drew, who had been quiet until now, pleaded sweetly, tucking her wet hair behind her ears. "We can't have secrets." She had a point.

"Promise," I said to her.

So we told them how we'd come to rely on the messages, how we had learned the hard way that we needed to trust them, and how they had given us hope by convincing us something was looking out for us. We read a few of the most recent texts, and when we'd answered everyone's questions, River passed the phone to Tom to have a look while Dante tucked his away again.

"I wish Connor was still here," Emma sighed, hugging her legs to her chest, curling up in a near-fetal position.

"He's gone. Suck it up," River shot back. "So you—" she looked right at Lucian. He still wore his tuxedo, weathered now from the party at the Lexington eight months ago and tonight's events. He sat leaning forward, elbows on his knees. "You're the 'flame'?"

He looked at me as my eyes darted away shyly, then he nodded at River.

"Scandal! Haven, you're full of surprises. I kind of love that."

Drew shook her head and Emma craned her neck, looking at Lucian as though for the first time and then giving me a conspiratorial nod.

"Hang on," Tom said, squinting at the phone as though he was thinking so hard he might injure himself. "What's allonse-why?" he asked. He butchered the phrase so well it took me a moment to fully appreciate the change in subject.

"I took Spanish," Dante shrugged as he settled onto the arm of the chair Max had nestled into. "Hav?"

"Oh. *Allons-y*," I repeated. "Let's go. French." It got me thinking.

"Why is it in French?" Emma asked.

"*Pourquoi?*" Drew said, quietly.

I turned it over and over in my mind, searching through what scraps I could call up, I sensed the answer was in there somewhere, but the wheels were turning so slowly now. All I could register in my mind and body was an overwhelming void. I could only think about Lance. I felt myself shutting down, finally surrendering to the physical strain and emotional devastation of the past several hours, hopelessness creeping over me like a sheet pulled over a cadaver. I wanted to curl up in a corner and sleep. Forever. But I knew that was the wrong thing to feel. I needed to be stronger than that; I needed to be stronger than ever to find him.

The answer was there, lurking in the background of another memory. Yes, that night at the cemetery, the transformation ritual for the devils. No wonder I had buried it: that had been a night with Lance I would've rather forgotten. When we had made the mistake of not treasuring each other enough. If I ever saw him again—I caught myself. *When.* When I saw him next, we would know better than to ever repeat that same mistake.

"Père-Lachaise," I heard myself say out loud, trancelike. "Père-Lachaise," I said again, my voice more solid this time. "In Paris. Cemetery." I turned to Lucian: "What do you know about it?"

"I've heard of it, of course, I mean, just from my studies," he looked at the ceiling, closed his eyes, thinking. "But I'm not sure what—"

"The Krewe, they mentioned it during the ritual that one night. During Jimmy's transformation," I said it quietly, not wanting to hurt Emma. "Just in passing, they said something about meeting—"

That triggered something in him. He sprung forward, hand to his mouth, a grave expression clouding his eyes as if pieces were falling into place and regrettably so. "So that's where it will be," he said in a whisper, as though the realization was too much to even say out loud. No one spoke, collectively allowing him the time and space to work it out. "That's it. That will be the start of it. The revolution." He stared into my eyes. "They must intend for Lance to be their sacrifice." A lump formed in my throat, a catch interrupting my heartbeat. I couldn't fully process what he was saying. I suspected the others were facing the same kind of system overload as I surveyed their dropped jaws and dark eyes.

"But...what..." I couldn't form a complete thought, there were too many questions. Lucian went on in choppy, rattled sentences, addressing the group now.

"They like to begin with an angel sacrifice, since they only revolt every few hundred years. But, it's a challenge, capturing an angel to sacrifice."

"They had Sabine. Brody. Jimmy. Why not them?" I could hear the mania in my voice, shooting out the names of our fellow angels-in-training who had been wooed to the dark side. I wanted Lucian to be wrong. I could barely calm the tremor as I spoke.

He shook his head. "No. They all fell prey, they didn't fight. Or at least, not hard enough. For the sacrifice, they want a real capture. Someone who fought tooth and nail. It's a celebration," he said, shaking his head in regret. "They feel that ensnaring someone who's a true enemy helps unify their cause."

"What happens at this sacrifice?" I spat it out, disgusted.

"It's the first time the portals below reopen after the last Metamorphosi Day," he spoke slowly, eyes traveling around the group. "It's the beginning of the end. They will gather to launch the revolution, which plays out over a course of weeks, nightmarish weeks, where they try to gain control, bodies, souls, angels. They will try to claim new devils in the most barbaric, violent ways."

"Spectacle." Dante said flatly.

"So the sacrifice revs them up. He'll die for this. For *this*." It was hitting me now.

"It's a frigging pep rally," Dante said.

"Fuck that." River said, pointing, as angry as I'd ever seen her. "Fuck. That."

"River," Drew shushed her. But I appreciated it. I needed it, to hear that. I needed to feel that everyone cared as much as I did.

"No, she's right," Emma said.

"I never liked pep rallies," River spat.

"Well, I mean, for football they're OK, you know?" Tom offered. "They can be cool, you know to get everyone rooting for—"

"Don't even—" River didn't have to finish. Tom just shrugged and swigged his water bottle. Everyone was talking now, asking questions: *What are we supposed to do? How do we stop it? What do we do?*

"So if there aren't any portals open before then—?" Dante asked.

"Right." Lucian answered.

"Then that's it," I said firmly. "We have to crash this. Are you with me?" I asked the group. They looked at each other and then at me, silent. I needed them all. Refusal was not an option.

2

Keep A Quiet Vigil

I looked around the room and as I made eye contact with each of them, one by one they nodded solemnly back at me.

"Good," I said. Then to Lucian: "What do we need to know?"

"It's a rough scene," he shook his head. "The sacrifice is a meeting of the most powerful. So it means the Prince is there, with his closest confidantes and those who have been rehabilitated following the battles of the previous Metamorphosi Days—"

"You don't mean—" Dante asked, frozen.

"Yes. Any devils you've fought and banished to the underworld could potentially come back. Depending on their strength. Newer devils are the weakest, but some...the more formidable, would likely have had time to renew their powers." At this, Max placed his hand on Dante's leg. He had surely heard of Etan, Dante's first love—evil though he was—the demon who had nearly claimed Dante's soul in Chicago. I still couldn't bring myself to think of that time. And then another face pushed to the forefront of my thoughts.

"Aurelia," I whispered. The woman I had admired, whose approval I had sought when we first began work at the Lexington Hotel in Chicago. The demon who had tried so skillfully to lure me to her cause with her promises and her glamour and her power, and of course, her assistant, Lucian.

He nodded slowly. "I would suspect so. As I told you, they stopped letting me in a long time ago. I've seen Aurelia only once since you banished her. It was in the very beginning, when she was still withered. She came to my cell to taunt me and…" he shook his head, as though regretting having shared this much.

"And what?" I asked, steeling myself.

"She said something? About Haven?" Dante prodded.

"She vowed to regenerate," he said finally. But I could tell he was holding back.

"So she could kill me. She wants a second chance at me," I said, no emotion in my voice.

"She wants to make you suffer," he said softly. I understood the subtext. She could accept me battling her, as angels and demons are born and bred to want to cleanse the world of each other. But what had been unforgiveable in her eyes, what had truly enflamed her, had been on a far more personal level. I had not only rejected her world, even with its glamorous trappings, but I had managed to woo one of her own, her favorite, her pet and plaything, Lucian, from the dark side. Rather than him stealing my soul, I had instead awakened in him a desire to be in *my* world, to repent and escape from below. I had also accused her of needing Lucian's attention. She wasn't the kind of woman who wanted to be seen as *needing* anything. I had undermined her authority and power. Yes, it was personal. As I considered it all now, the twists and turns that had led us here, the possibility of encountering this vicious figure from the past, another realization burned through the haze of my mind.

"It was her idea," I said, and as I did, one of the phones in our circle of light turned off. "Taking Lance instead of me. She knew that would devastate me. She would understand that even more than the Prince." That act was a particular form of violence only a woman would think to inflict on another. A man would underestimate the power of taking a loved one. Aurelia had always known how to prey on emotions, to go for the heart rather than the jugular.

"I don't know. I don't have any more. I've failed you so much. All of you," Lucian looked around the room. "I'm so sorry. I have caused so much pain." I had never seen him like this, so defeated, so weakened. He bowed his head, as though in shame. In all we had been through together, this wasn't a side of him I had seen. No one spoke for several long seconds. Outside, sirens I had neglected to notice before roared. The storm now subsided, the city roused again, help on its way, ready to rebuild.

"Wait," Dante broke the silence. "What did you mean, outside? You said you couldn't believe he would risk it?"

I had heard that too but had been too jarred by Lance and the Prince to process it.

Lucian brightened, a flicker of hope lighting his stormy eyes. "I'd almost forgotten. Maybe…" He seemed to be thinking aloud. His gaze fixed somewhere across the room and he left his place beside me, drifting over toward the windows. He stopped in the far corner and knelt, picking up something shiny from the floor: the chrome wall clock. The piece, which looked like an oversized pocket watch, usually hung on this wall a few feet from the flat screen TV but must have been knocked down by the gusts that had blown out the windows. A lightning bolt-shaped crack now ran across its glass face. "I'd almost forgotten, it was so close," he said. We all leaned in, quiet, waiting.

He looked at the clock in his hands then placed it carefully on the side table, like a precious artifact. "The timing was so close." Scanning the room at each of our curious faces, he went on: "It all happened so fast, you know? You were there, at midnight, you saw," he said to me. I only nodded. "The timing was close. More than close. He was *late*," he said, leaning against the windowsill. "Those minutes are lethal. It was just past midnight, and the Prince stayed behind. He didn't claim Lance until *after* midnight. And I know that because I saw it from just past the threshold of the house—I could not leave that house until midnight, when I became mortal. *You* know," he gestured to me again. "It was like an invisible wall keeping me there, sealing every door and window. All of …us…" He seemed to struggle to avoid using the word "devil" or "demon" and I couldn't blame him. "…we had to return below by midnight or risk becoming mortal and being locked out. The Prince, as the most powerful, wouldn't become mortal as instantaneously of course, nor could he be locked out so immediately—" his words had been picking up steam and now he pulled off his tuxedo jacket, folding it in half and laying it beside the clock.

"But for him," he went on, pushing up his sleeves, excited, hopeful. "Each minute would bring an irreversible draining of power. He must've realized he wouldn't have time to fight and capture you," he gestured toward me. "But he could take a prisoner and a good one at that. Even if he had to sacrifice something in order to do it. So he risked it," he shook his head, seemingly shocked. "He took that gamble even though he had no idea how it might impact him. It's unprecedented."

"So that's how desperate he is—they are—to destroy me," I said, not intending to be a killjoy overlooking the positive here—that the Prince had been weakened—but rather, just trying to wrap my head around that level of passion, the wrath I could expect to be up against.

He waited a beat, searching for a response and then, finding none, ignored me. "What matters is: he's wounded. It's impossible to know just how impaired he might be, but if ever he were to be defeated, this is the time."

"This revolution," Dante cut in. "Am I right in thinking that it's a total free-for-all? Like, everyone fighting, the Prince, everyone on the battlefield?"

Lucian nodded. "That's my understanding. I've, of course, never been through one of these. I'm new to all this. But from what I had always been told, yes."

"So, when? When?" I asked, shaking my head, coming back to life. "How long do we have to wait till the start? The sacrifice? Until we can get to Lance?"

Lucian sighed, hands behind his head. "Soon, I imagine. They've been waiting a long time and they were anxious even before Metamorphosi Day. If I had to guess?" he thought for a moment, making silent calculations until finally: "My best guess would be the summer solstice. The portals are always open on each solstice anyway. And in this case, I would be surprised if they would open any sooner than that."

"So, June," Dante said.

"But why?" Max asked, scratching at that scar on his head. It matched the scar on Dante's arm and above my heart and beneath Lance's eye. We all had swipes like these along with matching hatch marks on our shoulder blades, three on each side, where wings would hopefully attach one day. Max preferred to cover his marking beneath his trademark fedora or another of his many hats, but the one he had worn so many hours ago had likely become another casualty of this wild night. "I mean, how can you be sure? And, what—" I imagined he was secretly asking on Dante's behalf, preparing himself to aid Dante through Etan's renaissance.

"Yeah, what's the deal with those portals anyway?" Dante liked to finish Max's sentences; he was good at it.

"They're sort of like the tides. There's a schedule but external forces affect it. Instead of the moon cycles, the portals are controlled by the charge of the air in the underworld. The portals open when the heat and poison, the strength of the collective evil, reach a certain level."

"You know who was all over tides and that stuff? Lance," Dante said, with regret. It was true; he would have thrown

AIMEE AGRESTI

himself into this challenge. He loved science, math, the relationships in nature. He loved how things were built. He was the architect among us. *The architect, the alchemist and the illuminator must stay together.* I recalled that message from my phone just before Metamorphosi Day. Lance, Dante and me. I forced myself back into the present, back among the living. I couldn't imagine how slowly time would move between now and then. It seemed so far away. But I would keep my focus steady on that day when we could steal him back. I needed to think like Lance would in order to get him back.

"So it's decided," I said, my eyes connecting with each angel again and landing finally on Lucian. "We're going to Paris. In June. All in?"

Drew nodded first. "Of course, Haven."

"Damn straight," said River, lifting her head from Tom's shoulder. After a moment, she smacked the back of her hand against his arm.

"Ow! Yeah. Got it. I'm in," he said.

"Paris," Emma said with a hint of dreaminess. "There are worse places."

"You know what they say about Paris in springtime," Dante said.

"What exactly do they say?" Max asked.

"Well…I don't really know," he admitted. "I just know that something is said about Paris in springtime. Not that it'll be much of a vacation."

"Yeah, that's true, actually," Emma said, her tone somber now.

"What are we supposed to do between now and then, though? It seems like kind of a long time. I mean, it isn't, but it is," Drew said in that serious, sensitive way of hers.

"We do what Lance would've done if he were here," I said. "We prepare. We keep our heads down. We plan." I was surrounded by this group of angels and Lucian, but I could not have felt more alone. I was so accustomed to plotting something like this *with* Lance. I didn't have all the answers on my own. Everyone seemed to be looking to me to fill in the blanks, to bring order and impose structure, to move us forward. I had to work to suffocate that sentimental part of myself; it would only bring me down, slow me down. I needed to grow armor around my heart. And I needed to lean on my friends too. "There will be logistics to deal with. I'll need someone who can be our facilitator," I said, using the word Connor had once used to reference the mysterious man who helped arrange some of our more ambitious training assignments—fending off gators in the bayou, leaping down from the rafters of the Superdome— only to vanish back into the shadows when we were finished.

"I'll do it," Drew raised her hand.

"Thanks, Drew. We'll need somewhere to stay, and, like, credit cards to book some insanely expensive flights, practical stuff. We'll talk," I said. She nodded and grabbed her phone, turning it off flashlight mode to tap a few notes. "In the meantime, we need a script for what went on here. The storm can explain a lot. Just like the fire did, back at the Lex," I said the loaded name with quiet reverence. At the mention of his former home, Lucian whipped back around to look at me with pursed lips. One of the phones died, the room growing even dimmer.

"Yeah, and by the way," Dante hopped to his feet, flipping the nearest light switch again and again before giving up. "Really, no one could bother to predict even the chance of rain, let alone, like, a hurricane today? All that fancy Doppler business. I mean, seriously." He ducked into the kitchen to pillage some more. I hadn't thought about it, but the storm truly had come out of nowhere.

"Actually," Lucian started, apologetic. "I think we're to blame for that." He had been quiet for a long time, sitting on the windowsill staring out into that black, hot night, the empty road below naked without the glow of its streetlamps or the pulse of late-night revelers. Emma, who had had her back to him curled up on the love seat nearby, straightened up at the sound of his voice, as though she'd forgotten he was there. The thick, wet air outside had wafted in, hanging in the room. He had our attention.

"It's like the tides again, right?" Max asked. Dante returned with a pint of melting ice cream and two spoons, taking his seat beside Max.

"Yeah. Kind of. When you get a bunch of us in one place, it tends to mess with the natural order of things."

I considered that for a moment and realized: "It was kind of unseasonably hot in Chicago when you were there."

"Yeah," he said, regret in his voice.

"But, then, so, what's our story?" Drew asked, keeping us on task, phone poised for more note-taking.

"Right. Well, let's lean on the chaos of the storm, right? There will be plenty of…people…lost." I didn't know how to phrase it. "I know the Krewe was *at work* tonight," I finally said, landing on a euphemism for the killing that likely went on despite our efforts. "But I think the storm erased evidence of their violence." As I went on, Emma grabbed her phone from among the flashlights, causing the glow of our room to fade so we looked like an old sepia-toned photograph. She typed frantically. "I imagine there are plenty of destroyed homes and things. It was enough of a storm that there will be people who just aren't accounted for."

"Did you see the floats flying? And from, like, uptown? I don't even understand," Drew shook her head.

"Exactly," I said.

"Parts of the city were leveled. The garden district got it bad," Emma paraphrased, reading from a news story on her phone. "I've got pictures."

"Pass it here," Tom said, reaching out. River intercepted it to look herself.

"So people will be unaccounted for," I repeated. "Lance will be one of those, OK?"

"What about any of the bystanders who saw you guys jump off the float and start chasing people?" River asked, smirking.

"A, that could've all been part of the show. And B, no one knows we were actually chasing people."

"Wasn't that you who came crashing through the skylight next door?" Dante asked, tongue-in-cheek, looking at me.

"Whoa," Drew said.

"When this one gets going, she kicks total ass," Dante said like a proud father. I was oddly touched, my heart swelling by his faith in me.

"But, dude, it was a skylight," Tom shook his head.

"Listen, the ballroom had totally cleared by the time Sabine...." I shook my head, not wanting to rehash something so grisly. They understood. I had fought her and won, banishing her to the underworld. It hadn't been a pretty affair, but it had been done and, as far as I could tell, without an audience. "If anyone asks, she and I had climbed to the roof to get a view of the city on Mardi Gras, the storm picked up before we could safely get down and we got thrown around. And after a fall like that, if I 'don't remember' a whole lot, it will make sense, right?" I made the quotation marks with my fingers to underscore my point. "It doesn't really matter. The issue is, we need to be set on Lance. So here's the story: He and I jumped off the float to rile up the crowd and toss out more trinkets or whatever, and then we never saw him again. Got it? That's all anyone needs to know. And then, between us, we'll just keep a quiet vigil. We'll figure this out and we'll get him back." I noticed from the expressions on their frozen faces that there was nothing quiet about my vigil. I was getting angry. It occurred to me that I was standing now.

I turned away for a moment, taking a deep breath. I just didn't like any of this. Talking in the past tense. This need to create a fiction about what had happened to him—a horrible fiction—because the reality was too terrifying to even be fathomed. I wasn't sure how I would make it through the night, the week, the next few months. My leaden heart fell, over and over again, sinking. My whole body rejected what had happened. It drowned in it. Nausea set in, and then I felt a shooting pain in my chest, my lungs straining against my ribcage. But whereas everyone else looked fearful, Lucian stood, taking a step toward me, reaching out as if to comfort me from across the room.

"Are you all right?" he asked in a gentle tone as though it were just the two of us in the room. I could not afford to have anyone doubt me or to doubt that it was possible to get Lance back. I needed to be strong for everyone here, from this moment forward.

"I'm fine. Fine." The line sounded rocky and unbelievable now, but I vowed to practice. He looked deep into my eyes. Even in this relative darkness I could tell he was searching for a way to help, pledging himself to the struggle ahead, to me. When it became clear that I wasn't going to say anything more, he nodded and took a step back again.

"It's late. Maybe we should get some rest," he addressed the group. "How much more can really be accomplished tonight?"

We all agreed, but the curious thing was no one actually moved for many minutes. We each sat there in our respective places, shifting on creaky furniture, trying to get more comfortable. Lucian finally joined me on the sofa again. After many quiet minutes, Emma spoke, yawning as she did: "I kind of want to sleep and kind of don't want to sleep and kind of am scared to be in my room," she said, like a child who had in fact faced monsters and had every right to be afraid of the dark. None of us had bothered to assess the state of our rooms yet. I could only imagine that tour would involve more broken glass, damp floors and damaged belongings. I was in no rush.

"I'll go with you," Drew offered. "It's too quiet out there," she nodded toward the street. "It's creeping me out." It was true, it was eerie to not hear the constant buzz of activity coming from outside. A soft murmur hummed from the dark house next door, where some of the partygoers must have decided to wait it out until morning. Though they were also high school interns in our program, their dorms were further away than our home and would have required a shuttle or streetcar ride to get there. The only modes of transportation that seemed to be operating were emergency vehicles, their sirens still blaring every few minutes.

"Thanks, Drew," Emma said drowsily, bidding us a, "Night-night," as they found their way back down the main hallway, Drew lighting the way with her phone.

River flicked on her pocket lighter, the flame illuminating her face, and slapped Tom on the shoulder. He snarfled a snore as his head jerked up. "What? Hey. Huh?"

"Let's go," she ordered. "Catch you in the morning, kids," she said to us as they were swallowed into the darkened hallway. I felt Dante and Max, shifting, gesturing, deciding wordlessly whether to go and I got that feeling, butterflies I suppose, but not the same variety I was used to. This was more of a queasy flutter. It occurred to me that for the first time since we'd met, I actually didn't want to be alone with Lucian. Over the past few months, we had had an intense sort of reflex when faced with the combination of low lighting and privacy, a magnetic pull that neither of us had bothered to fight. I had blamed some of it on the turbulence with Lance. As for Lucian, whether he realized it or not, I think he might have been swept up in the idea that I happened to be the only one capable of freeing him from the shackles of the underworld. That certainly seemed like the sort of trait that could amp up a girl's allure. But now, it was as if that magnet had been flipped to the side that repelled, pushing me away from him.

"Are you guys staying here?" Max asked from across the darkness.

"You can totally stay with me, Hav," Dante said. "If your room is a mess and all." Ever the good friend, he didn't want to abandon me. He offered me an out, in the event I needed one. But the rational part of me knew I couldn't take it. I felt Lucian watching me. At some point, if not now then in the coming days, Lucian and I would inevitably be left alone together, and there would surely be things that needed to be said. I just wasn't certain if I wanted that moment to be now, when I felt so physically and emotionally depleted. I couldn't handle any sort of confrontation. A breeze swirled the curtains, and a sliver of the moon peeked from behind the clouds, lighting the room. I caught a glimpse of Lucian's eyes, hopeful and translucent, before the sky shifted, plunging us into near darkness once more.

"I'm good. Thanks, though," I said, a tentative quiver to my voice. I wouldn't run away. I would face this now.

"If you're sure," he said, not entirely convinced. He extended a hand, pulling Max to his feet. "Night, guys."

Lucian and I mumbled shy goodbyes. I curled up, gathering my strength and waited until I could no longer hear their footsteps. Then I waited some more. And then I decided I just didn't feel much like talking. Lucian took a deep breath and exhaled like he might say something. But instead the quiet minutes, with their faintly wailing sirens in the distance and their gentle breezes and their buttery moonbeams, stretched on. I didn't move, I barely breathed. I just wanted to skip ahead to June, to Paris. I had no interest in the hours and days between now and then. They would be excruciating.

He was the first to speak.

"You're pretending to be asleep aren't you?" he asked quietly, his voice eased now that it was just the two of us.

"No," I lied. But I was disappointed with myself. "Maybe."

"You have every right—absolutely every right—to blame me for Lance's capture," he said, weary.

"I don't." That was true, actually. "I blame myself." I hugged my legs to my chest and stared straight ahead into the nothingness. I picked at my cuticles, needing an outlet for my nervous energy. The last of the phones died out and the moon hid again, plunging us into pure black. I appreciated the cover. "It's my fault," I said, lifeless. "And it makes me sick so I'd rather not think about it. The only thing I can do to keep from actively hating myself is to think of how to make it better. Even though that's months away and—" I felt him shift on the sofa, leaning toward me.

"How is it your fault?" he asked, gently cutting me off.

"This is about me. They took him instead of me. To hurt me," I said, frustration behind every syllable. "We already went over this." I didn't want to rehash it all.

"You were helping *me* though," he sighed. He paused a moment, then in a freshly wounded tone: "And now you won't even look at me."

"It's dark, I can't see you."

"You don't want to look at me." It may have been true, but I wouldn't tell him that. When I looked at him, I kept replaying that scene of the Prince morphing back into his own image, shapeshifting from his guise as Lucian, which had fooled Lance. I felt the gaping wounds from tonight scarring up almost immediately and changing me. It was setting in now: our trio—Dante, Lance and I—had been shattered, and I had to lead this group of angels. I had to take control in a way I never had before. Lucian's hand found mine across the darkness and the emotional divide, his fingers interlocking with mine. My hand remained limp, not sure it felt right about participating but not wanting to pull away either. "I know you love him," he said. "I know you're afraid for him. I promise we'll get him. If you don't believe me then at least believe in *you*. In how strong you are, in how much you've already accomplished against them all. OK?" I rolled my eyes. He must have known. "This isn't the first time I've told you that, we've already been over this." He borrowed my language to make his point. I shrugged and gave a staccato laugh.

"OK, then what about this," he shifted, changing tack. "If there's one thing I'm sure of, it's that he will not be....killed." He seemed to be trying to find another word, as he had earlier, and again had come up short. I could tell the burden he felt for Lance's capture. "They want him for the sacrifice, and for that they want someone vital, strong. It's a better show in their eyes. I would venture to guess he'll be better cared for than a great percentage of captives down there right now."

"That's comforting. Being treated better than other prisoners of hell." I shook my head. "So what's that mean, he only has to be tortured through eight circles instead of nine? Why don't I feel better?"

"No." He let go of my hand and crouched down to grab the last phone that had died on the ground, fiddled with it, and got it going again. I watched him from the corner of my eye, but as soon as the light brightened, I turned away again. "There. Better. No, actually, it's probably nicer accommodations there than here at the moment."

"Now you're definitely just telling me what I want to hear," I said flatly, though secretly encouraged.

He must have detected a thawing. "Some of them, as you recall, do appreciate comfortable surroundings. The Prince especially. It's ingrained in him, the love of beauty and opulence. You saw the Lexington, after all. There *is* a version of luxury available to the upper crust of the lowest realm. And Lance could be held there. There's more hope in our situation than you realize. Honest."

I liked so much about that statement. *Our situation.* The idea that it was a shared struggle. The talk of hope. I felt a tiny section of my charred heart begin to regenerate again. It almost sounded possible that they might not want to break him. They might not want to harm him too much in advance of the horrific day that lay ahead. "Well, now you're flirting with me." My tone was still too heavy to be read as flip, though, and he seemed concerned that I didn't believe him.

"No, it's true. I think they'll go easy on him. I'm not just saying that. I wouldn't say it if I didn't believe it. It wouldn't do you any good to lie to you."

"How tough is this going to be? In June?" I asked. "Truth."

He exhaled and took a moment, as though constructing just the right response to not surrender what gains he had made. "It won't be easy, but it can absolutely be done," he said carefully. "You will be outnumbered. Even if they aren't all at their strongest, there will still be dozens of them. Maybe even scores—I'm not sure how the recruiting progressed after Chicago. But if you are all as strong as you can be, if you use everything in your arsenal, if you have a solid escape plan, then you can free him."

"Great. Sounds like a cakewalk. *Très facile,*" I said, coating my words with the necessary sarcasm. He wasn't amused.

"Listen to me." He grabbed my hand again, gazing at me with those once-sparkling gray eyes. This was how he had looked at me during those talks strategizing his own release from below. My head turned away but he still held my hand, leaning toward me. "It can be done. I know you can do it. Look at how far you've come already. Don't you remember? When we met I was supposed to be pulling you into my world, and instead you changed me. So deeply. You can't even possibly understand what you did for me. You don't realize how many lives you've saved. You need to know how incredible it is, what you've done."

"Thanks." It came out as a whisper. For the first time all night I felt tears well up, so fast and full I couldn't contain them. I choked them back as best I could, swallowing them, fighting. He squeezed my hand again. A runaway drop fell, and then another, each streaking my face and landing salty on my lip. I wiped them away, fast, before they could spur others to follow. I had no time for tears or for regret or for lamenting what could have been done differently tonight. I had to push forward.

"Lance has something else to get him through: the thought of seeing you again. And I know for a fact that can go a long way." He bowed his head, his eyes trying to find mine. My eyes connected with his for a moment. "And that's not me flirting, that's just me stating the facts," he said firmly, with a shrug.

"Thank you."

"So. There's just one last thing. I know I'm always asking for something."

I nodded.

"I know it's selfish of me, but if you can forgive me for causing all of this…I just…it would mean a lot to me. I don't know how much time I'll have now—"

My head snapped in his direction. What did that mean? "I don't understand," I cut him off.

"It's just…I'm mortal now. I'm not like I was before. I feel it, a weakness, a fatigue. I'm not like I was and I'm not like all of you here. And I've got a price on my head. I want you to know that I'm in this fight, body and soul."

"Well, good. That last part was nice. But I don't want to hear any of that other stuff. Ever again. OK?" If I was going to make it through until June, and then survive freeing Lance, there were certain things I just couldn't allow myself to hear or think. I wasn't equipped to hear Lucian doubting himself. And it was about time I started to lay down some rules. Tonight had been a game change, a life change. I felt the shift in my cells, in the synapses of my brain, everywhere. This event, losing Lance, would push me to become a new person, I could sense it. "That's counterproductive. Got it?"

He nodded. "I think you're going to be just fine, actually," he said.

"You too."

"We're all right then?"

"Yeah."

"Thank you. Haven." He leaned over, kissing me on the top of the head, then retreated again to his side of the couch.

We drifted off to sleep, neither of us bothering to go to my room. It had taken every bit of my remaining energy reserves to have that talk. Now that it was over, I didn't want to shatter the calm. Every once in a while something important wraps up in such a way that you just want to leave it alone. I closed my eyes, vowing that tomorrow I would wake up as the strongest version of me I could be. It would take everything I had to free Lance. I couldn't let anything hold me back, least of all myself.

3

What Are We Going To Do With Him?

BANG-BANG-BANG. The pounding shook my heart awake. The door. "*Connor, leave us alone,*" I thought. It had to be Connor waking us for another early morning training session. Just couldn't give us a morning off. Ready to whisk us away to another part of the city to practice "cultivating our fearlessness." Wasn't that how he put it, shorthand for the business of trying to harness our freakish new angel powers—leaping, swimming, battling native beasts, whatever it took—to test what we were made of? *BANG-BANG.* I reached for the pillow to pull over my head. But if I didn't get the door, then Sabine sure wouldn't. She probably hadn't even heard it. When she was out, she was out. Or else she heard it but knew I would take care of it. That's what I do. I take care of things. *BANG-BANG.* Connor had a low threshold for being ignored, didn't he? He would probably barge right in any minute. I opened my eyes, surprised to see daylight streaming in through the shattered windows of the living room. I pushed myself up on my elbows, looking around. I felt something jabbing me in the back: a foot.

On the other side of the couch: Lucian.

It all came rushing back at me—where I was, what had happened, that it had all been real. And Sabine was gone—by my hand. And Connor was gone, for now at least. And Lance....

BANG-BANG.

Lucian lay on his back, one arm over his eyes, the corners of his mouth turned down into a grimace as though he hadn't wanted to let himself fall asleep and had been taken against his will, succumbing to the once-forgotten fatigue of being human. His tuxedo shirt still on, he had propped his folded jacket beneath his head.

I sat up, getting my bearings, my muscles a little tight and sore. It felt as though each part of my body was waking up on its own time. Like Lucian, I had stretched out in the night, my legs reaching toward him. One of my feet, still in its combat boot, was wedged under his arm and against his chest, an imprint of its dirty sole stamped on his white rumpled shirt.

Then came the voice, shouting but gentle in tone:

"Anyone in here? I'm with Tulane. Volunteer Program. I'm coming in," he said, pushing the unlocked front door. It creaked open. "OK, that was easier than I thought. I'm an idiot," the man added under his breath. "OK. Mirrors need fixing." I heard pen scribbling on paper. He was in the foyer. "Hello?" he called out. "Brett from Tulane."

In a flash, Lucian's arm flung out against the sofa, his eyes now open and manic, and he bolted up. He looked at me with that terrified frozen shock of someone waking up who hadn't realized he'd been sleeping.

"It's OK." I whispered. "Good morning." And he sat back down, exhaling.

He was probably as confused as I had been, and maybe more so. That was the first night in years that he had awoken as a mortal. I wondered how different it felt for him and what kinds of memories might have haunted him in his sleep. My dreams had whirled and buzzed from the specific horrors of last night to the general mundanities of living and training here, back when it had been so much simpler.

"Sorry, man, didn't mean to startle you guys," Brett said, stepping out from the foyer. "Crazy stuff last night. Totally understand being jumpy. Guess we came from the same party." Brunet with a wrestler's stocky build, he wore a rumpled, untucked and unbuttoned tuxedo shirt and pants. I recognized him from last night's masquerade ball next door and from that first night in New Orleans, that lavish New Year's party in the garden district to welcome those of us in the volunteer program. He was one of Connor's friends, a fellow counselor. "Hey, I'm Brett." He waved. "Guess my man Connor deserted you all, huh?"

"He said something about a family emergency," I said, as Connor had instructed us. He had told us his cover and explained that as our guide, as our link between the lives we had been leading and these new angel selves we were becoming, he wasn't permitted to be here among us during our test on Metamorphosi Day. Yesterday had been the second of the three tests we would need to pass in order to earn our wings, and it had to be fought alone. He had reminded me a bit of the comforting SAT prep instructor I'd once had, who I had wished could've just sat quietly in the corner of the room on exam day. But of course, proctors don't allow that kind of thing, and I had been nervous and hadn't done as well as I'd hoped. Joan, my adoptive mom, always said not to worry, some people just don't test well. I smiled to myself now: I had passed my test last night, though, surviving that battle even without Connor.

"Yeah, he left me a message, too," Brett went on. "I just didn't get it till this morning with the storm and all. Cell service is kinda out, you might have noticed. We'll get everything sorted out with the school, figure out where everyone will be stationed.

There's a ton of damage, from what I've heard. Sounds like this thing was like Katrina's little sister," he shook his head. "Anyway, we'll get everything settled with you guys and all the volunteers and all, it'll just take a little time, you know?" We just nodded, not wanting to engage too much and be forced to answer any questions, like, *Is everyone accounted for?* He said everyone was still next door; they hadn't been able to get back to their residences last night. Their electricity was still out but they invited us to come over if we needed anything. They still had plenty of food and drink left over from the party. He suspected that our group would be folded into his group once the school and the volunteer program got up and running again. "In the meantime, you know where to find me," he said, and held out a cocktail napkin with his contact information. "In case the phones come back." I took it from him with a smile and no intention of getting in touch. He waved goodbye, letting himself out.

As soon as he was gone, the door rattling shut against its frame, Lucian sat down, running his fingers through his hair. The color had drained from his face, leaving him a pasty shade of pale, and he looked like he was going to be sick.

"You OK?"

"It's a strange reflex," he said in a trance, head in his hands. "I kept expecting him to shapeshift into someone I recognize who wants to kill me." He looked up, staring into the empty space in front of him. "It isn't even really logistically possible because they are all locked away now, for at least a little while," he reasoned with himself. "But…I don't know. I just hope every day isn't going to feel like this." He looked at me: "I guess when we get what we want it never feels exactly like we expected, right?" He laughed one dry laugh, camouflage for something that wasn't actually funny at all.

"That's probably true," I said, I couldn't remember the last time anything felt like I expected it to. I kneeled on the ground near him and went on in a gentle tone. "You'll shake that fear though. You're just getting used to this new you. You've still got, like, a mortality hangover. You had this wild night, escaping hell and all, and your body is probably a little confused. No big deal," I smiled, trying to comfort him and diffuse his darkness.

"Right. There's probably some kind of remedy for this, like Hair of the Dog," he joked.

"Exactly, I'm sure Dante can whip something up. You'll be feeling human again in no time."

He shook his head at this exchange, as though appreciating the lightness. "Haven, Haven, Haven. How did a couple of nice midwestern kids get caught up in all this?" he said wistfully, like he was talking about other people. But of course, he was talking about us, or the people we had been before finding ourselves conscripted into this war of angels and demons. In all this time I had never thought of us as peers, even though, despite all he'd been through, he was only a few years older than me. He had once been simply an Iowa farm boy angel-in-training, before he fell in with Aurelia. I remembered hearing his story, but it had always been so difficult to imagine him as anything other than the worldly, confident operator I had met at the Lexington.

"You know what you need?" I asked in a brighter tone, changing course. He looked up, curious. "You need to get outta here. I know it's, you know, a state of emergency outside. But… it's still got to be better than what you're used to." I shrugged and gave him the slightest smile.

"Well, you're right about that," he said. I could see the cloud cover in his eyes, a flashback of what he had endured. I hoped that Lance wasn't facing those trials right now. I pushed that thought away just as fast, though. I had promised myself to snuff out anything defeatist. I had to extinguish any thoughts that weren't going to help.

"Good," I said, pushing forward. "Then it's decided, we'll go out—"

"You know what else I think I need?" he said, a serious look in those eyes.

"Breakfast!" Dante appeared in the hallway, stretching his arms up, still waking up. Max trailed behind him, yawning.

"Morning," Max said.

"Who wants some breakfast?" Dante greeted us.

Lucian stood up, whispering quick in my ear: "I need a new name. New start, right?" He finished his thought and I nodded. It would be necessary. "Lucian Grove" was already assumed dead, just like whoever he'd been before that. A new life, a new identity. Then, as though resolving not to waste any time starting over, he answered his housemates with a lighter tone. "I'm starved. I forgot what it was to be really hungry."

"You guys are just where we left you. Did you sleep at all?" Dante asked. He wore his favorite plaid pajama pants and a tee advertising "Priestess Mariette's Voodoo Temple," on Rampart Street, where he worked.

"I'm gonna see what's in the kitchen," Max said, wandering away.

"I'll help," Lucian said, following him past the broken windows where warm air and sunlight peeked in. "I'm familiar with Dante's work from the hotel. Let's see what raw materials we've got for him."

"What do you mean 'where you left us'?" I said to Dante when they were out of earshot, almost taking offense. There had been a time, not so long ago, when he would've been justified in asking that. But we were in a different place, and hearing that doubt in his voice only deepened the hollow in my heart left by Lance. Dante read my tone.

"No, jeez, Hav," he shook his head. "I mean, these couches are not comfortable, they're more style than function so...."

"We got to talking and then just passed out," I said with finality.

He stared me down, conducting a scan on my eyes to be sure I wasn't leaving anything out. Analysis complete and response accepted, he nodded. "Last night was just…intense," he said, allowing Serious Dante to creep in for a moment. "I woke up today and I, I don't know, I expected to see Lance in his bed. I kind of can't wrap my head around what happened." He whispered—probably out of habit since we had grown so accustomed to having secrets over the course of the past year—even though everyone in this house knew exactly what had happened.

"I know," I said, sinking into the sofa. Dante plopped down next to me. "It's like I'm OK and I'm thinking about the future, how we'll get him back…somehow…but just when I'm feeling like it will be all right, I suddenly just fall off a cliff. My heart just drops and it feels…" I was about to say "impossible," but I stopped myself.

"…It feels like, how the hell are we supposed to pull this off?" He finished my thought, but in that over-the-top Dante way that always made me feel like we were in it together. I put my head on his shoulder and he leaned his head against mine.

Max poked his head out of the kitchen. "Lucian found the Nutella, it was in the back on the top shelf," he reported.

"That's where it went. No wonder," Dante said, pulling me up to my feet now. The sunlight flared, pouring in and reaching all the way to where I stood, licking my arm with its heat.

Lucian appeared in the doorway: "And we've got loads of bread," he said, before stepping out of sight again. But seeing him there, in the kitchen of our storm-trodden house, in his beat-up formal-wear, ready to help make breakfast out of whatever wasn't spoiled in our kitchen, was just another of the sights of the past 24 hours that I couldn't fully comprehend. He was still beautiful, even as exhausted and worn as he now appeared, but he did seem human now. I had only ever seen him in fantastical settings where he had some level of control: the hotel with all of its delicious luxury, the mansion next door which even as a construction site had held a promise of much mystery in its walls, even the cemetery crypt. This was the only time he had ever been on my turf. It set me off-balance.

"Nutella sandwiches all around. I'll see if I can jazz 'em up somehow," Dante called out. And then to me, barely audible with his back to the kitchen doorway: "What are we going to do with him?"

"With Lucian?"

He nodded.

"I know," I said, my eyes fixed behind him. "He's one of us but—"

"Not totally one of us. Like in the most basic ways."

"Yeah, there will be some…challenges," I said. It was an understatement, to say the least.

"And what the heck do we do with him when we go home? Which we will inevitably be doing before we find Lance. I mean, right?" He started walking away toward the kitchen.

"We've got some logistics to deal with," I said sarcastically.

"Right, logistics," Dante said, with a smile. He shook his head.

Max poked his head out of the kitchen again. "We could make these ourselves, but you'll reject them," Max joked.

"You're probably right about that," Dante laughed, ever the perfectionist.

As Dante whipped up the sandwiches, bulking them up by embedding things like apple slices ("We need some sort of crunch factor," he instructed as we all played sous chef), I filled the men in on our introduction to Brett. Drew soon joined us, then River and Tom and finally a weary Emma, still yawning, who chastised us: "Next time you have a family meeting, would someone please wake me?"

"We had to wait until we finished talking about you," River deadpanned.

By now we had moved out of the cramped kitchen and back into the living room, everyone taking their spots from the night before, like assigned seats in class, imposing mild structure on the madness of our world. Lucian remained quiet, and darkly so. He looked like I felt—though I was doing a much better job of masking it. We all were doing a better job: I imagined everyone still felt the sting of last night. He glanced at me, brow furrowed like he wanted to speak but was wrestling with something. I watched him out of the corner of my eye, connecting with him for a moment. "You OK?" I mouthed, not wanting to draw attention.

"I need a name," he said. Though he directed it to me, he was loud enough to interrupt the debate going on about whether we should go next door to introduce everyone to Brett. Lucian turned to the group. "I think I need a name. A different one. I don't know any other way to do this, to be here, without a new identity. I'm kind of not sure who I am right now." There was something painful and true in his candor. It caught us off guard.

"That's understandable," I said finally, adding lightly to ease him: "If ever there was a time for an identity crisis…"

"Right?" Dante answered. I smiled. Lucian had gone from mortal to angel—before I even knew him—to demon, then back to mortal in the span of a few short years. That could wreak havoc on anyone's sense of self. "We've gotta kick this witness protection style—"

"—yes, and give you a cover," I finished the thought.

Lucian brightened. "Yes. Please."

"Oooh, can we name you?" Emma lit up.

"Sure, that works for me," he shrugged. "I'd like that actually, if you don't mind."

"Good team-building activity," Max said to Dante. "If we were also simultaneously defying death in some way, it would be a Connor-worthy exercise." Dante chuckled, slapping him on the back. Tom, who was occupied throwing grapes in the air and catching them in his mouth, overheard and laughed.

"What do you look like?" Emma asked herself, twirling a lock of her auburn hair around her finger. "Something really fun. And, like, nicknamey."

"He's not a puppy, guys," I smiled at him. "Be nice."

"So, like, Fluffy is out?" River joked, stone-faced.

"No, but, just like, something friends would call you, like you're part of the group, you know?" Emma said.

"Thanks," he said seriously, sounding touched.

"I don't know, I would say something formal, regal," Drew offered thoughtfully. "But maybe that's just how you're dressed." I realized that he and I were the only ones still in our clothes from the night before.

"I've got one!" Dante said. "Al. Like for Capone. Chicago, you know?" He tried to sell it, but his suggestion was met with groans.

"That's, like, a parent's name, Dan," I shook my head.

"Alistair? Alvin? Albert? Alex?" Dante went on.

"Give it up," Max smiled.

"Wait. Chicago. Sure, why didn't I think of it sooner?" I thought aloud and looked at him. "Lex," I said, matter-of-factly like there was no other option. We would name him for the hotel where we met him.

His gray eyes shone, "Perfect."

"Unless it's too…loaded," I added, just in case.

"No," he said slowly. "Lex. I like it. It's part of my history."

"You can own it," Dante nodded.

He took a deep breath and then looked at me, stretching out his hand, "Hi, I'm Lex," he said. His body seemed to relax, the crinkle between his brows smoothed, his eyes became more translucent, the darkness draining from them. I understood now just how much healing he needed to do, why this was so urgent, this first step.

"Haven," I introduced myself, holding out my hand. "Lovely to meet you." I smiled shyly as he leaned over to shake my hand.

Dante leapt up from his seat, lunging with his arm extended. "Dante. *Enchanté*," he said. One by one, each came over to shake his hand, as though meeting him for the first time. He looked in their eyes, his smile growing brighter with each introduction, touched by their inclusion. Watching him, the way even his posture eased, you could feel his walls beginning to come down.

We tossed our breakfast dishes in the sink, dressed, and decided to venture out into the Quarter to have a look around, gauge the damage. Our phones had all died by now and with the electricity still out, we just needed to feel like we were back in touch with civilization. We needed to be put to work doing something useful for someone. It didn't make sense to sit around. By now it was already early afternoon on a day so sunny, warm and still, it made it even harder to believe that just twelve hours earlier a storm had raged.

My room was pretty much as I expected. The window had been blown out. Glass spikes and jagged bits lay sprinkled across the carpet, which was still drying out. Sabine's bare bed was still damp, and some of my papers, books, and clothes that had been lying about were now scattered throughout the room. My bed, which was lofted in a nook opposite the window, had been kept out of harm's way. The ladder leading up to the hideaway was still bolted in place but was now missing its bottom two rungs. It appeared that the floor lamp, which now lay in pieces, had been employed as a weapon by the wind.

Without a word, Lucian knelt down and began picking up the glass.

"You don't have to do that," I said, embarrassed.

"I wouldn't want you thinking chivalry is dead," he said, placing the shards on the desk against the opposite wall.

"Don't worry. I'll let you open some doors later if you want, but we'll just leave all this for now."

"Whatever you say," he smiled. We stared at each other a moment, still figuring out exactly where we fit in this new chapter, how to relate to each other. Those leftover sparks didn't know where to go. It was odd to be in such close proximity, for once neither of us on the clock needing to return to the underworld for the equivalent of bed checks or home to curfew, no secret meetings. But now, much as I cared for him, I wanted Lance here. I wanted Lucian safe, but I longed for Lance.

"So, *Lex*," I tested it out. It worked. I liked it, even if it still felt a little foreign. He cocked an eyebrow, in agreement. "Obviously, we've got to get you out of that tux." I shook my head. "I mean, you know what I mean."

"Right, of course," he smiled, ruffling his hair.

"So, this place ain't so bad," Dante joked, wandering in through the open door. He sipped what had to be a warm can of soda. "Ours was about the same. Part of the balcony got ripped off, though." He leaned out the window and pointed to the opposite side of the courtyard. In the area outside Connor's room, a half-moon bite a few feet long had been taken out of the wooden platform. Tracing the path of destruction on the ground, I found the patio furniture overturned. The chaise—the likely culprit—now lay in pieces. A metal side table sat twisted in the fountain.

"I never liked that chaise anyway," I said. Dante smiled conspiratorially. We had once spied Lance on there, lounging with Sabine during what I thought at the time was our nadir. But this right now had to be worse.

"Anyway, sorry to interrupt, just came to rock-paper-scissors for the next shower after Max."

"How about it's all yours if we can borrow some clothes," I nodded at Lucian.

"Sorry," Lucian said. "For some reason, Haven thinks this isn't going to work," he gestured to his suit.

"You would certainly be the best dressed one in our group. You're welcome to any of my stuff, but," he folded his arms, sizing Lucian up. "I think we might not have exactly the same build," he said with just the right amount of self-deprecation. He was several inches shorter than Lucian.

"That's OK," Lucian said. "You know, anything is an improvement here, honestly."

"But..." Dante hesitated, looking at me expectantly like I had the next line in a play, but I had no idea what that might be. I crinkled my brow, confused. Finally he went on, looking disappointed in my failure to read him. "But we've kind of got all of Lance's stuff," he said quietly.

It hadn't occurred to me. They certainly shared a tall and lean frame. It would all fit, but I wasn't sure how I felt about that. An emptiness set into the center of my chest.

Lucian didn't seem to know whether to except the offer. He looked at me for approval or at least guidance. After a beat too long, I shook my head, rattling the thoughts loose again.

"Of course, that makes sense. Help yourself to anything in there."

"You're sure?" he asked, tentative.

"Absolutely. Someone ought to be wearing it," I said, just to fill up the air.

"C'mon in, I'll show you," Dante said, leading Lucian away.

"Thanks, that's really nice," he said.

I stayed behind a moment, leaning against Sabine's bed, just feeling the need to brace myself. I wasn't sure if it would be comforting or more upsetting to see Lance's clothes on another body. I worried it would just make him feel further away.

———◆———

I waited until Lucian was in the shower and Dante out of his room and I crept inside, rummaging through the bureau drawers for my own keepsakes. It felt wrong, like disturbing a museum exhibit, but I had to. I pulled a few of Lance's favorite tee shirts, neatly folded. They had that clean, freshly laundered scent I recognized as pure him. Nestled in among them, cushioned in their cotton, I found an artifact of our past. The terracotta disc that had fallen from the Lexington Hotel the night it burned to the ground. I had caught it when he and I were in the alleyway, safe at last, having escaped through the tunnels just in time. It bore the hotel emblem, the L and H entwined. Our initials. I had given it to him for his birthday. I hadn't realized he had brought it here.

I was only in there a few minutes when I heard footsteps in the hallway. I closed the drawers and sneaked out as Max came down the hall. I pretended to be looking for Dante. I would come back for more later.

4

We're All Just Fine

When I heard the knock at the door, I steadied myself and tried to settle the queasiness in the pit of my stomach.

"So…is this OK?" Lucian asked, his arms outstretched. He looked truly unsure, carrying himself in that stiff way of someone wearing a costume.

I was secretly relieved to find him in the blue plaid button-down that Lance hadn't actually worn since we had been here, and a pair of his dark jeans. "Yeah, looks good," I said, nonchalant. I was lucky: Lucian wasn't the t-shirt and hooded zip-up type. If he had shown up in the faded Cubs t-shirt, I might have had trouble. For just that reason, Lance's most beloved shirt now lay tucked into the bottom of my sock drawer for safekeeping.

We all went next door en masse so the others could meet Brett. The school had managed to send shuttle buses to the house to bring everyone back to their dorms. He was waiting with the final group, once glowing, now bedraggled in their party attire, like glitter stuck to the bottom of a shoe. Most of the guys had stripped down to their undershirts by now, crumpled jackets and French cuffed shirts in hand, their pants still damp at the bottom hem. Girls in smeared makeup, their silk and satin dresses puckered in spots where they had come into contact with the rain, held their spiky heels like weapons, tiptoeing in their bare feet out onto the street and into the awaiting van. Brett said word had traveled down to him that we would all be offered the chance to stay in New Orleans and aid in the relief efforts or be allowed to go home from the program early. That would not be a difficult decision for me. I hoped the others felt the same way.

"You guys wanna grab your stuff and head back with us now?" he asked.

River and I spoke at precisely the same time.

"Awesome," she said, as I said, "No, thank you."

"We're just fine," I pushed, politely, speaking for the group before they had a chance to weigh in, and shooting River a quick look. Like the oldest and wisest among orphaned siblings, I couldn't bear to leave our home or risk being split up. I saw Tom grab River's arm as she was about to speak up again. Brett squinted his eyes, considering whether he might get into some sort of trouble leaving us behind.

"I'm supposed to bring you guys back," he said, inner-monologue creeping out. "It sounds like your place isn't any worse than ours at least, but I'm not sure." He looked us over. "If you change your minds we can send a shuttle bus anytime and put you in the common room of our dorm for the time being. But if you say you're OK…"

"We're all just fine. Promise," I said in my most convincing tone, glancing at the others and relieved to find them wearing their sweetest, most well-adjusted grins.

"…then you're OK. Be back tomorrow," he said with a shrug, boarding his ride, the door snapping shut behind him.

And so we were left to explore the muddy, wet streets of the French Quarter on our own. River and I effectively froze each other out for the afternoon. She quietly seethed, whispering in sharp hisses to Tom as we walked. I pushed it aside, hoping her resentment would pass as quickly as it had sprung up. The scene around us was a distraction, though not a welcome one: evidence of the storm lay everywhere. Street signs were thrown to the ground, street lamps uprooted and shattered, storefronts beat-up and looking like they'd be shuttered for some time. A few shopkeepers had returned, picking up glass and debris, assessing the damage. We asked if we could help and received news reports in return: Other parts of the city were flooded and under water, but it was receding now, one said. So many people missing, said another. Could've been worse but could've been better, said another.

At Mariette's voodoo shop, we found the windows blown and items thrown off the shelves, broken and scattered. It seemed that no glass in the entire city had remained intact. But the place was still standing, which was what really mattered. Dante climbed in through the jagged front window and found Mariette herself tending to the remnants of the mason jars in her pantry—their contents, from alligator teeth to rare plant stamens, all swirled together. I followed him and she hugged us both so tightly in her long, reed-like arms. "I knew you would succeed," she said quietly, simply. She knew our plight and had worked with Dante to develop substances to guard against the toxins from the underworld. She wasn't exactly one of us, but she was most certainly part of us.

We introduced her to the group and when we got to Lucian, before he could tell her his name, she cradled his face in her hands and gazed into his eyes.

"I know who you are. Welcome. Welcome back to the living. Your soul, I can feel, is well and renewed."

"Thank you," he said solemnly. She looked at me and nodded. She and I had spoken of Lucian many times. She had seen his notes to me; she understood his journey. Before we left, as the others headed out to the street, I hung back.

"I know one of you is missing," she said, before I could say a word. "Do not lose faith. Remember what you've learned, fall back on those skills and they will carry you through. Be strong for Lance and for all of them, they need you." And with that she sent me out to the group again.

As we continued on, toward the cemetery and then all the way up to the warehouse district where we had once built our Mardi Gras float, Lucian trailed the group, quiet, eyes focused ahead taking it all in.

I slowed my pace, walking beside him, trying to read his thoughts. "It usually looks a lot better than this," I smiled.

"No, it's incredible, even like this," he said sincerely. "To be walking out here and to be safe." He shook his head, in awe, his hands in his pockets. I just nodded. The sun beat down on us, unusually strong for March.

We spent the rest of the day touring, stopping to sweep up glass, hang fallen signs, and cart away broken furniture. It wasn't until nearly dusk when anyone brought up the decision I had made for us. We had just unlocked the gate back into our courtyard, home at last.

"So I'd like to think things were democratic here," River started in her usual aggressive tone. She stopped near the fountain filled with debris blown from the storm, and faced me. The group slowed to a halt around us, like kids in a schoolyard who sense a fight is coming. "Thanks for telling Brett we're staying."

I stood still and tall, prepared to defend my decision and myself. "Listen," I started. "Sometimes I need—"

"No," she snapped, then shook her head. "Thank you," she said it forcefully, but without sarcasm. I didn't understand. "For real. I think we all need to be here, just us. No outsiders. No tiptoeing around, worried about saying all that we know about what's going on or about who we are or about what really happened to Lance. We need to be together. I get it." Her face was stony, her voice firm. I could tell it took a lot for her to say that.

"Thanks," I said simply. She nodded.

"It just happened fast and I would've liked to be part of the decision, you know?"

"Got it. Fair enough," I said, still a little rigid.

"Is everyone good with that? We stay together?" she looked around the circle. "And I'm in no rush to leave, either."

I had to agree. "Stay here," I gestured to the house. "And here, in New Orleans, as long as possible. Everyone in?" The five angels all quickly answered in the affirmative, no prodding needed. Lucian nodded, averting his eyes. I imagined he was probably wondering where else he would even have gone. I hoped he knew that I would keep watch over him. I had that figured out the minute Dante brought it up this morning. "Good, then that's settled," I offered but the group still felt off balance.

"Awesome," Dante said. "Anyone hungry?" He bounded up the steps to the house, diffusing the tension in the air as only he could and giving everyone an excuse to go inside and, in a grander sense, to coexist here, as alike and as different as we all might be.

"See, we're angels but we still know how to bring the drama," Emma said with a shrug as she passed Lucian to skip up the steps.

Lucian and I exchanged a look.

"Nostalgic for your old home yet?" I asked, joking.

"Not even close."

The electricity came on later that night. All at once it seemed every light bulb and TV blazed on, a jarring return to normalcy that reminded me I needed to call Joan. It felt like time had stood still, even though of course it hadn't. A paralysis had set into my bones and muscles and mind with Lance gone, and the city so torn up and quiet. But now that we could watch the news—and the images weren't pretty—now that our phones were charging and we were reconnected to the world, it occurred to me that my uneasiness wouldn't be going away so quickly. I was going to have to talk to Joan and make it seem like everything was OK, and carry on that way until Lance returned to us. It was going to be a tall order.

———

Twenty-three. I had twenty-three missed calls from Joan and seven messages. I certainly couldn't blame her. I turned my phone over and over in my palm as I slouched in my bed. Steeling myself, I tested my calmest tone. *Hi, everything's fine. Everything's fine. Everyone's good. It's not as bad as it looks.* I took a deep breath and dialed.

As usual, Joan picked up on the first ring, caller ID doing its job and delivering the number she had been waiting for.

"Haven! Are you OK? Where are you? Are you all right? I've been calling. The news is terrifying. Are you OK?" The questions shot out rapid-fire. I waited for the first pause.

"I'm fine. We're all just fine—" I invoked my new mantra again, as though saying it over and over might will it to be true.

"Ruthie called asking if I'd heard anything," she interrupted. This was Dante's mom. "And Lance's mother, and no one had heard anything. None of you could call or send an email or something? You know I can text now; you could always send a text the way that one girl did who was kidnapped and hidden in a cave and she texted her mother. Remember that story? And they were able to find her and it was such a short text, one of those with the letters and numbers that usually don't make sense to me—G? R? Number 8?—something along those lines except it was a 9-1-1 sort of message, you know what I mean? But they found her!" I had to smile. Joan was off on one of her tangents. This is what she did when she got excited. I had never found it so comforting as now. I curled up on my bed, felt the smile turning up the corners of my mouth as the slightest hint of tears began to well.

"I know. I'm sorry, Joan. We had no phones, no electricity, nothing. It all just came back. But we're totally fine," I said, impressing myself with the steadiness of my voice.

I was met with such perfect silence I thought for a moment that my phone might have died again. Then a slow, skeptical, "Really?"

"Yes. I promise," I was almost believing it myself. "I know it must look scary on TV. But where we are, we're fine. I swear. It's just been….a weird 24 hours." That wasn't a lie at least.

"Weren't we just talking about this, Haven? How it's always a weird 24 hours for you?" She wasn't angry necessarily, she was just venting in that way that you can when everything seems roughly OK. "Why do I feel like you're always in the middle of all of these disasters?"

I didn't really have an answer for that. It was true. We had had this conversation before. We had had so many of these talks now, which required my greatest acting skills, because there was no way to tell her the truth. But I needed to, and soon. I couldn't take this lying anymore. But for now, I just let her go on. "I'm so glad you have Lance and Dante there," she said, softening again. "Thank goodness you kids have each other at times like this."

I chewed on my bottom lip, anything to distract me. I needed to hold it all together, to keep even a single tear from falling. A single tear would beget a sea of them. "I know," I said, my voice tense. And then I knew I had to do it. I had to cover. "And, you know there's a lot of stuff to do here, to help and all,"

I stammered. "So, Lance actually is with the first group that went out to aid some of the hardest hit areas. He still doesn't have a working phone. Can you tell his mom he's fine?"

"He isn't *with* you?" I could hear the alarm beginning to sound in her voice.

"He was but, you know, we're a volunteer program, so obviously we're going to be helping now that there's, you know, more to do," I was not at my most eloquent, but I just hoped my tone sounded easy enough to slip through her sharp sensor for trouble.

She paused, thinking. "Next time you hear from him, tell him he needs to call Roberta as soon as possible. She is NOT going to like this," Joan said firmly. She and Lance's adoptive mom had a lot in common. It was still surprising to me that we had managed to get ourselves into such dire situations considering how overprotective our parents were.

"Of course."

"And Haven, I know you're not insinuating that you all intend to stay in this disaster area. I want you on the first flight out of there."

"Well—"

"Don't start with me," she was exasperated now. "Don't you know they've declared a state of emergency there?"

"Sure, but that's why—"

"We'll talk about this tomorrow," she silenced me. "I'm just glad you're safe. Please be careful, honey. I don't think you realize how dangerous this is." I had to stop myself from protesting. "I love you."

"Love you too, Joan."

I snuggled up beneath the covers, still in my jeans and thin v-neck sweater I'd worn all day, and stayed there as the minutes stretched on, not quite ready to rejoin the group yet. I thought again of what Lucian had said: I was the leader here. I needed to be strong in their eyes, to give them hope and make them feel that our goals were achievable. Even if, in these quiet moments of solitude, I wished I could feel more certain. I climbed down the ladder, rifled to the bottom of that one drawer, and retrieved that hidden Cubs t-shirt from its resting place. Then I slipped off my clothes and pulled on the soft cotton shirt, feeling at home in its embrace.

⟫◦◈◦⟪

I dreamt feverish dreams of reality, replaying those images of the night of the storm again and again until I awoke with a jolt, panting like I'd been running through the French Quarter again, digging up the dirt of the cemetery, hopeless. My clock read three in the morning. Dante's comforting snore greeted me from the bed below.

Would I have those dreams every day until I saw Lance again? Yes, I supposed. I probably would. Well, then I would use them for something good. Wide awake, I crept down the ladder through the black of the night-filled room.

I showered, dressed and made my way to that padded sanctuary that had once seemed so mysterious: the levitation room where we had saved each other after each of us had been poisoned by the toxins administered by the Krewe. We had focused our strength to lift out the blackened halves of each other's souls. We had only recently acquired those wild freewheeling powers. We had learned to harness them, but they still needed to be strengthened and refined.

So I focused my gaze on a basketball on the opposite side of the room, studied it a moment and then, with my mind, threw it easily, warming up with the same effort one might use for an underhanded toss to a child learning to play catch. The ball slammed against the ceiling with such force it popped it like a balloon, its hollow carcass smacking against the padded floor.

The bang echoed like a gun shot, making me jump. I had done this trick plenty of times, always expending far more energy with far more modest results. But this? This felt like I had merely tapped an accelerator and sent a car speeding at 100 miles per hour. I caught my breath, eyes to the ceiling, and noticed that the impact of the ball had left a half-moon shaped indentation above.

The thought crossed my mind: if that had been so effortless, what else had changed over the course of the past day? What had the passing of this Metamorphosi Day done to me? Suspended a foot below that dent, a metal lighting track ran parallel to the center of the ceiling. I took a hop, swinging my arms as though on a trampoline, and on the second bounce I pushed off and rocketed up. Fast. Too fast. Up I flew. The ceiling was probably 18 feet and my head would have crashed against it in an instant if I hadn't grabbed that track. My legs kept moving, the centrifugal force slamming me against the ceiling and ricocheting back down again. I held on for the briefest moment, then fell just as fast, the kinetic energy sending me right back down.

I landed on my feet, crouching. My heart beat loud, the adrenaline that I loved beginning to course through me again. Without thinking, I ran. Straight at the wall, faster and faster, and when it neared, my legs surged just as fast up, up, reaching the ceiling and then flipping me backwards so that I floated back down to the floor again. When my feet hit the ground, more softly than they should have, I couldn't quite process what had happened. I couldn't help but smile, thrilled by this new power. This was just the kind of thing that could help take a girl's mind off of the boy she was missing.

<hr />

It became my new routine. I would be at the sanctuary every morning at 3 am. I would run circles around the place, like a stunt motorcyclist enclosed in a steel cage. I would explode off of every flat surface, and then, when I tired of that room and felt even those wide walls closing in, I would go outside to run, jump, launch myself against the sides of our home and the fence of our courtyard. I would skip up to the roof and skitter down onto the balcony railing, then onto the ledge of the fountain and then right back up to the main doorstep. My landings and points of contact grew softer as time wore on, at first sounding like a single, assertive knock against the door, then later like a pebble against a window.

If I woke anyone, no one ever said a word. With one exception: Emma. One evening, early on, when I had been only a week or so into my nocturnal training sessions, she had sought me out in my room. She looked nervous when I opened the door, like she had seen something she shouldn't have.

"I just wanted to let you know that I'm up sometimes at night too. Thinking about Jimmy, even though I know I shouldn't be because he really is gone," she said, launching right in with no warning as her fingers fidgeted. I was so shocked, I didn't say a word, just let her talk. We had always gotten along fine, but had never been close. She tucked her auburn waves behind her ear. "I just mean to say, I know how it feels to lose someone. I know it's different, what happened to Lance, and that there's still hope for him and all. But I know how it feels when a piece of you is missing. And I don't want you to feel as alone as I did. So if you ever want to hang out or just need to talk to someone who understands…" She nodded, as though glad to have gotten that out. "So that's all." Then just as she was about to turn and leave, she paused a beat and threw her arms around me instead, taking me by surprise. I thanked her and told her I was here for her too. It wasn't the way I tended to operate, this sort of reaching out, which is why it meant something to me that she had sought me out. I made a mental note to take her up on her invitation. She had been putting on even more of a brave face than I had realized: she had seemed so stoic ever since those shocking early days of Jimmy's transition into a creature of the underworld. I didn't want her feeling alone either. And it was true, she would understand more than anyone.

The only other person who seemed to notice my activities was a dark figure I would catch peeking out from the window in Dante's old room from time to time. I had grown accustomed to his silhouette, from all those nights gazing up at the window of the mansion next door, where he had been trapped during his tenure in the underworld. He would watch me for a while, then disappear again. And each morning, as the sun rose and we all gathered in the living room with our breakfast and our new ideas for conquering our future tests, he and I would go on each pretending we hadn't spied one another the night before.

5

Business as Usual

The next couple of months were the most normal, relatively speaking, that I had experienced in quite some time. It reminded me of those months in the fall back in Evanston as we wrapped up high school early and awaited the start of the volunteer program, knowing somewhere deep that nothing would probably happen to us until we got to New Orleans. If that had been the calm before the storm, this was both the calm after that storm and before the next. We felt as safe as we possibly could.

With some convincing we had gotten Brett to agree to let us remain in the house. He moved in for a while, taking dinner with us in the dining room—which we only used when he was there because it felt too formal. We preferred the easy comforts of the living room for sentimental reasons; it felt like the place where we had committed ourselves to each other. Brett bunked in Connor's vacated room several nights, switching off between us and the dorm with his other group of high school volunteers. But slowly he came to trust us, for better or worse, and he left. It helped that, as Tom learned during a pick-up basketball game, Brett had apparently broken up with his girlfriend on nearby St. Ann's Street and begun dating a sophomore closer to the Tulane campus. So our house just wasn't convenient anymore, thankfully.

We would still see him at our various projects, though. The first few days he had us aid the rest of his group in fixing up the dorm they shared with some of the other interns. Then they came to our place to return the favor. Though it felt oddly intrusive to have our home overrun with relative strangers, it was a relief to not have to wear shoes all the time to protect our feet from the constant crunching of broken glass. After that, there were other buildings on campus to tend to. We replaced windows, patched up walls, and repaired what furniture could be salvaged. Brett, it turned out, was a skilled carpenter, leading us through our work along with a handful of professional contractors. Emma flirted tirelessly with him, telling him he belonged on one of those home makeover reality shows, and he seemed to enjoy the attention even though he still went home to his girlfriend at night. I understood now, just as I ran myself ragged in the nighttime hours, this was *her* way of handling Jimmy's absence.

Every morning a shuttle bus arrived and we were whisked away to spend the day cleaning, building, distributing supplies, cooking, delivering meals, and on and on. We worked in many of the places we already knew, from the food bank to Our Lady of Guadalupe Church near the cemetery, to the Superdome where so many were staying—this time with greater success and comfort than during Katrina. There was no shortage of work, and it was all much easier knowing that we wouldn't need to fight demons simultaneously.

We had relied on the chaos and confusion of the storm's aftermath to gloss over certain details with Brett and it had worked: he had a list of who lived here but when he asked about the mysterious Lance, we told him his information was outdated, that Lance had left and Lex had arrived. We kept out of the levitation room when Brett was around and called it a gym, which is what it had been before Connor had moved the equipment to a storage room on the first floor.

I checked my smartphone obsessively, to no avail. We received no new text messages during that whole time. This life felt so foreign because it was entirely *normal*: we had work to do; we had a counselor checking in on us; we didn't have any of those training exercises; we didn't live under the threat of attack. And life during that time was virtually monastic. In the evenings, since a city-wide curfew was in effect and the Quarter still hadn't fully reopened, we gathered in the common room to eat dinner and watch TV.

We talked about things like where we had gotten into college and where we had decided to go. When Brett wasn't around, we spoke more openly about whether we should all try to accept schools located near each other, just in case we survived and would actually be able to go to them. Our list of questions grew and grew like a tree in need of pruning, with no one available to pluck these inquiries and answer them.

So we just focused on what we did know: when our time here was through we would all go home and then reconvene in Paris. We met nightly in each other's rooms or in the courtyard, quietly plotting and planning. June 21. That date was circled in blood red on the calendar in my mind.

We all independently laid the foundation with our parental units, selling the trip as a graduation gift. Some were already on board. River had had no trouble getting permission. She welcomed the challenge of running away, making it sound like her single, adoptive mom was laissez-faire enough that she could get away with escaping to another country. "I'm always glad for anything that might keep you out of trouble," she had apparently told River. Emma's folks were tougher but seemed to appreciate that it had sounded more educational than the beach trips she usually pushed for. Tom's parents had been convinced it was a joke. Max, Drew, and, of course, Dante, had all left parents like my Joan—the kind who asked questions and had opinions about the answers you gave—back home. The phone calls could be exhausting.

Lucian often kept quiet during our strategy sessions, much in the way I used to before becoming the person who had to run these meetings. But the reason why hit me during one of our talks debating how long to stay at home before going to Paris. Of course: he didn't have anywhere to go. I had been so consumed with the grander plans, I had overlooked the fact that I hadn't yet actually invited him. "You know you're coming home with me, right?" I said to him easily, interrupting Drew's report on potential flight itineraries. "So don't worry, OK?" Dante looked at me across the patio table, horrified, as though anticipating how Joan would handle a handsome stranger moving in, even for a couple weeks. "Don't give me that look," I smiled, then ordered: "You're going to host him."

"Wow, you're getting bossy," Dante said. "I kinda like it. Works on you, Hav."

"Thanks," I laughed. "And River, we need to talk about IDs."

"We sure do. Lex, man, you're gonna need a passport, you know," River said. "My services don't come cheap, but I'm worth it." I planned to keep her very busy.

"Works for me, thanks," he said.

When Lucian did speak, it was with caution, and only on issues on which he was an expert.

"How early do we get there?"

"Will they appear before the solstice?"

"Will the revolution begin immediately after the sacrifice ritual?"

These concerns all fell to him. He would always preface his answers with, "I can't be sure," as though nervous about leading us astray. I could see the toll the guilt of Lance's disappearance had taken on him. It had settled on his shoulders, shrouding him like a heavy cloak, trailing him when he walked. It encased him. His spirit felt leaden and diminished. Whereas I used to feel a *presence* when he walked in the room, a sense of control emanating from him like he had a hold over you and knew it, now he felt like a ghost. His gray eyes had gone dark, a spark missing and replaced with the kind of daze I used to see in hospital patients coping with constant, chronic pain.

I wasn't sure whether it comforted me to know that, like me, he continued to feel the burn of that loss every day, or if it concerned me. I hoped that I hid the strain better than he did, but I couldn't be sure.

The only time I saw the old, commanding Lucian was at work. He wasn't as physically strong as the rest of us, but you wouldn't have known it to watch him. He worked alongside Brett as though he were one of the program directors. He seemed familiar with the mechanics of whatever task we had been assigned and directed us with respectful authority. I couldn't help but get the sense he was trying to redeem himself and make amends by devoting every scrap of energy and life force to these projects. Most of us didn't mind his taking charge. I saw it as a nice respite from the decision making and wrangling we had to do during our nocturnal war-room discussions. But as we inched closer to going home, some people started to bristle.

On a particularly hot May day, just a week before we were to leave, we were all punchy. The blazing sun singed our skin and burned up the clouds as we toiled, sweating as we rebuilt homes in a devastated part of town. Tom, on edge like the rest of us with our time winding down, began shouting. I heard him from the next room and caught sight of him and Lucian between the vertical beams of the house's framework, where I was helping the group hang drywall.

"Lay off, OK?" Tom barked, pushing Lucian's shoulder with one hand. Lucian just stood there, stone-faced as though he'd felt nothing more than a strong gust of wind blowing through. He put his hands up in unemotional surrender. "You aren't even supposed to *be* here," Tom said. "I've been listening to you for weeks. I'm sick of it. You should know your place." I felt a dagger in my heart and rose to my feet, on reflex. But something held me back, not wanting to make it worse.

"Just meant we could use you for some demolition work at the place down the street," Lucian said. "We need to tear it down before rebuilding and you seemed to know what you were doing on that other rebuild last week."

But Tom ignored him and flung his hammer, putting such a spin on it that it slammed against a beam a few feet behind Lucian's head and stuck into it. Then he walked off the platform of the home, straight across the street, and kept going. Lucian quietly pried the hammer out of the wood. After a few moments, I saw River trailing Tom, following at a distance behind him at an urgent pace. Lucian caught me watching and I looked away a moment, not wanting to see the defeat in his eyes. He walked out to the back of the house.

"Whoa," Dante whispered beside me. "We may all kill each other before we give any demons a chance."

I followed Lucian and found him sitting on the muddy ground, watching the work underway on the ramshackle house neighboring this one. He glanced at me only a moment, as though telling me it was alright, he wanted to be left alone. So I squeezed his shoulder and then slipped back into the house.

<hr/>

Tom and River reappeared just in time to take the shuttle bus home. None of us said a word on the ride back. I sat beside a silent Lucian, who gazed out the window, then closed his eyes, a tense crease between his brows. I thought about Dante's words. I had been so busy trying to hold myself together, so proud of not crumbling in these many weeks, I had failed to notice that as we marched closer to our end date here, our fuses had all grown shorter. We all felt the loss of control, a shared dread of time running out. Tom had just acted on it, but we were all spiraling in our own way. Some more quietly than others.

I cornered Lucian that night before meeting the others in the courtyard. I knocked on the door of what had once been Dante's room but had become just Lucian's room following the storm when Dante opted to stay with Max down the hall. Hearing nothing inside, I tried again then turned the door-knob and found it unlocked. I pushed it gently open. Lucian sat on the bed, back against the wall, lost in a book. He looked up in my direction, trying out the slightest smile. But I wasn't buying it.

"Are you hiding out?" I asked, leaning against the doorframe.

"I prefer to call it reading," he said, holding up a copy of *The Time Machine*. It wasn't one of Lance's titles so it must have come from the shelves in the common room.

"That's a good one," I nodded. "But not so good that it should keep you cooped up on one of our last nights here."

He stared at the ceiling like he'd been caught. I still wasn't entirely sure how to comfort him. What would I have said to Lance now if it had been him?

"So, are you Team Eloi or Team Morlock?" I joked, the first thing that came to mind.

"Who knows anymore," he said. I worried that my stab at small talk might've hit too close to home. But then he smiled and shook his head. A promising sign at least.

"Tell me about it," I returned the smile. "Did you know—" I wandered in, letting the door close behind me. "—that the original version was all about the time traveler himself and sort of being this guy who didn't fit in anywhere and dealing with that?" A few long seconds passed. I took a seat beside him and finally filled up the silence. "But then Wells changed it to be more about the world he encountered when he traveled and less about him, which I think is kind of a shame, I guess maybe because that's how I feel, like, all the time."

"I actually found a book once that had some of that first draft in it," he said, his tone still a little dulled. "And I agree, it was exactly what you would've hoped…" He stopped himself. He looked at me a moment then stared into the space in front of us. There across the room the closet door was ajar, Lance's clothes and belongings tucked inside. "It's OK. You don't have to say anything."

I abided for a moment and then, quietly: "So, you know, Tom is just freaking out because he and River live on opposite ends of the country and we're all going home in a couple of days, right?"

"Sure," he said, unconvinced. "That's fine. I don't blame him. He was right anyway."

"No he wasn't. He was just looking for a punching bag. So I'm not going to let you beat *yourself* up, it's a really bad use of time."

"Haven, haven, haven," he sighed, looking at me in that way he had so many times before. "I just…I wish I could start over. I wish so many things—So. Many. Things.—had been so very different."

He put his hand to my face, locking his eyes on mine, studying me for a few long seconds. In that time I felt I could see the whole history of us unfold against the gray screens of his eyes. If this had been a few months ago, this moment might have been very different. But now he ran his thumb across my cheek, as though catching an invisible tear, and then simply took his hand away, casting his eyes downward again.

I had no words. I could not summon the right ones to soothe him. Ever since Lance's capture, I had been struggling to avoid playing that game with myself: considering what might have happened if things had gone differently, replaying the scene over and over. It was such a dangerous business and always led you somewhere dark, feeling the weight of your failure, tallying up mistakes and what ifs. I had to steer him away.

"We have to look forward, that's all we've got," I said, as light as I could muster. "It will be easier when we get to Evanston. Calmer. Fewer personalities to manage. And then, I know these guys, everyone will rally for…" I struggled to put the right spin on this battle we faced. "…for Lance," I said simply.

He just nodded, looking like he wanted to say something more, only to come up with: "See you tonight then. Courtyard," he nodded. I hopped off the bed.

"You want to…?" I pointed toward the door, hoping he might join me.

He held up the book, "I think I'll finish." I nodded, not wanting to leave him there but also not prepared to stay and possibly be lead into the talk we had been avoiding for so long.

I found Tom and River in the common room, which seemed encouraging: at least they weren't cutting themselves off from us. Tom was watching ESPN, unwinding. Neither looked at me, so I stood in front of the TV screen. Their lifeless eyes fell on me. "Cool?" I asked, easily.

He nodded, expressionless.

"Courtyard tonight?" I asked.

Both nodded again. River, who was curled up beside him, smoothed his hair in a loving way, a show of affection I rarely saw from her. I continued on to the levitation room, thinking about the gesture. I wondered if that was how things were when they were alone together. He got to see a side of her that none of us knew. You never knew what really went on between two people. Everyone, I was sure, had formulated plenty of opinions about Lucian and me and about Lance and me. But the truth was so much more complex than anyone could know from looking. I had always quietly scoffed when I had heard people writing college admissions essays about how love had changed them. It had been the first rule of what not to do, as far as I was concerned. But I was beginning to understand. That power, so transformative, was the impetus for everything, wasn't it? It could lead you into fire and death and danger to preserve it.

———◆———

Brett had stopped by in the early evening, as the volume turned up on the street outside, the resilient French Quarter now returning to some of its pre-storm buoyancy. The revelry may have been muted, but it was a comfort. More normalcy. He had been armed with airport shuttle pick-up times, flight numbers, and checklists of what we needed to turn in at our move-out inspection. Nothing new, it was all information that sat in my email in-box untouched. I hadn't been prepared to open any of it, to go over the details that would take me back home, where I would be spinning many more lies. It had grown exhausting maintaining so many elaborate fictions.

As we all gathered by the fountain, it set in that this was it until Paris. The chaise and patio chairs still forming the circle from our last meeting, we sat in the same seats, whether we intended to or not. Dante and Lucian on either side of me perched on the ledge of the fountain.

"This is probably the last chance we'll have together, just us, before leaving," I started, but shook my head. "Not to be dramatic or anything." I tried to lighten up, and they smiled. "But, so, where is everyone on the trip? Passports?" I looked around the circle. Everyone nodded. With the exception of Lucian, we had all gone over the course of the past few weeks to secure our passports. It still seemed unbelievable that someone like me who had barely ventured outside of the Midwest would be making this trip. I still hadn't quite gotten Joan's approval, but it didn't really matter. Nothing would keep me from getting there.

River cleared her throat for attention and leaned in, brandishing a navy booklet at me, its golden seal glinting in the light of the porch. I thought it was going to be for Lucian but she nodded for me to take it. When I opened it, I realized why. It was an olive branch. I flipped through. It looked just like mine, except of course, the identification page bore a headshot of Lance. It made me shiver, like I had seen a ghost. Holding it in my hands, this falsified document, gave me hope: it implied that he would be coming home with us. I hoped it would be a self-fulfilling prophecy. I pictured it in his strong, smooth hands, pictured him striding through the airport with us, perfect and beautiful, returned to us where he belonged. I didn't want to fall too deeply into the rabbit hole of that comforting fantasy though. I would bump up against too many questions to which I didn't know the answer. Even if all did go smoothly, it would only be the beginning of our battle. Sometimes it did no good to look too far into the future. I returned to the present. The others were watching me silently. Dante placed his hand on mine and I snapped out of my thoughts.

"How did you…?" I asked.

"It's surprisingly easy to get the raw materials," River said with a shrug, adding cryptically. "If you know what to say and where to look. And then it's just an arts and crafts project. Thanks for your design expertise, Drew," she gestured. Drew shook her head, modest. "We'll copy the stamp when we get there," she went on.

"Will it scan?" I asked, studying the identification page.

"Absolutely. I've got friends in low places."

"It's incredible," I said, solemn. "Thank you."

"No problem," River offered the slightest proud smile. "Oh! And for you," she shook her head, almost forgetting. She handed Lucian a laminated card and booklet. I leaned in, looking over his shoulder. An Illinois driver's license and a passport, both in Lex's name. They looked shockingly real.

"Nice work, River," I said. I could understand why she had such a bustling fake ID business back home.

"Thanks, this is perfect," he said sincerely. "I owe you."

"No sweat," she said. "Now there's no getting out of it. See you at Père-Lachaise."

"No place I'd rather be," he said. And I felt like he meant it.

"So, that's all set," I said. "Drew, how's travel and accommodations?"

And so we had gone on, running through all of the details in our shorthand, everything we had established so far and pledging to check in during the few weeks between now and then. When we had covered everything, we stayed outside for a while, gazing up at the stars, yawning, even closing our eyes. It felt as though we all didn't want to go back inside, to sleep, knowing that we would wake up and be closing this chapter, going home and then into so much uncertainty.

⟡

The farewell party the following night could not have felt more different than the fête that had greeted us when we arrived on New Year's Eve. Instead of a lavish soirée at a home in the leafy garden district, this time the volunteers and program leaders all crowded into a meeting room in Tulane's student union. We stayed for only a short time then trickled out, taking a bus back to the French Quarter to wander the streets one last time.

That night, like every other night since Lance's disappearance, I stepped out of my jeans, peeled off my top, and pulled on one of those few shirts I had pilfered from his closet. Tonight it was my favorite: the faded black one bearing the dates of Nirvana's tour in a year before we were born. He had gotten it at the same thrift shop in Chicago where he had found the cuff with the angel wing that matched my necklace. We had been together that day, back when we had already discovered how much we needed each other, but were just beginning to understand how very much we also had in common.

The worn cotton so soft against my skin, I climbed into my bed, willing myself to sleep, knowing I needed strength not just for my early morning training, but for all that lay ahead.

My room was bare, my bags packed, my clothes for the next day the only items left in my dresser.

6

It Doesn't Hurt to Keep People Guessing

I smoothed my dress—black, knee-length with thin straps. Plain and somber, it looked like I was going to a funeral. I placed the square satin cap on my head. I felt like one of those pencils with an elaborate eraser on top. I cocked it to one side then the other, trying to fix it. Nothing was right. But it was because *I* wasn't right.

"Haven, we're going to be late. Two-minute warning!" Joan yelled up from downstairs, her heels clicking against the floor in the kitchen.

"Coming, Joan!" I yelled into my reflection in the mirror but made no attempt to move. The morning sun streamed in the window, the air already warm, the conditions, unfortunately, ideal for this kind of thing.

Being home without Lance was even worse than being in New Orleans without him. His absence was more jarring here. After all that had happened, to be back in Evanston—in our old neighborhood near our old school, in a house a few blocks from his—confused my body. I couldn't remember how to be me here without him. I kept pulling out my phone to call him and realizing he wasn't there. I kept tucking things away that I wished I could tell him. I supposed this kind of thing happened to anyone who had lost someone, even if it wasn't through an act of pure otherworldly terror. It changes you. It had changed me. And it was near impossible to act as though it was no big deal that he wasn't here, unable to talk about it. Under normal circumstances, I imagined scar tissue would build up over time to let you move on, and you would eventually learn to carry on despite the void. But what happens when that person might be able to return to you if you can find a way to steal him back? I felt my skin harden into a shell, preventing me from engaging with the world. I wanted to retreat from it all and focus entirely on preparing for Père-Lachaise.

Today's events were the last thing I felt like doing. It was all for show anyway. It didn't matter. The piece of paper was still mine. But I couldn't do that to Joan, or to Dante for that matter. I sighed at my reflection, blowing a strand of hair from my face in the process. I placed the cap on again and shook my head.

Joan appeared in the doorway, smiling. "Don't worry, honey, those caps are meant to look ridiculous," she said, fishing for something in her purse. "You look beautiful."

"Thanks. That's pretty, is it new?" I asked. She loved girl talk. Her excitement at having me back had bought me extra time, but she would start asking questions soon. She had been far too accepting of our Lance cover.

"Why thank you, it is." She posed, then waved for me to follow. "Come on now, let's go. How would it look if the salutatorian was late?" she asked, beaming.

⸻◈⸻

For the first time I could remember, Dante had arrived before me. "You know you only wanted to be salutatorian so you could sit next to me," he greeted me with a hug, as I found my seat beside him in the front row. A stage and rows of chairs had been set up on the football field, families and friends packing the bleachers.

"That B in AP Euro will haunt me forever," I joked.

"Seriously, what happened there?" he laughed.

"You got the only A in that class. The final was multiple choice, remember? The really crazy kind where you second-guess yourself because all of the options are almost correct—" My competitive streak was flaring.

"Oh, yeah, not your strong suit," he said. "Your loss."

"Most people didn't even finish." I said, defending myself but laughing that it was still a sore point. I elbowed him. "Are you super nervous?" I asked, joking.

"Yeah, this is definitely worse than battling demons," he whispered with a roll of the eyes, slapping me on the arm. Dante had written his valedictory speech out on the flight home. He had scribbled it out in no time into a notebook he had bought in the airport gift shop. Classic, brilliant Dante. Then he had set it on my tray table. "I'm so not going up there alone," he had ordered. "Make whatever changes and get an apron." And with that he had settled in to sleep through the rest of the trip.

Now he said, "How much do you wish we could just sneak outta here after getting our diplomas and not wait for the whole class?"

"Yes, please," I smiled.

On stage the teachers took their places while behind us our fellow students found their seats. The class president took his place beside me without a word, in the seat that would have been Lance's if he had been here. I looked out of the corner of my eye considering saying hello, in the spirit of the day, even though we never spoke, but he ignored me. I looked back through all the faces of our classmates and then into the crowd to where Joan sat with some of the ladies from the hospital. A few rows above I spotted Lucian, in more of Lance's clothes, seated beside Dante's mom. His brow was furrowed and he looked far away, as he often did these days. I wondered if all of this felt familiar to him, if it reminded him of those days not so long ago before meeting Aurelia. I wondered how much this now-mortal Lucian was like that boy who had been recruited. I had found my mind wandering. What would they have said if they really knew what had happened to Lance? *Please join us as we take a moment of silence for our dear student, who was abducted and....*

Dante elbowed me, snapping me out of it: "Hav," he whispered. It was my cue: I was in charge of props and special effects.

Principal Tollman, helmet-like hair bouncing joyfully as she spoke, was introducing Dante as "one of the best and brightest in the history of Evanston Township High School. We expect great things from this young man, who will be attending Northwestern University in the fall."

Dante jogged up the steps to shake her hand, dreadlocks shimmying, his grin lighting up the stage. From the wings, I wheeled out a small table I had set up for him with a working hot plate and several items he had brought from his kitchen at home. He pulled the microphone from the podium and took his place behind the table.

"Thank you, Principal Tollman. Hi, fellow soon-to-be graduates. I promise this is going to be nice and short because it's hot out here and these caps and gowns are not made of breathable fabrics. But most important, high school has already gone on way too long, so I don't know about you but I'm pretty anxious to get out of here."

I was already prepared to whoop it up for him, as he had instructed, to make sure his jokes weren't met with complete silence and to try to get the crowd going. But I didn't have to. They did it on their own. My heart swelled with pride for him. The audience was listening and responding.

"So, I actually spent the past semester in New Orleans working on some community service projects, and spent some time at a food bank and soup kitchen," at this, he pulled out a chef's hat from behind the podium and put it on in place of his graduation cap to some chuckling from the audience. I tied an apron over my gown. It read "Hats off, Wildkits!" featuring our feline mascot in a graduation cap. When Dante had given it to me I had assured him I wouldn't have done this for anyone else. "So I can now make a pretty mean gumbo—which is basically a spicy stew full of all sorts of good stuff that takes a crazy long time to cook.

"And while I was making these day after day, it hit me that it's kinda like how we've become who we are over these past four years. Each of us is our own gumbo. I know, I know, it sounds crazy. But, listen, we've been tossing in all these experiences and simmering here at Evanston Township for four years and now we're done....or are we?

"See, we've all learned a lot about ourselves here, right? But now that we're all moving on, it's exciting, and a little scary too. So I thought we could use a recipe for success going forward. So with the help of my lovely assistant and your salutatorian, Haven—" I waved shyly, looking out into that crowd of hundreds of faces watching, and gestured toward the pot on the hot plate like a game show hostess, as we had rehearsed. "—who is tending to this roux I've already made, I thought I'd offer five steps for the perfect Graduation Gumbo to get us through the next chapter in our lives. No two gumbos are alike, you know.

"First, find your passion, something you love that can define you. This is the heart and soul of your gumbo. This is your chicken or seafood or sausage or what have you." I tossed in a bowl of chicken and stirred.

"Second: add your own flavor to everything you do," he said. I held up a spice rack and then one by one sprinkled several of the small canisters into the pot. "Don't be afraid to be bold and to be you, no matter how spicy that is. Someone will appreciate it.

"Third: always have a few people you can count on, the kind of people who make you better, smarter, stronger," he said. I held up salt and pepper and sprinkled each in. "And remember you don't actually need that many friends. You just need one or two really, really good ones that are there all the time.

"Fourth: Strive to be better. Remember to keep learning every day." At this he pried the microphone from the podium and strolled over to the table. I pretended to take a bite and then he did too. "Keep working, don't give up, take your time," he said as we added bits of chopped vegetables and more spices. An egg timer on the table went off. "You'll get it just right." We sampled again and nodded to each other. Some of our class-mates snickered at our show, but it didn't matter to us. We were getting to the good part.

"And, finally, above all, make your mark. Make a difference, have an impact," he said. This was what I had been hired to do. I took a handful of cinnamon, he took a handful of ground car-damom, though it didn't matter what we used. "Always, always know you're something special. And it doesn't hurt to keep people guessing." When we each tossed our final ingredients in, I focused on the pot for only a moment before it flared. A fiery burst shot straight up nearly licking the "Congratulations, ETHS Graduates!" banner strung up above the stage, then flamed out with a puff of gray smoke and a POP so loud it shook the entire platform. In the audience, some of our fellow classmates, who had begun to zone out, jerked at the display. A few yelped. In the bleachers, some parents' jaws dropped and others nodded, as though this were evidence that we had gotten a good enough education here to know how to do something like this.

Dante and I looked at each other and had to suppress the nervous laughter. When we had practiced it in his backyard, with Lucian our audience, it had been a more modest explosion. But this was definitely a lot more fun. After a second to process that that was in fact part of the act, the audience applauded, impressed and, judging from some of their stunned faces, a little unsure of whether it might have been a fire code violation.

Dante, proud of himself, took a bow as my favorite English teacher left his seat to help me wheel the table away. As he did, the cord from the hot plate unwound. He gathered it up, looking at it curiously, expecting it to have been plugged in to the power source on the platform.

I overheard one of the chemistry teachers on stage leaning forward to whisper to a concerned Principal Tollman, a crease now visible between her eyes, that there was nothing to worry about; it was easy to pull that off with the right basic household chemicals.

"Wasn't that so liberating?!" Dante said softly with wide, wild eyes as we took our seats again. This had been our own private senior prank, as far as he was concerned. Something symbolic he had proposed in order to, quite literally, go out with a bang. "It's like, 'Guess what? We've got this whole secret life that you guys know nothing about. We're so much stronger than anyone would guess,'" he had said when he tried to sell me on the idea. I liked his thinking, just as I liked that it was something we could share. We had gotten each other through high school, so it was so fitting we got to have a moment like this to cap it off.

After the ceremony, as everyone milled around the field with their families, congratulating each other and taking pictures, we were asked many times for our secret. "Just a simple chemistry experiment," we said. "Hardly more complicated than when we all had to make volcanos erupt in fifth grade science class."

———◆◇◆———

A teary-eyed Joan had rushed the field and swept Dante and me into a proud embrace after the ceremony, gushing about the speech and about all the clubs we had led and the grades we'd racked up through our four years. But by the time she and I got home, she had flipped into full party-planning mode. We only had a short time before the house would be overrun with all the family and friends she had invited to my celebration and, though she had, naturally, made all the food already and hung the decorations the night before, there was still plenty to do. She was already barking orders as we walked in the door.

"I think, flow-wise, we're going to want the food on the table in the dining room and then let's put the cake on the server by itself. Don't forget to fan the napkins," she said as she dropped her keys on the table by the door.

"I'm on it," I said, ditching my cap and gown on the coat rack. She stopped and looked at it.

"Normally I'd tell you to put that in your room, but actually I like that there today. It's artistic, isn't it?" she smiled, considering it. "You certainly learned a few things during your time as a *gallerina*. Isn't that what *Chicago* magazine called you?" she joked, squeezing my shoulders as she recalled my time at the Lexington, which had landed me a cameo in a story in the magazine. She had been so proud of me getting that internship and she had loved bragging about it to the ladies at the hospital. It gave me chills though, thinking about it. But Joan just went on to the living room, humming, so upbeat, as she fluffed pillows. I headed to the kitchen.

"Oh, Haven," she said, calling me back in. "Before we start on the food, I need you to do something…" I rolled my eyes, ready for more orders. But as soon as I poked my head in the room, she grinned, pulling a "Congrats, Grad!" gift bag from behind her back. "Open your graduation gift! Surprise!" she said, shaking it at me.

"What's this? You're already throwing me a party," I laughed.

"Go on, go on!" she motioned for me to open it, as she took a seat on the sofa. I sat beside her, pulling out purple and white tissue paper. "Northwestern colors!" she said, proudly. Nestled below, I pulled out a book: a travel guidebook of Paris. I looked at her and she nodded.

"Does this mean…?" She still hadn't given me permission to go on the trip, though she must have gotten the sense I would be going either way, and she knew I still had some savings left from working at the hotel.

"I know you're trying to fly away again," she said, in a serious tone. "And I want you to know that you have my blessing to go. Only because I worry if I don't let you go, you'll just go on your own and then I'll lose you." Her eyes welled up at this.

"You're not going to lose me, Joan," I said, even though I knew it wasn't a promise I could actually make.

"Just be careful, Haven," she grabbed my hand. "You find yourself in such dangerous situations. You've given me a series of heart attacks over the past year and a half—fires and storms and living away from home. I'm hoping it will stop. But I'm beginning to accept that I can't protect you from things, and I'm not supposed to, now that you're going off to school."

"I'll be so close by," I said, once again wishing it to be true. I had no idea what lay ahead though and it hurt me to not be able to tell her that. When would I tell her? Would I tell her?

"I know it's just down the street, but you know what I mean, in the grander sense," she went on, flitting her hand. "I just have to hope you know how to handle whatever is thrown your way as the smart and capable young woman I've raised."

"I promise," I said, softly. Finally, a promise I could keep.

"So you can go, if you promise to be careful and keep your wits about you," she said just stern enough but allowing a smile. Hard as it had been to hide so much from her this past year or so, I knew I would miss having her keep such close watch, being there with her admonishments when I looked over my shoulder. As stifling as it could be to know someone is watching, it can also be comforting.

"So, it's OK, then?"

"Happy graduation, honey," she said. "I needed to get you a gift anyway."

I didn't know how to thank her. I just threw my arms around her, not just for the trip, but for all of it, for her patience and for the long leash she had given me during these past many months to try to become this strange, powerful creature I was expected to become, for having the right words even when I couldn't fully tell her the truth about the horrors I had faced and the ones that lay ahead. "You know I'm going to miss you though," she said, pulling back but still holding my hands. "So," she looked like she was about to scold me. "I'm going to expect to hear details about it all because you know I've always wanted to go. I need to plan that trip one of these days, finally," she said the last part as though to herself.

"I promise."

"You're lucky, you know. If it wasn't such an organized thing and a big group and everything, I would be threatening to come with you. But I don't want you to be the only one with your own personal chaperone there."

"I know. Thank you. Believe me, thank you," I joked.

"How about this? We'll take a trip together sometime, supposing you like it there," her eyes lit up.

"Deal," I smiled.

"Paris!" she gushed, leaning back now. "Oh, how incredible! You have to bring me something back. Some madeleines or those little macarons in the pretty colors that look so delicious? And something fashionable, whatever everyone is wearing, so I can say, 'Oh, this? Yes, well, Haven brought this back for me from *Paris*." She laughed and I did too. Sometimes it made it harder to have her so understanding. The guilt of lying to her ate away at me. But I pushed it aside for now. She pulled me up to my feet. "OK, now, back to work!" she smiled. "We've got a party to throw."

Joan had invited everyone we knew—from the cousins in Peoria who came in for the day to, seemingly, the whole hospital or at least anyone who could get the afternoon off or be spared a few minutes—so many nurses I had grown up with. They had treated me back when I was just a child found abandoned on the side of Lake Shore Drive and then taught me so much as I worked alongside them. Joan had made her classic tea sandwiches, hundreds of them it seemed, and ordered my favorite red velvet cake, which read, "Happy Graduation, Haven!" in more Northwestern purple and white.

"Oh, Haven! Paris! It's to die for!" Nurse Sanders said. I bristled on reflex at her word choice, but caught myself and smiled.

"I know! I've always wanted to go. I'm really looking forward to practicing my French." I had been playing my role so well I was almost beginning to forget the real purpose of my trip.

"She should be practicing her French kissing there—French men are *très beau*!" Nurse Calloway piped up, winking.

"Darlene!" Joan scolded her. Even in the middle of another conversation across the room, she had an ear tuned to us. At just that moment, I spotted Dante at the door with Lucian and excused myself, grabbing two pieces of cake on the way over.

"Hey, Hav! Would've been here sooner but my family wants to adopt this guy," he gestured to Lucian, who looked at the ground. "Did you know he plays the piano? So *someone* dusts off the upright that's totally been out of tune and plays a few bars of 'Pomp and Circumstance' when I walk down the stairs—"

"Because you were late to a party in your house—" I filled in, guessing the backstory. I handed them slices of cake.

"Of course," he said. "But it totally mellowed my mom, who was going crazy dealing with the whole fam. So, meet my new brother."

"It was no big deal," Lucian said, shaking his head.

Dante leaned in to me. "Joan, 12 o'clock," he said, just as she appeared behind me.

"Hello, boys! So nice of you to stop by!" she said, too excited. I could see the wheels turning. "Oh, good, you have cake! There are sandwiches too, Lex, are you hungry? Let's get you something to eat." Dante just shot me a look.

***

It was dusk by the time the last of the guests left. The three of us wandered by Jason Abington's house, where a party was just getting underway. Everyone would be there. Anyone was invited. That is how your parties are when you're captain of the basketball team and the football team and the epicenter of all social activity. We could easily have gone in, our classmates were already flowing up the driveway in packs. Cars lined the street. We slowed our pace as we neared the scene, music trickling out, but none of us bothered to stop. Instead, we just walked back to Dante's house where his family was still gathered. Through the window, we could see them huddled around the piano, drinks in hand as Dante's uncle played.

"I should probably hang with this crowd," he said at the front door. "It's just going to be a lot of gushing about how great I am in there," he joked. "You guys should go do something fun." We looked at each other unsure. "See *you* later," he pointed to Lucian. "And catch you tomorrow. Thanks for being my sous-chef today, we were totally amazing." He hugged me and kissed me on the cheek, then pushed me. "Now, go!"

7

This Is From Lance

The evening air warm and sweet, we decided to walk along the lake instead of heading back into town, which would surely be bustling with so many out celebrating. We talked about easy things, like we were just two classmates catching up after an exciting day rather than two people with such a dark and heavy history.

"So you'll be here in the fall then," he asked as we walked along the beach on the university campus. The water so still as the sun faded from the sky.

"Yeah, I mean, I guess. Who knows, right?" I shrugged. "Depending on how things go." I couldn't really imagine it.

"No," he said, nearly scolding me. He stopped walking to look at me. "You *will*. It's that simple. OK?" He seemed to be waiting for an answer. I nodded.

"OK."

"That doesn't sound like the girl who was keeping everyone else going in New Orleans," he said, more gently.

"Yeah, well, hate to break it to you, but she might've been faking it."

"I don't think you were."

"You've always had an awful lot of unwarranted confidence in me," I said, joking.

"You're welcome," he said. We made our way up a hill now. I watched the sky as we walked. It was easier that way. Looking at him, still in Lance's wardrobe, continued to confuse my lonely heart even after these months. It was a mind trick that I had given up trying to understand. When I looked at him I saw Lance, and I saw glimmers of the old Lucian, and then I also saw this new, mortal, beaten-down Lucian. I wondered what he saw when he looked at me. If he still saw the unsure girl who had begun work at the Lexington and fallen for him or the one who had saved him in New Orleans, after a dalliance, and returned heart and soul to Lance.

The field was empty except for a stargazing couple up near the student union. Crickets chirped and a pack of fireflies buzzed by us. Lucian stopped when we reached the top of a hill, the dark water of the lake glistening below in the moonlight. He pulled something from his pocket and tucked it under his arm, then spread his jacket out and took a seat beside it, looking at me as though waiting for me. "Where else do you have to be right now?" he asked, patting his jacket.

I sat down, hugging my legs to my chest. Elbows propped on his knees, he gazed out into the deep blue evening sky. "So," he started, his tone easing as he spoke into the space ahead. "It occurred to me that if Lance were here, you two probably would've exchanged gifts of some sort. Yours, of course, is risking your life to save him." He said this lightly, as though it would be easily accomplished so there was no need to discuss it any further. "So, you're covered. But he owes you."

"Oh, is that right?"

"Yes, so this is technically from Lance because, you know, I've been wearing his clothes and he had a tendency to leave cash in all his pockets." That made me smile. He pulled a velvet box from his shirt pocket and handed it to me. I recognized the style from Joan's favorite jewelry store in the center of town.

The one where she had bought the angel wing necklace for me. I touched it now, on reflex. It lay on my chest just above my scars and beside the fleur-de-lis charm Lance had given me for my birthday.

"You know, it's practical, and a classic graduation gift. But I'm sure you'll appreciate its depth, because you're…you."

I opened the box and found a watch nestled inside. Gold with tiny roman numerals in red, its face was the size of a silver dollar. I checked the time and found it off by about seven hours.

"It's on Paris time," he said, explaining. I slipped the slim gold band on, not needing to unfasten the clasp since it was a little big. "I figured," he said. "But we can size it."

"I love it," I said. "Thank you."

"It's not me," he corrected.

"Right," I shook my head. "Lance."

"And you'll thank him yourself soon," he said. "This," he grabbed what was beside him. "This is from me." He handed me the book he had been reading that night after Tom walked off the construction site: *The Time Machine*. "Thanks for looking out for me that day, and so many days since we've met," he said in the tone of someone speaking at a funeral. He looked at me now, for the first time since we'd sat down.

"Thank you," I fanned the pages. He watched me, intense concern behind that gaze. I thought of the things he had said that day, about feeling out of place. I worried he was feeling dark now and wanted to pull him out of it. "So, you stole this from the house," I tested the waters.

He smiled. "I prefer to call it a souvenir."

"I love it," I held it to my chest, folding my arms around it. A breeze blew in from the water, a chill setting into the night air. I felt the goose bumps rise on my skin but even so, I didn't want to leave. It was nearly six in the morning in Paris, so it was late here, but I didn't care. I sensed there would be few moments like this, moments of peace and calm, in the next several weeks or perhaps months.

"It's strange to be back here, after everything that's happened," Lucian said, as though to himself, breaking the silence at last. He kicked the heel of his shoe—Lance's black converse sneakers, which still looked like a costume on him—against the dewy grass, making a divot.

"We used to go to the ruins of the Lex a lot," I said. "Just to remind ourselves that all of that really did happen. It was comforting in a sort of heavy way, I guess."

"Yeah, but I mean, *here*," he looked at me, to underscore it. His gray eyes squinting, pained.

"Here?" I didn't understand.

"This was it, where I met Aurelia. I was visiting here."

"I thought you went to Iowa." That's all I had ever known, that he went to college near his hometown and met Aurelia during his freshman year. It surprised me that there was information of this magnitude that I could be learning for the first time about him. I felt like I had been remiss somewhere along the line, but then again, we had spent little time talking about the past and much more about the future. "When were you here?"

"It was a visit with this club at school, a Model UN," he shook his head as though this were embarrassing in some way. "I was joining things, trying to find people like me, you know? But it kept not working out. I suppose I liked the activities just fine, but the people part just wasn't so easy."

It sent a jolt through me, this idea that he had walked these streets, blocks from my home, before I knew him. Before I knew what he was or what I was or what kind of horror I would fall into. It killed me to think I had been so nearby when he had been recruited. If only there had been something I could have done. But I couldn't have.

"I wish I had been strong enough to stay away from them." He was far away now, fingers to his lips, thinking back. "It happened so fast." That I understood.

"Of course it did. That's how these things work."

"I just wish I'd been stronger—"

"Stop thinking that way—"

"Like you. And Lance and Dante. Maybe if it hadn't been just me," he seemed to be thinking aloud. "I don't know. I just keep going over it all."

"Well, you can't," I bolted up, surprising even myself. "And I'll leave if you're going to be defeatist like that." Anything to show him how futile that thinking was. In my efforts to shift him into this platonic sector of my life, I had given myself free rein to fight with him. But if I had learned anything in the past year it was to not waste time on the many things out of our control, to not waste time at all, because people can be taken from you at any moment. He grabbed my wrist.

"Please," he said, tugging me to sit down again. I did.

"You have to stop blaming yourself. Without you we wouldn't have even survived the Lexington. You got us through that. Just like you're the reason we know where to find Lance." I knew where he was coming from. I understood his guilt, just as I could read that he was as nervous as I was, and that worried me.

"Why won't you just let me say everything I need to?" he asked, frustrated.

"Because I can't hear it right now," I said honestly. I knew he wanted to say those things that people often wait to say until moments of tragedy and crisis and death. If we had that talk now, it would suffocate the warrior in me, the animal capable of destroying any obstacle littering the path to Lance. It would soften me; it would blunt the edge I needed now. It was selfish, yes, but also self-preservation. I needed to maintain this laser focus. I was a soldier.

"I understand," he said softly. "Sometime, please, promise me."

"Of course."

We didn't say another word and so many quiet minutes passed that I stopped trying to think of something to say. Instead I just breathed in the sweet night air, savoring these moments and the comfort of having Lucian beside me, alive, his heart beating, his soul reclaimed. This was a victory, this living, breathing man who had once been lost to the underworld. I had done this. Just as I could lead us to Lance.

Finally he stood up and reached for my hand to pull me to my feet. He grabbed his jacket and we walked back. I left him at Dante's house, saying our quiet goodnights, then took the long way home past Lance's house.

The lights were off inside the brown-and-white row house, only a porch lamp illuminating the swing where we had spent so many evenings rehashing our old war stories of the Lexington as I curled up beside him, his arm looped around me. I crept up onto that porch now, took a seat on that swing, careful not to let it creak as it always did. His mother and father were likely sleeping soundly with thoughts of their son, who had wanted to be a firefighter ever since he was found as an infant at the nearby fire station, now nobly aiding the displaced of Louisiana, as we had told them. I hoped we would be able to stop writing emails to them from his account soon. I hoped we weren't going to have to make up another story, a sad one, to explain why they wouldn't see him again. I hoped that I could save him.

I shouldn't have been surprised to see the halo of the living room lamp glowing through the gauzy front curtains when I got home. I tucked the watch up into my sweater sleeve; it would just be easier that way.

"You know you don't have to wait up for me," I said, smiling as I dropped the book on the table.

"Of course I know that, but how many more opportunities am I going to get? Besides, it's a good excuse to watch reruns of this terrible show," she shook her head, flipping off the TV. She wore a bathrobe over her pajamas, her glasses on. "How was your night?" she asked in that expectant way.

"Fine," I said, drawing it out, hoping the extra syllables would make up for the lack of information.

"Did you go to the party?"

"We went near the party," I shrugged. "Good enough."

"Just you and Dante and that Lex?"

"Yes," I said in a guarded way.

"He's awfully cute, Haven." She gave me a look. "You must have noticed that."

I said nothing, hoping not to encourage this discussion. We had told her and Dante's mom that we were coming home with one of our roommates from New Orleans who had also graduated early and had always wanted to visit Chicago. No big deal. But I knew there was no way that Joan, who was so attuned to everything and happened to love girl talk, would let me get away with that story so easily.

I was suddenly glad that I had hidden that watch. I resisted the urge to touch my concealed wrist.

She went on: "And he seems to hang around you a lot." I just smiled innocently. She was not easily deterred. "Maybe a summer fling is what you need," she said, in the same tone she used when she encouraged me to incorporate more antioxidants into my diet.

"Joan."

"I just mean, something light and breezy. A fling!" she said it with such glee.

"Yes, I know what a fling is," I smiled, embarrassed. "I don't... fling. It's just, it's not me. I'm not programmed for it. I don't want to talk about this." What could I say? I've got a lot on my mind. In a matter of days I'm going to be flying to Paris to try to save the angel I love from the gates of hell?

"I just don't like to see you get so hung up on this one boy, who must not be very smart if he didn't come back to be with you. You're too young for that. Forget about Lance, honey."

"I thought you loved him," I snapped. I wanted to say that I loved him, but I pulled myself back, it would just fuel the fire. "I don't want to talk about this."

"You never want to talk about the fun stuff. Why can't we talk about the fun stuff? Tell me about Lex."

"No."

"Well, I know something's up because you've been avoiding talking about Lance and he never calls anymore. I don't understand why he isn't here now. It doesn't make sense to me. All I can think is he's just not thinking of your feelings. And why be tied down? You're young. There are so many boys out there, I'm sure, who are just like Lance." I wanted to tell her how wrong she was, about what he and I had been through. But this was not the time.

"I'm going to bed," I said flatly, heading toward the stairs. "Thank you for today and for the trip and for everything. I'm exhausted and I'm going to get some sleep."

"Fine, I didn't mean to get you worked up," she said to herself as I walked up the stairs. "I just don't get it."

8

The City of Light

"So you got all of these today?" Dante asked, rifling through the shopping bags from my day in Chicago with Joan.

"You know Joan," I laughed. She had insisted we have a girls' day, running around Michigan Avenue for any last-minute things I might need for the trip. I guessed it was a peace offering, and I appreciated it. Just as I appreciated that she hadn't mentioned a word about Lance—or Lex for that matter—since graduation night. So we had had our day of shopping. I would've been happy to just go out for pizza at Gino's East and spend the day at the Art Institute but she argued that, "A girl can't wear just any ol' thing in Paris." She had bought me a trio of dresses, even though I tried to talk her out of it. I felt a little guilty. I couldn't quite imagine having the occasion to wear them given the real purpose of my trip, but it made her so happy. I had chickened out again, wanting so badly to tell her everything, but just not able to find the words. The business of secret-keeping had once been so foreign and was something my entire being seemed to reject. It made me skittish and short-tempered to carry this around with me, as it had on graduation night. What if I didn't come back this time? She deserved to know what was really going on.

AIMEE AGRESTI

"Joan is so sweet, she's never going to give up trying to turn you into, like, a real girl," Dante said, shaking his head. "Bless her heart."

Lucian sat on my bed, flipping through one of my poetry anthologies. He looked up and gave the slightest smile. "You do all right," he said, almost to himself. I smiled back at him, but he had returned to his book. My luggage from New Orleans lay open and nearly full, ready to digest the last of my things, most of which lay scattered on the floor.

"You're rereading this?" Dante asked, picking up The *Time Machine* and tossing it in, where it landed atop my worn copy of *Les Misérables* and a file folder. "I'm very disappointed in you, Hav. You need to be reading some sexy Collette in its original French or something," he joked. "It's a pretty long flight, mademoiselle."

"Collette is good," Lucian said, under his breath again.

"Relax, D, I've got that too," I said, pulling a slim volume from my bookshelf. I had told Dante about the watch—which hadn't been news to him. "Who do you think told him where to go for that?" he had said, with that smirk. But for some reason, I found myself excluding the book. It felt especially private to me. I already had a terrible history of not being honest with Dante about Lucian, but I didn't think there was any harm in withholding this little bit this time. I dropped in the dresses and stared down the suitcase again. I had told Joan six weeks—hoping it would be more like six days away.

"Passports?" he asked, plural, meaning mine and the one for Lance.

"Yep."

"You got the itineraries and tickets from Drew?"

"Got 'em."

I had taken her up on the offer to handle the logistics and she had booked everyone's flights, lined up our lodging, metro

96

passes, everything. We had been getting daily emails from her with details about our new neighborhood—Montmartre, the 18th arrondissement, as I had instructed—and links to maps of Père-Lachaise to get us started. We would be arriving three weeks early to get our bearings and fully wrap our heads around what we had to accomplish.

"Then we're good to go," Dante said. "Now you can come over and help me pack, I need help editing."

A day later, I managed to hold it together as I said goodbye to Joan curbside at O'Hare Airport. She had wanted to come in, of course, but I convinced her not to and she acquiesced this time. "You're a high school graduate, you're the boss," she said, upbeat, her perky gray ponytail bouncing. Then she pulled my bag from the trunk and gave me one of those strong hugs that could crush you if you weren't ready for it. "Have so much fun, honey!" she trilled. "And I won't tell you again to be careful... but be careful. And for the record, I do love Lance, of course. I love anyone you love who treats you well. I just haven't known what to think the past few weeks, that's all. I happen to think Lex is lovely too." She winked. It was pure Joan to say exactly what I needed to hear when I needed to hear it. "Now give me another hug."

As I waved and watched the car drive off, I felt the shell harden around me again. I crossed through the automatic doors and had the sense of shifting into a new mode, crossing into a new world. A new kind of fear-laced energy coursed through me. Perhaps I wasn't the only one: Dante, perpetually late for as long as I had known him, stood at a ticket kiosk with Lucian. Early. I should've been relieved to see him, but it chilled me. He knew it too: we were heading into the battle of our lives.

We breezed through security, Lex's passport drawing no second glances, and at 5 pm we boarded our flight to Paris.

———✦———

"Did you have any trouble getting here? The directions were OK?" Drew asked as she greeted us with hugs at the door of our new home.

"It was all perfect, thank you," I said, newly energized now that the group was reassembling and we were here.

I had managed to sleep only an hour on the plane. The rest of the time I spent watching a movie (the kind of thing Dante and I would've caught on one of our nights in eating home-made gourmet pizza) and reading Lucian's *Time Machine*. It was shorter than I remembered, so I read it twice as he dozed peacefully to one side of me and Dante snored on the other. I had noticed some markings in the margins, a name scribbled in, a few check marks here and there. I had been lulled into a hazy dream state during the flight, my mind fixed on Lance despite not actually sleeping much, but as soon as we stepped off the plane the hum returned, adrenaline charging me like an IV drip. I thought I could feel it being released into my bloodstream. This used to only happen immediately before a battle or even mid-attack, like that time I'd been ambushed in the cemetery. But this was new. I didn't know what to do with it. I felt hyperaware of everything—the scent of fresh paint from the apartment two doors down, the sound of children on a field trip singing as they crossed the street several stories below our seventh floor apartment, the aroma of warm bread wafting up from the bakery below us.

The neighborhood was as charming and bohemian as I had imagined. The three of us had ascended from the depths of the Abbesses metro station, luggage in tow, and been deposited into an idyllic Sunday afternoon. A flea market sprawled in the park at the metro's mouth, tables and tables full of wares and odd, old treasures—records, books, guitars, chairs, alarm clocks bearing cartoon characters, dresses and blazers from bygone eras in pristine condition, old maps of non-existent countries, warped mirrors. Bikes wheeled by and people strolled along the sidewalks smiling as they gabbed into their cell phones and toted baguettes. The pace didn't feel like that of anywhere I had been. It felt warm, comfortable, welcoming. "Nice call on the 18th arrondissement," Lucian said as we reached the top of our street, Rue des Martyrs. A steep slope lined with shops and cafes, the narrow cobblestone road rolled down, down, down endlessly. A few blocks in the opposite direction, I knew from my studying, would be the hill up to the Sacré-Coeur, the white, domed church overlooking Paris. When Drew had asked, during one of those early meetings in the courtyard back in New Orleans, if I knew where I wanted us situated, it had taken only a second for this area to come to mind. A place I had remembered from our French class studies and tucked away.

"Not near Père-Lachaise?" she had asked.

"No, I want us away from there. I want a home base. I want to think a few steps ahead." They had all watched me, listening closely. It had been a heady thing to feel that they trusted me and had faith in my decisions. Not something I was used to. This wasn't quite like being an officer in French Honor Society. "I sense that if," I caught myself. "Or, rather, *when* we free Lance, it's going to be the first of many challenges as the revolution gets under way. Right?" I looked at Lucian.

"Yes," he said serious and firm.

"And those events will be carried out throughout the city?"

"Yes," he said again.

"Then I think we need a perch where we can address everything. I want to feel like we're thinking beyond this one event

with Lance. That will help convince us that we're going to survive it and get him out of there. That there will be days to follow,
for us all. It's impossible to know where they'll be—"

"Anywhere, everywhere," Lucian cut in. "They will be
everywhere."

"Then that's it. I want to feel as though we're above them,
looking down on them, watching." I had looked at Drew: "We
need to be in the 18th arrondissement."

⋯◈⋯

We buzzed into the doorway nestled beside the Bistro des
Martyrs and stopped before a winding staircase. "Yeah, good
call on Montmartre, but bad call on a place with no elevator,"
Dante said.

I pushed ahead of him. "You could use the workout," I
joked, aware of the sweat on my forehead. But carrying suit-
cases up seven flights of stairs wasn't the hardship it once
would have been for Dante and me. We had the strength to
make it quickly and effortlessly. Our biggest complaint was
its tediousness.

Drew ushered us inside, so excited to show us around she
was almost jumpy.

"So this is it! I thought an apartment made sense, fewer
people to monitor our comings and goings than a hostel or
hotel or whatever—"

"Absolutely," I said. "This looks great. Really nice job finding this." I took it all in: modern and luxurious, located on the
top floor, it boasted windows in the living room spanning the
corner of the building with a clear view all the way down that
long street, and a delicate wrought-iron balcony. Perfect.

She walked us through the furnished apartment—the kind
of place meant for business travelers staying in town for a while

and hoping to live like a local. With sleek pull-out couches in splashy colors, it managed to sleep eight even though it wasn't all that large: a small kitchen, living room, one bathroom, and one bedroom. A skinny spiral staircase led up onto the roof. The bedroom held a desk and king size bed. "We can fit a few of us in there," Dante joked. "Who's with me?" A strip of windows faced the back of the building.

"Was this what you had in mind?" Drew asked, leading us back to the living room. She had set bottles of soda and a plate of baguette sandwiches out. It reminded me of Connor feeding and housing us in that hidden cabin in the bayou after our first swim through the gator-infested swamp.

"This is amazing. Thank you," I climbed the spiral staircase, opening up a trapdoor onto the roof for a peek. A brick wall separated our space from the building next door. I liked the idea of this private spot. I imagined that—beautiful as the apartment was—it might get claustrophobic at times. I pulled the hatch back. "Perfect."

"Totally kickass," Dante agreed, already nibbling a sandwich as he opened the oven door to peek in. Lucian poked his head out the window, watching the quiet street below.

"I looked into a bunch of places, but I liked the location of this one—the metro is so close and the layout was the best," she explained. "It's gotten to be a pretty popular place here, I guess. It was a home to artists and writers, so there's that whole bohemian vibe."

"Van Gogh. Degas. Picasso. They all hung out here," Dante said.

"Is that why you wanted to be here?" Drew asked.

"I like those guys, but no," I smiled. "It's kind of just a symbolic thing: Montmartre, it's the 'hill of the martyr,' you know?" Which reminded me, there was someone I needed to see. But I went on, "And also—"

"It's the highest point in the city," Lucian added, speaking into the window. "Or, I mean, overlooking Paris."

"Exactly," I said, surprised to have him finish my thought. "So I felt like it was a good vantage point, you know?" I joined him at the window. Beneath us a girl in a flowing dress on a bicycle zipped around the bend onto our street. Beyond her, the city fanned out. She seemed so carefree, her wavy chestnut hair blowing in the breeze, her polka dot sundress billowing. In the basket in front of her, paper sacks of produce from a market. I imagined her going home to a nearby flat where her Parisian love would greet her with an open bottle of wine. They would fix a lunch involving baguettes and fancy, mysterious cheeses for a picnic in the sun.

"I like that," Drew said, busy gazing outside, leaning her elbow on the windowsill. "That's smart."

But just as fast as that image flashed in my mind, another image seared my eyes and set the scars above my heart and at my back burning. I gasped from the sharp sudden pain. Dante, still in the kitchen, whipped his head around to look at me. The beautiful woman on the bike flickered and for an instant she was a rotting corpse, her skin sallow and diseased, melting from her skeleton to leave puddles on the street. I blinked and she had returned to herself, glowing and perfect as she coasted around the corner and out of sight. Lucian, noticing the exchange, crinkled a questioning brow at me.

I had had this feeling before, leading into Metamorphosi Day. I knew what it meant. It seemed we had come to the right place at least. They would be here soon: the underworld finding its way here to recruit again for their cause.

"Who's ready to see the town?" Dante asked, his voice hesitant.

"Have you gotten to look around yet?" I asked Drew with as much ease as I could muster, the pain now dissipating.

Drew shook her head: "I'm dying to, but the others should be coming in the next hour or two." As if on cue, the buzzer zapped.

"Bonjour, *mes amis*," Emma said as she peeked in the unlocked door. "Is that right?" she asked the person behind her on the landing.

"Yeah, just like I taught you, perfect," came the voice. Max appeared, in his signature fedora. "This place is très gorgeous."

"I picked up this guy at Charles de Gaulle," Emma joked, saying the airport in an exaggerated accent.

"*You're* très gorgeous," Dante said, pushing past us beelining for Max and greeting him with a kiss. They were the only couple I had ever encountered whose PDA wasn't off-putting. It was so sweet it gave you hope for love instead of just making you feel resentful.

"Hey, you," Max said, glowing. "I missed you," he said it making each word count.

"Me too. So much, I can't even tell you," Dante said. Then he shifted into his light mode again. "Thought you might've swapped this for a beret by now." Dante stole his hat and tried it on himself.

"You mean, like this one?" Max pulled a beret from his bag. Dante grabbed it, laughing. "That's for you. Got it at the airport waiting for her." He swatted Max with it, then put it on his head. They were instantly in their own world, catching up.

———⊰•◦۞◦•⊱———

Drew stayed behind to wait for River and Tom, but she didn't mind us having a look at our new city. She just had one request. "I wondered, do you have to go to Père-Lachaise now?" she asked, almost nervous to bring it up. "I understand if you want to go right away, of course, but I was just hoping to do that all together. I didn't want to be left out, you know?"

"We can wait, of course," I said, no hesitation. I liked the idea of us all going together. I wanted everyone to feel included and feel how vital they were to this mission. I needed them all in order to get Lance back.

Our quintet set out, wandering the main artery, Rue des Abbesses, where the sidewalk cafés were packed with leisurely diners facing out to watch the world pass by. Between those were so many boulangeries, fromageries, and produce markets, their front windows all displaying breads, sweets, cheeses and fruits so beautiful they looked like still life paintings.

But we had gone only a few blocks when I saw her again: the girl on the bicycle. She pedaled ahead of us, her form flickering.

I didn't think, I just ran.

My instinct was telling me I had to act. *Now.* My legs sped off, so much faster than seemed right for the amount of effort I felt my muscles putting forth. Wind whipping my hair, I tore past those fruit stands and cafes, dodging couples strolling the streets. I caught up with her at the end of the next block, running alongside her and following her as she turned a corner. I got close enough to clamp my hand down on one of the handlebars, my other hand grabbing her arm, to keep her from bolting forward at the sudden stop. The bicycle fell and she stumbled over it but remained upright as I held her. She screamed, but couldn't pull away from my iron grip. Only now did it set in: I had no idea what to say and worse, she probably thought I was trying to steal her bike.

"You're in danger," I blurted out. For some reason she let me speak. Perhaps because, now that we were stopped, she could see that I was several inches shorter than her, unarmed and likely looked as startled as she did. "Someone is coming for you," I said quickly. "You're in danger. I know it sounds crazy but beware of new friends, people promising you the world. Your soul is in danger." Her eyes wide, she looked at me like I was insane, the kind of person who talks to themselves in loud voices about the coming apocalypse, someone you cross the street to avoid. I loosened my hold on her. There was no way she would believe this kind of person accosting her. I couldn't blame her; I would've felt the same way.

She wriggled away from me, and I let her go. As she sped off, shouting something in French and running over my foot in the process—though it didn't hurt, of course. It would take more than that to register on this new body of mine. I watched her until she disappeared down the street toward that grand red windmill I knew from so many pictures—the Moulin Rouge. A sense of defeat replaced the adrenaline and hope I'd felt only a few minutes ago.

I had tried, but that wasn't good enough. I didn't like starting our trip this way. It felt like arriving at the game of my life and having a disastrous warm-up. I would need to do more than just try on June 21.

Slowly I turned, knowing the other angels were there behind me and wishing I hadn't had an audience. The four of them were stone-faced. "In my mind, that went differently," I said, trying to mask my disappointment. "I probably should've thought about that before I just…yeah." I shook my head.

"Well, I kind of like Impulsive Haven," Dante shrugged. "But you might get us run out of our new neighborhood." And then, his voice serious, whispering, "She'll be a target. You saw it?" A few tourists walked by, muttering something and shooting me curious looks.

I nodded. "Just like in New Orleans."

"And you see their souls rotting? Like a prediction of what could happen?" Max asked, clarifying what Dante must have explained to him.

Lucian let the slightest smirk curl his lips, as though trying to suppress it. I didn't understand why he was looking at me this way.

"So at least you don't have to lug your camera around everywhere anymore," Dante shrugged. "I mean, unless you're actually sightseeing." Always looking on the bright side, I couldn't help but smile now. Back in Chicago, when I had just learned what I was, I had discovered that my photos could show a person's true soul. When I had photographed the beautiful demons of the Lexington Hotel, the pictures had morphed into horrific portraits of decay. Before the battle in New Orleans, my power had grown stronger: I could see the decay in person, identify souls in danger of being claimed before they were taken. That is what had happened with the girl on the bike. Lucian studied me in a way I couldn't read and found offensive.

"Why are you looking at me like that?" I asked, sensitive, feeling exposed like I was something caged in a circus of freaks.

"You really are as powerful as they feared," he said, his eyes a brighter gray than I'd seen since the night Lance was lost. "This is what they always said. But they had never seen a soul illuminator at work to their full potential." He used the term I had learned from the demons themselves to describe the special talent that had made me their target and now their greatest nemesis. "They knew you would be a step ahead of them. They feared it would cripple their recruiting efforts. And it will. This ability is…extraordinary."

"Maybe just tone it down a little," Emma said, lightly, as though advising me on accessories. With a glance back toward the Moulin Rouge, I set us walking in the opposite direction, needing to flee this scene.

"I guess I need to work on my delivery," I said, embarrassed.

"That part is easy," Max said, kindly. "I wish I could do what you do."

"It's a major time saver," Emma said.

"Yeah, we'll work on making you a little less aggressive," Dante said. "Not a concern I ever thought we'd have with you." He put his arm around me, shaking my shoulders.

As we looped back toward the metro station, we passed a wall with the sculpture of a man walking through it. I stopped for a moment. This is how I felt, moving between these two worlds, trying to appear to live a regular life while having this secret one where the stakes were life and death.

9

I'm Not Here to See The Sights

The metro rattled along, picking up its chic patrons and bohemians as we rolled into the center of the city, passing through stop after stop bearing floor to ceiling ads for Parisian department stores, French-titled American movies, and local products like Orangina. But I just kept seeing that rotting face in my mind, replaying the scene I had made. I mostly tuned out the group as they brainstormed where to hit first.

"Yeah, but I'm thinking more Champs-Élysées," Dante was explaining. "I need to do some retail therapy." He looked at me seriously now, like this was an itch that needed scratching. I knew that look and it actually meant that he was scared and needed soothing. He understood they were coming. Max put his hand lightly on Dante's back.

"Can we go to Chanel?" Emma asked, her eyes set on a pair of girls in short boots, dresses and scarves.

"*Mais oui!*" Dante said, perky again. Only Max and I got to see serious Dante. "You know what, we should totally swing by—what is it? I marked it in your book, Hav?" he snapped his fingers and it came to him. "Rue Cambon! We'll go there after—Coco's *appartement* is there." He looked at me. "You know you're dying to see it, Hav. I'm sure some of this chicness is bound to infect you."

"Yeah, I want to get infected, really, but there's just something I have to do first," I said. He nodded, not pushing. "But I'll catch up with you later."

"You want company or…?" Lucian asked.

"Sure," I said, trying to sound casual. I didn't plan to let him out of my sight. I checked the map lit up above the doors. We were nearing our stop. "We can probably walk from here," I said to myself as the train slowed. And then to Dante: "We'll give you a call."

"Good, because, seriously, we need to get you looking the part here. You're in Paris, if ever there was a time to kick things up, it's now." Outfitting me was his favorite distraction. I could always be sure something terrifying was on the horizon if Dante was proposing a style overhaul. With a wave goodbye, Lucian and I jumped off the train.

———◆◆◆———

I dug the museum passes out from my pocket. I had asked Drew to secure a couple, along with the metro passes, just in case we needed to get in to any of these spots. Any of these sites would surely be prime targets for demons in search of "spectacle," as Lucian had advised us. He and I slipped past the line waiting near the grand glass pyramid gleaming in the afternoon sunlight outside the Louvre, and took the escalator down. "You don't think you were wrong on the date, right? The portal?"

"I really don't think so," Lucian said, firmly as he looked out into the sea of tourists buzzing through the marble lobby. A swell of them surged toward the wing marked "Denon," where we were also headed. "The amount of rehabilitation that needed to occur. The fact that the Prince himself has been weakened.

They need everyone ready. They waited a while to send anyone out after Chicago even though the demons from the Lexington wouldn't be going on that tour. They had hoped to have them prepared, just in case they needed the extra reinforcements, but they weren't ready. They were still getting their powers returned when I was there. But you can look for the other signs. For example, the temperature will spike."

"We'll be ready. We'll have to be." We would scope the place out together and then go every night of that week if we had to. We would not miss it.

But I could tell Lucian's mind had wandered. He walked with his hands in his pockets, gazing up at the ceiling, as we drifted with the masses. I had looked online so I wouldn't waste any time getting lost in the vast complex, with its rich marble columns and its stunning sculptures at every turn. It helped that what I wanted to see was apparently located adjacent to the room that the rest of the world came here to see.

"I always wanted to come here," Lucian said quietly, awe in his voice.

"Me too." I had always dreamed I might study in this city one day, tour this and every museum, wander each neighborhood and discover all those precious little shops and eateries, places I could call my favorites when people would ask what I loved most about it here.

I knew we were in the right place when we turned a corner and stepped into a room with velvet ropes and throngs of people clustered, cameras poised, to see one woman. What I had come for lay just on the other side of this. But I paused anyway. The painting was so much smaller than I expected. I did like that something so powerful took up so little space on this grand, otherwise empty wall.

"She does have a nice smile, I'll give her that," I said, with a passing glance but anxious to move on.

"I don't know, I've seen nicer," he said, looking at me a moment and then back at the painting. "Go on," he said, giving me space. "I'll be here." I nodded and slipped away into the room next door.

With its crimson walls and painted ceiling studded with gilded eagles, this space enveloped me. It was as intimate as the other room had been vast and over-populated. Many who drifted in here were just passing through and, like clouds on a sunny day, they cleared away and there she was: "*La Jeune Martyre*," the painting I loved. That ethereal girl, who seemed to be my age, left lifeless, floating in water on a black night, her wrists bound, a halo glowing over her head and casting light on the rippling river. It felt like a reunion with an old friend. She seemed somehow different than when I had seen her in Chicago, at the Art Institute, when I had just begun at the Lexington. But now that I thought about it, it was me who had changed. I wanted to say to her, "I have to tell you all that's happened since I last saw you. I'm such a different person now. You wouldn't even recognize me; I don't even recognize me. And I'm changing still, right now. I will be a different person tomorrow."

I felt like she was part of me, like we had been through so much together. I had once been left for dead as she had, when Joan had found me. But I would not end up like her.

I stood there, watching her as the minutes ticked by, not quite able to pull myself away. To his credit, Lucian left me alone, as though wanting to be sure not to rush me. Finally, though, I said a quiet goodbye, and returned to the bustle of the adjacent room.

As soon as I stepped over the threshold, I felt it, that stabbing pain. I stopped in my tracks a moment, catching my breath. Regaining control, I found a place at the very back of the group and scanned the crowd, bracing myself for what I might find. My eyes settled on a handsome boy, also hanging back, pencil working furiously on the sketchbook in his hands. He had short wavy hair and the scruffy chin of an art major. After just a few seconds of watching him, his image morphed into the x-ray of a decaying soul, his features melting, lesions multiplying like freckles. *His soul is in danger*, I said to myself with certainty. *He will be a target.*

I had a chance to redeem myself. I needed a different approach than I'd taken with the cyclist, but what? The boy flipped the pages of his book, looking as though he might be wrapping up. I had no time to waste. I drifted over toward him and stood nearby. It was almost too painful to stand there: his form flickered fast, a strobe effect so intense he should have carried a warning that he could cause seizures.

"*Elle est belle*," I whispered.

"Yes, she is," he said in accented English. British. "Although, not in my rendering I'm afraid." He looked at his work, then flashed it at me. "Rubbish."

"Hardly. I think she looks a lot happier in yours. Are you studying here?" The crowd continued to regenerate, a few people finally getting their fill and heading to the next room, just as new admirers arrived.

"Yes. On an exchange from St. Andrews."

"Scotland. Nice. Always wanted to go there."

"It's lovely, you should. And you? Studying or on holiday?" He closed his notebook again and slipped it into his messenger bag, zipping it up.

"I like how you guys call it a 'holiday.'" I smiled.

"Ahhh, so you know a lot of Scots? A lot of 'us guys' as you say? Perhaps spent some time chatting up patrons of the British Museum, for instance?" he joked.

"No, you know, I just read a lot." The gray-haired tourist on the other side of him caught my eye for a moment, raising an eyebrow as though in appreciation of how well this seemed to be going, before she wandered away. How funny. I had never thought I'd been particularly good at flirting but now, as a cover, I had managed it just fine. If I could learn how to do this, then maybe there was hope for me mastering the more useful skills of flying, and destroying demons. I could still feel the strobe effect beside me but kept my eyes focused on the painting as much as possible, to avoid looking directly my target.

"The British Museum, that's the one with the Rosetta Stone, am I right?" I looked over from the corner of my eye.

"So you *have* been there."

"No," I was thinking for a way in to this heavier matter without it feeling like too sharp a turn. "But I know it unlocked the secrets to hieroglyphics. And I've got a secret to tell you," I grabbed his arm now and his image steadied, first freezing on that horrific version forecasting what his soul would become, then shifting back to normal and staying there. "And you have to listen to me, as crazy as this sounds," I looked in his eyes, whispering. "Be careful here. In this city. Now. Be very careful. Beware beautiful things. Follow your gut if something feels off. Keep focused on what matters, don't be led astray." I didn't even know exactly what to tell him to look for, and it occurred to me that the more I tried to get my point across, the more off I began to sound. I didn't know how it would happen, if he would be carefully wooed as by the orderly Outfit, or brutally attacked as by the feral Krewe, or perhaps he'd fall prey to some terrifying new method of control. His brow furrowed, then he smiled like he just might turn up on one of those hidden camera shows.

"You are one of the strangest girls I've ever met. I'm oddly intrigued. Part of me wants to run far away, and part enjoys this brand of crazy emanating from someone so seemingly normal." He added, as though thinking aloud, "I've actually just described my last two girlfriends."

I smiled now. I couldn't help it. "Just be careful," I said, pulling away. "It won't make sense now, but trust me." With that, I walked away. I hoped to at least have given him something to think about, something that might resonate if he found himself walking in a deserted part of town or encountering a mysterious stranger offering him the world in exchange for the simple promise of his soul.

I was nearly to the staircase when I heard soft footsteps behind me and felt that sharp pain again.

"Excuse me," he said in a stage whisper. I slowed, turning around. "So just to clarify, you would probably, for instance, advise against partying in the catacombs, then?"

"Funny," I deadpanned.

"And how do I find you when I do encounter this unexpected trouble?"

"Oh, well…" I started, but he was already taking out his phone and typing something.

"Here, just in case you and your friends are in need of tour guides. Best to exchange our information, right?" he smiled, handing it to me. He had already keyed in my name: he had christened me "Rosetta."

"Hilarious," I said, typing in my number. Before saying goodbye, I asked him to do the same, but I let him type his own name: Gavin.

Within seconds of Gavin leaving, Lucian appeared at my side again.

"That looked interesting," he said, waiting for me to fill in the blanks as he watched Gavin walk away. To my eyes, he vacillated again between the charming student and the rotting soul.

"He's another one," I said as I led us away.

Lucian only nodded. "There will be more, I'm sorry to say."

"I know." We descended the steps heading back the way we had come and I stopped on the landing, pulling out my phone to text Dante. "This is going to sound crazy, because we're at the Louvre and all, but I feel like I'm set now and I need to just…" I felt that adrenaline coursing again and felt like even this grand museum couldn't contain me. I wanted to help Gavin now, I wanted to slay demons now, I wanted to save Lance now. And it made my blood boil to have to wait for all of it.

"Haven," Lucian said firmly, gray eyes piercing mine. "I'm not here to see the sights. And I know you're not either. I'm here for Lance. And for you." He held my arm in his strong grip, trying to make me understand. "Do you understand?" I nodded. His gaze drifted up in the space behind me. "Look," he said, turning me around by my shoulders so I faced the majestic sculpture sharing the landing with us. It was raised up on a pedestal and reached at least ten feet into the air. It was an angel standing there so proud, wings stretched out behind her as though in triumph. The plaque read "Winged Victory." "This is you," Lucian whispered in my ear, his voice almost angry, as we both watched her. "*This* is what you are. Don't forget that. You are stronger than any of the others, than anyone I have ever known. All you have to do is realize it. OK?"

I nodded, studying the figure. Wings resplendent and powerful carrying her skyward, she wore a long billowing dress, seeming at once delicate and a force of nature. She was made of stone but felt lighter than any of us.

His tone softened now, as though worried he might have been too harsh trying to get his point across: "So I just want you to know that, this is what you're becoming."

I wanted him to know that I had heard him, and also that we were fine. Eyes still on the sculpture, I leaned back to whisper, taking a chance to lighten the charge in the air between us: "But she has no head," I said, with the slightest smile. It was true, this was one of those many sculptures in this place that happened to be missing a vital piece. He shook his head, smiling too: "You're her with a good head on your shoulders," he joked. "C'mon, let's get out of here."

⋯⋯◇⋯⋯

I called Dante and was surprised to discover he and the others were nearby, grabbing a snack at Angelina, a tearoom just a few blocks away on the Rue de Rivoli, a strip full of posh hotels, charming cafes and souvenir shops. "If you hurry, I'll save you a bite of this amazing cake I'm eating," he had joked. The air had turned crisp as evening approached, though the sun still blazed high in the sky.

As soon as we sat down, Dante threw a thin cotton scarf around my neck, "*Trés jolie*," he said. It was pink, a color I never wore. But I knew what he was doing. "Don't give me that look," he said, laughing. "I'm broadening your style horizons. Besides, it's practical too. It's chilly out there." Emma had a matching one in violet wrapped around her neck. She smiled as she and Max sipped the remnants of the blackest hot chocolate I had ever seen. Max now wore a gray fedora with a black band.

"Nice, Max," I nodded. He tipped it toward me.

Two cups arrived, set down before Lucian and me. "Here, drink up, you'll thank me," Dante said. I took a sip. Thick as tar, it tasted like drinking the richest candy bar.

"So what did you get?" I asked Dante.

"Emma got a ton of magazines," Dante reported instead. I detected a darkness streak across his eyes. She pulled a stack of four fashion magazines out of a bag.

"Aren't they gorgeous? All of the secrets of French women are in here," she fanned the pages, wistful. "It's tragic that I can't read them. Can you translate for me, Haven?"

I laughed, "Of course, we'll have a study hall later." Dante quietly stabbed what was left of his cake with a fork. "Hey, what's up?"

"I've lost my mojo," he said, letting the facade crumble. I had been bracing for it. On the rare occasions that Dante showed this side, it cut deep into my soul. And it always made me realize just how much I depended on him to keep me buoyant. "I can't even distract myself. It's just, I'm freaked out being here. I just want to get Lance, I don't want to wait. I don't want to do anything else." He pulled the smartphone out of his pocket and tossed it on the table. "And this worthless thing can't bother to tell us anything."

"I know," I said, my hand on his back. It was true. I had that smartphone nestled in my bag right now. I had looked at it daily since Metamorphosi Day, hoping for some of the guidance and comfort I'd come to rely on, to no avail. "Believe me, I know." This was his version of how I had felt at the Louvre. Lucian seemed to read my thoughts.

"The waiting is the worst part. It always was, even below, waiting for the portal to open," Lucian said in a hushed tone. We hung on his words. He was almost in a trance, as though describing the flashback running through his mind. "There it was different because we had this madness running through us, so anxious to get out to do these dark deeds. But what makes them wild and animalistic, out for blood and ultimately out for themselves, is what gives you the advantage. You're a unit and you will have a strategy. You'll see the cemetery tomorrow, you all will be together. It'll make a difference. It'll give you a sense of control." He looked at me. "Tell them what you saw today."

When we arrived back at the house, River and Tom were there, chatting with Drew and eating dinner. We greeted each other with hugs, Dante pulling from his shopping bags scarves for Drew—who was touched—and River, who looked confused.

He tossed something blue at Tom, who held it up. "Paris Saint-Germain. Awesome, thanks," Tom said, holding the soccer jersey over his chest. He pulled it on over his t-shirt. "You guys want?" He munched on a French fry and gestured to a pair of McDonald's bags, ripped open on the coffee table. "I got homesick," he said with a shrug, in explanation.

"I didn't even know they had those here," I laughed.

"Yeah, we passed one today," Dante said. "And it's no Angelina obviously, I mean, hello, but I gotta give it to them, they did have some shockingly good looking macarons and pains au chocolat."

"Guess we're not in Evanston anymore," I smiled at him.

"That's for sure," he shook his head. I was glad he had said what he did earlier. I thought about Lucian's words too. He stood at the living room window gazing out, night finally falling. It gave me an idea.

I found my bag, slipped into my favorite cropped running pants and a tank top and poked my head back into the living room. The group had splintered into pairs. I clapped my hands. "Five minutes! Wear something you can move in and meet me downstairs." They shot questions at me, looking for details.

"Really?" Dante asked. But I just took my phone and left, double checking the map as I headed down the stairs. Yes, so very close. Good.

When they came down to me, I didn't say a word, I just started running. Fast. Without trying. I hadn't intended to sprint like this, but this was the pace that now felt natural and easy to me. The streets had quieted and the sky dimmed at last. My watch read ten o'clock. The wind whipped my hair as I led the pack a few blocks back to the funicular that lifted visitors up the hill to the Sacré-Coeur. It had stopped for the day and the last of the tourists had gone. There was no one left to be swept up in our stampede. I didn't slow down as I climbed up the steep steps beside it, taking them two and three at a time, the others following behind me. I reached the top and kept running until I reached a spot just before the church. I leapt up onto the ledge overlooking the hill and all of Paris. The lights below twinkled, the city stretching out endlessly. The illuminated Eiffel Tower peeked from behind trees, spearing the sky. The group slowed to a halt, looking at me like I was crazy. But then their eyes focused behind me.

"This is why we're all here," I said. "To watch over this place." I had chosen my words carefully and though I wanted to say more, I sensed that I didn't need to. They understood. We were in this together, and we were here for even more than Lance. And so I let them all gaze out, lost in their thoughts for a few long minutes. The sounds of the city muted, the world at peace. Finally I turned around to face them again. "We'll be doing this every night." With that, I burst down from the ledge, running past them and leading them all back around the church—I wouldn't make them scale it tonight—and down the other side of the hill, taking the long way home.

10

I Need to Redeem Myself

Back in New Orleans, I had spent a considerable amount of time with the volunteer program painting graves at the most famous cemetery in town, Saint Louis Number One. They had referred to it as a "city of the dead," which had always sounded especially eerie, though I suppose I liked the sense of community it inspired. But Père-Lachaise—this really felt like a city. I had printed maps for us, so I had an idea of the scope, but standing there within its walls as it sprawled out endlessly before us, it truly felt like a city, complete with street signs to aid in finding the more popular gravesites. We stood quietly clustered just inside the front gate deciding where to go first. Lucian, Dante and I had spent hours back home looking at pictures of the tombs online and had amassed a list of potential spots. It was the kind of thing Lance would have loved to have done, pinpointing the best location and setting our plans in motion. "They need a large gathering place, somewhere to set a stage of sorts, so everyone sees him," Lucian had said softly, referring to the lamb in this sacrifice.

The group huddled up with their maps now but I stepped away from them, gazing out. There was some nervous, idle chatter. "Can we swing by Jim Morrison's grave to pay our respects? The Doors were a huge influence for me," River, who had been playing in a band in her hometown when the demons tried to recruit her, had asked. I paid no attention though, my eyes set in the distance.

"So, we marked some of the crypts here that seem like they could be good meeting spots," Dante began to explain in a tense voice, after waiting too long for me to start. I had done endless work to prepare, but now that I was here, standing in this place where Lance would be returned to me, all of that seemed unnecessary. I knew where he would be; it could not have been clearer. I felt it. I didn't need to see anything else. I set off walking straight down the path leading back from the main entrance. On either side, trees reached up into the sky and narrow streets fanned out leading to more and more mossy tombs and crumbling crypts. In the distance, the earth rose into steep hills covered with even more graves. But I needed only to keep to this one path: at the end of it lay a grand tomb that I knew in my soul would be it. It looked like a wall from here, a long marble bookend. Steps led up to a platform where sculpted figures stood as though already gathered for an event. I recognized it from my research as the Monument Aux Morts—the Monument to the Dead. Flanking this gathering place, densely packed trees stretched their full leafy branches and rained twigs and seeds onto the ground. Tiny bugs buzzed around us. So much life where there was so much death.

The group had followed me without a word, their soft footsteps crunching behind me until they reached this spot. They gazed up, spinning around to see every side of the space as though visualizing what it might look like at night filled with demons.

I shot Lucian a look, seeking confirmation, and he nodded solemnly.

"Then this is it," I said.

We spent the rest of the afternoon roaming the other paths, searching out the best hiding spots, mapping escape routes and entry points, taking pictures, surveying every inch of the sprawling cemetery. We stayed until just before the heavy gates swung closed for the night. It began to rain, soft heavy drops slowly soaking us as we made our way to the metro station, weary from a day of climbing chipped stone steps and wandering bumpy cobblestones past tombs of writers, artists, scholars and even starcrossed lovers. One question answered, my mind worked over the many others. I had tuned out everyone else, retreating inward. We reached a crosswalk and I kept walking, thinking—*it's not enough to save Lance, we need to keep him safe, we'll need to get away from them*—and not watching the light.

Lucian grabbed my arm, yanking me back and pulling me out of my thoughts for a moment. A dozen motorcycles zipped by, roaring.

"Whoa, watch it, Hav!" Dante said. "Where are you?"

"Sorry," I shook my head. "Wasn't paying attention. Thanks."

"I know you guys can technically survive being hit by a gang of motorcyclists," Lucian said softly, letting go of my arm and returning his hands to his pockets. "But even so, it's just easier not to risk it, I figure."

I watched the machines zoom down the road until they were out of sight, obstructed by a bus. Our group walked on.

"Drew!" I called out as I sped ahead. She stopped, turning around. "I have another project I could use your help on."

⬦

The next week we fell into a pattern: early morning jogs through the village of Montmartre and up the steps toward the Sacré-Coeur as the sun ascended. At night we returned to climb the church, leaping down from the spire at the top just to keep ourselves limber and fearless, recalling the kinds of nocturnal adventures we used to go on in New Orleans. We turned the living room into a war room, posting pictures from our scouting trip to Père-Lachaise. Nearly every day we split into groups to visit the cemetery and fine-tune our plan. We took day and evening trips there, running drills like we were staging some kind of covert military operation. We ran home, using different paths, mapping the possibilities, figuring going on foot would give us the greatest flexibility. The distance wouldn't be a problem—or at least for most of us. We practiced shadowing, which I had done in New Orleans but was new to the others. Dante picked up cheap Eiffel Tower trinkets for the group to wear which he fortified with the solution needed to pull off this feat. I preferred to use the fleur-de-lis charm Lance had given me, which had always worked just fine. I was as superstitious as I was sentimental.

We considered every variable: if our disguises didn't work; if we were being chased; if we freed Lance but he was physically in bad shape. We rented a pair of motorcycles as getaway vehicles, in case injuries prevented us from running. Lucian would drive one of them. If I allowed him to come with us.

<hr/>

When the day finally arrived, we felt as prepared as we possibly could. Even so, a nervous energy pulsed through the house, the way it used to at school before finals, rising through the day until we were a tinderbox awaiting the inevitable spark. We had gone over the timeline and were now just waiting it out until the hour came to leave. Everyone had paired off, searching for comfort and distraction. Drew and Emma paged through Emma's magazines—which I hadn't quite found the time to translate—polishing their nails. Tom and River snuggled on the sofa talking and paying no attention to the bad American reality show, dubbed in French, that was on TV. Dante had set to work rearranging the cabinets in the kitchen, his clanging the perfect soundtrack for rattled nerves. "It doesn't make sense that the pots and pans are so far away from the stove," he shook his head. To Max's credit, he bit his tongue, understanding that this was how Dante kept calm, and he stood patiently by as Dante passed saucepans to him.

I had searched through my bag, which I had never bothered to unpack, over and over still missing the one item I needed: that fallen disc from the Lexington Hotel that I'd taken from Lance's room in New Orleans. I couldn't explain to myself why I needed it so desperately, I just did. I needed to look at it now before heading into whatever tonight would bring. Finally I found it, folded up in one of my cardigans for cushioning. I propped it up on the desk, leaning it against the wall and the few books I'd brought. I was missing one but looked over and saw that Lucian had it. He sat on the bed flipping through channels, the abandoned novel flipped over beside him, seemingly too on edge even to read. Emma came into the room, pulled her makeup bag from the shelf above me, grabbed a new nail polish and returned to the living room. I refolded all of my clothes, pulling out what I planned to wear tonight. River came in and grabbed her laptop from under the bed and left again. I folded and folded again, and lined up my combat boots—a new pair identical to the ones I'd sufficiently destroyed in New Orleans, and paged through the cemetery maps I had highlighted, and put them away, and pulled them out again. Lucian changed some more channels—soccer, soccer, soccer, news in French, news in English, bad reality show—fast, fast, fast and then switched it off. He tossed the remote control on the bed.

"Stop!" Lucian said, making me jump, loudly enough that the others in the living room craned their necks to look in and the clinking stopped in the kitchen. "I need to talk to you." He ran his fingers through his hair and closed his eyes a moment. Drew had stepped into the doorway but turned around to leave.

"You've been avoiding me all day. All week. You've been avoiding me for months now," he said, closing the door.

"I've spent nearly every minute with you," I said in my calmest voice.

"You know what I mean," he said, too loudly again.

I opened my mouth to speak but he was right.

I felt like a criminal caught after years on the run. I knew he would call me out on it at some point. And I knew he had waited a good long time to do it. But if we were going to have this talk, finally, it wasn't going to be with such pure silence on the other side of that door. It wasn't going to be in this claustrophobic war room of an apartment.

"First of all, I'm coming tonight," he said. "But it's not just about—"

"No. I don't want—" I snapped but he cut me off.

"*Listen* to me," he shot back in that voice again.

I looked at him. "I will. But *not* here," I said, just as firmly.

I burst up from the floor, flung the door open and blew past everyone in the living room. They stared at me as I passed, the TV on mute. I stomped up the spiral staircase so fast the metal rattled and shook. I didn't have to tell him to follow me. When we reached the top, he pushed the hatch shut. I kept walking clear across the roof until I reached the ledge overlooking the street corner. My eyes followed the few cars traveling down the slope of our quiet street. The days had grown warmer and now this last day of spring felt like the high heat of summer. The air had grown warmer as the day had worn on and hung heavy and still, sauna-like around us now. I wiped the sweat already beading up on my forehead. I heard him take a few footsteps toward me.

"I want to be part of this. It means everything to me to be part of this," he said, his voice much more controlled now. I turned to face him. He stood there, arms at his sides, watching me.

"I don't want you coming tonight," I said, calm but clear, nearly pleading. "I don't want you there."

"I'm coming." We had been at an impasse ever since we had developed this plan with the group to ambush the sacrifice and steal Lance back. I had hoped his silence on the subject meant he was coming around to my way of thinking. Apparently I had been wrong. I changed tack.

"I'll leave someone here to watch you if I have to."

"Then I'll do what I have to to get away."

"What does that mean?"

"It means everything you think it means. That's how important this is."

"I care about you too much."

"If you care about me, you'll let me—"The frustration in his voice building like a rushing wave, ready to crash.

I raised my voice. "Why won't you listen to—" I raised my voice. He didn't let me finish.

"Because I'm not going to sit back and let you clean up this mess I made," he shouted at me again. "I need to be there. I need to redeem myself."

"You already have!" I yelled back. I had never been so angry at someone I loved so much. I spun back around, my hands on the ledge, trying to calm myself. The kinetic energy and anger I felt made me want to jump from here. I understood. I didn't want to, but I did. I couldn't rob him of what he needed in order to feel at peace with himself. He stepped closer. I could feel him at my back.

"I wouldn't be able to live with myself if I wasn't there," he said softly.

"You know how I feel," I said into the street below, my eyes squinting in the late day sun. I waited a long moment, still weighing it all. And then: "I don't agree with this. But I won't stop you from going."

"Thank you," he said sincerely, slowly. "Thank you, Haven, it means more than you could ever know."

I leaned on my elbows and bowed my head, shaking it out. I felt like I had lost something. He took a place beside me. He went on, in his gentlest voice.

"There's something else, too." He stood next to me, leaning on the ledge, watching the city, his hands clasped just like mine. "It's just…" he took a moment, looking for the words. Here it was, the moment I had been trying to run from these past couple of months. I couldn't take any conversation that had that air of finality. I had gotten used to them in the past year and a half. I was too familiar now with the impulse to leave nothing unsaid on the precipice of big events like these. But it implied that you were preparing for the worst, that some sort of failure lay ahead. "There's so much I've always wanted to tell you and now we're here and—"

"Lucian—" I stopped him, without even thinking. There was a time when I would have died to hear words like that cross his lips. But now I couldn't let myself. I feared that whatever he might say would set me back, make me lose my nerve and my focus going into tonight. "It's OK, we're—"

"Remember when I said I would love you forever?" he asked, determined.

"Sure." It had been in New Orleans, just before Metamorphosi Day. "That's not the kind of thing a girl forgets." I thought for a moment. "Why, are you taking it back?" I looked at him from the corner of my eye.

He smiled. "No. I just wanted to tell you again."

"Oh," I said, surprised. "Good—"

He cut me off. "And I just wanted you to know you've changed my life. That's all." He said it simply, as though glad to have gotten it out without interruption.

"You've changed me too," I said.

"Good," he echoed me. We looked at each other a moment and then, as though both deciding at the same time, we drifted back toward the hatch. He put his hand on my back, allowing me to go first.

I heard the TV volume go up again and felt everyone's eyes on us. I was sure they had heard some of what had gone on. And who could blame them for listening? When you are both people who don't raise your voices too often, others find it especially interesting and worrisome when you do. I needed to clear my head, so I just kept walking through the apartment, down the stairs and out the door.

I followed the path I knew so well, to the hill near the Sacré-Coeur, jogging the uneven steps upward on Rue Foyatier, racing the funicular as it lifted its patrons. I kept running until I found my favorite spot, the perfect vantage point: far enough from the Sacré-Coeur to avoid the throngs of tourists still out sightseeing, but nestled in between the trees so my view was clear. I climbed onto the wall, letting my legs dangle over the edge, and took a deep breath. The city below twinkled, Paris' lights just turning on as dusk set in. The tower stared back at me and in a blink, its lights came on too, glowing as it dwarfed all else in the skyline.

We were here. We were ready. We would soon have Lance with us again. And Lucian—stubborn Lucian. I understood, of course. It was going to take a lot for him to feel like his soul had been cleansed. I hoped that tonight would give him the redemption he sought. I hoped he would finally feel like he had shed his past and could move forward, with all of us.

11

Le Commencement de la Fin

We took the metro there, adding a welcome dose of the mundane to balance out the otherworldly horror we would soon be encountering. We arrived just before 11 o'clock, well after the cemetery's closing hour. The air stuck to us like flypaper. The humidity smothered us. Though the sun had set, the night grew hotter. We had expected this, of course, and dressed as appropriately as possible considering the physical challenges ahead. I wore my combat boots, black cargo pants cropped at the knee, my new watch, and Lance's Cubs t-shirt for luck. Dante had found this tribute both touching and appalling: "You haven't seen him in months and you're wearing that shirt?" he had scolded me at first. Then he had set to work, cutting it so that one shoulder peeked out here, cinching it in there, to make it more form-fitting and flattering. It had been a sweet gesture and a welcome distraction. And I had to admit, it did look much better. Around my neck, along with my usual necklace, I wore an extra chain bearing one of those ridiculous Eiffel Tower charms for Lance. "Function over style, I'm afraid," Dante had said as he fortified it. Now Lance would be able to shadow too.

We emerged from the Père-Lachaise metro station to find every sidewalk café along our path boasting full tables. Smiling patrons swilled wine and reveled in a summerlike night, the season itself just a mere two hours away.

"It's gotta be friggin' 90 degrees out here," Dante said, wiping his brow.

"This is like a cold spell where I'm from," Lucian said, almost smiling. He had a serene air about him now, after that talk on the roof. He was as calm as I had seen in some time. The torment that had clouded his eyes these many months had lifted, like a fog burning up in the morning sunlight.

The cemetery's fortress-like stone walls stood nearly twenty feet high, but we had had no trouble scaling them during our dress rehearsal two nights earlier. Lucian had been determined to do this himself, in his newly mortal body and with no help, even though he had needed a boost from Tom during our practice sessions. "I don't want anyone wasting their strength on me on that night," Lucian had told us stubbornly. When we had proposed hiding out in the cemetery just before closing time and being locked in, he had shot it down. "You're not spending one minute longer in that place than you have to. Certainly not for me."

Tonight we had decided not to set foot in the cemetery until we were in shadow form, so we found a leafy spot outside the front gates and each of us took hold of the talismans that Dante had fortified. For me it was akin to muscle memory, my body slipping back into this invisible form without trouble. But it had taken the others a few days to master the principles of shadowing. It could take tremendous focus to change states and maintain it. I had seen the ups and downs as the group had practiced. Drew and Emma had been quick to dematerialize, only to come back into view minutes later. Tom, on the other hand, had worked many minutes to get it right, but once he succeeded he was gone until he decided to be visible again. River had had mixed results. She had disappeared in a flash on her first try and maintained it for an hour. But on the second try, she had been unable to disappear even after a good twenty minutes and had to stop and pick up the work again later that day. And so it had been all week, my friends' shadowy forms wandering the apartment, getting in practice time whenever possible, during those late night jogs, while fixing a meal or sending an email home. It was a fantastical display of multi-tasking, our version of reading while running on a treadmill.

The work, though, seemed to have paid off. One by one, each person faded away leaving behind only silhouettes in the darkness. I held my fleur-de-lis charm, closed my eyes for a moment, and then looked at my hands. Or rather, looked to where they ought to be. I was no more than a smudge on the tapestry of this black night. Done.

"Watch the lights," I reminded the group before we threw ourselves over top of the gates. Dante had warned me of this when he first developed the practice. There's a false sense of security: you still exist. You aren't invisible, and if you fall into any direct ray of light you can be seen. That can be useful at times but, of course, could be deadly too.

One by one they went over, each quietly counting off as they reached the other side. It was our way of keeping track of each other. And then Lucian. Over the course of the past week I had caught him pulling himself up on the metal twists of the spiral staircase, on the shower curtain rod, practicing every-where he could. He flung himself up onto the gate, a huge door that offered some footholds in its architecture. I watched him climb as though on the face of a cliff, and when he reached the top, I took a breath. He swung his leg over and leapt down. The landing was soft, and I knew that our team had looked out for him. "Seven," I heard him say. With no more than a leap and then a push off the wall, I propelled myself over, floating down almost silently on the other side. So far it was all much easier than I ever would have thought, evidence that I had changed in a short time into something I still didn't fully understand.

"Eight," I said with a whisper when I was over. All here. We made our way back to the tomb silently, the gravel softly crunching under our feet. Lucian the only one we could all see. He felt for my fingers as we passed a lamp and looked at me, squeezing my hand then letting go again.

We reached the Monument Aux Morts, the imposing marble tomb glowing in the haze of the moonlight. Lucian had said that the demons would likely appear immediately after midnight so in the unlikely event that we had guessed wrong on the location and didn't see anything, we would quickly move on. We had ranked the five most probable locations and would hit them one by one until we found what we were looking for. I heard our footsteps collectively stop and then felt our group dividing, pairs splitting off to their respective places to wait out the start of this dark ritual.

Dante, Lucian, and I had flagged a nearby tree as our post. Its full branches shaded the far corner of the crypt providing, we hoped, a perfect vantage point for the proceedings. We made our way there, Lucian climbing up first and taking a seat on a low branch. The branches rustled again, like a brush on a drum, which I took to mean Dante was taking his place on another perch. I swept up the trunk, barely needing to use my arms, the same way I had run up the wall in the levitation room during all those nights of quiet practice. I knelt on Lucian's branch, just behind him. His eyes remained trained on the stage before us.

"I know you can climb higher than this," I whispered. He jumped, startled and whipped his head around, looking through me, camouflaged as I was by the black night.

"Don't you have more important things to worry about?" he whispered back.

"Not at the moment," I said. "Go." He pulled himself up, clasping his hands around another branch directly above ready to weave himself up higher through its network. "Dante," I said, just one notch louder.

"I'm on it," Dante answered back, his tone assured. He would keep an eye on Lucian, who was like a child looking for every opportunity to run out into traffic. "Up here, man. Keep climbing."

Lucian, still standing on our branch, shimmied up. Without thinking, I reached out and let my hand graze his calf as he disappeared up into the clouds. It was involuntary, a last move toward quiet comfort and connection before I was left alone with my thoughts. My watch—his watch—showed we had twenty minutes left. I felt my mind and body focus as I applied my mental war paint.

I pictured the others doing the same from their treetops and tucked behind nearby crypts and watching from that spot on the cemetery wall. Silent. Ready.

<hr />

At one minute after midnight, I heard it, the scrape of stone against stone, the unmistakable grind of the door to a tomb being slid open after being sealed for so long. Then came the footsteps, soft and light, barely audible, a ladybug crawling on your earlobe. And then that low hum, steady and rhythmic. My skin slicked up with sweat. I smoothed back my damp hair, pulling my ponytail tighter. The temperature in the cemetery had to have cranked up ten degrees in the past few minutes. Scores of figures swept past wearing heavy black cloaks that flapped softly like a flock of birds. The guttural hum grew louder.

They formed neat rows, half moons circling out from the monument. And then from the center of that grand tomb, a doorway pushed open and a sextet stepped out, heads bowed, taking places on either side of the entryway. One by one they each pulled down the hoods of their cloaks to reveal their faces. My heart stopped. I recognized beautiful Clio first, still perfect with her pixie cut. The others were mangled, ghastly, but still recognizable to me, burned as they were in my memory: Kip, whom we had banished just before Lance was taken; Beckett, pure evil and one of the chief henchmen of the Outfit in Chicago; and finally the most chilling, Aurelia herself. My blood ran cold to see her there, memories and horrors flooding back. Lucian had tried to prepare me for this, but still, it was overwhelming to see her, to see them all here in one place, led by the Prince. I felt my fear infect me, stopping my heartbeat and lungs and breath for a moment, giving me a chill even in this intense heat. I flashed back, remembering a similar feeling in the tunnels at the Lexington, and then another time when I had wandered too far into the crypt in New Orleans, down into the tunnels leading to hell. I felt trapped. I didn't know the other two faces in this group, but something told me my compatriots would.

The hum crescendoed, so loud it rattled my bones. The group on the platform turned to face the crypt entrance again and a flame flashed, momentarily turning the monument a fiery red. The heat flew at us all, like we had opened the door of a burning building. It seared me fast and sharp, then subsided just as quickly.

The fire instantly flamed out and in its place stood the Prince.

He wore all black: a three-piece suit and a cloak like the others but of a reflective luscious satin. His hood down, I could see his square jaw and chiseled features lit lovingly by the low-glowing security lamps. He commanded all eyes and got them. It was this showmanship, confidence and beauty that had built his empire. I had encountered him only a few times and never witnessed his full power, his complete mesmerizing charm. This was the alluring package necessary to seduce good people into bad things. He walked forward, slowly, his arms outstretched as though conducting. Row by row, those before him kneeled, bowing their heads. He swept his arms down fast and sharp, then raised them again and the hum stopped. Everyone bolted back to their feet again.

"*Bonsoir*, my lethal creatures of the underworld, esteemed members of the Court," he began in French, "*Bienvenue au commencement de la révolution. C'est le commencement de la fin.*" He let it hang there, grinning proudly. I translated in my head. *Commencement.* It meant beginning, of course. I had always liked that a graduation ceremony was referred to as commencement, the start of something. But now this word jolted me: what they considered a beginning was actually the end—*la fin.* They hoped for death, destruction. His words were crystal clear. I would have understood him even without four years of French. His tone was smooth and hypnotic, like reading a bedtime story.

He went on, "You've no idea how it thrills my soul to gaze upon you all and know that this shall mark a new beginning for us. We could not hope for a more auspicious start than this one." He smiled now, wooing them all with his gleaming teeth and sparkling eyes. He pulled them all in. I could feel it too, as though he were speaking just to me. "You are all to be commended on what you have accomplished in these years. We are more powerful than ever before. We have welcomed so many new souls. All. Because. Of. You." He said those four words with such care and passion. "And now on this blessed night we mark this time of revolution in grand fashion with the most stunning sacrifice."

If he had been weakened at all by the events of Metamorphosi Day, as Lucian had claimed, I certainly couldn't tell. He was all bravado—part ringmaster, part cult leader. He had that spark that begged you to watch, invited you in and then stripped your defenses. I couldn't be sure how much was true mind control, otherworldly power unique to him, and how much was just his stunning brand of showmanship. "In coming weeks and months, you will be called upon to recruit, to kill, to fight to preserve our way and spread it to the masses." As he spoke—slow, clear, emphatic—he paced, his eyes connecting with his followers, holding everyone in his grasp. "Though we have small victories, soul captures every day, and we celebrate them, the opportunity to seize power on this scale comes only every several hundred years. The time we have waited for is here at last and so much is ours for the taking. Each of you will be leading your own soldiers in this war. It will be difficult, to be sure, but success is in our sights and the rewards for your service will be sweet. This city is important to me, so we begin here and after conquering this, we shall continue on, swiftly obliterating our nemeses and claiming the rest."

He paused for a moment for effect, his tone shifting. "Tonight though, we rejoice in what is to come by partaking in the most anointed of rituals…"

His words seemed to be a signal. On cue, a handful of cloaked figures, carrying wooden beams under each arm, converged on the crypt. As they placed the beams on the ground, like spokes of a wheel, another five figures brought beams forward, leaning them up against each other, creating a spike pointing up to the sky and securing them with rope. Meanwhile the original five brought forth more beams, fastening them to each other on the ground. Their steps had a floating lightness, like dancing; this was a joyful moment for them. As one hooded figure drove the stake into the ground in one sharp stab, I felt it go into my heart. They finished in minutes. I was at the perfect height to see it: they had created a pentagram with a stake pointing up from its center.

He went on, arms in the air: "A sacrifice of the highest order: The sacrifice of the young angel. One of their most prized." The group answered him with a chant, words I didn't recognize, perhaps Latin. But the joy rang out so clear.

My jaw clenched and my chest constricted like I'd been kicked. I forced a deep breath, steeling myself.

"And so I beg you: What is your greatest desire?"

Again they chanted these words, pumping their fists three times in the air to punctuate them. In the space behind the Prince, the same doorway from which he had come, three cloaked figures now stepped out, the two on the ends holding up the one in the middle by his arms. Their heads were bowed and their hoods were up, shielding their faces, but the one in the center had his head up, staring directly into the crowd, fearless. I couldn't see his face in the shadows but I didn't need to. My heart knew it, and it beat as though trying to burst from my chest.

It was Lance. And they were going to burn him.

My mind turned it over and over, as though I were watching a horror film. The cloaked figures led him forward, taking down their hoods now to reveal the disfigured faces of our fallen compatriots Jimmy and Brody. They had been our roommates in New Orleans, our fellow angels, but had let themselves be taken by the other side. Lance had defeated them himself on Metamorphosi Day, and now they would repay him for it by leading him to his death. I wanted to run to him now. Seeing him brought it all rushing back, all that emotion that had been simmering these past months. Even weathered as he was from what he may have encountered in that world below, he was so achingly beautiful. Seeing him now, my heart and mind, my body and soul understood how deeply I had missed him. I wanted to touch him, to hear his voice, to be near him again.

He betrayed no emotion, standing strong, his eyes steady, his chin cocked at the slightest angle as though looking down at these creatures. Adrenaline surged within me. I wanted desperately to run to him right now. I had waited so long for him. I could destroy every evil, rotted soul that stood between him and me. I could fight them with my bare hands, ripping them apart. I felt my body lunge, about to pounce, but stopped myself.

No. There was a plan here. Abandoning our carefully considered strategy would be like tripping a wire, detonating the whole thing and losing our opportunity, losing him. I would only have one chance at him. I had to wait for the sign. I had to wait for her. I hoped she could do it. I hoped they all could.

Jimmy pulled off Lance's cloak, shoving him toward the stake, while Brody tugged his arms behind him, tying him there with fast, deft hands. As he was pulled against the stake, Lance's body went slack for a moment. He looked like he was fighting to remain on his feet. There had to be some sort of toxin at work or he surely would have broken free. He wore the black jeans and t-shirt he had worn on that last day, when he was taken prisoner. I ached for him. I hadn't seen him in so long; my thirsty eyes drank him in. He was close now, but so much needed to happen in order for me to get to him. I watched him as he scanned the crowd, and I tried to read his thoughts. He was looking for us or at the very least, looking for some possible escape. Then he returned his gaze into the distance.

"Enter into record that our sacrifice has been offered the opportunity to join us and refused," the Prince said, as though it were an official declaration. Lance stood stonefaced but seething. He struggled against the stake, trying to pry himself from it.

"He is not only the upper echelon of those on the verge of earning their wings, but he is the paramour of the one we have long been chasing. The recruit who intends to lead them, and who herself will be killed for it." I had to stifle my gasp. This was me. They were cheering my demise, their voices growing more buoyant. Each chant taunted me. This is how they would destroy him: slowly and painfully, as they rejoiced around him.

The blood burned in my veins, my temperature rising. I wanted to tear their limbs apart. I felt a violent impulse rising within me unlike anything I had ever experienced. It almost terrified me. Almost. But instead I siphoned it into a reserve, determined to stockpile it until I needed it. This feeling, this mad passion would keep me alive tonight. I slithered down from my perch, purposely snapping a branch as I did. At the sharp crack, Lance's eyes darted in my direction. A few of the cloaked figures nearby looked over. The Prince interrupted his speech for just a moment, then went on riling them up some more, conducting their chants, playing one side of the crowd against the other. But Lance kept looking my way. For the briefest second I stepped into the halo of light around the nearest security lamp. His eyes speared mine sharp and fast. Then he looked away just as quickly, and I ran back into the safety of darkness. He had seen me. I felt a calm relief. He knew we were here. At least he knew we were here.

And then, I heard it. I had never been so happy to hear River's voice. She had campaigned for this role. I couldn't have done it myself, though I wished to. I wanted to be the one to go in after Lance. But if you're leading that mission, you can't be the diversion, too.

"Hey there," she shouted loud and deep, the sarcastic bit of those two words cutting through the chants. "Mind if we crash this party?" The cloaked masses and the Prince swiveled their heads toward the opposite side of the crypt, further back from where I was positioned. And I ran.

"Of course, they are here," the Prince said softly, as though to himself. "And so it begins." He threw his arm toward the stake and sent a flame to one spoke of the pentagram. It burned around the circle and charged toward Lance as I bolted to him. The crowd lunged toward River, who took off running. Then Drew appeared, back in the distance.

"Anyone remember me?" she called out sweetly from a patch of light. Another surge pushed over toward her and then she disappeared. Next came Emma's voice in another part of the grassy gathering area, leaning against a lamppost like she was waiting for her favorite boutique to open for a sale: "I love Paris in the summer," she gushed, drawing even more demons charging toward her. It went on this way for some time, all of them appearing and disappearing, tormenting the demons.

They were angry now, running in every direction like a mischief of mice dropped into a maze, some blindly shooting bolts into the air. Still in shadow form, I pushed upstream, brushing past the swarming demons as their cloaks swished against me. I struggled to keep Lance in my sights. The flames licked at his feet now, the fire would be on him soon. In the space behind me I heard the angels continue to appear throughout the crowd, taunting them then fading to become shadows again. The prince shot a burst of fire encasing Lance within cylindrical flames to keep us away. The Prince's confidantes charged out into the crowd dispensing more bolts, trying to catch us all presumably before we could get to Lance. But I was closer than they knew. I reached the platform of the tomb, squinting against the bright, raging flames. I was sure that I was now visible. I had to work fast or I would be attacked. A woman's voice pierced the air. Raw and gasping. Emma. It sounded as if someone had grabbed her. But I had to free Lance, I was just steps away from him now, near enough that our eyes locked through the bands of the roaring fire. His face was stony, his expression stoic, I didn't understand how he could withstand it. I could get no reading on his level of pain. His image started to sway: it was me. I felt woozy for a moment. Now I understood—the fire had released some sort of opiate as it burned, something to hinder our efforts. If we didn't do this fast, it wouldn't be done at all.

The fire bands were crosshatched, a grid, impossible to slip through. But between their dancing rays I could see they seemed to stop nearly two feet from Lance's body, creating a small radius of breathing room. For now. The flames would only creep closer. Already they were reaching up ten feet into the sky. I ran to the monument wall, where the Prince and his inner circle had emerged. Pulling myself up on weakened limbs, I climbed to the top of the slippery marble, using more effort and less speed than I expected. I steadied myself, then pushed off, flinging myself out toward the stake. I caught the top of it to stop my momentum, thick splinters digging into my fingers like staples, then I dropped straight down landing in front of Lance. It felt like being in the center rack of an industrial strength oven. Lance's head had bobbed forward as though he were drugged.

"You're a tough guy to get to," I shouted over the roar of the fire with a smile, squeezing his arm to pump some life back into him, wake him up. He didn't quite feel like Lance yet.

"Thanks for dropping by," he said drowsily, shaking his head.

"Anytime." I pulled frantically at the steel-like rope that bound him. It burned when I touched it, like a seat belt buckle of an old car on a summer afternoon.

Through the wall of fire I spotted Tom, my backup, sprinting to the tomb, then halting as though his legs were entwined in vines. Emma screamed again somewhere in the distance. "Go on!" I yelled at him through the blaze. "I got this!" He gave me a look, then stumbled and ran back toward the lawn, the screams, and the chaos.

I pulled and pulled, loosening the bind around Lance's wrists but this rope was more than mere steel and the way his arms were pulled back behind the post made it especially hard to free enough slack for him to slip through. The flames burned closer, licking his feet. He was barely moving now. Then, I thought of something else: "Duck!" I shouted into his ear. He slouched to the side, nearly folding himself in half, and I kicked the stake he was tied to. One sharp, strong snap, and it splintered and broke, falling away from us as the hungry flames bent to consume it.

I grabbed Lance's wrist and pulled him, running away from the flamethrowing masses, away from the screams. I thought I heard Dante's voice above the din, a roaring "NO!" and perhaps River answering, "I'm here, I'll get him." And then a, "She's OK," from Tom. I could only imagine it was about Emma, whose scream I had heard first. It felt strange to be running *away*, but this had been our plan: as soon as Tom or I had freed Lance, we were to remove him from the scene and head home, taking whatever measures necessary to avoid being followed. And as soon as the others saw that Lance was no longer a captive, as soon as the ritual had been adequately disrupted, they were to escape. We didn't need to wage a revolution-scale war tonight; we just needed to get Lance. But still, I felt a tug. I needed to be everywhere at once, to finish this. But I couldn't. We were so greatly outnumbered. I had learned my lesson from the final battle at the Lexington—all you could do at a certain point was divide and conquer and hope that your plan looked as good in reality as it did on paper. I needed to get Lance away. Our diversions would all be for naught if we still lost him. I had to get him somewhere safe, get him shadowed, make sure he was all right.

We wove between crypts, taking a series of sharp sudden turns as we let ourselves get lost in this city of the dead. The noise of the fight was fading behind us. With each step away from the paralyzing effects of the pyre, I felt Lance's strength return. Our pace sped up, though I looked at my feet and found

I still hadn't returned to shadow form, my system likely still recovering from the toxins of the fire.

Lance grabbed my arm as he darted into the quiet nook beside an imposing stone crypt whose facade was covered in lipstick kisses. He tugged me with such force I lost my balance a moment. Without a word, he pulled me against him, his strong arms closing so fast and firm around me it knocked the wind out of me. He pressed his lips to mine, feverish, pushing me against the tomb and crushing me against him in a way that made me not care about things like breathing. I wound my arms around his neck, pulling him closer, closer, holding on fiercely as though he might still be taken from me and using his weight to keep myself from melting on my unsteady legs.

His hands wound in my hair, pulling it from its ponytail, the layers falling around my shoulders. He looped my hair in his hand, pulling it back from my ear to whisper. It was all so fast, that feeling that either of us could be killed or captured at any moment and time couldn't be wasted. I felt his hot sweet breath on my neck:

"I missed you," he said, a rasp of desperation.

"I missed you too," I echoed him. We spoke with a choppy urgency, our eyes scanning each other's, manic, knowing we could be interrupted, ambushed at any moment. "It was hell."

He smiled. "It was hell," he repeated. "Literally." He kissed me again.

"Wait," I pulled the chain from my neck, the one meant for him, and placed it around his. "Shadow yourself."

"Shadow YOURself," he kissed me again, not paying any attention. I clasped my arms around his neck once more, losing myself again in that sweet, swirling frenzy of reunion. The rest of the world felt put on pause. I gave myself permission not to think, just to act, and I let myself drown in his arms, in his kiss, in the heady feeling that he wouldn't let me go. The air around us was perfectly still and tropical.

"I thought I'd never see you again," he said, his lips still on mine as he spoke.

"I know," I answered.

He pulled away just enough to look in my eyes: "I thought of you every day. All day," he said, needing to be understood.

"Me too. Every day."

Then he shifted, apologetic: "We were so stupid. I was so stupid."

"I was too," I gasped. I knew what he meant. We had lost sight of each other in New Orleans, briefly. We had been… confused. We were dealing with so much. Yes, we had become more powerful than anyone we knew—we were new creatures entirely. But we were still seventeen. We were still figuring so much out. So we had made mistakes, we had strayed mildly. We would not do that again. We had a new start now. We had changed for the better. We had grown up.

"Every day should feel like this," he whispered, his lips on mine again.

"Except without the burning at the stake," I whispered back.

"Right," he placed his hand on my neck then spoke into my ear again. "We're always good under the threat of death, aren't we?" It was something we often said, our inside joke—and it was true—but it had never sounded quite like this. And it had never been truer than now. This was us. This was us at our best.

"Yeah, we—" I started but was interrupted. By a guttural, bone-chilling scream. It ripped into the air, tearing my heart. It was a man's scream and it shook us instantly out of our reverie and returned us to the present. I knew even then, much as I pushed the thought aside. I just knew. Lance and I took off running. As we did, he grasped that pendant and transformed himself into a shadow for safety. But it did little good. As soon as the Monument aux Morts came into view, we found the pentagram-shaped stake engulfed in roaring flames, burning so boldly it illuminated the entire area, rendering our shadowing useless. Sirens rang out in the night air. In the distance, I spotted some of the nameless, weaker devils slinking back into crypts. Others hung back to canvass the space around the pyre just in case they could make an easy kill or better yet, find their escaped prisoner. We ran along the periphery, trying to guess where the scream may have come from, Lance trailing behind me. I swerved behind a boxy tomb to avoid a pack of cloaked figures darting out from around a bend. Lance put his hand protectively on my shoulder. They thrust their fists in the air, chanting those words from the ritual. The language was unfamiliar, but the voice...I feared that I knew it. One of them slapped the other on the back, congratulating him. I ducked down the alleyway they had just come from. And in the glow of the street lamp I saw him. The sight stabbed me, stopped me in my tracks. I opened my mouth expecting to scream but found I didn't have enough breath, I gasped instead, nearly choking on instant tears.

We had walked by this crypt on our scouting missions, the memorial to the lovers Heloise and Abelard. Laying before it, on his back with his arms splayed and blood pooling around him, was Lucian.

PART TWO

12

Everything I Love is Taken From Me

I ran to him. Throwing myself to the ground, I put my head to his wet chest, blood adhering to my ear. But there was nothing. I took his limp wrist in my hand. Checking. *No. No. Please. No.*

Lance dropped to his knees beside me. "Is he...?" he asked, his voice raw. "What can we do for him? There must be something."

I tore open the tatters of his blood-soaked, burned shirt to find a wound more grisly than any I'd ever seen—a gaping gash at his heart and charred skin as though he had been both stabbed and burned. I had to look away, steadying my breath.

Soft footsteps came running, halting just a few feet from us. I felt the others, flickering in and out of shadow form, collect around us. I heard their gasps, felt their disbelief. And then that voice behind me, one that I hadn't heard for months:

"They're coming, Haven. We've gotta go. C'mon."

Lance turned around: "Hey, wow!" he said in recognition.

I looked up and found Connor.

I was too numb to process the full shock of seeing our guide from New Orleans, the one who had been charged with training and shepherding us through the second of our three trials toward earning our wings. My body and soul had been so beaten, no feeling remained. I worried for a moment that the devils might simply be shapeshifting into this trusted figure in order to finish us off, but my telltale scars lay silent. It felt like him. But, still, I didn't move.

"Now." He grabbed my arm, yanking me up by the elbow.

"No!" My yell tore out of my lungs sounding jagged and bloody.

"Yes," he barked back. "If we don't go, we risk starting the revolution *right now*. You don't want that. You all," he gestured to the others, "Go! Meet us on top of the monument." He knelt down, looking me right in the eyes, gripping my upper arm. The sirens blared, closer now. And the footsteps neared, a herd of them. He shook me, waking me up: "They are coming back. They want to see the body. We have to be gone." Each word felt barbed. He spoke as though I wasn't familiar with this language. "There's nothing more you can do for him now."

"We have to bring him," I said, my hands sliding under his neck, around his chest, trying to scoop him up.

"We can't, he can't go where we're going—"

"Where—" I started, angry. He cut me off.

"His body won't be admitted entry—it's not my decision, it's a matter of science and chemical composition." He said, making no sense at all. But I didn't care. I only cared that he seemed unable to offer me the answer I needed.

Lance must have seen that Connor's words weren't connecting. He cupped his warm, smooth hand around my face and spoke into my eyes, slowly, as though I were catatonic.

"It'll be OK. I promise. But we have to go now," he said, the tension creasing that spot between his eyes. The chanting began, euphoric and celebratory.

"NOW, guys," Connor said flatly.

INITIATE

Lance stood and gave my hand a gentle tug, but Connor yanked my other elbow, getting me up onto my feet at once. "This way," he said, leading us back the way the others had gone. I stopped after just a few steps, looking back at him one last time, helplessness and hopelessness washing over me. "C'mon!" Connor yelled up ahead. My heart torn, I took off again running back to Lance and Connor just as that same group of cloaked demons turned down our way.

"Hey!" came a voice as one of them launched in our direction. *That voice.* Yes, it was Kip, the demon who had been so disappointed not to kill Lucian in New Orleans. The one Lance and I had banished below. He had seen us. The fire burned so bright in the distance now, our shadowing failed. He called out as he ran: "Come on, they're here! Hope you're keeping count, Beckett, I'm about to score my second kill."

Lance followed Connor climbing up the pillars of the tomb where the others were now grouped, jittery, bouncing from foot to foot, kneeling down looking for Connor and some guidance. I heard myself breathing, panting as I ran, but felt like I was watching the scene instead of actively participating in it. My heart had only just repaired itself after seeing Lance and now it was torn open again, spilling into my body. Again. Failure again. I couldn't keep doing this; my heart couldn't take it. My soul couldn't take it. Everyone I loved was in constant danger because of me. I wondered if I should even bother, just let the others go on. But they were waiting. They watched me, Connor gesturing into the sky, telling them something. But still they waited for me.

I pushed everything else aside for now. I couldn't risk hurting them all. I ran up the pillars on quick, sure feet, flinging myself up to the top.

"….no, you just jump, it's not as high as it looks," Connor was explaining to Tom in a clipped tone, no time to waste. The racing footsteps grew closer below.

"Sorry, what did I miss?" I asked, making my voice strong. River averted her eyes. Dante left Max's side to dart over to me. I noticed Emma had a bloody slash on her cheek. Our eyes connected for a flash. She read the concern in my look and shook her head that she was fine.

"We're going up there." Lance said, hand on my back, pointing upward to what looked like a hazy cluster of stars.

"It's a portal," Connor said. "You just have to shoot for it, jump. I'll go first and show you, but you've gotta follow me. One at a time, but fast, got it?"

"But we can't fly yet," Drew said, quietly as though she felt ashamed pointing out this shared flaw. She had a burn on her arm in the shape of a hand.

"Doesn't matter. It's like a magnet, it will recognize what you are and pull you through. Go! Now!"

"But where are we—" Emma started, but Connor took a warm-up bounce and then leapt, rocketing upward, arms at his side but moving fast. Sure enough, about twenty feet up, he was suddenly swallowed. He just disappeared into the glowing patch in the night sky. On either side of us now, we heard the footsteps.

"See you up there," Tom said, he took a running start then pushed off the ledge of the crypt and upward he flew, arms up as though he were beginning a high dive. He, too, was engulfed. The others went one by one and then finally Lance, who I told to go on first, and then me. I glanced back once more at that spot in the distance where Lucian lay and tried not to feel like I was abandoning him. I bounced a couple times, then set off running, just as the others had. I pushed off, leaping up, but something grabbed my ankle pulling me down, smacking me hard against the flat top of the tomb. I lifted my head, struggling to get back up to my feet, and found Kip there on the edge of the tomb. His disfigured, melting face, which had not had time to heal after we had banished him to the underworld back in New Orleans, grimaced at me. He clung to my foot. I grabbed onto the lip of the tomb for leverage and kicked, shaking him off. He landed with a thump on the ground below. On the other side of the tomb, two other heads appeared, climbing and running to converge on me.

"I got this, Kip, don't hurt yourself," Beckett said, snarling. His face wasn't fully returned either to the perfection it had been in Chicago before I had sent his blackened soul back down below.

I crouched, then bolted up, rocketing on strong legs, up, up so many feet, and just at the point when I expected gravity to set in and jerk me back to the ground like a snapping rubber band, as it always had, I suddenly felt a pull *up*, like an ocean current before a storm. There was no use fighting it. It lifted me through the air, the wind whipping my hair and pushing my arms down to my side. I felt the shift in power—for these brief seconds my body eased, making itself lighter to float upward. I felt guided by this force, and let myself be carried. Giving in seemed to allow it to pull me even faster. The haze, though, seemed to always be the same distance away until everything around me went blank. I couldn't imagine ever stopping; I certainly had no idea how I would know to put on any brakes. A flash of bright white light blinded me, and then, pure darkness. My body slammed full force against something cold and hard. I had stopped. Breathless, I couldn't be sure I was still alive.

The raw skin of my cheek felt as if it would need to be scraped from the ground. The bones on the side of my face felt brittle. My tongue checked to be sure my teeth hadn't been knocked out and, surprisingly, found all still in place. I moved my arm and a sharp pain shot through my chest. I imagined all of my ribs shattered and clinking like wind chimes loose within my body. Slowly, I curled myself into a ball. Everything ached and throbbed. I reasoned with my eyes, trying to urge them open, and was greeted by a warm glow, the color of melted honey and just as comforting. Silence. Peace. My eyes focused in front of me, on an outstretched arm, that hand with its long fingers and the cuff on its wrist, the one with the angel wing, beside the leather strap bearing a fleur-de-lis charm: Lance. So still. I couldn't be sure he was breathing and didn't have the strength to crawl to him yet. I reached out slowly and my fingertips brushed his. Instantly his hand snapped shut around mine. Relief flooded me, giving me the strength to pull my head up. The others were all there sprawled out on the grass beside us, like items left behind after a party.

I tried again to flip through the pages of my memories searching for which parts might have been a dream and which real—something I had often had to do over the past year and a half. And then, like so many other times, I felt my heart stop once more. Yes, it had all been *real*. Lance shifted his arms and legs, turning his head toward me. I was grateful that this one part had not been a fantasy: Lance was all right, as far as I could tell. And we had freed him from the Prince and his underworld. But there was a new hole in my heart: why could only Lance or Lucian seem to be with us? It had not occurred to me that we would be replacing one with the other. They weren't interchangeable. They were meant to both live. I needed both. For different reasons they were both part of me.

Why was it that everything I loved was constantly being taken from me? Lance's warm chocolate eyes lasered at me from behind his glasses, silently asking if I was OK. I offered the slightest smile and he closed his eyes, relieved.

I heard the quiet muffle of shifting limbs around us, a communal attempt at rousing. I tested my voice:

"One," I said just loud enough, hoping to be followed.

"Two," Lance said, not moving.

A long pause, and then a gravelly "Three," from River. Then Dante. Tom. Drew. Emma. And finally "Eight"—which had come after many torturous seconds from Max, who had been thrown several yards away, judging from the distant sound of his crackling voice. Slowly, we all began to make the tiny movements necessary to pull ourselves up onto our feet. Everyone was even nearer than I expected, all of us almost touching, except for Max, whose sneakered feet poked out from behind a patch of blooming trees, its flowers elaborate ruffles of turquoise and fuchsia unlike any I had ever seen. As soon as I righted myself, stretching out my sore limbs and massaging my shoulder, which had taken the brunt of my smack against the ground, I jogged over to offer Max a hand, pulling him up. "Well, you found a romantic spot," Dante said, reaching us just as Max was dusting himself off. He gave Max a kiss on the cheek. "Had me worried though. Don't do that again."

"Sorry, guess I lost my way," Max said, shaking his head. I picked up his fedora and set it on his head.

"Good as new," I said, nodding to him. I shook my limbs out and stretched again, hopping up and down. I felt back to myself, so unusually fast. "How's everyone?" I scanned them all, in various stages of stretching, standing, and tending to achy limbs. Lance helped Drew test out what seemed to be a sprained ankle. The air was warm, perfect, and the sky a shocking cloudless blue. We had landed in a field, surrounded by trees with star shaped leaves and flowers in shades and shapes I wasn't familiar with. Everything seemed just one step beyond what was recognizable. An imposing, palatial columned building shone in the distance. It looked as though it were made entirely of glass or crystal.

"It's OK, I'm good," Drew said, hobbling, then shaking it out and walking just fine. Lance patted her on the back. We all looked at each other, everyone wearing the same surprised and confused expression.

"Strangely, I'm feeling not terrible," Emma said. "If that makes sense."

"Yeah. I mean, it hurt getting here, but now it's all good," Tom said with a shrug.

"Wherever here is," River added.

"Yeah, where are we anyway?" Max asked, running his fingers along one of many mossy trees, lime green and so densely packed they created a wall interspersed with low hedges and more vibrantly hued flowering plants. Midway along this stretch, a bare patch had been cut out. It appeared to be a doorway of some sort.

"Wherever it is, they've done some lovely landscaping," Dante said.

"And it's better than the scene we just left," Emma said, shivering. The bloody streak on her face had hardened into a ragged red fault line.

A whooshing came from a spot along the greenery where a pair of reflective doors opened on smooth tracks. Connor stepped out. He walked toward us, looking as he always had in New Orleans, as he had last night, in the casual clothes of a college man. But he had a different air about him now, regal. I noticed there was a glow above his head. It wasn't as pronounced as the halos you see in paintings, it was more subtle, a bright spot that cast a faint light over his whole body.

"You're awake. Good," he said, as though we had simply stumbled into the living room of our old house after a good night's sleep. "They're anxious to see you. We've got a lot to talk about. C'mon." He gestured for us to follow him through the doors.

13

I Give You The Administration

Once inside the chrome vestibule, the doors snapped shut. We stood still but sensed we were moving, though we had no idea how. When the doors opened again, we were deposited into a long hallway rolling endlessly before us. We were in the crystal fortress. On all sides now we could look out and see views of the field and gardens. The structure felt airy, part of the world outside. And it too had a glow, not unlike what encased Connor.

He kept talking, his footsteps echoing as he walked. "Sorry about that bumpy ride. It can be a little rough before you're full-fledged angels, but I thought it was the best way to go. That was getting dicey," he shook his head. "Good work though. I would've liked to get there sooner, but our portals have greater security measures so the journey is longer for us than it is for those coming up from below."

"Might want to get that looked at," Dante said under his breath.

He walked at a quick clip and we were silent for a few moments, trying to gather our thoughts and make sense of our surroundings. Paintings in ornate, gilded frames adorned the walls on either side of us, some very familiar. Reaching back to the beginning of civilization, their names were engraved on gold plaques underneath. Some of the ones I recognized on my quick survey were Joan of Arc, Cleopatra, Pierre and Marie Curie, Hippocrates, Galileo, an architect of ancient Greece that Lance worshipped named Ictinus. On closer inspection later I would learn there were knights and saints and artists and inventors, people who had changed the world throughout the history of time.

The expansive walkway was dotted with many sets of grand double doors, all closed and imposing with no sign of what might be behind them. It looked like a museum, except for that honey glow that lit the entire vast space. As we walked, the group took it all in, slowing to get a better look at some of the paintings, gazing up at the crystal, prismatic ceiling that let the light flood through in beams. I barely paid attention though. Something was nagging at me. I couldn't shake it. I walked beside Lance, so close our hands brushed against each other. My heart beat stronger to be near him, to know he was safe. I wanted time to revel in that, to fully appreciate what had been returned to me. But still I couldn't stop thinking about the scene I had left. It felt wrong to have fled, to be here and safe now. The guilt hung heavy on me. Around me, the others posed questions that didn't matter to me right now.

"So we're not full-fledged angels yet?" Drew asked, the disappointment knocking her voice down a register. Connor shook his head.

"Not quite," he said.

"I was sorta hoping getting Lance was our third test," she looked at him out of the corner of her eye, as though it was wrong of her to even suggest such a thing.

"'Fraid not," Connor smiled. "But hopefully it was still worth it to get this guy back." He squeezed Lance's shoulder, like a big brother.

"How do we get to be one? What's the next test?" Emma asked, prodding like an impatient child. "I'm so sick of tests."

"We'll get to that. We'll get to all that. I want to get everyone together first."

"Everyone?" Max said to himself.

"Where are we?" River asked, an undercurrent of anger.

"I'm just gonna go and ask, because you know you all want to," Dante stopped in his tracks, setting it up. "So Connor, dude, is this Heaven?" he looked Connor in the eye, as serious as I had ever seen.

We had stopped before a set of glowing chrome doors. Connor faced us all. "No. It isn't. And I'm not sure there even is one. None of us have ever seen it, or any sign of it," he said gently, knowing how earth-shattering a statement like that could be. He started again, hope in his voice: "But I like to think this is even better. This is the realm of the angels." He held his arms out and we looked out onto that field we had landed in. It stretched on forever it seemed. "And you are home. This is where you belong."

"Is that, like, in Paris?" Dante asked.

"No, Dante," he laughed.

"So where is it then?" Lance asked, pushing his glasses up on his nose. "I suspect it isn't located on any map we're familiar with."

"It's everywhere and nowhere," Connor said, letting it hang there for a few seconds, reading our faces. He put his hands on his waist, like a coach explaining a new play. "Portals exist everywhere, but this place exists on another plane. You can only reach it if you are an angel of your level or greater—" My mind wandered as he spoke. Now that I felt back to normal, in one piece and strong again, I felt even more unsettled. That familiar boiling roiled my blood, making me skittish. I was feeling trapped, far away, as time ticked on and my opportunity faded.

Connor must have sensed this somehow. His eyes landed on me as he went on. "...And so that's why even Lucian's body couldn't be brought here." He said it softly, like a eulogy, as though he expected this subject matter be put to rest now. But I refused to believe it.

Connor touched his palm to the door and it glowed golden and slid open. Inside, the sleek space was all glass, Lucite, crystal and chrome burning with that same glow. Here it illuminated so many books lined floor to ceiling in built-in shelves. Spiral staircases twirled up in each corner to reach the top and ladders on mechanized tracks sat ready to zip around. Where there were no bookcases, there were those all-encompassing windows out into the peaceful calm of this new world.

In the sunken living room in the center of the space, chairs and a long oval table sat awaiting a group. "Go on in and take a seat down there," he directed us as he walked straight to the back of the library, pulling down a tome. A ring around the periphery lit up, a balcony level with five ornate metallic thrones, each carved with figures of angels, the back and seat made of a luscious bright white velveteen.

Our group found their seats, gazing with dropped jaws around the room, but I caught up with Connor. He typed into a keyboard embedded in the Lucite desk. I glanced at the screen: *All present and assembled in the annex and ready to begin.* He ignored me and continued typing. As he did, the windows onto the outside clouded to a bright white and the glow around the living room brightened.

"Look," I said, leaning in front of the screen. He looked at me, but with a blank expression. "I'm getting the idea this is going to take a little while."

"Haven," he said, in that scolding tone that he had used with me in the past when I was about to ask something he wouldn't approve. His eyes were stony.

"I can't just leave him there," I said, my fingers jittery, looking for an outlet for this energy. Lance's eyes were on me, curious. The others sat, quietly talking, trying to guess what would come next. "Can't I go back and at least take his body somewhere? I just can't leave it—him—there, for them. I—"

"You *will* go back," he said, his sharp tone cutting through me to make his point. "If you really want to go back. You *will*. But not to the cemetery. And not now. Take a seat." I looked into his eyes, but they were unwavering. I slunk back down to the space where the others sat, taking a place next to Lance, my eyes still set on Connor. Lance put his hand on my knee and looked at me with that furrowed brow. He could read my thoughts, I was sure. And I didn't want him to misunderstand. It wasn't about loving him any less; it was about needing to at least feel that Lucian's body could be at peace, not left as a souvenir for the demons. I couldn't bear for them to use him in one of their dark rituals. I opened my mouth to explain but he squeezed my knee and cut me off, softly.

"I promise, we'll figure something out," he said, those comforting words again, he put his hand around the back of my neck and pulled me in, kissing the top of my head. "I promise."

Connor took a seat with us just as the lights of the room went black. The balcony encircling the room now lit up like a halo above us all. It only just occurred to me that there was no railing around it. A small cluster of figures—a woman and three men—clad in white filed in through the door. They looked our age, perhaps a few years older, but carried themselves with an otherworldly tranquility. There was a presence and maturity about them, the kind that usually divides the high school students from the collegians in a crowd. Just steps inside the doorway, the panels slid shut again and in a flash the three figures took flight. One by one, their backs erupted with blinding white wings as they floated up to the seats along the balcony. I glanced quickly at Connor for explanation. He shrugged, nonchalant: "I give you the Administration," he whispered, standing. We all followed his lead.

They raised their arms, serene smiles on their faces, and lifted our sunken area up to their level. We hovered there for a moment, and then the man in the center nodded at us, and they lowered their arms once more, this time taking their own circle down almost to the floor below us. It was like a theater-in-the-round and we were now the attraction. We were still standing but Connor motioned for us to sit down.

"You all could have raised yourselves up like that, but you're very polite so it hasn't occurred to you to try something like that," the man smiled, looking from side to side at the others, who nodded at this joke. Connor shook his head, smiling, also in on it. I didn't understand. The others traded confused glances. "It's a pleasure to meet you," he went on. "We are the Administration, the governing body of angels at the moment." He looked around the circle to his fellow angels. Their pristine white wings framed them grandly, each wing seeming equal to the height of the angel wearing it. Their halos were the same shade as the glow that had followed us everywhere. "I'm Henry," he said kindly. He had mocha skin, close cropped dark hair and a wide, warm smile. "This is Jackson, logistics," he pointed to the man with the chin length dark hair, olive-toned skin and serious expression seated on the end. He wore a leather jacket and looked familiar. Yes: he had been the one we had seen in New Orleans. Connor had called him the "Facilitator" and he had helped arrange some of our large-scale training missions like racing steamboats. "Elodie, weaponry and mechanics." The woman, with full, wavy blond hair smiled and bowed her head with the careful grace of a ballerina at a curtain call. "The empty seat is for Connor, of course. Research and Intel." We all looked at him now, awe in each of our faces. He was one of *them*? He just shrugged like it was no big deal.

Henry went on, speaking carefully but without the stuffy pomp. His was a natural, welcoming tone: "We congratulate you on completing your first two tests. We know how difficult this path is. You will be part of us soon, I'm certain." I had never heard those words spoken by anyone other than a representative of the underworld, so it surprised me to find them so comforting in this context. "As you are well aware, revolution is coming and it is our responsibility to prevent evil from seizing control. For now, I'll leave the proceedings to Connor. We look forward to hearing of your travels and wing-seeking trials. Welcome and thank you for your service." He bowed to us. We weren't quite sure what to do. Emma curtsied as the rest of us nodded awkwardly. Connor took a seat and gestured for us to do the same. Dante stood motionless, watching the Administration until I tugged on his arm to get him to take a seat. The light of the track below us dimmed and our own circle grew brighter, the transparent furniture adopting the same glowing hue.

"So, guys, I want you to pretend it's just us," Connor said easily. "You've been on the front lines against the underworld and whether you realize it or not, you're going to help lead us in the revolution." He was back to being Connor our friend, our guide, not the man who barked orders at us or snapped at my questions. This Connor was always capable of injecting a sense of calm into the atmosphere. I felt myself ease just enough. This could have been just another debriefing in our French Quarter living room after a night of demon-shadowing.

"I'm sure you guys have questions," he went on, scanning our faces. "We do too. So first, we're going to get our questions answered. And then it'll be open season for you guys. Good?" He waited for us all to agree. "So, Lance, good to have you back with us."

"Thanks," Lance nodded. "Thanks to all you guys," he looked around the table.

"We're all very curious to hear what you might have seen and heard where you were—" At this, Lance bowed his head, looking at his hands folded in his lap. Connor didn't miss this. "You don't know yet."

Lance looked up. "I'm sorry, it's like a total blank right now. Just like after we were tagged in New Orleans." I shuddered, remembering how during our second test we had each been attacked by the band of demons running wild in the French Quarter, their toxins invading our souls and threatening to poison the good in us and replace it with a thirst for evil. The eight of us here had made it through but some of our fellow angels had not. In the days following each of our attacks, none of us had had any recollection of what had happened. But it had all flooded back later on in the form of dark dreams and chilling flashbacks of the killings we had witnessed.

"It'll come back," Connor said, disappointment shading his voice. "And the minute it does, I want you to find me."

"Got it," he said, shame in his voice.

Connor nodded and looked at the rest of us, moving on: "What we need—"

"I've been wracking my brain," Lance interrupted, as if he were talking to himself. "But I just wasn't all there, you know? They used some kind of toxin on me. I barely knew who Haven was when she showed up tonight."

"That was from the fire," Tom said. "When I got up there, it knocked me out. They were burning something in it to keep us away. And man, how are your feet not destroyed? That fire was *on you*. Looked like it, at least."

"Our skin is really tough now," Lance said, perking up, glad to have a concrete piece of news to share. "I saw it but I didn't feel it until just before Haven got me out."

"Tougher than when we wrestled the gators?" Drew asked, recalling our adventures in the bayou.

Lance nodded.

"Whoa," Max said. "Nice."

"OK, so moving on, what we—" Connor started again.

But it was all bubbling up in me: "We have to retrace what happened tonight," I blurted out. Everyone looked at me.

"There will be losses, Haven," Connor said sternly.

"I know. I get it. But I'm not accepting this one," I said.

"We have a lot to get to. I told you we'll discuss—"

I cut him off: "I need to know where it went wrong."

The man who had welcomed us spoke now. "If you don't mind, I would like to hear."

Connor looked down at him. "Of course," he said and took a deep breath. "All right, Haven."

"I just need to know where *I* went wrong," I said, my tone softening, the guilt so heavy on me I cast my eyes down. I forced myself to look around the table. Everyone's faces had fallen again too. No one spoke for several seconds.

"Listen," Connor said at last. "This is what happens in battle. I will not let any one person take the fall. All we can do is learn as much as possible about what we're up against and adapt ourselves to fight our hardest." He looked each of us in the eye.

Dante spoke into his fidgeting hands: "Lucian took off running." He looked up at me from across the table. "I called to him, but he was gone before I could even get to him."

"He heard me. Jimmy had found me," Emma interrupted, shaking her head. "I don't know how he found me, there were so many people in his way and I thought I was so fast. But all of a sudden Jimmy was there, and he pinned me and he was going to kill me or, or, or, burn me with his bare hands." She stammered, trying to push the words out, and held up her wrists, which had been hidden under the table. I noticed now they were red and raw. It looked like she was wearing two pink cuffs.

Drew, seated beside her, took hold of her arm, concern in her eyes.

With her other hand, Emma wiped a tear as it ran down slicking up that ragged scratch on her face. She patted at it, and shook her head: "This is Jimmy, too."

"He's a monster now. Literally, a monster," River said, leaning into the table, as comforting as I'd ever seen her.

"I feel like I've lost him twice," Emma said. "It was enough when they took him and he was gone, and I dealt with that. But now he's something so evil and…" She shook her head, unable to go on. "I'm not sure I can take this. Whatever is coming next."

"Does this hurt?" Drew asked, patting her arm. Emma shook her head.

"No, I mean it did at first, but now it's just ugly," she said, then looked at Lance. "But I feel like, what's wrong with me? You said your skin is so tough, why isn't mine?"

Lance looked away, pushing up his glasses, that nervous tick showing how sorry he was to not have an answer. Connor had been listening, letting us talk and console each other, but now he cut in. "None of you have reached your full potential yet. You're all at different stages, even now. But this is not the time to lose faith in yourselves."

"That's what they want," I said. "They want to chip away at every part of us, mind, body and soul, right? They want to turn every one of our weaknesses against us. And they know they have limited time because we'll be strong enough soon. Once we get our wings?" I looked at Connor for confirmation.

"That's exactly right," he said, reassuring.

"I'm sorry, Haven," Emma said, crying now. "Lucian was coming to help me. I heard him come out of nowhere to distract them. Can you forgive me?"

I nodded. "It's not your fault. He knew they would be seeking him out."

"He ended up near us," River said, gesturing to Max. "But they all went after him."

"They were already on him by the time I got to you," Tom shook his head with regret.

"We were so close to getting away," Max said, head heavy.

"We saw you up there with Lance, we saw you tell Tom you had it covered, we were ready to retreat when it all went bad," River finished his thought. They spoke like war vets recalling a hazy, chaotic battle. I pictured it all.

"I tried to hold them back. I used everything in my arsenal, things that had worked in New Orleans," Dante pleaded. "They're stronger now. They are. And they didn't even care about us, they went for Lucian. I mean, savagely. We were surrounded by them and couldn't push through them all fast enough to get to him."

"Kip got him only because he beat that other guy to it," River said. "He was so pissed off, did you hear him? That guy who had been on the stage."

"Beckett," I said. I could picture this rivalry playing out over Lucian. I could see Kip, so anxious to get in the Prince's good graces, descending like a vulture to a rotting corpse.

"You knew that guy? Because I saw some familiar faces too, from when I was first recruited or whatever," River said.

"Me too," said Drew.

"I heard Lucian. Did you hear him? He said to them, 'Wouldn't you rather go after me?'" Max said.

Emma hung her head: "He was trying to get them away from me." She went on, angry now, "We just couldn't fight them all. We weren't prepared."

"I saw Kip from one of the trees, he blasted through the group," Drew said. "He stabbed Lucian with something on fire. It sent up this spark." She shook, a chill sweeping over her.

AIMEE AGRESTI

One by one, they each offered a piece to complete the puzzle. I thought of our talk, that last talk up on the roof. Lucian had been so set on going, so unafraid to throw himself into the fray. Reckless, even, in his need for redemption. The chaos and confusion of that scene had given him all the opportunity he needed to scrap our plan. And now, just as I needed someone to absolve me of the guilt I felt at what happened, I was comforted to see that they did too. We were in this together, in a way I had never felt so completely. They were all still talking, going over the minutiae obsessively, looking for ways to have avoided this. Connor looked at me, as though expecting me to take control here. And I realized, yes, that was it: he had told me once that I would eventually be more powerful than even him. I just had to have confidence in my abilities.

"No," I said, perhaps too loudly. I had the answers I needed now and I couldn't allow them to beat themselves up. "He was going to do this, he knew how dangerous it was. He wanted to be part of it and he wanted to put himself, his life, on the line. I understand now. Thank you all. I wasn't there and you did more than I ever could've hoped."

We had set this plan in order to save Lance and get him out alive. It had all happened in the span of minutes, the longest minutes I had ever felt. It wouldn't be possible to scrub the image of Lucian from my mind or to stop feeling that loss. Just as I now understood the timeline of what had happened, I also realized that there was no comfort in that: this new life meant absorbing this kind of pain. I wasn't sure yet that I was strong enough—just as Emma's skin felt too thin—but I couldn't let them see that.

"If I may?" Henry's voice came from below us.

"Of course," Connor said, with reverence.

"You've all been brought together because you are stronger together, greater than the sum of your parts," he said. "It has been tremendously difficult to find you and to unite you. But you are unlike anything we have seen. What happened tonight, despite the loss you suffered," he looked at me as he said this, kindness in his eyes, "fills me with great hope for what you can accomplish in the future. I suspect you will all pass your third test with little difficulty. And that is all that stands in the way of you becoming guardians." He nodded to Connor, ceding the floor back to him.

"So, the third test," Connor started. "You will be required to free a repentant soul already claimed for the underworld." I looked up at this and our eyes connected. "Everyone will receive a dossier of a target repentant-devil: someone who made a mistake and wants a second chance. These have been sussed out by careful research and are being prepared right now."

"Can we choose someone?" I interrupted him.

"You will be able to choose from among several dos—"

"Do they have to be…living?" I cut in again.

Connor didn't answer right away. "Historically, they have all been living," he said slowly. I sensed it wasn't an absolute. He glanced down toward the Administration. "Our angels-in-training have been very successful with these…"

I thought of what he said before the meeting began. "However," I said, prompting him. "There must be a however here." I nodded.

"However…."

"No, Connor," a sharp voice came from below. It was the man with the chin-length hair, who hadn't said a word yet.

"However…attempts involving going back to the past have been unsuccessful."

"What does that mean?" I asked. It wasn't the kind of "no" I had expected. I didn't know whether to be encouraged.

"It means there *is* a way," Connor said, looking down, unsure of whether he had permission to go on. "But so far, testing this procedure has resulted in *failure*. Do you know what I mean when I say that?" He gave me a cross look. I nodded. "We think some of you—you, Dante and Lance specifically—may be able to complete the puzzle to make it possible. But we're not sure we can risk losing you, especially before the revolution. It's a decision you shouldn't take lightly, so I want—"

"I'm in," I said, my voice strong and steady.

"We're in," Lance said, backing me. He looked at me and nodded as though pledging himself to me. "You?" he asked Dante.

"For sure," Dante said.

Connor leaned back in his chair, sighing, as though disappointed by this turn. He looked at me like I was a problem child. It wasn't a look I was used to getting from anyone else in my life, but one he gave me often. Finally he spoke: "Well, the decision isn't really up to me."

Henry cut in: "Might I suggest we adjourn now and let our newest angels get acquainted with their surroundings? We'll reconvene shortly."

Connor nodded, standing, "Of course, sir." We all stood as the Administration filed out, our platform sinking back to the floor again and theirs rising above us. Connor shook his head at me as he filed out, leading the group ahead.

I found Dante standing before a wall adorned with four rows and four columns of evenly spaced glowing halos, each set above an etching of a face. No names, just faces and burning halos. The rest of our group continued down the hallway away from us, their footsteps growing more distant, their words a hum.

"This is like what they have at the CIA, right?" Dante asked. I didn't know the answer, but it seemed possible. I remembered it from our Contemporary Issues class: the CIA had a wall marking each of their fallen heroes with a star. I didn't need to reply though.

"Yes, winged one," came the voice behind us. I felt his glow and serenity in the air. My spine lengthened, my posture straightening before I turned around. Henry stood there. He placed his hand on Dante's shoulder. "And you see him, don't you?" he asked. Dante nodded in response, eyes fixed to an image in the second row, just above our heads. A man who looked just like Dante, with the same playful eyes, same sparkling grin. "I knew you were his son the moment I saw you."

Henry held his hand up against the picture and it glowed, then changed to writing. *Michael Dennis. Beloved warrior.* No dates were given. "I worked with him, fought alongside him several times, saw his bravery. That was my last battle as well," he said with a thick sense of loss. "This nemesis of ours…this is an evil unlike any you have ever known. The depth and breadth of it," he shook his head, "The corrosion of soul and charring of the heart," his voice tensed with anger. He shook his head, starting again. "The losses we have suffered I feel personally in every cell of my being. They will not be in vain. I promise you." He calmed himself again, looking in Dante's eyes. "He was a great man," Henry continued. "It is an honor for me to meet his son. I have been waiting for your arrival for many, many years. As great a warrior as he was, I suspect you will be his greatest accomplishment and legacy." He gave the slightest bow to Dante. Dante's eyes welled up. I could feel him fighting those tears. I grabbed his hand for a moment. He nodded back at Henry, no words, it seemed, necessary. With that, Henry turned, floating back toward the library. We stood motionless until he was out of sight, then, with a look that said, *No, I don't want to talk just yet*, Dante nodded at me and we found our way back to the group.

14

So How've You Been?

"Well, that was heavy," I said bursting into Lance's room without knocking as soon as Connor left us at last. He had led us to a suite of sleek chrome and crystal rooms, urging us to get some rest because we still needed to regain our strength after crossing through the portal. I found Lance standing right in front of the door. I nearly hit him with it.

"You read my mind, I was just on my way to you," he said. I let the door close and he kissed me. It was the first time we had been alone since the cemetery. We had so much time to make up for.

"So, how've you been?" I asked, making a joke. But he looked at me, his eyes clouded. "Wait, what is it?"

"I can't believe what you went through to get to me."

"Of course," I said. "I would do anything." I didn't want to think about Lucian right now. My heart needed a reprieve from what it had endured in the past 24 hours, 48 hours, or however long we'd been here. My watch seemed to have stopped the minute we crossed through the portal. Lance pulled me to sit down on the bed, holding my hand and looking deep into my eyes.

"I just have to make sure you know I was trying to keep the Prince away from you. That night."

I shook my head, not understanding. "What are you talking about?"

"On Mardi Gras. I kept him away as long as I could," he said, urgently. "I ran him all over the French Quarter trying to kill time before we finally got back to Royal Street."

I flipped through those files in my memory, calling up all I remembered of the chaos of that night. I thought back to that moment, Lance appearing just in time to help destroy Kip as he closed in on Lucian...and me.

"It's killed me to be away from you all this time, these months. That was harder than anything they put me through there. But what destroyed me the most was thinking that there was any chance you might've thought I'd been stupid enough to lead that monster right to you."

I had always wondered why Lance had fallen for the Prince's trick shapeshifting to look like Lucian. Lance was so much smarter than that. I should never have doubted him. My hand flew to my mouth, in shock at what he had endured for *me*. All along he had been trying to protect me.

"He showed up saying, 'Haven's in trouble, we have to get to her.' And I was surprised of course, because I knew that technically the real Lucian should not be physically capable of leaving that house until midnight. So I told him to lead the way. And he said they were taking you somewhere, he didn't know where, he had lost track while chasing you and Kip and that I would know where they would be going. He, of course, expected me to lead them to you. I lead him all over the city pretending to look for you—back to the cemetery, to Bourbon Street, over to that bar on St. Peter, but when it got close to midnight I started to freak out. I started thinking what if you *were* in trouble. I tried to time it so he would have to disappear before he could cause you any harm. I kept him away as long as I could." He squeezed my hands in his. In my mind

I watched that night unfold again, this time with the blanks filled in and the burning questions answered. He kept going, as though needing to get it all out.

"I knew it was him. He could've killed me anytime, but I knew I'd probably be OK until we got to you, but then we'd be in trouble for sure. But I couldn't bear the thought of something happening to you if I could've been there to help. It was a gamble, I know. But I went back to check on you."

I let it all set in. "You sacrificed yourself."

"I don't know that I would put it that way. I just did the best I could to keep him away. You were the one he wanted."

"You went through so much for me."

"I would do it all again. And you went through so much for me."

"I would do it all again," I repeated.

After a beat, he spoke again. "I like this, by the way," he tugged at the sleeve of my Cubs shirt. "Never knew you were such a fan."

"Well, I'm a fan of yours."

"It looks better on you than it ever did on me."

"Thank you," I said, shyly. "So, I have something to say, too."

"OK," he squared up, as though expecting it to be about that night, the Prince, some tiny wrinkle in the story.

"You've just literally been through living hell for the past two months, two weeks, three days and four hours, give or take."

"Right." He sounded touched that I had been counting.

"Don't take this the wrong way. But I am so sick of talking to you," I said, with a smile.

"Good. Me too," he laughed. And like magnets snapped together, those lips I had missed were on mine again.

A knock rattled the door and just as fast we bolted away from each other, as if someone were watching. We both sprung up and he opened the door.

Connor glanced from him to me and back again. "We need you guys, OK?"

As we followed him out, we shot each other a look behind his back.

⸻◆⸻

He led our group to the library again. We took the same seats. Pristine white folders lay at each spot, and an additional stack of them lay at the center of the table.

"In the coming days, you will be setting out on your third test."

"When would that be? How long have we been here?" Lance asked before I could. "I'm sorry, but after coming from where I was, with no weather and no sun and all nights and no days, I'm a little confused." It occurred to me that I had lost all sense of time. It felt like we had been here for weeks, months, the way you feel when you go away on a trip. It takes such a short time to feel such a great distance from home. But the sun hadn't set or even dimmed.

"Perfectly understandable, Lance. You guys left the cemetery about 48 hours ago. It's easy to lose track when you cross over here. You'll notice your watches don't work." I looked at mine again. Lance noticed it now, too. I wondered if I could get away with not telling him where it had come from. Connor went on. "The only time that matters is the zone where you need to be going to. So, it's about 2 am in Paris now. I'm glad you mentioned that, actually, Lance, because you all might also have noticed that your body clocks have reset up here. Anyone tired or hungry?" he asked with that smirk that accompanies rhetorical questions. For the first time it occurred to me that none of us had eaten for a very long time. And aside from being knocked out when we arrived here, we hadn't really slept. In fact, I now realized I had been trying to ignore an electric buzz in my veins.

"I kind of feel like I've been consuming nothing but coffee and, like, speed for days," I said, hoping I wasn't alone. "I mean, not that I've ever tried speed, but I would guess it's like this."

"It is," River said flatly.

"Good, because I feel like I'm going to have a heart attack," Dante said, shaking his head and shimmying his limbs. "It's like when I got a little overzealous making my own chocolate-covered espresso beans—remember that, Hav?—and I ate all the ugly ones. And then all the pretty ones too." I had to smile. I did remember.

"You'll get used to it," Connor said. "Being here is like putting your phone in a charging station. There is a current here that you pick up, that you feed on. You are at your strongest here. It's the same for *them* below, from what I've gathered. You'll learn to harness it and to not be overwhelmed by it. You're designed that way."

At this we all stopped and looked up. His face was stoic, making sure everyone had caught his word choice. He looked at each of us and nodded. "You all are something new. Something we have tried for the coming revolution. A new kind of angel, one that has in its makeup centuries' worth of power of mind and body."

"So, we're, like, superangels?" Dante asked, eyes wide.

"I guess you could say that."

"How?"

"I hadn't planned to go down this road right now, guys," Connor said, watching the door. "But, all of our souls are recycled through time. Angel souls pass through here before searching out host bodies in the world. A host is basically a body left abandoned somewhere dead or alive, someone that no one is going to look for. There are more of these in the world than there should be. Each generation of angel is by nature stronger than the one before it. But with you all we identified the strongest souls—they might have been warriors, visionaries, geniuses—and directed multiple souls to the same host body. Those souls were cobbled together to form a new supremely powerful soul in each of you. Every angel's powers begin to manifest when the host turns 16, but none have ever been as strong as all of yours. The things that you're doing come from powers usually reserved for full-fledged winged angels. And it's a good thing you can do these things because the demons have gotten stronger too."

But before he could go on, the doors opened and the Administration floated in again. We rose in greeting and they took their places once more.

"So, we have dossiers here for repentant souls, those recruited and sold to the Prince in recent days, that can still be reclaimed." He walked around the table, tossing smart-phones at each of us: they looked exactly like the ones Lance, Dante and I had been given before heading to New Orleans. The three of us shot glances at each other. I gave Connor a look of understanding as he approached to hand me mine: so it must have been him sending us those messages all along? That certainly made sense.

But he just furrowed his brow at me. "Look alive, Terra," he barked before tossing a phone at me. "What's with you?"

I hit the Home button on my phone, expecting to see a painting of a drowned angelic girl flicker on the screen, as it had on my old device. Instead, I saw a photo of a girl walking on a city sidewalk. I couldn't tell exactly where but from the slope of the street, it seemed to be Montmartre. She looked haunted, hollow, but beautiful. And familiar. Brunette and lovely. Yes, she was the girl on the bike, from our first day in Paris.

"This test will require each of you to track down your subject and inject them with a protectant serum while extracting the portion of their soul that has already been diseased."

"Like in NOLA?" Tom asked, recalling the levitation rituals we had once performed, saving each other's souls after being hit by the demons of the Krewe.

"Right, except, this time you're doing it all yourself."

"What if we can't do it?"

"If you stab them with the serum without lifting the diseased soul then you kill them," he said matter-of-factly. "A repentant soul still has a good portion to it. It's still fighting, it's just almost overrun. In the past we've done these exercises in teams, but you all are stronger and the danger is more pressing: the revolution is coming and we need every possible soul on our side. So you each have your own target. Study up, everything you need is in there. These files are more souls. Once you finish, you may be asked to keep hunting. As you head out, someone from the lab will be waiting to escort you to pick up the supplies you'll need."

"Good luck and stay safe," Henry said to our group. Everyone bowed and filtered out. I let them go. Lance stood but took only a few steps away, still watching me.

I held up my phone at Connor. "Does this mean I'm not—"

Connor sighed when he looked at me, arms behind his head, exasperated. "I know what you're going to ask me."

"You have to let me try. I'll save her soul too," I said to the phone. "But—"

"That's why I've asked the Administration to be here, Haven."

"Oh," I stopped and sat down again.

"This is something we've been working on but have not successfully tested yet," Henry spoke now, seated at the center of the Administration. A grave look set in Connor's eyes.

I nodded. "I'm guessing it means you've lost people."

"Yes," Connor said. "And I personally am not in favor of this. But—" There it was, hope. "But others are," he glanced at Henry. "And it's something we have been working to achieve, so we are willing to let you go provided you follow our rules."

"I understand," I said solemnly.

"Because I don't want you stranded there. We can't afford it. You have to parachute in to the right time, get his attention, thwart their attack and get out. If you get hurt you might not have the strength to return on your own and I certainly don't want to have to send someone else after you. Lance—" Connor addressed him now, he had been standing at the opposite end of the table, waiting, listening. "We're going to need you on this. And Dante!" Connor called. Sure enough, Dante had been listening with the door ajar.

"You rang?" Dante appeared.

"You all can wait on your test assignments for now," he sighed, as though he'd been talked into something he knew he shouldn't be going along with. "I'll show you to your workrooms."

"Take good care. We need you back with us," Henry said before we left. I bowed toward him. I wasn't sure if I was allowed to speak to him, but I did anyway:

"Of course. And thank you, sir. I won't disappoint you."

Connor dropped Lance off in the workshop a few doors down, where a group of 15 angels toiling on mysterious machines and gadgets all stopped what they were doing to greet him with the reverence reserved for the Dalai Lama. Dante asked to tag along with me before taking up residence in the lab, where he too would have his own staff. Connor led us into a grand room the size of a banquet hall with every inch of wall space covered in flat screen TVs lined side by side, hundreds and hundreds of them showing what looked like security camera footage. People walking along city sidewalks, people riding buses, people checking the mail on their leafy suburban streets. At the bottom of each screen read the geographic coordinates of each location along with the city and country.

"Whoa. This is just a little Orwellian," I said under my breath, leaning into one of the screens.

"We're gonna party like it's 1984," Dante said. "You must have one heck of a cable bill up here." I scanned the screens: Los Angeles, Sao Paulo, Toronto, Paris. So many. I glanced at the Paris screen, testing myself to see if I knew where it might be. I recognized the statue: it was Joan of Arc. Yes, I knew that. Along the Rue de Rivoli, I thought to myself, proud.

"So this is the Illumination Chamber. This is where…" Connor began to explain. But I wasn't listening. Something else caught my eye. I leaned into that same screen, and saw it again: someone flickering back at me. I shook my head. "Wait—" I blurted out, hands on the screen. For a moment, a boy skateboarding past the statue morphed into a grotesque rotting figure, his skin dripping from his skeleton. A hazy gray static surrounded him. I blinked and he was on the skateboard again.

Connor stopped midsentence: "What is it?"

"This guy."

"We've got one. Screen 53," he called out.

"On it!" a girl's voice rang out from a nearby desk. She wore glasses and had her short platinum blonde hair pulled up in a messy ponytail, a stylus tucked behind her ear. The image I had just been looking at came up on her screen now. She typed something in and the picture shrank, filling the top of the screen as text scrolled in a document on the bottom. She pulled out one of the smartphones, aimed it at the screen and with the press of a button, a laser beam shot between the two electronics. She stood up, attaching the phone to her belt with a clip, pulled the sweater from the back of her chair, and ran out the door. On her computer screen it now read: "Portal 53."

"What just happened there?" I whispered to Connor. Before he could answer, I heard another voice behind us.

"Wow. Just like you promised," came a voice from behind Connor.

"I'm a man of my word, these guys are on their game," he said to the boy, apparently talking about us. He had spiked black hair and sparkling, lively green eyes.

"Hello there," he bowed his head to me in greeting.

"Hi, I'm—" I was about to introduce myself.

"Haven, I know," he said with a smile. "And Dante, hi." He shook our hands. "We've been waiting for you. For all of you. I'm Nathan. Tech support."

"You must be a busy guy," I said, gesturing to the room.

"We've got desks already set for all you guys, for after initiation if you want to see." I didn't entirely know what he was talking about, but Dante and I followed. The workspaces were equal parts streamlined and cozy. Each had a chrome laptop and a Lucite chair with a white cushion. Everything was sleek, modern, and crisp but with comforting touches: floor pillows, white banquettes along the walls, a sign for a meditation room. "It gets intense in here. It's like a stock market for souls," Nathan said. "It moves so fast and it can wear you down. But this is it, this is what we do. If we don't do this then the demon realm will gain more followers every day. If we don't do this then a simple mistake made at 16 can end a life, kill a soul. We are guardians. It's the best job in town."

"And it's about to get revolutionized," Connor said. "Think of this as command central of the soul-saving factory. This will be your domain, Haven."

"Wow, thanks," I said, awed. It felt like getting a Ferrari as a birthday present before you had a license.

The room seemed to hold at least 50 of these stations. At its center on a circular raised platform sat another workstation, with a larger chair that looked like it swiveled to view screens on all sides of the room. Just below that, another ring of just a handful of stations orbited this pedestal.

Connor and Nathan led the way to the center of the room, climbing a tight spiral staircase up. Once up there, Connor pressed a lit silver button, and in a flash the screens went dark. Everyone turned to face him, all conversations hushed, as though understanding this signal.

"Hi guys," Connor got their attention. "Just wanted to take this opportunity to introduce you to someone: Our illuminator is in." He put his hands on my shoulders, pushing me in front of him. The room erupted into cheers, as though the football team had just taken the field at the Homecoming game. It took a moment to process that this reception was meant for me. I gave a wave, nodding at them in shy appreciation.

"Whoa, Hav," Dante said, smiling.

"Your jobs are about to get a whole lot easier: Haven's gonna get to work," he said, looking at me. "But it's also about to get faster. You may feel overloaded at first. Remember to recharge as often as possible. And as always, be careful. I don't need to remind you that each and every one of you is an integral part of what's coming. Make me proud!" He hit the button again and the screens all erupted back to life. "What do you say? Want to get started? You've gotta kill time before this guy—" he nodded at Dante,

"—and Lance can figure out how to shoot you back to the past anyway," he shrugged.

"Sure, sign me up," I said, shocked by their collective confidence in me.

"Here's how this works," he gestured for me to take a seat. "What you just did? Spotting that guy? That quick work got an angel dispatched to him. That soul may be saved. You're going to do this every day. You'll be the one to locate anyone needing help, anyone in need of a guardian."

I couldn't quite formulate a response yet. It sounded so grand, the responsibility too tremendous to even fully comprehend. Me. I was the safety net. For everyone.

"How do I do that? There's so much going on."

"You'll need this," Nathan said, handing me a remote control.

"Great," I exhaled. "I was wondering how to change the channel."

He smiled and kneeled beside me, looking at the screens on the wall before us. "So, you basically just watch," he pointed before us, then rose to his feet and turned me to face another wall, "And watch." He turned me again: "And watch."

"But, what if I miss some?"

"Others are watching, and they have the gut checks and instincts every angel has—which is something—but it's still a slow business for them. For you, it's instant." He snapped his fingers. "I wouldn't have believed it if I hadn't just seen it."

"But what if I miss some?" I asked again, this time my voice flat, serious. I thought of all my days at the hospital when someone didn't make it, when one of those beloved doctors I knew so well had to tell a family news they desperately didn't want to hear. In all my years there I never got used to seeing that. I never got better at navigating the hollowness that came when I found an empty bed while delivering meals and learned that someone I'd seen hours before had not gone home. I turned the remote control over in my hands, delicately, as though it were a scalpel. No one spoke in our small cluster for several long seconds.

"Tell me something: What do you see when you notice one of these souls?" Connor asked me.

I thought about it. "A sort of flicker into this ugly sort of corpse and a haze," I shrugged.

"They will find YOU, these images. They will reach out to you. Just like what you saw in that one screen. You could have been looking at any of a handful of screens at your eye level, but you latched onto that one and you were right."

I turned that over in my mind. It was true, I had never thought of it that way. "So maybe things that feel like luck are actually something more?"

"Instinct, gut check and illumination—and that's something only you can do. That's what will save us time," he patted me on the shoulder. "We identify the folks who need us, we send someone in to assess the situation, and they lead that person out of whatever darkness they're in."

"I always thought a guardian angel could also just kind of, like, help you out of a jam, you know?" Dante asked. "Like if you're depressed or you're going through something tough. I didn't think you had to be on the verge of selling your soul to the Prince in order to get one of us to show up."

"Absolutely, yes, good question," he said gently. "You'll find, as you guys start to review the footage, which you'll also have on your screens here," he tapped at the laptop on the desk, "that all of us, you, me, all of these guys, we recognize those people the same way. Because, if you think about it, if you're in a rough place, and you need some help and some answers and some comfort, you're also in a position where the underworld could move in on you and could offer you the wrong kind of solace."

Dante nodded. It made sense.

"We get in there and see what's up and then we get them out of it, however we need to: in some cases, we may need to physically spring them out from a den of demons—like Brandon did just last week," he pointed to a baby-faced red-head just below our perch, leaning into his screen intently, like he was playing a video game. "In other cases, it's just offering them other ways out of where they are. All of it keeps them from falling in with the Prince's network. Because they are everywhere. We get a respite after Metamorphosi, but then the portals open again and it's a free-for-all."

"So Haven, eventually you'll be sending assignments to others from your angel class," Nathan said. "But for now, if you want to, just watch the screens and get the hang of what you're looking for. The majority of our targets are between 13 and 21 or so."

"Ever the coveted demographic," I said.

"Why's that?" Dante asked.

"Because those are the most vulnerable," Connor explained. "They're the most recruited by the underworld. There's enough natural upheaval during those years that souls are often in flux. Think about yourselves, right? You're all figuring stuff out, it's tough, it's emotional, there are ups and downs."

"When you see something like that skateboarding guy, who went demonic earlier," Nathan leaned in, looking ahead as he took the remote control from me. "All you have to do is flag it," he aimed at one of the screens and a border lit up around it. "Hit it once more and it's sent to one of the terminals below. And another soul is saved." He said like it was no big deal.

"Right, piece of cake," I said, with a laugh. "Then what?"

"Someone below gets it on their screen," Nathan pointed. "They pull up all the necessary information attached to that image: who it is, where they are, they sync it up to their phone and then follow the assigned portal to the location." They certainly made it sound easy. "I'm here if you have any problems. Have fun," he laughed.

I settled into my chair and focused on the wall in front of me. For at least half an hour I sat there staring, swiveling to study screens on all four walls, before I spotted the first one. A girl with long hair, she looked my age, walking along a body of water alone, dipping her toes in and gazing out at the horizon. The bottom of the screen read Hilton Head. I pointed the control at her, isolating that screen then clicked again and it disappeared. I noticed a golden glow around one of the terminals below: a boy with a long blond forelock over one eye leaned into his screen then looked up toward me for a moment, nodding. I waved and said, "Thank you," and though he probably couldn't hear it, he smiled in an easy way as if to say, "No big deal, it's my job." Then he focused again on the girl on his screen, and in minutes he was gone. He leapt up so fast his chair was left slowly spinning to a stop.

My eyes returned to my screens, the endless souls parading by. Eventually, after what felt like many hours, the screens went dark, a mandatory break time. I remained in my seat, leaning my head back gazing at the ceiling, then closed my eyes. There were very few people left in the room now. But others were starting to filter in, perhaps the new shift. I felt emotionally spent. Something else had been wearing away at me too: I didn't like the feeling of sitting here while others were in the field. How long would it take until I could get to Lucian? The screens flicked back on.

15

Just Another Day
At The Office

I worked, searching out endangered souls so long I lost track of time—and my timepiece. Nathan climbed the spiral staircase up to me at one point asking me to hand over my watch: "We heard from the workshop. They need it, for what Lance is constructing for your travels."

"Oh, wow, OK, I guess," I said, unfastening it. "Do you know if I'll get it back?"

"I suspect it will be new and improved when it's returned to you," he said.

Reluctantly I handed it over. The next interruption came from Connor, who popped his head up just as I had found a soul in Chicago. "Check this out, right by the hospital where I always beat you at poker," I said, still looking at the screen. Connor had employed a series of covers to come to personally round us all up and bring us to New Orleans. For me, he had posed as an injured college student being treated at my hospital. It worked.

"Good times," he said, watching the screen. "Sorry to pull you away from your hometown. But, it's time for you to hit the road." I looked at him, wondering if I'd heard right. He nodded.

Since Lance's workshop was clear on the other side of the complex, Connor suggested we walk outside. I had been waiting for this but now that the time had come, my nerves rattled under my skin. The air was perfectly warm and carried the sweet scent of summer blooms—I breathed it in deeply and exhaled, feeling it fill my lungs and seep into my blood, calming me.

"Healing properties, everything out here," Connor said, gesturing at the field. "That's why this is where you all land when you cross over, it heals you fast."

That made sense now that I thought about it. We had recovered nearly instantly.

"What else is out here? I mean, you know, if you kept just walking?" I pointed out toward the horizon.

He laughed to himself, "If you want to really mess with your head, go for a long walk. Whatever direction you go in, you end up back here," he pointed to the complex.

"Seriously?" I looked out. "Whoa." I shook my head. "Well, you just saved me a lot of time exploring."

"You're welcome," he said. "So, about today, here's what you need to know."

"Right, so I'll jet back to when? New Orleans of a few months ago, before he turned mortal again? And just stab him with the antidote from Dante then lift out that bad part of his soul," I went through what I imagined the plan would be. I had always done well with the levitation rituals, so I hoped this wouldn't be too bad.

"No," Connor said firmly, stopping in his tracks. He could read my complete confusion. "No, it's not like a typical 'third test' for wings. Lucian is dead, Haven. His *life cycle* is complete and that changes the options available to us. It's not like the girl whose file you received today. She is repentant but still living, her soul has been promised to the underworld but it has not been delivered to them yet." He flipped into

Socratic method mode: "How does that differ from Lucian's situation?"

"I freed his *soul* in New Orleans by helping him escape the underworld and by helping him become mortal again," I said slowly. "But now his *body* is dead." I looked at him, understanding. "So what I'm doing now isn't saving his soul. That's done. It's about saving his body? His actual life and allowing him to live again."

"Yes," he said, proud. "And when we're dealing with someone whose life cycle is complete, the only entry available to us is the beginning of that cycle."

"The beginning?"

"When he first pledged himself to the underworld."

"When he met Aurelia," I said with a chill.

"Yes." He started walking again. The young woman with the blonde ponytail who had gone in search of the skateboarder suddenly appeared, picking herself up from the tall grass in the distance. She walked toward us. Connor looked over and held out a thumbs up. She nodded and he smiled. She had gotten to the skateboarder in time.

"Right, Lucian, so he fell out of touch with family, he stopped going to school and eventually he was considered gone."

"That is still going to happen," Connor said.

"What?"

"You're not changing every event of his life. You're just *returning* him to his life. You're showing up at a point in his life when he needed a guardian, you're making enough of a difference in his life in that day to prevent him from making the decision to sell his soul. His life cycle is complete so you're not creating a ripple in it, you are just changing that one decision of his." He changed tack. "What happens when a soul is pledged to the underworld, sold to them? What happens to that person?"

I didn't know where he was going with this. "They start pulling away from the life they knew and eventually are considered to have run away or gone missing. Sometimes there's some sort of accident, a fire or natural disaster that can easily explain these disappearances."

"Right. So that happened to Lucian in the weeks after meeting Aurelia."

"So then what happens to him?"

"Then, if you succeed, he is returned body and soul to wherever he considered home before selling his soul. But he's returned there *now*, today. You won't be freeing all the people he recruited for the underworld or anything. Those are all individual cases. And only truly repentant demons even stand the chance of being turned. If something catastrophic shook the underworld, then all the repentant demons would be returned, but otherwise, this is what we're dealing with. It's a very difficult business. I hope you know that. You could be risking it all for nothing." His tone was so serious, almost chastising me.

"I know," I said sincerely. But couldn't leave it at that: "Just another day at the office, right?"

He broke into a smile for a moment, giving me a look that said he wanted to suppress it but couldn't. "The bottom line is: your goal in this exercise is to give your target a second chance. Give them a reason to NOT strike a deal with the devil. If you can get him to make it through that day without joining their ranks, then he will be protected from them."

"And he'll be free to live a mortal life?"

"Yes, and his soul will be guarded against falling to them again." We reached a shimmering crystal door on the opposite side of the building now. It slid open on its tracks as we approached.

"Got it," I nodded. I felt ready now. I understood the full scope of what this meant. Lucian deserved this chance; I had to make it happen for him. "So, how do you know so much about this anyway, if it hasn't, you know, worked before?"

"This is how it was explained to us by one who traveled back but died hours after his return," he said softly. I had no words. Somehow that seemed even worse than not making it back at all, coming so close.

"So just promise me you'll be careful—"

"I will."

"—and you'll conserve enough energy to make it back. This is a taxing journey, it's going to take a lot out of you." I nodded. He looked at me as though debating whether to say something more, not dismissing me just yet. I shifted my weight from one foot to the other, expectantly. "And you've got to do this as quietly as possible. Time is fragile. You could upset the balance of things. Try not to talk to anyone but him. And this is serious," he looked at me. "*Don't* touch him. At all. Don't touch anyone, but definitely don't touch him. You need boundaries, got it? It's safest that way. Be like a ghost that only he can see. You know, in other words, just try not to break anything. Do you understand?"

"Yes. I promise," I said solemnly. He nodded, his brow still furrowed, reluctantly allowing me to go. I nodded back and stepped inside the door. Before I closed it behind me, he called out:

"And Haven?" he said. "Good luck."

***

I stopped off to pick up Dante first. He carried a tray of supplies for Lance and me. I needed him to pump me up, distract me and keep me calm, but he barely said a word as I filled him in on my talk with Connor.

"...And apparently if I physically touch him or anyone else then I'm causing some kind of rupture in the time/space continuum or whatever. I don't know how I'm supposed to steal him from Aurelia."

"C'mon, Haven, appeal to his mind. You're so used to always just using your body to get what you want," he joked, but his voice wasn't as buoyant as usual. It was the lightest strain, probably only noticeable to someone who knew him as well as I did, but it was there.

"Oh, you know me," I smiled, rolling my eyes.

"Just think about it though, he's not going to be the same guy we were with before midnight on Mardi Gras. He's going to be probably even more conflicted than the guy we spent the past couple months with, you know? Imagine how different *we* are in just a year."

He had a point. He opened the door ushering me into Lance's workshop. As soon as I stepped inside, a hush fell and the angels gathered up, all halting their various projects and blueprint drawing and experiments to watch me. "Great, who's ready to skip time?" Lance said in greeting.

⊰◈⊱

I sat on a stool beside a large flat screen, Lucian's picture displayed on it. "...So based on the information you provided to us about Lucian, and the research conducted into his past, the team here has managed to make a pretty solid determination of the date and time of his soul capture," he said, typing into the screen. Photos of the location popped up. Home.

"Really? I mean, how? I had a school and a rough guess at the year, but not even a name."

"These guys are good," he pointed to the dozen fellow angels in the room. Some smiled proudly, others shyly, while some wore grave expressions that concerned me. "And they had a good prototype too. I just added some of Dante's firepower and made a few tweaks in the engineering. But Owen led the charge." He gestured and a boy with dark hair waved his hand, embarrassed.

"Thanks," I said to him and then to the room, "all you guys, thanks. I owe you."

"That's what we do," Owen said, no big deal. "Happy to show you around the data collection protocol anytime." Then he added shaking his head: "When you get back, of course."

"Thanks," I said, secretly as grateful for the offer as I was for his assumption that I would, in fact, be capable of coming back.

"So, this will take you there," Lance held up a small pocket watch, which I realized on closer inspection was actually my watch mounted on what looked like a stopwatch. It hung from a chain. "You'll be able to speed it up or slow it down manually, within reason, if you find that you're not in the right place." He pointed to the tiny buttons.

"Is that something I should worry about?" I felt like I was about to fly a plane but didn't know how to land.

"No, it should be properly programmed—"

"I have total faith in that," I said, cutting him off without meaning to. "And I like the aesthetic and all, nice to see my piece repurposed...but it looks a little old school." It just didn't look like this was going to be capable of shooting me back to an entirely different time, really a different world. "I had envisioned a whole sort of contraption."

"Really, because you're not the best driver, and I didn't know you to be much of a pilot either," Lance's lips curved into a smirk, as though he had been testing me. "But, you'll be comforted to know, I've inserted a mechanism here," he pressed a button on the side of the watch and the face opened up on a hinge to reveal a touch screen below. It looked like a tiny circular smartphone screen. "This is like your command center. You can also adjust specifications here in the event that you were ever far off-course. Or in the future if you wanted to make multiple stops, that kind of thing."

"Which won't be necessary right now," Connor appeared in the doorway. The others in the room straightened up their posture.

"Of course," I said. It warmed me to see him there. I had thought that since he didn't entirely approve of this he didn't want to be part of my send-off. I felt stronger having him here.

"Right," Lance went on. "But anyway, it's all basically an elaborate alarm clock, sending you there and back...." Lance explained again what I would need to do. As he wrapped up, Dante started fidgeting, like something had been left out.

"So, his name is John Miller," he said, pointing at the screen. I nodded, letting that sink in, his real name. So simple, giving no hint of all that he was—complicated, tortured and also, in the end, selfless. It would be an entirely different him that I would be searching for, one that didn't know who I was. I wasn't the only one thinking this. "But Hav, we can only get so specific. You're going to be dropped onto this campus, you're going to have to find him."

"No problem," I said. I had some ideas. "And the illumination ought to help."

He snapped his fingers at me. "Yes!" he sounded relieved.

"Definitely comes in handy. I knew there was a reason we were sending you," Connor said.

"I've packed up all these," Dante handed me three slim tins the size of pillboxes, each containing a different antidote or weapon. He even gave me a few miniature versions of the star-shaped plants I had used to slow down my demonic rivals, Sabine and Clio, in New Orleans. "Just in case you run into...." He didn't seem to want to say "trouble," "...a reason to need them. And this is something new we're working on." He pulled out a thin clear strip. It looked like plastic printed with a drawing of angel wings. He held it by the edges, as though it were a microscope slide of some sort of abnormal cell.

"Is that a tattoo?" I almost laughed, but his face was as serious as it had ever been.

"Sort of. Get him to put this on any of his pressure points, wrist, neck, heart, it will be absorbed into his bloodstream and basically prevent the demons from killing him. This is what allows him to come back. This keeps the good part of his soul from being cannibalized by the evil part."

"So this is the reason he won't die the next time at Père-Lachaise?"

"Yeah, as a mortal it'll act kinda like a shield to keep him from succumbing to their toxins. At least, theoretically. Fingers crossed it works and all."

"Wow, OK, that's pretty incredible, Dan. Thanks." He handed it to me and I received it in the palm of my hand like something fragile.

"It's OK, it won't be activated until it's held on skin. You can throw it in your pocket." I shrugged and patted it inside my pocket, still nervous. He went on. "As soon as he puts it on and it activates, that stops the clock. Everything after that point carries on like it would have." I nodded. "And I've coated the watch itself with a variation of the substance used for shadowing. It's the same principle. A little of my magic, a little of yours."

"Got it." I tucked everything in my pockets. He had outfitted me in black skinny cargo pants and a slim black sweater, suspecting I would need to look at least passable at a nice event.

"Your focus, you know? That's how you steer this. Because it is YOU steering. It could run off-course if you're not entirely focused," he said, a little jittery. He leaned in now brushing two different liquids onto other charms. "I'm fortifying, to ward off toxins, and also for shadowing, in case it could be useful. But the effects of the time travel may nullify it. It's a wildcard."

"Got it," I said again. I was beginning to give up hope that Dante would be keeping me calm. "I'll be fine, you did the hard pa—"

He cut me off: "Maybe you should do a travel practice, Hav," he blurted out. "Just to make sure maybe, you know? Like when you started shadowing." I was about to answer that maybe it sounded like a good idea. But before I could agree, Connor interrupted us.

"Actually, Dante and I have discussed this," he said, leaning against the doorframe, arms folded across his chest as he shot Dante a look. "And if you don't mind, Haven, I think it could actually be more dangerous to practice—"

"Respectfully disagree!" Dante said, hands up, as though it were his final protest. A tiny cell of doubt implanted itself inside me like a cancer. I didn't want to question my abilities. If I had learned anything during the past two years as my physical strength and powers had grown, it was that you had to throw yourself into these kinds of challenges fully, completely, with blind, dumb faith, in order for them to work out.

"She may burn out all of her strength," he said to Dante. Then to me: "I think you should just go for it. You will be fine, Haven. I'm not saying it will be easy, but you will be fine."

I didn't know whether to be encouraged by his faith in me, or terrified that the journey alone would sap all my reserves of energy. Lance placed the necklace with the clock charm around my neck with all the gravitas of awarding a medal. I stood in the center of the workshop, everyone studying me like I was a mouse injected with some new wonder drug. He looked over my head at this audience for just a moment, then pulled me closer, speaking into my ear.

"You've got this, OK? Just watch the clock, don't overstay your welcome. I want you back here, where you belong," he said, then added: "With me." He looked in my eyes for a moment, as though wanting to be sure I understood what he meant by those two words. I did. He had given my trip his blessing and he had even engineered a way for me to get there. But he did that with the unspoken agreement that after saving Lucian's life I would leave him in the past. In MY past. And that Lance and I would move forward, eyes set on the challenges ahead.

He kissed me firm and fast, then whispered before letting go of me: "Ready to get this show started?" I nodded. "Sorry about the audience," he added with a smile, "they're excited." Indeed they had formed a tight circle around us, staring, waiting to see the fruits of their labor in the form of this disappearing act I was about to pull. He backed away. "Give the girl a little space, guys," he ordered everyone. "See you soon. And I mean it." He backed up.

I clasped the watch around my neck and closed my eyes. It's a strange thing to know you are following in the footsteps of others who have been unsuccessful, who may have set out on this path well enough but then taken a misstep and failed to return. With no one to tell you what this should look or feel like, to guide you. There was, of course, always the chance that I might go no further than the spot I occupied now in Lance's workshop. But that, to me, would be such a stunning failure, it ranked as bad as not coming back. Possibly worse.

But that was all unproductive, wasn't it? Instead, I pictured the campus of the school that I planned to go to in the fall, the one Lucian had been visiting those days just before his soul was captured. I thought of how he might look and how he might act. And then I felt myself floating, my feet slowly peeling up from the floor, a sweet weightlessness.

And then just as fast, I felt leaden. Something grabbed me, pulling me as though I'd been lassoed around the waist. My hair flew behind me, my clothes felt like they were being glued to me. I had not yet learned to fly, so I didn't know what that felt like, but this did not feel like flying. There was a struggle to this. My body felt heavy, so heavy. I tried to work with this force, hoping that it might ease the pressure, but I felt powerless. It tugged me with such strength I feared it might rip my skin clear from my bones. I tried to open my eyes, but the rush was too much. I could not pry them open but could feel flashes of light igniting around me. Faster and faster still. As though I sat on the wing of a shuttle crashing through the earth's atmosphere.

Then I hit something, so hard I thought I had been shot in the chest simultaneously by hundreds of machine guns. There had been no winding down, no indication at all that my destination was near. Just full, mad, hurtling velocity, as I slammed into what felt like a steel wall.

I couldn't feel any part of my body. I couldn't feel myself breathe, I couldn't feel my lungs doing their work or my chest expanding. I couldn't feel my heart beating. It began to make me nervous, not feeling these things you're supposed to feel to know that you're alive. I couldn't even feel my eyes to open them. My mind flashed to those stories of St. Denis of Montmartre, the martyr I had read so much about, carrying his decapitated head as he walked up the hill. I did not feel there was any part of me still intact, nothing for me to carry anywhere. I had thought it was hard crossing over into the angel realm—that had been nothing. I pictured myself now shattered into pieces, nothing to reassemble. Then I thought of this failed mission. And of the revolution—not being there.

But I could still think. That had to be something. *I have too much to do and too many people who still need me*, I told myself. *I can't go now.* My anger rose. And I felt myself gasping, my body unsure how to take in air. My heart struggled as though it had been wrapped in a box that was too small and it needed to beat its way out. It pushed and pushed and broke through and then it raced. In a flash, everything went on. An operating system rebooting, lights blazing.

Before I could even feel my legs again, they had already sprung me upright. Before I could focus on regulating my breathing, my body sucked in a gulp of air so purifying it felt like it contained every flower and tree and blade of grass, every possible living thing around me. I heard the buzz of voices in the distance, people coming and going. I felt a crisp snap to the air, cooling my sweat-slicked skin. My eyes flung open. I stood in a patch of trees, in a ditch at least three feet deep, left by the impact of my body thrown against it. I unwound my arms and legs, stretching them and cracking them back into place and leaned against the broad trunk of an oak to catch my breath. Through the branches I could see the hill overlooking the lake in one direction and the library in another.

I was home, in Evanston, but it wasn't home. It was the home of a few years ago. Just a few blocks away from here, I was probably leaving school for the day, catching a bus to the hospital to work and meet up with Joan. I wanted desperately to go now, to see her and, I suppose, to see me. To warn myself what was to come or just to relive a day without the responsibilities I had now, without the things I'd seen. There had been a time when I hadn't had to face down battles every day. But I tucked those thoughts away.

16

This is How a Lot of My Dreams Look

I checked my clock charm—it was late afternoon here. October. I dusted myself off, pleased to find that the earth was dry so I wasn't muddy, and smoothed my hair, picking a crunchy autumn leaf from its tangles. I climbed out of my crater and stumbled from the wooded patch onto a pathway I recognized. This was the main artery through Northwestern's campus. I had been here many times on trips back to the apparel store to pick up sweatshirts through the years. A banner strung from the archway read "Welcome, Model UN Participants!" A line beneath listed the dates—it ended today.

I remembered reading about this a few years ago—Northwestern had hosted a conference. The schools involved had effectively taken over the town—every hotel was full, every restaurant packed. They had been meeting at the student union. I set out that way, looking into the face of each student I passed, at anyone who could possibly be him. Anyone tall enough. Anyone with light hair and his fair complexion. Especially, from what I understood of him then, anyone walking alone. I spotted a boy with his books open, studying beneath a tree and ran to him, only to get there and discover this person, who wasn't him at all, was sitting with a girl who had been concealed against the tree trunk.

I broke into a jog, passing a sign that confirmed I was headed in the right direction. As I got nearer, I felt an uptick in my pulse. He was here. I could feel it. It made sense to me, knowing what I did about who he was. He was where I would have been on the last day of this conference at a school that wasn't my own with sessions likely over and festivities soon to begin. Not in a hotel room that I was forced to share with others who probably weren't particularly good friends. Not out at one of the coffee shops in town. Not in any of the natural gathering places in the university center. I would have found somewhere for me.

I whipped through the turnstile of the library, checked the map, and ran past the elevators to the stairs, too impatient to wait. I headed for the history section but then thought better. He had spent the past several days thinking of nothing but international politics. I would go to Literature.

I reached the floor. Pin-drop silent, it had that stagnant musty scent of old books that I always found comforting. I weaved through the imposing bookcases, scouring every study carrel. I had walked the length of the building, it seemed, when I finally saw it, that sickly glow, a shade of gray I had begun to recognize now. It emanated from a workspace tucked back in a corner. It looked like the desk had been jammed in there, forgotten, a dimly lit hideaway stationed so far from where other such nooks were clustered back-to-back. A spot so remote it was still possible to have conversations amid the relentless studying.

I peeked over top of the wall and found him, asleep, his cheek against the open book on the desktop. Glasses in one hand. His hair was more closely cropped than usual and his long sleeved shirt, possibly two sizes too big, hung messily on his thin frame. His jeans were just a shade or two off from the majority I had seen in my walk here.

But there I found him, the boy who had once confessed that the hundreds of books in the library at the Lexington were his personal collection. My heart swelled to see him. I thought of the last time I had seen him, at Père-Lachaise, the pain of its memory still raw and ragged, a stake in my chest. He looked so peaceful now. I studied that face, youthful and vibrant, his smooth skin rosy in a way I hadn't seen since I had first met him. The Lucian I knew before his death had been worn by his time in the underworld, by his return to the mortal world after so many dark days. But within seconds his beautiful face flashed into the grotesque version that I had seen in the pictures I had taken at the Lex. This was what he would become, this is what I had to prevent today. And then just as fast he was back to that sweet looking boy again. I watched him as he flickered between these two versions. I would not be able to spend the entire day with him like this, the strobe effect was too distracting, jarring, and frightening with its festering lesions and rotting skin. I focused on him, thinking of only that good Lucian, the real him. His image steadied now, flickering only every once in a while. Much better. Now that he was stable, my eyes snagged on an imperfection I had never seen: a line marred his top lip, like an apostrophe interfering with its otherwise pillowy fullness. A scar I had never noticed because it had not been there when I had known him. If I looked at his back now, I was certain I would find those telltale shoulder scars as well. As he had told me, he had been one of us once.

I could have admired him all afternoon. I would have liked nothing more than to pull up a chair beside him and read and listen to him breathe and know that right now he was alive and safe. But he wouldn't be for long, and I had precious little time to make things right. I reached out to wake him and stopped myself just inches away, remembering what Connor had said. It was so hard not to touch him.

Instead, I leaned near to him, blowing on his ear. He twitched, but kept sleeping. I tried again. He swatted as though at a fly, eyes still shut. Finally I kicked the leg of his chair. That did it.

He woke with a start, his head popping up, and pushed his chair back. "WhereamIwhattimeisit?" He looked at me. I was so jarred to see no flash of recognition in his eyes that I didn't speak for a moment. "Am I dreaming?" he asked. "Because this is how a lot of my dreams look. I'm in the library and—" I interrupted him, my mind working again.

"I'm curious about those dreams but, no, actually," I looked at the clock overhead. "You're at Northwestern. It's 4:45." Outside the window on the far wall, the sky had already begun to dim.

"Shoot!" he said, gathering his things and throwing them all into his backpack. He stood up—still so tall but lankier, not as filled out as the Lucian I knew—and took off through the library to the stairs.

"Where are we going?" I asked, keeping pace with him. He was nearly running.

"I'm late. Why are you following me?"

"I'm going there too."

"Going where?"

"Where you're going." We were downstairs already.

"Really? I didn't see you at the conference."

"Yeah, no, I mean, there were a lot of people there."

"That's true. Where were you from?"

"Uhhh, here, Northwestern?"

"No, I mean, what country? I was Uganda."

"Oh, yeah, I was…on the other side of world." He gave me a pitying look, aware that I didn't know what I was talking about.

But I just kept on. "So tonight sounds like fun. Going into the city, right?" I guessed, but it was a pretty safe bet.

"Yeah, boat tour and then a reception at the John Hancock." He opened up his backpack and pulled out a wadded up blazer, throwing it on over his rumpled shirt as we hustled up the hill.

"It's beautiful up there, the Hancock building."

"Yeah, whatever," he said, not caring. We walked silently through the wooded path, the air cooling as afternoon faded into dusk. He wasn't one for small talk, this version of Lucian. I wasn't used to having to control our interactions; that had been his role for much of our time together. I hadn't realized how disconcerting it would feel to be with this person I knew who didn't know me. I found myself retreating into my natural awkwardness. I thought back to the Louvre, how I had built a quick camaraderie with Gavin before dropping a bombshell on him, and how somehow it had worked and he had taken me seriously. There had to be a way to get to Lucian, to quickly chisel through this wall, be let in and listened to.

We crossed the street, making our way up the hill to the student union. A sextet of charter buses idled out front, rumbling as chirping students boarded. Each had signs posted in their windows of the various schools participating: "Iowa," "Illinois," "Northwestern," all Midwestern. It felt warmer than it had when I had landed, surprisingly so for fall. By early October it was often already starting to get chilly.

"John! Where've you been? Let's go!" A boy in a crisp button-down and khakis leaned out the door of the "Iowa" bus, yelling to Lucian. He didn't answer. He just picked up his pace. I couldn't reconcile this version of him with the person I knew. He looked younger than the others and from his slouch to his downcast eyes, gave the impression of wanting to fade into the backdrop and be left alone. I followed him, but a group was just getting out of the union. They spilled onto the front walkway, swarming toward the last bus in the line, near us. Out of nowhere, she sidled up to him. The blood froze in my veins and I felt my stomach drop, sickened. I turned my back and took a few steps away, hiding among the masses. Aurelia grabbed his arm, stopping him without giving me so much as a passing glance. I peeked back enough to see her eyes lasering into his: "There you are," she purred, squeezing his bicep. "Great job today, even if you did make the rest of us look like total amateurs." His expression read that he wasn't sure why she was talking to him. "You owe me a drink to make up for it. I'll see you over there." He was mesmerized. I knew that look. I certainly couldn't blame him. She wore black pants, a tight sweater and heeled boots. She looked looser, her flaxen hair longer, wavier than I remembered. I was sure that was all calculated, like everything was with her. She was by far the best-dressed, most polished girl I had seen here and yet she still looked like she belonged in this group. Even in the wardrobe of a college student instead of the sleek dresses of a powerful hotel magnate, she still commanded complete attention. She turned and talked and laughed with a pair of equally stunning creatures—wait, I thought, looking more closely. Yes. The strawberry blonde, I knew her. It had to be her. Calliope. The beautiful artist demon I had photographed at the Lexington. She had disappeared soon after I had arrived, trying to escape the chains of the underworld, but her charred and mangled body had materialized on the hotel's doorstep on its opening night. I didn't know the other girl with them. Perhaps she had yet to be recruited, or perhaps some fate had befallen her before I had entered the picture. The women boarded a bus marked "Illinois."

I had lost track of Lucian. I scanned through the crowd and found him stepping onto the Iowa bus. I followed, but as I reached the first step, that same khaki-clad sentry stopped me. "We're going by schools. Sorry, no room on here," the boy said turning me away. The doors snapped shut before me and I backed up onto the sidewalk, just before it rolled out. Through the tinted glass I could make out Lucian's silhouette, sliding into a seat at the front. He pulled out a book and began reading. I wanted to jump up onto the bus, pull him off of there, tell him to stay away from this woman who would woo him to the dark side before the night was through. I could run and catch it now. I could hold on to the back of it and ride all the way into the city. But I remembered what Connor had said about not drawing too much attention, not leaving a mark. Instead, I went for the bike rack outside the student center. With my bare hands, I calmly ripped the metal chain from the fastest looking bike I found—a rather expensive looking racing bike. Desperate times, I said to myself. Surely a bike theft on a college campus hardly qualified as making waves. I hopped on as the rest of the buses navigated their way off campus, like ducks slowly following each other into a lake.

I took off, pedaling at a comfortable rate, but actually moving much faster than I should have been. The wind swept my hair back so it trailed behind me. Dusk falling now, I blazed into the city, going against the crush of weekday afternoon traffic. I arrived at the dock just minutes after Lucian's bus. The doors were just opening as I ditched the bike. The boat's captain stood on the dock greeting the crowd, and I let myself get swallowed into the group making its way on deck.

<hr>

I found Lucian on the upper deck and psyched myself up, prepared this time. "Hey, good spot. Great view, right?" I burst into the space beside him, talking like he'd been waiting for me. He looked surprised to see me. "I haven't been on one of these tours in forever. Have you ever been? It's a great way to see the city, and the architecture is amazing. I bet you'll like the Merchandise Mart; it's got an art deco thing going on. But the sleekness of the Mies van der Rohe is kind of stunning too. Good stuff." Without a word, he started walking away from me. In the distance below, I saw Aurelia just stepping off the bus and striding along the riverwalk, eyes lasering into Lucian's, pulling him to her even from so far away. I turned my back as I had before near the buses. She didn't know me here, in the past, and wouldn't recognize me. But still, she terrified me. At the back of my mind I couldn't help thinking of the future: if I made it through here and made it back, then I would have to face her all over again. My life had become a series of battles.

I had already seen enough to know the foundation had been laid. I felt like I was watching myself at the Lex that first day of my internship, when Lucian had looked at me and into me, back when I was so attuned to him that I could even feel the heat of his demon blood when he stood near to me. I knew how out of my league he was, just as I was sure he felt the same way now as he watched Aurelia watch him. In his heart he must have known something was not right. And that would be my way in, to take advantage of that doubt he already must feel even though he didn't want to believe it. I thought of how often I had let myself go against my gut in the past two years.

"I also really like the Frank Lloyd Wright," I said as I caught up to him. Lucian kept going. I followed, continuing—"Hey, there are refreshments up here, you know,"—saying anything I could to slow his progress, but he led the way down the narrow staircase, dodging the flow of students coming up. Aurelia's had been the last bus to arrive and there would be a gap of a few minutes before the first students from that bus reached the boat. There was very little time, and I needed to spend it with him. I needed time alone. I needed to keep him away from her. I wished Connor could have sent someone with me. I missed having a teammate, someone to run interference. I would simply have to make Lucian an accomplice in his own soul saving. I pushed past the students and swung around in front of Lucian, walking backwards down the stairs.

"Hey, whoa," he said, almost tripping over me.

"Can you do me a favor?" I asked, stopping in the middle of the staircase. "I get a little seasick. Could you ask the captain how fast the boat goes? I know it's not a speedboat or anything, but I just wondered how much he cranks up the engine, you know?" I could see the captain from here, back in the boat for the moment. "Ask him if I were to stand over there." I pointed on the opposite side of the boat, away from the dock. "If it would be a less bumpy ride. Be sure to ask about the engine." I needed him and the captain to be as far away from me as possible.

"Are you kidding?" he asked, looking completely baffled. But he was also, at heart, too kind to say no.

"Do you mind? I'm…embarrassed. Too embarrassed to ask myself." I smiled, a sweet, nervous smile.

He sighed. "Hang on," he said curtly, rolling his eyes but giving in. Ever the perfect messenger, he pulled the captain to that spot I had indicated on the other side of the boat. As I guessed, the man was so excited to see someone take such a keen interest in the mechanics of his boat that he was completely taken. I was as alone as I could hope to be. The students were all consumed by their own conversations, relaxing now that the conference was wrapped up, ready for a night of celebration. Music blared on the boat as the sky darkened. I thought back to New Orleans. Connor liked to force us to propel one of the mammoth steamboats on the Mississippi using no more than our arms and legs. This boat was practically a dinghy by comparison. I ought to be able to get us out of here. I revved myself up.

I picked up the walkway platform and gripped the boat's thin metal railing. I climbed over the railing, positioning myself in a tight spot between the boat and the dock. Aurelia was ten yards away. I firmly and securely wrapped my arms around the railing, curled my legs tightly into my body to make myself into a ball, like a grenade set to explode. And then I pushed off, kicking my legs so hard against the wooden dock I heard a plank snap. I threw myself into it with enough force to break the boat free of its anchor. We lurched forward. A collective "whoa" came from the group as their drinks sloshed and ladies stumbled in their uncomfortable footwear. But we were moving now. And fast. As I landed, one of my hands slipped off the railing, and for a split second I wondered if I'd plunge into the water. But then I recovered, snapping my hand back into place on the metal rail as I dangled outside the boat. Footsteps raced past. I guessed it must be the captain. I pulled the rest of my body up and climbed over the railing onto the lower deck. The boat began to slow now as the captain regained control.

"Greetings and welcome to Chicago's most exciting architectural tour," the captain's voice boomed from the speakers. "Sorry for the sudden start, it looks like we had some technical difficulties but we're set and on our way now. So enjoy the ride and the sights. Thanks for joining us tonight." I caught my breath as the confused group on the walkway stopped in their tracks, watching the boat race away without them. Aurelia's jaw dropped in shock; she was not the kind of girl used to being left behind. I couldn't help but smile. Luckily the majority of the group who had made it on were so busy getting refreshments and admiring the view from the upper deck there had been no one around to pay me any mind other than a quintet of girls, nearly matching in slim sheath dresses and tending to a sixth girl seated on a bench with her head in her hands, looking like she might vomit. "When did you even have time to drink, Christine? I mean, we were with you all day," said one.

"I bet those girls had something. They totally look like it, right?" said another. They gave me a look, pausing in their conversation.

"Just made it, phew!" I said with a smile, scurrying up the steps.

I found Lucian alone, leaning on the railing at the back of the boat, straining his neck to see the shore as he gazed longingly at those left in our wake. I followed his line of vision to her. That face—so beautiful and flawless—looked horrific to me. I turned my back.

"I don't understand how we can just leave a whole bus full of people," he said into the space in front of him, disappointment clouding his eyes.

"They literally missed the boat," I said, with a shrug. "It happens. They'll meet us there."

"You're awfully tough for someone who I don't think even belongs here," he tried to smile. He gave me a look like he was in on a secret.

"You caught me. I'm kind of a conference crasher. I guess the lack of a badge was a dead giveaway," I pointed to the one that still hung around his neck.

He pulled it off and dropped it into the river. "I don't really belong either," he said wistfully, still looking out at the water. He said it with enough honesty that it cut me. I wanted to tell him that I understood. I had to make him know. Over the loudspeaker, the tour guide directed us to Navy Pier. The lights of the Ferris wheel glowed as it rolled in the sky. Lucian spoke before I could find the words, dutifully reporting with a forlorn twinge in his voice all he had learned while hijacking our vessel.

"I think if you survived that rough start, you should be just fine," he started. "Captain Gary says we go pretty slow in order to appreciate the sights, and today is a pretty still day so there shouldn't be much rocking. The lower deck is the best place for someone with trouble though."

"Thanks," I said. "I figured that would be the case, but always best to know what you're getting into."

"Yeah," he said, not paying attention, "Do you know her?" he asked, changing course as jerkily as the boat had launched. "Aurelia?"

"We….um…travel in different circles," I said, struggling to construct the right response. He didn't seem like he was planning to share anything more. "Why do you ask?" I prodded in my most innocent voice.

He continued to look out into the water, not bothering to pay attention to any of the sights we passed. I had somehow forgotten how lovely it was here. I didn't even mind the chill that had set in now that the sky had darkened. I folded my arms across my chest for warmth. He looked at me from the corner of his eye, then back at the water.

"No, it's just…I don't know, it sounds stupid, but we've been here a couple of days and all and she's been looking at me. Her. At me. Does that sound ridiculous?"

I shook my head. I couldn't believe he was speaking so openly about this when he had just met me.

"And then, you know, she just talked to me right before we got on the bus and I just don't know if I'm just imagining things. I probably am. But what does it matter anyway because she's obviously not at my school, so it's just not a practical thing. These things never really work out for me. So I shouldn't be surprised, I suppose." A gust of wind blew through us, whipping my hair. He took off his blazer and handed it to me, looking in my eyes for only a quick moment, as shy as I had ever seen him.

"Thanks," I said, wrapping it around my shoulders.

He shrugged, resting his chin on his folded arms, as the city lights twinkled by. "Anyway." He let it hang there for a while until finally he said, "I don't know why I'm telling you any of this." I did though. It was because there was no one else. For this sweet and beautiful boy, there was no one else anywhere to listen.

"I know why," I started, unsure. I thought of what I would want to hear. "Because you must know that that's why I'm here." He looked at me with curious gray eyes. "I'm here to tell you that she is exactly the wrong kind of person for you to be focusing on at this particular time in your life."

"Really," he said, his tone biting. "Thank you. I tell you all this stuff and now you're basically making fun of me," he said flatly. "I've enjoyed getting to know you, whoever you are that's been stalking me today, and I hope to never see you again. Goodbye." He started to walk away. I reached my hand out, on reflex again, but stopped just short of his arm.

"Wait!" I called out and he turned around. He just stood there, looking away from me as though not really expecting me to say much worth listening to.

"I just mean, I want you to know ...." We were nearing the John Hancock building now. I could see the tower reaching into the sky. I would soon be running out of time. So I would have to be honest. "There's no way you could understand this, but I care about you. I'm here because of you. And I know that there is so much ahead for you but not with her. It's that simple. I know this won't make any sense now, but I'm here to make you realize that you don't need whatever she's planning to offer you tonight."

"What are you talking about? Offer me? You are one of the strangest people I've ever met," he said, frustrated.

My hands shot out to grab him by the shoulders, but I caught myself in time, grabbing the air instead. My eyes speared his, not letting go. Each time he tried to look away, I found them again. "I'm trying to tell you that I know there's something missing in your life right now, and she's going to seem like the answer to that. She's going to say all the right things to fill that void but she's going to take more from you than she ever gives back. She's going to hurt you and she's going to…" I wanted to say, she's going to cost you your life, she's going to lead you to your death, but there is no way to say that to a stranger. He just shook his head and walked away as the boat coasted to a stop, docking not far from our dinner location. The time had gone too fast. Now I would be forced to share him.

17

I Blame the DJ

I kept a few strides behind him on the walk to the John Hancock Building. He looked over his shoulder from time to time to see if I was still there, but we didn't speak a word. Not through the bustling Friday night streets, not up in the elevator with the others and not when we reached the stunning top floor event space overlooking the city. Aurelia and those who had missed the tour were already there and had wasted no time making themselves at home. They were already feasting on the buffet of party fare—sliders, mini stuffed pizzas, frites with tangy sauces—and dancing. A DJ played in the corner of the room and tall cocktail tables had been arranged around a dance floor. Perched on the bar, a delicately scripted sign read that the beverages would be strictly non-alcoholic. I thought of the girl on the boat and then glanced at Aurelia's group, dancing with abandon. There was a lightness to them and an ease. The whole lot of them.

Lucian, too, hooked onto her the moment we stepped into the room. I glanced at the watch on his wrist: Already almost 9 pm. The masses from the boat swarmed in now, joining Aurelia's group, following their lead. They flocked to her and Calliope. Other groups, satellites, formed along their outskirts. A euphoria swept the room, not unlike how it used to feel at that nightclub at the Lex, the Vault, where as teen interns we were never carded and many patrons went home soulless. They cheered and chanted. The DJ, eager to take credit for their spirit, took to his microphone to pump them up further, telling them what to shout and how high to jump. Those who weren't dancing swayed and sang along, freewheeling as they queued up for the food. Even amid the throngs, Aurelia's eyes connected with Lucian's. He circled the floor, watching, but stopped near the floor-to-ceiling windows. I had allowed some space between us, when a man stepped into it.

"Hi, I'm Trevor," he said, reaching out his hand. He had turquoise eyes, sandy hair and tan skin. He looked like he belonged on a beach, not in Chicago with winter approaching. Even if I hadn't felt my scars flare into a burn, I would have known who had sent him. "And you are?"

"Hungry," I just shook my head, trying to step around him, but he got in my way again.

"Me too, let's go," he flashed a blinding grin.

"Grab something for me and I'll be right there." I lunged around him, just in time to see Aurelia join Lucian at the window. She handed him a drink. It occurred to me that I still wore his blazer—a literal target on my back. Trevor had been dispatched to keep me away, I was sure of it.

"Look they're bringing out more, c'mon," Trevor moved in front of me again, pointing.

I glanced toward the kitchen and had to do a double take. He looked younger and didn't have on the uniform of the head chef, as I had grown accustomed to, but it was Etan. The one who nearly stole Dante's soul. Had he already been transformed? Or is this where Aurelia would be meeting him? I scanned the room with new eyes. This time I noticed a girl who looked like a rundown version of Raphaella—the stunning blond model who was a fixture at the Vault and had even tried to woo Lance—cleaning up the drinks and small plates from a table. Aurelia was recruiting here.

All of these faces from the past, or rather, the future, closed in on me. Aurelia whispered something in Lucian's ear. Trevor produced a drink for me. I took it, with no intension of imbibing.

"So tell me about you," he said. "You shop in the men's department."

"Right," I laughed, shimmying off the blazer. "Tell me about you," I deflected. I needed to talk as little as possible. And if I kept him here I could watch them in the space behind him.

"Well, missed the boat tour, but I'm happy to try it again in the future, if you're interested." I just smiled blankly and he went on. "I'm a junior at…." He rocked back and forth on his feet, hands in his pockets, as though giving a speech he had given a million times. But he had plenty to say. I looked at him often enough that he didn't realize I wasn't paying attention. Aurelia fluffed up her impossibly shiny blond locks and lifted her glass to her pink-glossed lips. Lucian mirrored her, lifting his glass so it hovered there near his mouth. I was certain there were toxins in there. I didn't want him drinking that, it would make my job so much harder if he were impaired, but I couldn't exactly run over and knock it out of his hands. I watched over Trevor's shoulder, focusing on Lucian's glass as people filtered in and out of my line of vision. It shouldn't have taken this long. I should be able to do this fast. Trevor asked me something I didn't hear.

"…Chicago? You're from here?"

"Me? No." I had no intention of telling him anything about myself. "But you said you were from which neighborhood?"

I looked again. Lucian was talking now, his glass still full but closer to his lips, as though he was about to drink and she had asked him a question that stopped him. Deep in conversation, she had draped herself on him, her hand perched on his shoulder, cozying up to him in a way that nearly forced him to put an arm around her waist. They acted as though they were the only two people in the room. His eyes danced, wide with an awe that seemed to say, *I'm not sure how this happened but I'm not going to mess it up.* The volume of the music had gone up, forcing them to stand nearer to each other to be heard.

I kept my laser focus, visualizing that glass bursting. Every ounce of me poured into the beam I was trying to direct. I had been warned of this—the travel upsets your composition. You may not be able to control your powers in quite the same way. You may not even have some of the powers you've come to rely on. But I zeroed in and finally, with a sharp POP the glass shattered in Lucian's hand, raining shards onto the floor and the sleeve of his shirt.

He stared in disbelief. Then he brushed himself off and Aurelia's arm. She looked surprised; he apologized profusely, his cheeks crimson. Trevor turned around at the sound and then back to me, shrugging. If he had been paying close enough attention, he would have noticed that I had actually gasped—from the exertion—before the glass shattered, not after. To distract from this fact, I started talking:

"That can happen, you know, from high pitched frequencies," I rambled. "I blame the DJ."

"It was bad enough when he played that boy band song, now this," he said.

"He'll never work in this town again."

"Cheers," he clinked my glass. I put it to my lips but didn't sip. Aurelia handed Lucian her glass. I stared at that one and then came another POP. It shattered, so much faster this time. Lucian turned beet red. I couldn't keep doing this, but there was no easy way to get over to him with Dante's antidotes. I didn't have enough to prevent everyone here from ingesting all the toxins that might be in the food and drinks. The anger burned in me. How was I going to stop this without physically pulling him away from Aurelia? Another drink came by for Aurelia. She whispered something into Lucian's ear and he blushed again, and then she kissed him, right there as the party swirled around them. Both were so transported and lost in each other. It reminded me of the first day at the Lex, when I had caught a glimpse of the two of them together, when I had gone exploring the hotel. I had known that there was something intense there. How had I let this happen now? The clock read nearly 10. Nothing was official until midnight, and I didn't think he had pledged his soul yet. There hadn't been time for that, had there?

"…So do you agree?" Trevor asked me something, with eyes that I once might have fallen for. Though I could see the difference: when Lucian was recruiting souls he made you feel wanted by him, it was a true feat. But Trevor wasn't as skilled. He could make you feel lucky that he was giving you his attention, but it fell short of real connection.

"Agree with—?" I started to ask and he cut me off.

"Great, then let's get out of here," he reached for my arm but I turned and he got the blazer instead, pulling it off.

"No, this is a party, why leave?" I managed to say with a laugh.

"Well, a friend is having an after party…"

But I didn't listen. My anger poured into every cell. The ticking clock, Lucian falling deeper into Aurelia's gravitational pull, my grasp slipping, his life being lost by the minute. I stared at them as they disengaged from their kiss just long enough for another drink to arrive. Aurelia handed him her glass and whispered something else in his ear. At once he looked at me, his eyes wide, shooting a bewildered look that I understood: I had just predicted the future and he was no longer sure whom to trust. I could imagine what she might have said. I was sure it involved kindly asking for his soul in exchange for the world.

My blood boiled as I watched. Without thinking I began walking toward them. Trevor went on talking, following me, but my eyes remained steady. The fresh glass in Lucian's hand shattered, along with the one in my hand. I shook off the broken pieces. And then there went the one in Trevor's and Calliope's hands, and the couple who had been talking beside us, and the group huddled near the dance floor, and then all the empty stemware displayed along the bar. I stopped for a moment.

But then came the crash. The windows beside Lucian and Aurelia shattered, twinkling pieces to the floor and sending a gush of wind sweeping inside. Aurelia and Lucian lunged away from the destruction, getting swallowed into the crowd.

Another CRASH roared and the next set of panes shattered, and then the next and the next, a chain reaction sweeping the entire length of that wall. I pushed past Trevor toward them as the DJ ducked under his station and partygoers fled. With an entire side of the room now exposed, the swirling autumn night wind roared in, knocking over the tables and sending the glass dancing, catching the light like confetti in the air. Revelers screamed and wait staff led everyone back toward the elevators and stairs. Aurelia and Lucian had been separated in the fury and she called for him across the crowd running down the staircases. It was hundreds of steps down. The building hosted charity races every year. It would take a while. I had raced one year with Joan and a team from the hospital. Lucian was steps behind Aurelia and I was trapped a flight above them. Then Lucian's pace slowed. He stood still for a moment, the people flowing around him. And then he turned and ran back up. His eyes caught mine as he did. I nodded and gestured for him to follow me. I stepped aside, letting the others rush down as they were joined by guests from another room in the restaurant, everyone racing out amid talk of earthquakes, bombs, and all sorts of wild theories.

It sunk in. I had done this. I hadn't meant to. Something in my chemical composition had been affected by the journey here. I had lost some control of my powers and pushed too hard and this had happened. But if Lucian was running toward me instead of away from me, then it had been worth it. Aurelia had gotten at least a couple of flights down. I could no longer see her. I hoped she hadn't noticed Lucian was gone. Trevor had. "John, you're going the wrong way, man," he pushed a hand against Lucian's chest to halt him. But Lucian just pressed forward past him.

Aurelia must have heard. Within seconds she appeared below, coming back up the stairwell, against traffic, walking up with fire in her eyes to get to Lucian. I ducked off to the side out of sight.

Lucian reached the top of the steps and nodded at me, but I saw Aurelia making quick progress through the crowd. "C'mon!" I jogged ahead down the hallway away from everyone and made a sharp turn into a narrow corridor, toward the coat check but dangerously close to the kitchen. Just before the kitchen doors—through which I could see Etan, still inside—we ducked into another door and found a staircase that led up to the observation deck.

I just needed a few minutes with him. I threw the door open out into the eerily warm autumn air and suddenly it was quiet. I could hear none of the hysteria of below, just the sound of the rushing wind in our ears.

"We shouldn't be up here," Lucian said, panting from the run. He leaned on the ledge to catch his breath and as he did I scanned the lounge furniture: the chair would have to do. I lifted a wooden chair and crashed it against my knee. He looked back at the sound. I ignored him. The chair splinted into several long pieces, which I jammed through the door handle to bar the door. It wouldn't keep Aurelia away entirely, but it would buy a couple of seconds if necessary.

"Why not?" I asked.

"In case something else happens," he said, looking at me with confused eyes.

"It won't," I said, firm.

He shook his head. "I don't know what's going on tonight."

"I know," I said in a delicate tone. I felt a pang being up here. Our last conversation had been on the roof in Montmartre. My heart dropped to think of that day. "Listen—"

But he cut me off: "How did you know?" I brightened to hear that. I looked at him standing across from me, arms lifeless at his side. "How did you know what she would say? That she would ask for something like that? For my soul? I'm not sure whether to be afraid—"

"Yes, she—" I started but he kept going.

"Or angry with you—

"No, wait—"

"—for ruining that for me. Because I was having a good time, for once. And no one has ever said something like that to me and on the surface it sounds like something amazing. That should mean something, that someone wants your soul."

"No, but not that way—" I cut him off, but he kept talking.

"And this person tells you these incredible things that could be ahead for you, that they want to make things happen for you. They know there's something special about you. All things that you don't tend to hear in your daily life. And you should get to enjoy that, right?" He looked at me, seething. I didn't say a word letting him go on. "But then *you* come along and tell me not to trust any of this. So I'm angry." I was about to speak, but he leaned against the ledge, looking at the sky. "But then I have a feeling like it doesn't make sense anyway. Even though I want to believe it. And I wish I could just stop *thinking* all the time and just go with something fun for once, because it's exhausting to be responsible all the time and to do the smart thing. And I just want something in my life to be easy for once." This was where the battle had been lost for him. I understood now. He had decided to go against his gut. He had had reservations, but he was weary. He made what was probably the first bad decision of his life and it just happed to be lethal. He looked at me now: "She knew things too, you know," he said, accusatory. Clearly I did not have a monopoly on this.

I thought for a moment, searching what it could be. "About your scars? On your back?" I asked. Shock flashed across his face and his hand massaged his shoulder, as though he had a sore muscle. "I have them too. Listen…"

"Tonight is blowing my mind, kind of," he said, to himself, shaking his head and slumping down to sit on the ground. And then to me: "Do you understand? I'm not someone that people pay attention to, and I feel so different tonight. I want to feel *this way* all the time."

"I know." I went to sit next to him and took a place a foot or so away, inserting that necessary cushion of space between us. "You will. You will get there on your own, without giving yourself away, without compromising, without losing who you are. It may take longer and feel like a tougher journey, but you have so much ahead of you."

"You don't understand what life is like for me. I don't belong anywhere. My parents don't care. They're not really mine anyway. I don't know who mine are. And if I did, what would it matter anyway? This week, it was great. This week I meant something. I'm good at this. But I'll go back there and it still won't be right. I won't be right."

"I know. I get it. Believe me." I looked in those pained gray eyes. "I'm like you. We are the same. You have to believe me."

"I'm sixteen, I just started college? Did you know that?"

"I did actually," I said. I had to smile: "And so I guess we're not exactly the same, I only graduated a semester early. But we're fundamentally the same."

"Why does everyone else always look like they're having such a great time?" he said, wistful. "What is wrong with me? I feel like I'm not like anyone else and I don't want to feel that way anymore. I'm tired of it. I feel so much older than I am." It felt like talking to myself in that time before the Lexington.

"Something I've noticed," I started. "It's not much better on the inside for these people. At some point their world stops spinning at the same velocity and they're empty. They put on facades too. They are just as deeply unhappy," I smiled at this. "And the ones who aren't are self-medicating."

He smiled too.

"I've seen a lot, and I've seen people who seem to have everything go down these paths and self-destruct. Every choice matters. And it takes guts to not get swept up in all of that. Do you hear me?" It didn't seem like he did.

"Part of me feels like I'll never have another night like tonight."

"You will have so many, but not with her, not with them."

"I want to believe that. But I don't know."

"It's not worth trading your soul, your life. You can't even begin to understand what it would mean, what you would lose. Please trust me," I pleaded. He looked at me with questioning eyes, as though trying to make sense of why I was so invested. "I have something for you." I reached in my pocket and pulled out the tattoo-like angel wings. "Please trust me and put this on your wrist. I know it may not make sense right now, but consider this a promise that there's something better ahead." I held it out for him to take. Slowly he did. But he just looked at it. "If you just put it here," I cupped the inside of my wrist with my hand. "It will save your life."

"Why?"

"Think of it this way, it means someone is looking out for you," I tried. He didn't know the worlds of demons and angels yet; it would do no good to try to explain it all. What he needed was hope, the feeling that there was something better coming. It occurred to me in this moment as he studied me with those limitless gray eyes, that this was what it meant to be a guardian. Showing up to give that extra confirmation that it was worth hanging on, it was worth forgoing instant comfort and being strong. I could feel him working through this as he leaned his head back against the wall. I looked at my watch. I had ten minutes. I knelt in front of him now, facing him. "She is going to ask you. Promise me you will turn her down. Emphatically, with all your heart and soul. Promise me."

He just stared at me.

"I'm going to know if you don't," I said, in a more serious tone than he seemed to expect, judging by the way he squinted at me. "And put that on."

"You show up here with all your ideas, you won't leave me alone, you lose my jacket on top of everything else…" he started.

I had to smile. "I'm sorry, it's downstairs. I'm sure I can find it for you."

"But I kind of want to believe that you know something I don't," he said, as though convincing himself. "Like those dreams I had."

"In the library?"

"Where someone shows up and says 'come with me' and all of a sudden my life starts to look different. I never see their face. And they're gone."

"Well, then it's like that," I said easily. Sirens blared below. I imagined a crowd had formed as the restaurant patrons were finally reaching the bottom of the stairs. Except for one: A

AIMEE AGRESTI

banging sounded on the other side of the door. I tuned it out, quickly: "Come with me."

"I'm smart enough to know I'm probably not actually going to see you again, am I?" The banging rattled the door again. I whipped my head toward it. I had to go. But he grabbed my arm: "Am I?" I flipped back around frozen, looking at his hand around my wrist. I was too paralyzed to tell him to let go or shake him off. It was too late. Whatever damage this would cause had been done. His innocent eyes searched mine.

"No," I said with regret, knowing it was the right thing to say. He still held my wrist. "But I'll watch over you." I slipped his hand off like it was a bracelet, and he leaned toward me. Then, because it seemed the crime had already been committed, and I knew that this would be our last moment together even if he *was* saved, I met him halfway in one last kiss. It felt so unlike the others had been, more like a first kiss, tentative and sweet.

The door burst open, as though with just one kick—something very few women could have accomplished so forcefully in heels. Aurelia appeared, looking as though it had taken no exertion. I slipped around the corner, flattening myself against the wall, and grasped that fleur-de-lis charm Dante had fortified, trying to shadow. I focused my energy but I could still see myself. I kept trying while listening. Then glanced at the clock face: it was nearly midnight.

"What are you doing up here? I've been looking all over, I was worried about you," she said, her voice all sweet concern. I peeked out from my spot. He hopped up to his feet but didn't move toward her. She grabbed his arm and then ran her fingers through his hair.

He looked away, out into the city lights. The sirens blared with the sound of more emergency vehicles arriving. I hoped no one had gotten hurt. From what I had seen it seemed that everyone had gotten away all right. I hadn't intended to cause such damage as I had, but if that's what it had taken to get to this point then it had been worth it.

"C'mon, Trevor got a room at the Palmer House. A bunch of us are staying there tonight, it'll be fun," she cooed.

"I've gotta get back, you know, my stuff is still in Evanston and all," he said, still sounding a bit unsure. But I was proud of him. I tried to shadow again. I wanted to get closer to them. But I couldn't get my charm to work.

She weaved her arms around his neck. "Have you given any more thought to what I proposed?" she purred, wrapping herself around him. I wasn't sure I wanted to watch this. In fact, I was sure that I didn't want to watch this. But I also knew that I couldn't leave without knowing he was safe.

He just looked away, his arms at his side, trying not to respond to her in words or actions. She gazed at him, reading him. "I know you're not changing your mind."

"Well, I actually hadn't given you an answer," he said, clarifying. He stretched his arms around her now and I worried he was embracing her, and all she represented. But instead, behind her back, he placed those wings against his wrist, holding the strip until he wiggled his fingers. It evaporated, swallowed into his skin. I allowed myself a sigh of relief.

"I'm beginning to feel like we're back at the conference now," she smiled, so charming, always so charming. "With these negotiations." He shook his head now, biting his lip. I wanted to hear it though. I needed to hear those words.

"The answer is no, Aurelia," he said, clear as the bell we heard from Sacré-Coeur on Sunday mornings.

"I don't think I heard you right," she purred in his ear. "Tell me again." She was awfully persuasive, I had to admit, and sure enough she seemed truly to be expecting a different answer. I worried for a moment.

"No, thank you," he said, polite but firm. His manners at a time like this made me smile. She stared at him, into his eyes, and she seemed to see it, the certainty. She dropped her arms from him, recoiling as though he were the demon.

"What?" she spat at him. "You can't be serious," she laughed, bitter. "You must…" She was talking but I blanked out for a moment. I shook my head to regain vision. What was wrong with me? I pulled the clock from my neck. It was midnight. Curfew. The door downstairs was still open. I didn't want to draw any extra attention traveling so I slipped into the doorway, in search of a quiet spot to focus on transitioning. As I did, I passed Calliope running up the dimly lit stairwell to meet them on the roof, her auburn waves flowing in the breeze. My vision went out again and I felt woozy but still, I figured, what did I have to lose? "Calliope," I said in her direction, my vision fading in and out. She stopped, her initial surprise at a stranger knowing her name gave way to a serene smile. "You're better than this. Better than Aurelia, better than whatever she's offering you and promising you. You are talented, you don't need her," I said, proud of my boldness. I would have loved to see her reaction. But I felt my body slipping, preparing to be pulled through time once more. If she said anything in response, I didn't hear it. My legs gave out, and I tumbled down the stairs. The timepiece swung against the floor, knocking its buttons as it did. I couldn't move. My mind raced, rehashing all I had just witnessed, as my body hurtled.

As I traveled, I registered a bittersweet loss as a tug in my heart. He should be free now to live a full life, to return to the mortal world without that constant fear of being preyed upon. A new beginning for him, and so an end to our chapter, to our odd friendship and connection. I would watch, though, and I hoped that he would in time find all the joy and comfort that he deserved, that had eluded him up until now.

My mind wandered as my body shot through time and space. I stopped my train of thought for a moment to consider my trajectory again. This felt different than the journey here. I spun faster now, lighter, wilder whereas before I felt like a heavy object being pulled painfully fast through tar, with so much resistance to overcome that my skin burned and my body throbbed. But now I did feel like I was flying, and fast. I could open my eyes now, though it still wasn't easy with so much wind. My body tried to brace itself for the impact of the landing, sure to come again without warning. And then, there it was, that slam against—what was it? This time it felt like hot cobblestones. My body felt worn but not as knocked out as before, not as destroyed as it should have been.

I opened my eyes. And I was staring into my own eyes.

18

Close The Loop

I wanted to scream but couldn't find my voice. The other me lay on the ground facing where I had just landed. She stared into me without blinking, her wide eyes pained and helpless. The shock set me scrambling to my feet. The atmosphere around me was just as jarring: sirens in the distance and a relentless crackling above that I couldn't place. I looked up and discovered why: The sky was on fire.

The flames roared, the bass balancing the endless, terrifying soundtrack of a whole city screaming. It looked like we were on a battlefield, bolts of fire flew through the air, bodies lay everywhere, and dark creatures—grotesque disfigured demons-—ran past, chasing angels and people. The only light came from the fire. There was nothing else in this whole city, shrouded in a thick hovering blackness, the color of death. I took a step back and nearly fell but caught myself. The river. We were on the banks of the Seine.

The version of me on the ground writhed in pain and I noticed now she had wings. Grand, they were as tall as she was and would have been pristine white but for the glowing reflection of the fire burning from above. And they were broken, crushed and poking at all different angles, parts of them gone entirely. I kneeled down over myself, knowing that I was watching myself die and wanting desperately to do something to save me. Beside her, me, something glinted: the angel wing necklace had been torn off her, its three charms scattered nearby. The figure on the ground looked into my eyes, and then with great struggle, squinting against the strain, produced a tiny whisper: "Do not let this happen," she said to me, *I* said to me. Blood trickled from her mouth as she spoke. "Close the loop.... And then make a roadmap...that will guide you... away from this." The struggle to speak was so great she had to stop after every few words to summon the strength to go on. "Please...." she said. Her eyes froze open. I stood up again, stepping away on reflex, and fell back toward the river. My shaking hands grabbed my clock charm like it was a life preserver, and instead of touching down in the water, I was whisked away again.

Now I felt like I was skydiving, freewheeling as the air whipped past me and I dropped again, this time smacking against cold, hard, nearly frozen earth. I landed on my back and rolled over, lifting myself up as sirens pierced the air somewhere above me to see I was on Lake Shore Drive. I heard footsteps on the pavement and saw paramedics pulling out a gurney. Then a voice came from just below me, high-pitched and sweet: "It will be OK," it said, I said, calmly. I looked in through the darkness beside me: a small girl lay on her back staring up into the night sky, and into my face. She looked peaceful though she wore jeans and a sweater and no coat in the frigid January chill. Glowing through the sweater I saw three stripes, like freshly branded scars.

It was me. On the night I was found. She closed her eyes again and I backed up just as the paramedics came through. Joan would find her soon. In the distance I noticed someone on the hill above, a dark figure watching. He turned his back, cape swooshing, to stalk away and as he did a ring of fire flared on the ground around him and he was gone. It was the Prince.

So he had known where to find me. He had been looking for me all along. I had so much to tell them back home. Home. I thought of what that meant. This new world with Connor, Lance, Dante, this was a new home for me.

I grabbed my necklace again, focusing this time, focusing on where I truly wanted to be: the angel realm, please, return me to the angel realm, to the odd present. To Lance. To Dante and to Connor and to the others who are like me. To comfort. To somewhere where someone would tell me that this would be all right. I had seen my full life span and wished to see no more. I wished to scrub it all from my memory. But I knew these images would haunt me for as long as I lived.

Much sooner than expected, I felt the THUD of my body pummeling against a cold floor. My eyes opened to Lance above me. He reached out to push the hair away from my face.

"What time is it?" I asked. That action alone hurt my chest.

He leaned over, hitting his keyboard. A stopwatch filled the screen. He stopped it. "You left," he reported, "Twenty-three hours, 40 minutes and 6 seconds ago."

"Really? That's all? Because I feel like I've been gone for ages."

"You travel pretty fast," he smiled. I made no attempt to get up.

I worried for a moment though. Had I actually been there—back and then forward and then further back—or could it have been an elaborate dream like the recurring one that Lucian had? Slowly I tried to roll onto my side to get up. I felt something in my pocket and reached in: I pulled out a cocktail napkin, bearing the name of the restaurant where I had last seen Lucian. I tossed it onto the floor.

"A souvenir. Thanks," Lance said. "There's a fine for littering my workshop."

I tried to laugh, but it hurt my ribs and my chest too much and I winced. I wasn't sure I could move.

"Here, I'll help you up," he said, leaning in to scoop me up. That was the last thing I remembered.

⟡

When I finally woke up, feeling instantly strong, I found Lance asleep beside me. Energy coursed through me, humming, fully charged as Connor had promised. It was almost too much, it buzzed my veins like overworked harp strings. It demanded an outlet. My body was renewed, but even the powers of this place could do nothing to help my mind: I couldn't push out the images I had seen. The broken wings and the angel's request haunted me, giving me chills. I had so much to tell of my travels. I almost woke Lance but, instead, crept out of the bed thinking I might go looking for Connor. Apparently he had the same idea. Slipped under the door, a note waited: "See me when you're up—Connor" Why did it always sound ominous, that terseness of a "see me" with no punctuation? Instinct told me something was wrong, and if it was, I wasn't prepared for it yet. I stuffed it in my pocket and let myself quietly out. I made my way through the silence of those bright, clear hallways, the light of the strange new world outside filtering through. I found the door to the equivalent of our New Orleans levitation room here, our version of a gym.

A pair of girls was leaving as I went in. "Hi, Haven," one said. "We heard about your travels," said the other, with a solemn reverence. "Never been done before, way to go. We hope to hear all the details. It's inspiring to have you here."

"Thanks," I said awkwardly. I still wasn't quite used to the warmth, to people being kind to me for no reason. I would have thought it would feel insincere to be instantly welcomed and cared for, but it didn't. They all had made me feel as though I were a missing piece of their puzzle they were grateful to have found. I hoped I warranted that kind of reception.

But I had picked the right time to come here. With so many working, recharging or out on missions, I had the levitation room to myself. Just like everywhere else here, the space was perfectly airy: clear on all sides with views of the fields. A skylight encompassed the ceiling at least thirty feet up, and a seam running along the middle gave the impression that it might open up. The walls were studded with planks, pegs, loops—all manner of footholds, ledges, and handles set amid plenty of space for jumping, rigging up your own obstacle courses, and climbing. I heard a quick sizzle and whipped my head around: there were ropes and posts that would flame up, catching fire for a second and then extinguish, or occasionally shoot a switchblade out at your hand as you held on. Everything was designed to test your reflexes, strength, and your ability to remain cool under pressure. None of it would leave so much as a scrape on us, but a demon version of any of these tricks could maim us, so it always helped to be schooled in the art of quick thinking and dodging hazards. I sized it all up and dove in, anxious to test my skills.

I bounced a few times then set off, scurrying up the wall to one of the planks and then I jumped down, grabbing a flag from another perch as I did. "Back from the past and feeling better than ever, huh?" Connor said as I somersaulted onto a ledge just above him.

"Yeah, thanks." I leapt down, landing on my feet in front of him, wondering where he had come from.

"Good, glad to hear it," he said, arms folded across his chest. And then, after a beat: "We should talk."

I tried a joke, to lighten things: "You sound like you're breaking up with me."

He almost laughed. "C'mon, all this can wait," he said, holding the door open to lead me out.

"Seriously, should I be worried?" I asked.

"Do you think there's a reason you should be worried?" he parried.

"That sounds like a trick question. You're making me nervous."

We heard footsteps behind us. The boy to whom I had sent my first assignment in the Illumination Chamber appeared. He breezed in from the field, looking a little weathered but merrily tapping away on his angel-issued phone.

As we passed, he looked up from his phone and bowed to Connor and then to me. I was going to have to get them to stop doing that. I didn't even have my wings yet.

"All good, I assume?" Connor asked.

"Yes, soul saved," he said with a smile. "Just filing my report now."

"Wow, thanks," I said. It was shocking how fast things could happen here.

"Good work, get some rest," Connor said. The boy bowed again and then left, still keying into his phone.

It got me thinking. "You really didn't send us text messages, like, giving us extra information and pep talks and things in New Orleans?"

"Why would I do that, Haven?" Connor asked, barely paying attention. "I was living down the hall from you, I could talk to you any time. Remember me? I'm the one who wasn't afraid to bang the door down at 3 in the morning and drag you guys to a swamp."

"Good point," I said, a little disappointed. It worked away at my mind as we ducked into a narrow doorway I hadn't seen before. Inside was a little nook of an office: a Lucite desk, a few matching chairs, one of those exotic star-shaped plants from outside. I wondered, though. I thought about where I had been in the past 24 hours. And the direct command I'd given myself. Wait, I mean, it couldn't be....could it? Didn't everyone always wish to advise their younger selves? I thought of that time-re-lease ink Dante had worked out in New Orleans and Lance's comfort with the inner workings of our phones. Yes.

"Have a seat," he gestured, snapping me out of my thoughts. I took a seat before the desk. He hit a button and the wall behind me clouded from clear crystal into opaque white, offering privacy like our rooms.

I sniffed the plant. It smelled sweet, a mix of tropical flowers and cotton candy.

"Healing properties, even that little thing," Connor said by way of explanation.

"It's like drinking one of those power smoothies with the shot of protein powder or whatever."

"Even the smallest plants here will regenerate you," he said, all business.

I nodded and then looked at him, squaring my shoulders. "I know you don't want to talk about plants."

"First off, you made it. Congratulations. That is no small feat and, as you know, it is something that has never been accomplished. We like to think you're out of the woods now," he said, his voice tense, a reference to the friend he had lost. "So you should certainly be proud. We are all anxious to hear the details of your trip."

"Great," I said, trying to thaw him, not sure what he wasn't telling me. "I have a ton to tell you. You know, I had some trouble getting back and ended up—"

"However," he said cutting me off, letting it hang there. "The Administration is concerned."

"Oh?" I could guess what this was about, but I was hoping I was wrong. So instead I said: "Is this about the windows?"

"I don't care about the windows," he said with a sigh. So he knew. "Technical difficulties. It happens. We weren't thrilled about it, but our researchers assure us there were no actual casualties so the disturbance didn't register on a grand enough scale to fracture the past. You're lucky there."

"Oh."

"What we're concerned about is your recklessness and breach of power."

"My—?" I almost laughed.

"We've had one of our researchers trained on Lucian's last known whereabouts before his recruitment and so far there is no trace of him."

"What do you mean? Wouldn't it take a while for him to return?"

"That's just it. No, it should happen instantaneously. His body should dematerialize wherever it is, even if it's been turned to ash or anything else the demons might have done with it. And he should reappear with no memory of anything after that recruitment. It should be a clean break and fresh start."

"Right, so he shows up after having been missing," I said. I knew that part.

"But it's supposed to happen before the angel even makes it back home."

"Oh," I said, not wanting to accept what they were telling me.

"So our researchers have deduced that you must have gone against our orders in some way and now your souls are linked."

"What does that mean?"

"If you had simply gotten him to refuse Aurelia, he would be returned to a mortal life now. But your…transgression," he said it in such a loaded way, "means that he won't return until after the revolution. If you survive."

"So otherwise he would have come back right now? I delayed it?"

"Yes," he said, sighing.

"He grabbed my hand," I said, even though it wasn't the complete truth. But if he hadn't done *that* then I absolutely wouldn't have kissed him and that was the truth. I thought back to that kiss. I couldn't possibly explain it, but it had felt like it would mean something to Lucian at that moment, even though for me it was the most innocent goodbye peck. I certainly didn't intend to make a habit of kissing everything with a pulse when I was on a mission, but these had been extenuating circumstances if ever there were any.

"You can dodge fire bolts thrown at your head, but not someone holding your hand?"

"You can blame plenty on me but last time I checked no one had done this before and I did and I'm back and I'm alive," I was angry now, and I did little to try to control it. For some reason I had always felt able to lash out at Connor, in a way I didn't at anyone else. I could be purely honest with him—I didn't worry about his feelings, I didn't have to worry about protecting morale as I did with the others. I didn't worry that carrying out my duties would infect a friendship or a relationship. This was probably what it would have been like to have had a brother. "You've never been back there. None of you have. You can't begin to understand what it's like to have your powers not working properly, to already be off-balance from the traveling, and to have all of these restrictions placed on you on top of that. To know that you're going to be pulled out of that time and place at a certain hour. There is so little in your control."

"I understand, I'm just telling you that this is where we are."

"So now what?"

"It's easy, just survive the revolution," he said smiling.

"That was my plan." I stood up, pushing the chair back. "Can I go?"

"There's one more thing," he stopped me at the door. "While you were gone, Lance began remembering what he had encountered in the underworld. We need to take a look at the catacombs. They may be recruiting there, and it could be a way to gather information about their plans for the revolution."

"OK," I said, suddenly feeling needed.

"I hear you might have a connection."

"I might know someone who can get us in," I said confidently. "I'll make a call."

"Thanks."

"But first, I'm going to need to travel again."

"What?" he spat, as though he was sure he misheard.

"I just need to go back and drop a few things off...."

Lance was waiting outside Connor's door when I opened it to leave. As I did, Connor was still shaking his head. "I can't believe the stuff you guys are pulling. I never would've thought when I met you, that you'd be such trouble," he called out, nearly laughing but a sigh escaping instead. Then, as though rationalizing to himself, "But I guess, if you got those dispatches from yourself then it means I'm supposed to let you go."

"Hey, there you are," Lance said, giving me a kiss as I swung the door closed. "Everything OK?" he said in a heavy way. He must have known that the trip hadn't gone perfectly.

"Yeah, it will be," I said easily, and I believed it.

"So Connor told you: back to Paris? I heard you guys were having all this fun before you got to me. Thought it was time to see some tourist attractions."

"Yeah, I'm on it....there's just somewhere I have to go first," I said, as he raised an eyebrow at me. "I'm going to need some spare phones from the workshop. And some other supplies. And Dante...and you, of course."

"Well, it's always nice to be needed," he smiled. "What are you up to?"

Just two days after I'd returned from skipping across time, I was back in Lance's workshop ready to go again. I had assured Connor that I felt strong enough for it—and I did. I also felt like I understood the mechanics better this time, the pure focus you needed to have in order to direct yourself, and how to prepare for the sudden, violent landings.

I had waited until Lance and Dante were together to tell them the news, the answer to this mystery we had been chasing for so long. We were in Lance's workshop, everyone clearing out for the day. As soon as it was just us alone, I blurted it out, unable to keep it in any longer:

"I know who it is, who sent us the messages."

"How do you know? Who? Should we guess? Did you see them where you were, Hav?" Dante asked, hopping up and down, anxious.

"No, and yes. I saw me. And I told me," I said, shaking my head to try again. "We wrote them. We did. We wrote them to ourselves."

Lance had been standing at his computer but he sat down now, looking at me like I'd just told him DNA was actually a triple-helix instead of a double. "That doesn't seem…"

"Whoa," Dante said, hand to his head. "That is some crazy stuff. I can't. Even. Wow."

"But, so what do you mean?" Lance asked, wrapping his head around it.

"We need to write them all now: your postcards that you found at the Lex, my journal, and then the texts for the three of us. Then I drop them all off and we're all set."

"Heavy stuff," Dante shook his head.

"All right," Lance said, eyes brightening with acceptance, thrilled. "Sounds like we've got some work to do."

We had spent another day writing. First the text messages since they were fresh in our minds. "Oooh, we need to make them sound like they're coming from some high authority," Dante had said. He had a point, they didn't sound quite like us. "We should channel Mariette," he said of the voodoo priestess who had guided us all. "You know how she was always so strong and sure and Zen?" Lance set them to release on a timer and monogrammed the phones for himself, Dante and me so we would get the right messages. Then Lance had written the postcards to himself, which he would find…had found…at the Lex, and I took one of the journals, the style that all the angels used, and penned all those instructions and pep talks to myself.

After all of this, I took my place again in the workshop, this time armed with a backpack coated for travel and filled with these supplies. Lance and Dante had programmed my locations.

"No gallivanting this time," Connor said from the doorway, showing up again at the last minute to offer his support. "Stick to the itinerary, please."

I held my watch charm and felt that rush again, the freefall, and then the smack against the ground. I was at the Lexington, just inside its empty lobby. The scent of fresh paint was everywhere, and I heard no voices. It hadn't opened yet. Back behind the front desk would be the hallway to Aurelia's office. She may be in there with Lucian even now. I passed by it, beneath the grand chandelier, past the award-winning, poisonous restaurants, in the direction toward the elevator down to the nightclub, the Vault. So many memories flooded back, good and bad. Because there had been good ones here too. This is where I had fallen in love with Lance. This is where we had all learned how strong we truly were, in mind and body, and how different we were from everyone else, and how that wasn't such a bad thing.

I ducked into the library, the books still in boxes. Lance would be here later today and would be tasked with unpacking them. I buried the stack of postcards, marked "For Lance," and the journal for me, in one of the boxes. I heard voices, Aurelia and Lucian, emerging from the hallway as I suspected. Perhaps this was the moment they'd share that kiss I had witnessed. I grabbed my watch charm and disappeared again.

This time it was as though slamming the accelerator to hit 100 and stopping at the end of the block. My body came to a screeching halt on the worn carpet of my old room. The journal lay on the nightstand, in plain view of any demons that might steal inside for a look. I needed to learn to hide it and study every inch of my surroundings to unearth secrets. I grabbed it, tucking it in the closet beneath my duffel bags, right above what I had discovered was a trap door down to the tunnels. As I did, I heard the door unlock. Through the sliver of the open closet door, I saw myself step back into my room—a confused girl, reading a journal every night, in this strange place, trying to make sense of so much. I wanted to tell her—me—everything right now. But she would discover it all, and ever better, she would also learn how to see the world, how to uncover secrets and learn to intuit the true character of those around her, and how to learn to trust herself and her instincts, all as she read that journal.

She—I—looked for the misplaced journal. I grabbed the timepiece again, disappearing just as she opened the closet door.

My last stop was my easiest landing yet. I touched down on the plush carpet of Lance's room at home, the walls lined with models of architectural marvels he had constructed—several by Frank Lloyd Wright, the Sears tower, the Taj Mahal. The scent of cinnamon wafting up from downstairs where his mom was making her trademark hot cider, the cold December day chilling his room. I left the three phones on the green plaid comforter of his bed just as I heard him running up the steps.

For the last time, I focused on my escape and pulled myself out of the past, racing back to the angel realm.

I awoke on the floor of the workshop again, my strength drained. Both Dante and Lance were there this time. Seeing them filled me with pure relief: I had made it.

"OK, can you not do that for a little while now?" Dante asked.

"What he means to say is, thank you. Nice to have you back," Lance said, helping me up again. "That was a really long day."

19

Know Where I Can Get In Touch With A Cataphile?

After a day of convalescence, I awoke—energized once again—to two important pieces of news: the first was that the Administration needed to see me. They summoned me to a sort of open hearing, which my fellow angels-in-training and representatives of the other departments were welcome to attend. Connor sat among the Administration, along the ring hovering in the library. They asked me share the details of my travels and all I had seen, then helped me make sense of it. I finished describing my visit to the past and witnessing my soul finding its host as an eerie figure lurked in the shadows.

"That was the Prince," Henry said with certainty. "A new angel echoes in the underworld below and they often send one of their own to the source of the quake. It's their way of tracking all of you. Your soul likely reverberated where it landed as never before. And so the Prince went himself. It's no coincidence that he sent his strongest messengers to Chicago. They were searching for you. The three of you, specifically."

Finally they asked me about my trip forward in time. I wasn't quite sure I wanted to talk about the future; it was still too terrifying to process. I was afraid that sharing it before the group would make it even more real. But I had learned that terrifying things needed to be shared. When I began, my voice dropped to a darker tone. I hadn't told anyone but Connor—not Lance, not Dante—and I could hear the others gasp and whisper as I described what I had seen happen to me. When I finished, Henry leaned forward looking into me.

"It's my guess that you visited both the past and the future because subconsciously you were curious, which is only natural," he said calmly. I wanted to protest, but I knew he was probably right. "The past is one thing, it is done. But I would strongly caution against believing too deeply in this vision of the future. From what we know, they are only suggestions of what *may* be, not necessarily what *is*. The future is still changeable. What you saw was only a possible outcome, that's all we can see. The angel who went before you came back reporting that he had visited a bleak world as well, and that he, too, was in it and in the fight of his life. But his version of the future never happened. And I know that because while our angels have witnessed plenty of violence and bleakness, he was not there to see it or to fight those battles. He died the day after sharing his vision with me."

I found this story both horrifying and oddly, selfishly comforting, wrong as that seemed. But it was that simple: I didn't want to die. And I would wholeheartedly believe anyone who would tell me that I wouldn't.

They were wrapping up this part of the proceedings, thanking me for my "fearless service" despite the "occasional breach," which they hoped "would be righted in due time." They were sure that my experiences would "prove invaluable" as they continued to uncover the mysteries of this kind of travel. I heard only bits and pieces, my leg tapping beneath the table, anxious to return to Lance and Dante and to leave this interrogation chamber.

Then came the second bit of news, a suckerpunch:

"We have something of grave importance to share with you now," Henry began. "It concerns your fellow angel-in-training, Drew. She has not been heard from since embarking upon her third test."

"How can you be sure? Is it possible her test was just harder than the others?" I asked. It jarred me to hear this news. It could have been any of us. All of us were strong and smart, but we all needed each other, we couldn't afford to lose anyone, especially before the coming revolution. While I was away on my time-traveling trips, the others had been completing their tests to earn their wings: everyone else had returned and now could calmly await the initiation ceremony. Everyone, that is, except Lance and Dante, who had been asked to postpone their tests until I got back, since they were the only ones who could help me if I ran into trouble.

"Certainly. Anything is possible," he said, unconvinced. "But it's our experience that if someone does not return to us within 24 hours of that test, then they have often fallen into some sort of trouble. Connor?"

Connor pulled out his smartphone and, using it like a remote control, projected a map onto the wall above the door.

"We last traced her to the Denfert metro station," he said, lighting up a pinpoint in a Parisian neighborhood. I tried to get my bearings among the other nearby notable sites marked on the map. Then I noticed.

"It's near the catacombs," I said, thinking aloud, putting the pieces together. "She must've been going there then."

"We wouldn't be surprised. Considering what Lance told us on top of this development, we think they've been recruiting there," he went on.

I thought about the call I needed to make: parties in the catacombs, the joke made by that exchange student at the Louvre, Gavin.

"We suspect she may have gotten pulled in and could very well be in the underworld as we speak. If what Lance has told us is, in fact, true," Henry said.

"Haven—" Connor started, but I didn't need him to finish.

"I'm on it. I'll get down there, no problem," I promised.

"I'll go too." I heard Lance's voice behind me. I knew what he was doing. He didn't want me to go alone. I certainly wouldn't turn down the company. I looked back over my shoulder, my eyes connecting with his. I mouthed, "Thanks" to him.

He nodded at me, the slightest smile that said he didn't love the idea of having to go back there, but he wouldn't have it any other way.

And then another voice: "Absolutely," Dante piped up.

"If you're going, I'm going," I heard Max tell Dante.

"Yes, me too," Emma said simply.

"We're in," River called out.

"We are?" Tom asked, receiving a look. "I mean, we are," he said, as though he'd been schooled.

"Thanks guys. I do have to remind you that you're not angels yet, but I think if we waited then we would lose too much time. Agreed?" Connor asked.

We all nodded and answered in the affirmative.

"All right, then I leave it to you, Haven, to secure entry as soon as possible," Connor said.

"Take great precaution now, you are being hunted," Henry said. "The revolution could begin at any moment."

<hr />

Only a few hours later, the seven of us were gathered again, this time in a circular room I hadn't seen before, tucked at the end of a long sloped corridor behind the library. Unlike the other part of this grand compound, this space had none of the airiness, no views of the field, no feeling of peacefulness.

"This is like their O'Hare or, like, Union Station," Dante explained in a whisper as Connor stood before us typing into a terminal at the center of the space. There were ten oval chrome doorways surrounding us, each bearing a panel that would display the destination. The others had all been through this for their tests. It was strange to think I hadn't been back on familiar ground since rescuing Lance. I had been back to familiar *places*—Chicago, Paris—but not in the present. I thought of Joan. Of course, Joan. I was lucky that she hadn't expected to hear from me all that often on the supposed trip I was on. Over the past year and a half I had also conditioned her to be content with short bursts of emails that gave little actual information, and she had been astoundingly calm, considering. I had also gotten better at lying than I ever would have expected. A signboard, so seamless it appeared merely part of the stark-white walls, listed the destinations: a number, a city and an angel's name beside them. This was the equivalent of their departures board: "Portal 1 Paris."

The oval passageway directly before us lit up in that honey golden glow I had grown accustomed to since arriving here. The doorway opened to reveal a chrome vestibule. Above it, it now read our destination.

"Who's up first?" Connor asked. "Just like getting here, you can only go one at a time."

"I'll go!" Dante volunteered, then looked at me. "It's a great rush, you'll love it, Hav," he said before stepping forward. "Or, who knows, maybe it'll be a letdown after time travel." He elbowed me, smiling.

"For a girl who never liked roller coasters, you're getting quite the reputation for being a reckless adrenaline junkie, you know," Lance said, kidding.

"So that's what you guys have been talking about while I've been away? Nothing beats the thrill of careening into the apocalyptic future, the ultimate travel destination," I said. Dante gave Max a squeeze on the shoulder then stepped into the vestibule.

"Catch you on the other side," he said to us all as the metallic doors slid shut with a swoosh as though he had been vacuum-sealed inside. A BOOM sounded within and then seconds later the doors opened again.

"Magic," Lance said.

Connor watched us all go, calling us one by one until I was alone, last. Not a coincidence.

"I don't have to tell you to be careful?" he started, as though it were a question.

"No," I laughed. "I know."

"You know I'm only tough on you because you're the strongest?"

I nodded. It was the best compliment I could hope to receive. It meant he had faith in me and thought I was capable of more than I realized. It was comforting and a great luxury to have someone like this on my side. "Lead them well, use them well. Bring them all back as soon as possible. And do your best to bring back Drew and any information you can about what's to come. I want to see you back here fast, Terra. Got it?"

"No problem," I said, stepping into the passageway, testing a confident tone though my mind couldn't help replaying the words at the hearing: we were being hunted now, as never before.

The doors snapped shut and the glow filled the space around me. Then that rushing whoosh I had heard from the outside. A force swept me up, shooting me as though I were being catapulted. Jaws opened above me and for just a flash I was above the field, and then once again, I was assaulted by the light I'd seen on the way here.

I soared, and then my trajectory changed and I was falling, but without the violent velocity of the time travel. This felt manageable to my body and I wrapped my mind around it, controlling it. The bright white went dark as I dropped from the night sky, but the pressure pushing against me let up too, and I slowed, floating now, my feet positioned under me as the ground below came into view. The wind whipped my hair, the air a cushion around my body. As I closed in on the group below, I saw we were back at Père-Lachaise, at the same tomb where we had lost Lucian. My heart braced for this just as my body braced for the impact of landing.

Emma, Tom and Max were just stumbling on to their feet when I touched down, gently, my toes delicately kissing the gravel first, like a dancer landing a leap.

"Nice," Lance said as I floated down beside him.

"See, pay up," Dante said to River, holding out his hand.

"My cash is all on Rue des Martyrs," River rolled her eyes. "I'll owe you when we get back."

"I bet you'd have the smoothest landing," Dante explained.

"Beginner's luck," Emma laughed.

"Time travel was like a boot camp for this," I said, with a shy shrug. I was just relieved it had been easier than our trip to the angel realm or any of my travels since then. Maybe I really was getting better at this. "Everyone good?" I asked the group, receiving all affirmative answers. I glanced to that spot, still picturing Lucian's body there. I turned back to the others: "Let's get outta here."

<hr />

It seemed a bit anti-climactic to take the metro after our arrival through the portal, but we hadn't yet been outfitted with our wings so we had to do things the old-fashioned way: scaling the cemetery walls and picking up the train at the Père-Lachaise stop to head toward our appointed rendezvous with Gavin. I had written him immediately following my meeting with Connor:

"Remember that joke about the catacombs? Know where I could get in touch with a cataphile? Haven (Rosetta)" It had taken just a little research to school myself in the lingo. I thought it would be easier to stay under the radar going in with a group who knew the way and knew how this world operated than breaking in through the underground museum ourselves.

He had responded to my text in minutes: "Rosetta! Much to tell you. I can hook you up, if we can come along."

"Deal," I wrote back and we set the time and place. I didn't know who "we" were and it didn't matter.

We rattled along through the tunnels, making stop after stop to let Saturday night revelers on and off, many who looked our age or a little bit older, all different Parisian versions of us, just a degree off from what we might have found back at home on a Saturday night. They emanated a more aloof aura of cool. And of course, there was a different shoe here—a wedge hightop sneaker or an oxford—a different hat there, a skirt length just a little shorter in some cases, or longer in others. A supreme, easy confidence hung on everyone as effortlessly as the girls wore their scarves. But in my eyes, they did share one thing with their counterparts back in Chicago: none carried the weight that the seven of us carried. For a moment, as always when I saw groups like this, I wondered how it might feel to be among them. But for the first time, it now struck me that I wouldn't be happy at all. I didn't know what lay ahead for our group tonight but I knew that we were doing something that mattered, and that that had become something necessary in my life—to have my actions and my time add up to something. I had always planned to be a doctor, saving lives. But devoting my life to this instead, saving souls, felt just as vital. It might come without accolades, or without my targets even understanding the full extent of what I had saved them from or what I'd risked to do it. But it was something noble, and it now satisfied a certain desire, quenched a thirst. It was something I was meant to do.

We rode silently. I suspected the others were having as much trouble as I was trying to come up with some topic of discussion suitable for a crowded train. When we finally jumped out at our stop and into the warm, still night air, we launched in as though we were our own mobile war room.

"So, they didn't want me to spend much time below—" Lance started.

"In the Underworld Proper," I clarified, like it was a cool, new neighborhood.

"Right," he smiled. "They were scared I'd learn too much, even though I was pretty knocked out most of the time."

"So they kept you in the catacombs?" Max asked. "I mean, I still think that was taking a pretty big chance that someone would find you." As we walked on, the streets grew darker, emptier. This wasn't a destination like other parts of town; it was isolated, the storefronts and offices closed up for the night—the perfect backdrop for trouble.

"I know, but that's the thing, there are these extensive networks of tunnels that aren't even part of the museum part that everyone sees, they're just there. And there are these sort of cells, with bars and everything. Like a prison. They moved me around too. I remember being dragged through these dark, cold passageways and then shoved into these cells." He shook his head, as though trying to dislodge this memory.

"Except on their recruiting nights?" I prompted.

"The parties," Emma said.

"Exactly. On the nights of the parties, then they dragged me through the passageways and shoved me into these hot cells instead. Those I think were in Underworld Proper, as you call it."

"I can't even imagine feeling the way we did after being tagged in New Orleans except, like, for months," River said.

"Really, you can't?" Tom joked.

"Shut up," she smiled. "Seriously, that's really messed up."

"Tell me about it," Lance said.

"So that's why we're here and not, like, near the catacombs museum, like the part where Drew….you know," Dante started. "Because I know geography isn't my strong suit, Hav. But this is nowhere near that."

"And it's kinda deserted and weird here," Max said.

"And it's kinda deserted and weird here," Dante repeated.

"Yeah, no, I know," I said, distracted as I led us, looking at the map on my phone, and directing us down a narrow side street. No cafes, no stores, just sleepy city residences. Lance looked at the screen and nodded, we were almost there. "We're not taking a museum tour. We can get you some lovely souvenirs later, D."

He slapped my arm playfully.

"It makes sense they would get in somewhere off the beaten path," Lance said, eyes set ahead, thinking. "Should be here," he pointed, picking up his pace. We all followed until he stopped abruptly in the middle of the street. At his feet: a black lacquered manhole glistened in the lamplight. My watch read just after midnight. Up ahead, a handful of silhouettes turned down the street. My posture stiffened for a moment, involuntarily, poised to attack. One of them waved wildly to be seen in the darkness: Gavin.

"Greetings, new friends, meet my merry band of international misfits! Nile from London, Simon from Sydney, and your fellow countryman, Noah. And, of course, Olivier," he said, in a pretty passable French accent.

"Call me, O," the scruffy Frenchman clarified in his thickly accented English. He puffed on a cigarette, its smoky tail winding up into the dark night air. He wore all black from head to toe, and had his shaggy dyed black hair—bits of blond peeking through at his roots—tied back in a ponytail.

"This is our resident cataphile," Gavin said. Olivier nodded, expressionless and waving some kind of metal stick at us by way of greeting. It had an odd triangular-shaped handle. Without a word, he knelt on the ground, inserted the stick's rectangular edge into a groove in the manhole cover and began twisting and struggling.

"Delighted to get your text, Rosetta," Gavin said. "I knew you'd come around and let your hair down."

"Yeah, we thought it was time we had some fun," I said, almost believably. I introduced our group. I hoped he had been discreet about the talk we'd had at the Louvre, but if he said anything that threatened to blow our cover I intended to pretend I had been on some kind of drug when I met him and claim to remember nothing. No sooner had we met them than they all began slowly flickering, just as Gavin had at the Louvre, all four of them at different intervals. I wasn't surprised. I had imagined that there was a good chance his friends would be in a similar state. But I wished I could turn it off or tone it down somehow. It was like my own personal, horrific strobe light-show of freakish images. I closed my eyes just a moment and looked again. It had slowed a little. Maybe I would be able to control this. It hadn't occurred to me I had much control in my life at all. Lance looked at me from the corner of his eye, but I ignored him for now.

"Got another one of those?" River asked, mimicking a cigarette. "Gotta take the edge off if we're going in there," she shrugged. "*Je fume—S'il vous plaît?*" she managed to ask, the first words of French I'd heard her speak since we'd gotten here.

"Ouais," O slurred, digging in his pocket and lighting a cigarette off of his.

"Seriously?" I laughed. "*That* you know? But I've been translating menus and traffic signs for you?"

"Priorities," she said. I understood though: River was nervous. She asked our new friends about themselves, and everyone started talking. Emma sidled up to Noah to ask where he was from: Athens, Georgia, he responded with a twang, thrilling her.

With the exception of Olivier they all carried backpacks. Simon opened his: inside were several bottles of wine and beer.

"Nile has the harder stuff." Ginger Nile, the tallest of them, nodded at this, slapping the backpack on his back.

"Good to know," I said.

"What did you all bring?" Noah asked.

We all traded glances. Apparently we needed an offering to the gods. We hadn't thought of this, but we hadn't come entirely empty-handed. I looked at Dante and he read my mind.

"I'm the designated pharmaceutical rep," he said. "Check this out…" He pulled from his pocket the trusty Altoids tin and opened it to reveal the thin translucent leaves that could be used to ward off minor devil toxins. They crowded around this show-and- tell.

"Whoa, what *is* that?" Nile asked.

"Latest and greatest from the States," Dante said, nodding an invitation to try one.

"Dude, I've never seen anything like that," Noah said, holding up one of the leaves for a closer inspection.

"Well, I guess you haven't been to the right kind of parties," I said, playing against type, in the role of experienced reveler. I took one, letting it dissolve on my tongue. It tingled.

"All I can say is it'll make you feel good," Dante said, and it was true. Should there be any toxins tonight or in the next 24 hours, everyone who took one of these would, indeed, feel just fine. I hoped we wouldn't blow through them all tonight, but at least we had brought something that could pass as currency.

The others kept talking getting to know each other. I pretended to listen, but kept sneaking glances at O, still at work. I wondered if entering the catacombs could be accomplished without that tool, should we need to come back without an audience.

At last, he pulled up the triangular handle, managing to lift the manhole cover. He flicked his cigarette in the street, pulled something from inside his coat and dropped it on the ground with a dull clang—a metal pipe, it looked like—then slid the cover over it, with a low screech of metal sliding, to help distribute its weight. "*Voilá*," he said with a shrug, no big deal. He lowered himself into the hole. Gavin and his friends followed. I was about to go next when Lance pulled my elbow back, so I stood beside him. Tom slithered down instead and then River. He talked her down, "A few more steps and you're there." I liked that River had a vulnerable side and that it came out at the most unexpected times. I would have thought this would have been her kind of thing. She could throw herself into a portal, but descending this narrow passage into a dark, unknown abyss was just a shade out of her comfort zone.

Lance whispered interrupting my thoughts: "How do they look?" he asked in our shorthand, when Gavin and company were likely out of ear shot.

"In danger, all of them," I whispered back, short and clipped like a newscaster monitoring an ongoing disaster. He nodded, pushing up his glasses, his eyes squinting in concern.

One by one, we all made our way down the metal ladder into pure, thick darkness and finally touched down, splashing in a shallow puddle. I felt it seep through my socks and shoes, cool and wet.

We walked through the suffocating darkness of the narrow passageway for what felt like miles, no sound besides the smacking of our footsteps, like wet kisses along the damp ground. O led us, holding his phone as a flashlight. We all did the same but the light was just swallowed up, our phones barely managing to illuminate anything more than a foot in front of us. They had all the power of newborn fireflies. I tucked mine away, instead reaching my hands to either side of me, feeling the coarse, rocky terrain of these walls carved in the earth. After endless twists and turns, O stopped, with no more warning then a soft, "*Ici.* Here." His light was on the ground now, the others trained theirs downward. In the glow I saw a half-moon shaped tunnel, a human-sized mouse hole. "*Allons-y,*" he directed us. Gavin and his crew were already crawling through. They had been down this way before. I was first among our group. I knelt down and flattened out, following Simon's beat-up sneakers. The space was so tight, the only way through was by doing a military crawl, elbows and knees bearing the brunt of the work against the rough ground, my head occasionally lifting too high and bumping against the rock above us. A claustrophobic person would surely have had a panic attack by now—and I could hear Tom talking River through in the distance behind me. Up ahead though, I heard just the opposite: relief as those in front reached what lay on the other side. "All right!" Gavin cheered.

20

There Are Angels Among Us

One by one we all pushed through, landing just steps from a passageway that must have been part of the catacombs museum, judging by the plaque mounted on it. Once we all had slithered out and dusted ourselves off, O gestured for us to follow down another dark corridor until we reached a sign announcing the ossuary. We crossed the threshold and were instantly surrounded by bones and skulls lining either wall, hundreds of them along with signs reading where the bodies had been taken from. O walked on, as though these specimen were just wallpaper. Gavin and the others stopped to pick up the occasional skull, make jokes and take pictures, their spirits high. But our group remained solemn much as we tried to appear buoyant.

"Never thought I'd get nostalgic for the tunnels at the Lex," Lance said, shaking his head, through more twisting skull-adorned passageways. "But—"

"Yeah. Tell me about it. Those managed to be creepy enough. I could definitely do without this…decor," I said, finishing his sentence. I leaned closer to examine the artfully stacked bones and skulls. "How many did you—"

"Six million," he said, adjusting his glasses. "Six million bodies."

"Well, I'm impressed that they bothered to make a pattern here," I said, lightly.

Dante had caught up with us. "Design by Grim Reaper," he announced, as though it were one of the home improvement reality shows he loved. "You know the French, style is in their—"

"Bones?" Max offered.

"I was going to say genes," Dante smiled. "But that too."

Lights dotted the walls here and there now, for which I was grateful. Anything to lessen the shock of seeing all that death. We turned a corner past a nook sectioned off with bars, making a prison cell and Lance slowed down. I grabbed his hand and he looked at me and nodded. "Home sweet home," he whispered, his voice heavy. We would see several more of these before we reached the party. The most interesting of those cells came with its own well tucked behind the bars. An eerie green glow surrounded it as though it was a cauldron and something sinister might be bubbling inside. It was impossible to see too far down with the bars in the way, but it was unlike anything we had encountered so far. Gavin and his group slowed down to have a look too.

"What did you call this thing last time, O?" Noah asked. Olivier leaned against the opposite wall, like a tour guide who'd seen it all before and was left waiting for his group to get their fill.

"Ça? Là? Le Puits aux Fantômes," he shrugged.

"The Ghosts' Well?" I asked. "Well of the ghosts?"

"Yeah, that's it," Noah said, snapping his fingers. "Dude, we started hearing crazy stuff coming outta there. A couple weeks ago maybe?"

"How many times have you been down here?" I asked Gavin.

He looked away, as though he had been caught. "Just once," he said, clearly ashamed not to have heeded my warnings. "Really. You'd be proud of me, I didn't go with them the last two times. And I kept to myself when I was here, honest."

He nodded in a way that said he was serious. "But it's really something to see, I couldn't resist, you know?"

"Yeah, I get it," I said, looking around.

"Bloody fantastic here," he said.

"You really say 'bloody' this and 'bloody' that?" I laughed.

"Thought you'd appreciate that," he said with a smile. "But now I know my way around, so I'm a better tour guide for you."

"I suppose that's true. So I should be thanking you for ignoring what I told you?"

"That's the spirit," he said.

I let him walk ahead and drifted back over to the well where Noah was busy filling Emma in. She hung on his words and he spoke in an even more animated way, appreciating the attention. "It was like all about torture and death and murder, crazy stuff, this tirade," he said. "How this guy wanted to kill people. Something about souls. Crazy. Figured someone was just playing a joke. We heard screams and stuff too. Messed up," he shook his head. "Way messed up."

That was all I needed to hear. Much as it sent a shiver down my spine, hearing this also delivered a shot of adrenaline into my system. This would be our way in, I was sure of it. Lance read my look. The others walked on as we trailed behind.

"I think I need to check things out. Would you prefer—"

"No," he said in a dull tone, before I could go on. But I could tell his heart wasn't in it. He knew I was going. And he knew he would be joining me, even if he didn't love the idea of returning to that world. "I mean, not now. Let's at least get to the party first, have a look around. We'll come back."

"Well, of course. I didn't mean now," I said, walking away to rejoin the group. "I meant, in five, ten minutes."

Dante glanced my way, "Patience, mademoiselle," he said.

"Thank you," Lance said. "Someone's gotten awfully impulsive all of a sudden."

"Moi?" I asked, innocently. But it was true. I saw the world differently now than I once did. I trusted my instincts so unfailingly these days in a way I never would have imagined, and I hated the idea of wasting time. I understood the need to act, to not let opportunities pass. I had changed. Nearly losing Lance. Losing Lucian. Every minute and every action mattered. When I spoke again my voice had slipped a shade darker. "Life is short."

"I know," Lance said, matching my tone. His hand found the back of my neck. "C'mon." We caught up to the others, winding through more passages, some so low that Lance nearly had to duck to keep from scraping his head on the ceiling.

We heard the music first, the pulse of the bass so steady we could feel it in the stones and bones around us. Then the voices—mostly French but some English. At last, we spilled out into a cavernous part of the museum, its rocky ceiling at least 18 feet up. And here we saw many more bodies: alive, dancing, bouncing, joyful. At least four dozen fellow trespassers, all about our age, maybe a few years older, had turned the center of the space into a dance floor despite the damp, slick ground. Lights seemed to be pulsing too, but where were they coming from? In other nooks and offshoots, intimate groups nestled into cut-out sections of rock, imbibing what libations they had smuggled in and partaking of other illicit contraband. Sweat beaded up on my forehead. It was so much warmer here than it had been on our walk. I felt that tingling in my scars.

"The rules: when you leave take with you what you brought—" O said before setting us free.

"And who you brought?" Emma asked, looking at Noah. I shot her a smile.

"Must respect these people, this space," O said, gesturing to the bones, the deceased. We nodded, serious faces all around, then he sent us off, throwing his hand in the air: "*Amuse-toi bien!*" He patted Gavin on the back, lit another cigarette and stalked off vanishing into a dark corner to join equally dark characters.

Simon and Nile splintered off, eyes set in the distance, a clear destination in mind, as Gavin scrambled to follow: "We're going this way apparently," he shouted back to me. Noah invited Emma to join them, she looked at me as though for permission.

"We'll catch up!" I called out to them, waving. Emma could be my eyes and ears with that group, though I didn't like the idea of her being alone among them.

The rest of us traded glances and without a word, broke off into pairs to have a look around. Dante led Max straight into the center of the dancing mob. River and Tom grabbed a few leaves from Dante's tin and investigated a quintet populating the darkest, dankest nook. Lance and I set off around the periphery. I planned to do a couple of laps, then return to the well. Lance had other ideas.

"I know what you're thinking," he said, preemptively. "But we need to spend a little time here—"

"I know," I said, wandering toward the dancers. But as I neared them, I stopped short. There were so many endangered souls here. Nearly everyone seemed to be fluttering between their human forms and their grotesque figures. I closed my eyes and shook my head, then tried to refocus. The strobe light effect was blinding.

Lance moved in front of me. "What is it?"

"It's…everyone. *Everyone.*"

He looked out, but of course he couldn't see it. "Everyone?" he said in disbelief, as though watching a funnel cloud approach his home.

"It's too noisy. I mean the images, there are too many. They're almost bleeding into each other, I can't tell what's what." I rambled, but I felt overloaded. Too many to save, where would I begin? It was so bright, these images were assaulting me. I had to turn my head away.

"Here. Hey, come 'ere," he said, holding my biceps and moving me back to a spot in the shadows. He leaned down to look in my eyes. "Triage," he said, a firm directive. Of course, something I should have thought of myself. "Focus on a couple of people. Can you make sense of them?"

I watched two girls dancing nearest us. They wore tank tops and formfitting jeans still covered in dirt from their trek here, their long hair draped around their shoulders. As they jumped up and down to the thump of the techno music, they changed into rotting corpses—sagging skin, lesions, limbs dangling on nearly snapped tendons—and then back to normal. I studied them as my mind put a dimmer on them, allowing me to focus on two guys talking just behind them. One wearing a knit cap was telling the other one, who had a buzzcut, something that seemed important. He listened so intently, nodding. His image flickered too. The one in the cap smiled as though something had been decided, then turned, brushing right past us to a hideaway where a more intimate group gathered. It looked like a private party, a VIP room, if there could be such a thing in a place like this. Champagne bottles littered the ground. I wondered what might really be in there. One girl wore a slip dress—I couldn't imagine how she had crawled here wearing that. A glow followed them, encasing them. The man in the cap seemed to make an introduction and the girl draped herself on to the guy with the buzzcut, whispering in his ear as she wove one arm around his neck. I watched the group, my eyes lasering, trying to see *into* them. The man in the cap's image stabilized, now frozen in a decaying corpse-like form. I gasped and doubled over for a moment. Lance caught me.

"Hey!" he said, righting me. I was sweating, as though a fever had just broken. I looked at the hideaway again and now

I saw it. This was different; this was not a soul in danger. This was something I had never witnessed in the flesh before but had only seen in the photos I had taken: he was one of them, this man in the hat. He was a demon.

"Yes," I said to myself. His glow darkened, tinged with an eerie crimson light.

"What?"

"Him." He was a demon and he was recruiting right now. Buying and stealing souls *right now*. Lance followed my line of vision.

I set the same intense gaze on the woman: long-legged, reed thin, features so perfectly shaped they belonged on a doll's face. She, too, was glowing, and the more I stared, the stronger the glow until the horror erupted from her too. Her organs burst through her chest, hanging on the outside of her body like ornaments on a tree. Her scalp grew scaly, her hair turned haylike, shedding. Her eyes drooped, secreting bloody tears. Unlike the man she clung to, her image remained this way, strong and sure, her glow turned a bloody red. His image flickered though; he could still be saved. But not her. But I had watched, inactive, for too long. Her long arms pulled him back, deeper into the crevasse, and I knew it was too late for his soul. Their sickly combined glow soon extinguished, swallowed up into the shadows, and I vowed to investigate what might be lurking back there. The man in the cap, mission now accomplished, left their secluded spot and headed for the dance floor again, I imagined to continue recruiting.

"They're here then," Lance said. It was a statement, not a question.

"We need to find Dante. They are here, everywhere. He needs to distribute as many of those leaves as possible. We all need to."

"Could be time to blanket the place too," Lance said.

"Absolutely, Dante's got it all."

We shot through the center of the dance floor and found them, looking like they were doing no more than dancing. Dante and Max jumped up and down, arms in the air, smiles on their faces. But when we got close enough, Dante said in my ear: "There's a girl over there that just lured some guy back to the tunnel where we came from. He was all over her. She just now came back. *Alone.* We're gonna check it out." I thought of that well and wondered what the odds were that he had been thrown in there. I looked at her, working on another guy, a short and scrawny boy outfitted in all black who looked too young to be down here. She leaned into him and grabbed his hand, flashing a seductive smile, her eyes burning, and then walked him away from us, back in the direction of the well. I couldn't keep her in my sights long enough to get a firm reading on her, but my gut told me what she was. Lance was relaying what we had seen, telling Dante and Max to give leaves to Gavin to distribute and to take the powder form of the antidotes to distribute in the air. I pulled out the black, monogrammed phone and tapped out a quick text to River and Tom: "Distribute leaves, watch for demons." And to Emma: "Max will find you with antidotes. Demons everywhere."

"Operation Glitterbomb redux, got it," Dante said. This was the name he had coined when we had dispersed these materials into the crowd at Mardi Gras, our best shot at guarding against the mind control efforts of the demons. We had seen how they could work together to ensnare a target, root them in place and then send someone in to woo them or, worse, stab them with their own toxins and imprison them.

"We'll take the back if you've got it covered here," I said. Lance was distracted though. I tried to follow his line of vision. "Hey, what are you getting on that guy? Blue t-shirt, jeans," Lance said into my ear, his eyes darting straight to the back.

I needed to watch only a moment for that flicker and a few grotesque flourishes mottling his skin: "Endangered. Possibly already committed to them," I said. He pulled his phone from his pocket and flipped through. "Thought so," he said at the screen. "He's my test."

He looked at me. "You can take him," I smiled, trying not to appear nervous. The trick wouldn't be extracting the soul; it would be doing it amid a backdrop of demons.

"Back in five," he said, stalking off, not taking his eyes off the guy. Lance took a place beside him, at the mouth of one of the darkened tunnels. Then he pulled some of those translucent leaves from his pocket, offering to share. The guy looked nervous, his eyes skittish as though waiting to get caught by someone. He took a swig from his bottle and shrugged, not making eye contact, instead scanning the crowd. Lance glanced over his shoulder, back into the tunnel and, perhaps finding it clear— focused his gaze on the man. He froze, a stunned expression on his face and I knew Lance had gotten hold of his soul. To my eyes, the man's image flickered between the good and the grotesque. His body began to rise a few inches from the ground. Lance stepped back into the safe shadows of that tunnel now, before this became a spectacle. He pulled the man with him. I saw a flash flare and a few long seconds later, Lance emerged, striding out of that passageway. I hoped the man's wrist now bore those wings to protect him. Lance nodded at me, mission accomplished.

"Nice, how was that?" I met him halfway and we slithered through the throbbing crowd toward the back, finding the right spot to disperse our antidotes.

"Not bad, actually. I'm lucky we didn't have an audience. That helps." The man in the cap we had just seen reappeared talking to another guy on the dance floor just a few feet away from us. It looked like a repeat of what we had seen earlier, I imagined he would bring him back to that private party in the corner again and this new recruit would soon find himself wooed. But the demon stepped back for a moment, shocked by something his target said. He responded, but I couldn't hear the words. Then he grabbed a fistful of the boy's t-shirt shaking him and yelling in his face: "Are you or aren't you?" He shook him. The boy looked terrified, his face panic-stricken. "*Je ne comprend pas, je ne comprend pas,*" he kept saying. "You're the second one tonight. I don't understand," said the demon. Finally he let go, shoving the boy. He pushed him once more and the boy darted away. Those surrounding him on the dance floor stopped to look, which was a mistake. The demon grabbed one of these spectators, shouting the same question into his face and pushing him into the crowd, nearly knocking over a swath of them. Then he grabbed a woman by the arm, yelling at her too, and then another. Lance and I backed up, careful not to draw attention. It was jarring to see a demon come so unhinged during a recruiting session. This was when they were traditionally at their most alluring and hypnotic. That was the whole idea; that was how they accomplished what they did. I could sense Lance feeling as I did: we wouldn't be the ones to escalate this. The music was so loud and ebullient, not the soundtrack this scene should have had. I glanced back to that nook and a few of his fellow demons watched now. He had another victim in his grasp and I heard that question that stopped us in our tracks: "Devil or angel? Devil or angel?" He shook him. Then he threw him back too, just as another demon appeared at his side to stop him, pushing him to the edge of the dance floor. The party raged on again, returning to normal around them. We followed, carefully. They spoke in harsh voices, I wanted to hear but even here in the shadows, it wasn't safe. "I've been turned down," I thought I heard the demon say. Lance pulled me back, near enough to still be heard.

"Stay off the radar," he said, lunging to kiss me. He wrapped me up in his arms and turned us around so he could watch them and we both could listen while appearing to be nothing more than another couple lost in each other, caught up in the wild emotion of this free-spirited, macabre setting.

They spoke in harsh voices: "What's gotten into you? This wasn't the plan," the calmer of the two said. "You're going to upset him. He wants this done in a certain way." The other barked back, not listening: "I've been turned down. Something is wrong here. They're *here*." Looking over Lance's shoulder, I scanned for Dante and saw him throwing that glitter-like powder into the air, dancing in the distance. I hoped he was far enough away from this. No sign of the others. I heard the man shouting now: "They're here. And they will die for it." He pushed his fellow demon, knocking him down, then stomped past us. The other one got back onto his feet and followed. Lance pulled his lips away from mine.

The demon charged forward into the dancing masses shouting over the music, his voice thunderous and chilling: "There are angels among us!" Some glanced over but it seemed the majority were content to chalk it up to just another mad, drunken outburst. Until he tried again.

"There. Are. ANGELS. Among. Us!" he repeated, in a fury now, from the center of the floor. He unleashed a feral roar, well above the raging music. Everyone collectively paused for a long second, as though registering this tonal shift from harmless to threatening. He swung his arm out, turning in a circle, sending a ray of fire sweeping the cavernous space. The music hushed and everyone scattered past us, screaming as they ducked into the labyrinthine offshoots, fleeing this roaring, fire-shooting creature. For a split second, a blink, I thought the demon's eyes set on us.

We ran.

Lance and I shot back the way we had come on lightning feet, toward the one place we were sure they wouldn't suspect: the well. The chaos provided all the camouflage we needed to sneak away, swerving from the pack headed back through the museum, and veering around a corner to that spot. With everyone escaping, at least it seemed all recruiting efforts had been suspended.

By the time we reached it, we had made enough twists and turns to shake off the last of the fleeing partygoers. In the distance we still heard the clomp of running feet and voices calling out the way to the exit—"I was sure he brought us this way," said one lost soul—but where we now stood it was deserted and dim, only a pair of weak bulbs lighting our way.

The well glowed, locked behind bars, its water gurgling an eerie aquamarine. We had no key, but it didn't matter. The bars were a thin metal. We pulled them apart easily, leaving a large enough gap to slip through, and pushed them closed behind us, not wanting to leave evidence of our breach.

We gazed down. "The last place they'll look for us is in the underworld," I said, quick and clipped. Soft, fast footsteps sounded in the distance, getting closer. We looked at each other, we both heard it. We spoke with a hushed urgency.

"It's got to lead there, right?" Lance whispered, watching the water, which seemed to bubble as though in a boil. "I thought wells were supposed to be still."

"They are."

"Well, that answers it then," he said lightly. "Are you—" he started, but I quieted him. I bent down just over the well and closed my eyes to listen more closely. Yes, I did hear it now. Voices. They were muffled through the water, but I heard them.

There was something, someone down there. I detected at least two pitches, two speech patterns and the way they were conducted through the water, I could almost make out words.

I weighed the possibilities. There had to be another way down—Lance had surely been brought up here a different way than this—but we had no time to find alternatives. We were being hunted.

This idea, on the surface, seemed to not compute: the water looked like it could potentially be searing. And then there was the more obvious concern: There shouldn't be anywhere to go but down and into more and more water, no destination. But it nagged at me, my gut telling me to listen: why could we hear those voices? I knew the answer. It didn't matter that it didn't make sense. Lance read my mind.

"I mean, theoretically, this could be hundreds of feet deep and shouldn't really lead anywhere," he said. "But the voices are clearly coming from here, so my guess is there's some kind of off-shoot down there or something we're not able to see from here. Look," he pointed now. "The water level is fairly low."

He was right. When I had seen the glow from the other side of the bars, I thought I was looking at the water itself. I lowered myself, even though there was no hope of dipping my fingertips in. I could feel the heat rising up, some of the spray from the bubbling water misting my hand. I sat up again, dangling my legs over the pit.

"Strategically speaking, we should probably go one at a time," I said. "Just in case…" I didn't finish the sentence, I didn't know how. The array of horrors that could await us was just too wide.

"That does sound logical," Lance said, crouching opposite me. "But I don't care. You're not going without me. And I don't feel like going back there without you either."

"All right then," I said, secretly relieved. "Catch you on the other side?" The footsteps were nearly upon us now, echoing.

He nodded. We watched each other, took deep breaths and plunged in together, pushing off easily as though we had been perched on the side of a pool on a summer day.

The warm water coated us, enveloping our bodies—so much warmer than a well should ever be, more like how I imagined a hot spring would be. Not hot enough to burn us, though likely hot enough to burn mortal skin. That shade of green was even more sickly and viscous from inside, the color of something foul and poisoned. As we drifted down it darkened to a forest green. It swallowed us slowly until it turned to an inky, opaque black and then whipped us down, yanking us like we were things being dislodged in a drainpipe. It sucked us down, the water equivalent of the wind tunnel. Then the unexpected: my feet were on dry land again. A wall of hot air caught us as we crashed against black rock.

21

There's Our Prize

We landed in a heap. Lance spit out first and then me, smacking against the rocky, slick ground. We could have been in just another part of the catacombs, with these craggy surfaces, except for the eerie blood-hued glow and the otherworldly heat. Though I was soaked—my clothes sticking to me, my wet hair flattened against my face and neck—the air felt capable of drying us in minutes, as though we had fallen into a kiln and our clothes might harden around our bodies. It sapped my strength. I felt it pushing against me as I struggled to stand. Lance had picked himself up, lending me a hand as I got onto my feet. His glasses were gone, of course, but he didn't need them—their primary purpose was hiding that scar beneath his eye. He always seemed to have spares tucked away, like extra props for a school play.

We gave each other a look that said, *That wasn't so bad.* Above us, like a skylight, was the bottom of the well, the water suspended as though being held by glass, except there was none. The heat here seemed to act as a force holding it in place. My feet began tingling now, and looking down I understood why: We had landed at the center of a pentagram, the symbol burned in a low flame on the ground. We leapt off of it and noticed five dark corridors spun out from it.

From one of them we heard voices and footsteps coming at us. We motioned toward one of the other corridors, hoping it wouldn't be the one they would be taking. We flattened ourselves against the hot, damp rock of the passageway and listened. It felt, physically and metaphorically, like the inside of a volcano about to erupt.

"It was a failure of epic proportions. He'll surely be shackled here now until the revolution," a male voice said, gleeful, in French-accented English. "So foolish."

"That's what you get for losing your temper," another man said, this one with a bitter undercurrent to his tone.

"Check on the prisoners but don't be late, you know how he hates that." I was beginning to understand why we could hear them above: the acoustics in this hollow cavern allowed voices to carry and amplify even at normal speaking volumes.

"He's getting a little power-hungry for my taste. He's as bad as Beckett now." Lance and I traded glances at the familiar name.

"When you kill someone of Lucian's stature then you will earn some perquisites too."

"There are plenty of us who have been around longer than either of those two, that should count for something."

"I've been here longer than you," the content man laughed.

"Yeah, but, it's a little different when you're a Duke," the disgruntled man said.

"I suppose it is," the Duke answered with a dry laugh. "But you know how this works. This is the agreement you made when you sold. You knew that your time would be up at some point. Raphaella went around the time you did, didn't she?"

"Just after me," he corrected.

"Fine. She's been a model citizen here, well-respected and she'll have a fine role in the revolution. You need to follow her lead."

"I just wish I could switch to a different unit. I can't stand working under him."

"Maybe you should join with Beckett's group and commiserate over your deep hatred for Kip."

"I'm praying they'll just destroy each other. And that we'll all get to watch."

"I'd say you're certain to be wasting your time praying," the Duke laughed. "But it's not a terrible bet that they could indeed kill each other when the battle begins."

They stepped into the glow of the landing and stopped for a moment and I now saw the malcontent: blond and golden still, but his aura tarnished since I had last seen him. It was Trevor, the man who had tried to keep me away from Lucian when I had ventured into the past. My brain fired up, making so many connections, I could barely stand still. I wanted to talk to Lance and sort through all we had heard. He looked at me and nodded. He understood.

"For now, it would behoove you to do your job. See to the prisoners, make haste to the meeting and be useful to Kip. You are in good standing, don't let that change."

"Easy for you to say, you and the Prince go back a few hundred years." We heard other voices in the distance, both men looked over their shoulders falling silent for a moment as another pair of demons exited one corridor. They all nodded as this pair passed through that central landing, then headed down another passage. When they were out of earshot, the Duke spoke again his voice hushed.

"With time comes wisdom," he smiled. "So listen to me and you'll do well—"

"I always have." Trevor bowed to the man.

"Maintain your allegiance to both Beckett and Kip, do not take sides and you'll be safe," the Duke said quietly. He spoke as though he were from another time even though he looked like he, too, could have been our age. He wore his dark hair slicked back and an all-black three-piece suit.

"Thank you, sire," Trevor said respectfully, bowing again.

"I expect to see you in the war room shortly."

"Yes, your grace." With a nod toward one another, they parted. Lance and I stood firm, still, barely even breathing. I saw them in slow motion as they turned toward their respective destinations. The Duke went in the corridor just opposite ours. Trevor turned facing us. We flattened against the dark curves of the tunnel, each of us holding onto our pendants in hopes of shadowing, but to no avail. He took several long paces in our direction, then shifted just a degree to the left, disappearing into the hallway beside ours. I could feel myself silently exhale, my body ease. I looked at Lance; we had a decision to make now.

"He's going to Drew," I whispered. "But the other one—" I didn't have to finish, he understood, reading the regret in my voice.

"I know…we have to go to Kip, don't we? Even though it doesn't feel right," he said, with guilty eyes. Neither of us wanted to leave her. We knew we may have only a small window and we couldn't be sure that she was in a place that would be accessible to us without someone like Trevor leading the way. My gut said to take the chance.

"We do, except—" I started but Lance touched my arm to quiet me. More voices: a trio of men appeared on the landing heading in the direction of the war room. We waited for them to pass and another several seconds to be sure they were far enough away. As we listened, their footsteps and voices grew more faint. From the direction they went we heard more voices, muffled but audible—*"Are we waiting for him or shall we begin?"*—as they were greeted. "Hear that?" I whispered. "The room isn't that far."

"Take the gamble we can find it on our own?" Lance asked. I nodded. That decided, we crept out from our hideaway and ducked down an identical corridor, that same red haze lighting it. We walked with soft, quick steps to catch up, until we reached a fork in the pathway. We saw an opening, what looked to be a window with no view, just a cutout in the rocky surface, jagged and raw as though it had been made by a dull knife in skin. I didn't breathe, just listened and heard the tap ahead, to the left. Yes. Those were his footsteps. Lance heard it too and pointed down the same path. We began walking again but as we passed that opening, I reached my hand in, almost not thinking, as one might to graze a patch of tall sunflowers in a garden. A rushing wind tried to grab me, sweep me up. Lance spun around at the wild whoosh of it. I retracted my arm.

"Portal?" he asked.

"Think so."

"Good find," he said.

We walked on and with just one more turn, we caught sight of Trevor, his pace leisurely, as though in no hurry to complete his task and be forced to go to Kip's meeting. We followed him with light footsteps, keeping our distance, the red haze fading into a deeper darkness as we pressed on. I held my pendant, nodding to Lance that we might as well try once more. I was completely dry now after our swim through the well and could feel some of my strength returning. Grasping the necklace, I focused again and felt a burst of energy within my cells, as though they were changing and allowing me to shadow this time. I checked my hands: they were no more than dark smudges. Yes, at last, it was working. I looked for Lance, and was pleased to not be able to locate him. I felt the air beside me and found his arm. His hand grabbed mine and gave it a quick squeeze before letting go. Just ahead, Trevor stopped outside what looked to be a steel door, inserting a key and opening it up. He left it ajar behind him and we slipped in.

Inside lay a tunnel, both sides lined with the kinds of cells we had seen dotting the catacombs. Except here, the bars of the cells weren't metal at all: they were made of fire. A hint of weakness set into my muscles and bones as soon as we reached the passage. This fire had the same mind-numbing powers as the one that had encapsulated Lance at Père-Lachaise. He grabbed my hand again for a moment and I understood: we couldn't afford to spend much time here. Those crackling flames produced the only light and even so it was difficult to see into the cells. They all looked to hold slumbering captives. It was as though we were visiting the circus at night while the animals slept in their cages.

One generous compartment, easily the size of our living room in Montmartre, housed scores of bodies, all thrown on top of one another, a few bearing some manner of gruesome lethal injury—puncture wounds, limbs and necks bent at odd angles—and blood, thick and hardened. But many others looked perfect, no sign of trauma whatsoever. And all of them, it seemed, were just waiting to be put to some sort of horrific use. He stopped again a few cells down from this one and knelt.

"And there's our prize. Hello there. You're looking just as dazed as we hoped," he stood up again. We hung back, looking over his shoulder into that cell: golden hair glowing orange in the light of the flames, Drew lay on her side. Her eyes open, she stared out but didn't seem to be seeing anything, nothing registered. It was just how Lance had looked at me when he was tied to that stake. I thought of the fire that night: the flames had bent to consume the wooden post when I kicked it down. Like bees swarming, if given something to devour, the flames were trained to surround it and destroy it. But this created other open pockets. Could I find my way back to that pentagram and to that tunnel where the meeting was taking place? Yes, I could. I could do it without Trevor. I pulled one of Dante's spikes from my pocket and leaned in toward Trevor, who was still talking to himself. With a sharp swipe, I jabbed it into the back of his arm. He spun around for a moment, clawing my hand with his burning, iron grip. I felt my skin sizzle. Lance stepped into focus. I could see him—we were close enough that the fire cut through our shadowing efforts. Lance rammed his fist into Trevor's jaw and I kicked him in the gut, sending him clear across the tunnel. He hit the rocky wall, landing on the ground, knocked out.

I ripped off the t-shirt I had on over my tank top and fed it to the fire guarding Drew's cell, as though it were a hungry beast. I swept it across the flames then wedged it in the corner of the gate. The fiery ribbons swerved, snapping up the shirt. Lance did the same, pulling off the long-sleeve flannel he had tied around his waist and tucking it beside mine, leaving him in just his t-shirt. It created an opening large enough to reach in. I climbed in, the flames singeing my back, and grabbed Drew's twig-like arm, tugging quick and sharp. Lance pulled her other arm and we dragged her lifeless body just as the flames roared back, having devoured their meager snacks.

Her eyes were still open but her legs were jelly and her voice a hollow whisper. She mouthed "Thank you" as Lance swept her up in his arms and we ran for the door. I could feel the wooziness setting in, liquefying my limbs, and I saw Lance stumble. I was behind him when it hit me that I had to go back. I ran to Trevor and checked his pockets: inside I found a pentagram-shaped key the size of a tube of lipstick. I grabbed it and followed Lance, tripping over my own feet desperate to get away from that fire.

As soon as we left that room, our strength returned to us. We stopped just before reaching the central pentagram near the well portal, catching our breath, letting the energy trickle back into our veins, the blood flowing with its full force again.

Drew lifted her head, "I'm good, thanks," she whispered, wiggling out of Lance's hold and putting her feet back on the ground. "I don't know what happened but you have no idea how good it is to see you guys."

"I'm afraid we're not leaving just yet," I said.

"We've gotta get to the war room, can you make it?" Lance asked.

"No problem," she said. "And I can do better than that: I think I may know a way in."

"Will this help?" I pulled out the key.

She smiled.

We traced the path back the way the Duke had gone, that red haze filling the space again. We tried to shadow but our powers hadn't fully returned yet. At the end of the hallway, the haze faded and we reached a black iron door perched open. Kip occupied the head of a long onyx table, the Duke stationed at the opposing end. A dozen men sat huddled around it, waiting, listening. A few seats had been left empty. The space, all black like a dark canvas, looked simple at first glance but studying it I could see its camouflaged ornamentation: it was all rock and black marble. Pentagrams had been engraved as a border along the walls, shining in the glow of the room. The ceiling had been painted with a scene all in shades of black and gray depicting the Prince—an army of Princes—set against a backdrop of Parisian landmarks, killing people, pulling limbs from bodies, crushing winged figures with his hands. We hung back outside the doorway against the wall. Obviously we couldn't just walk right in. But I had learned a bit about how they operated in my time battling them. These were creatures that were fond of escape routes and secret entrances, nothing was ever quite what it appeared to be with them.

"I'm not waiting for him. He's lucky I haven't requested his transfer yet," Kip said, arguing with someone. If they were waiting for Trevor, they were going to be waiting for a while. "Shut it," he ordered. "He'll just have to catch up—" We didn't hear another word, the iron door swung closed.

"There's got to be another way," I said. I studied the pentagram key, turning it over in my hand. It resembled the master keys to some of the hideaways at the Lex. I had hope.

"I was in that room when I arrived," Drew whispered. "There should be a balcony or something on one side. I remember some of them looking down on me, and I was afraid they were going to attack me. All of a sudden they were there when they hadn't been."

"There's gotta be another way in," Lance said. "Remember that bookcase in Aurelia's office?"

"Absolutely," I said, already walking along the wall of the door, my hand skimming its rough, rocky surface. I studied the key again, this time holding it out like a flashlight pointed toward the wall. I wandered several yards from that door when the key burned red, illuminating a matching pentagram engraved on the wall.

"Nice," Lance said. I slid the key into the marking and a slim wedge of the wall popped. Lance pulled it open to reveal a stony staircase no wider than a couple of feet. The voices were clearer now, the meeting in progress somewhere within these layers of rock. I led the way up, Lance pulling the door shut behind the three of us. The steps were so steep, each a few feet tall and running nearly straight up the narrow space, like a skinny elevator shaft. I leapt up, anxious, feeling the energy coursing now that we were close. That eerie haze reappeared in the distance and in a few more steps I reached it, poking my head up, trying to get my bearings.

Drew had been right: a thin walkway extended along the wall facing Kip's side of the table. It was tucked behind the border up near the ceiling and it was just a few feet high. We wouldn't be able to sit here; we would need to lie down to listen without being detected. I slithered along the slick black surface, keeping low and careful to be as silent as I could. I felt the others file in after me. When I reached the end of the perch I stopped, lay on my stomach—glad to be able to take a position that would not have me staring into the horrors of the painted ceiling—and listened, committing every word to memory.

22

An Unknown Evil is Better Than A Known Evil

Kip seemed to be answering a question posed by a voice I hadn't recognized.

"No. He won't. Martin—" Kip said it with the accent on the second syllable, Mar-TAN. "—has been, uh, removed from our unit."

"In light of today's events, he has been reassigned," the Duke said.

"Beckett's in for it now!" I knew that voice—Brody. I could hear Kip try to stifle his snickering by clearing his throat. I peeked up just a moment and saw Brody balancing on the back legs of his chair, as he always used to, then slunk my head down again.

"I urge you not to judge your fellow demon by his actions today," the Duke said. "He's extremely capable. Shall we move on?"

"Yes, indeed, thank you," Kip sounded as though he were trying to appear as formal as his counterpart, like someone who knows they've been promoted to a position they aren't entirely suited for. "I spoke with the Prince and the plans are shaping up to begin at the...*chateau*," he said it with a flourish.

"And then continue on to assigned points throughout the city. If all goes well, we oughtta be up with the Prince on—"

"So he really is going back?" another man interrupted.

"Was there ever any doubt?" the Duke answered so quickly, the question must have been directed toward him. "Obsessions die hard and he always wanted the chateau—and all that went with it—to be his, as impossible—"

"You mean, absurd," the other man corrected.

"*Impossible*, as it was at the time," said the Duke, diplomatic.

"He's been insatiable ever since he put Charlotte up to it," said another.

"Who's Charlotte?" Brody asked.

"These new recruits have no sense of history. Or of the exquisite torture of history," said one of the men who seemed to be a contemporary of the Duke.

"The history of torture, they could stand to brush up on as well," another chuckled.

"Indeed, that will certainly be put to good use," the Duke said. "Have you seen the plans? Drawing and quartering."

"No. Fantastic!"

"What's that?" asked a more familiar voice. I didn't dare to look again but thought it might be our fallen angel Jimmy.

"You'll see," the Duke said.

"Whoa, back up. What's the story?" Brody asked again, cutting through all the chatter. "Who's Charlotte?"

"Corday," said one in a pitying tone, as though embarrassed for Brody. I pictured a man shaking his head. "Surely you've heard of her."

"Is she here? Have I met her?" he asked, as if speaking of someone at a party.

"No, she wouldn't give her soul to him in the end. So she died, just like any other mere mortal, and her soul went with her."

Charlotte. A French Charlotte in a castle. Why did that ring a bell?

"They were in love," said another. "How can you not know this by now?" he added, disgusted. Kip remained silent, I wondered if it might be because he didn't know the details either.

"Well, love is a strong word," the Duke began, in a tone suitable for school children. "He was in the king's court, you're aware—Louis, the sixteenth—but he had fallen out of favor with him." My eyes bulged, I thought I had heard wrong. How was this possible? But no one in the room seemed surprised by this, the man simply carried on. "He was not content to be that close to power, he wanted it himself—as you can imagine if you know anything of our liege. But, of course, it was just not possible. He came to detest everyone but still maintained that winning facade of his. He managed to appear so charming, affable, and loyal that no one suspected he was effectively playing both sides against each other in the war." I searched my mental files now, sure that some answers lay tucked away from my studies: AP Euro, one of the classes I had had with Lance before we really knew each other. Charlotte Corday, the war, Louis XVI, the *chateau*—the Duke wasn't talking about just any war; it was the French Revolution. That *house* was the palace of Versailles.

"He put her up to it, to the murder, and then he ended up falling more in love with the chaos that followed." He breathed in deep, as though recalling the sweetness of his preferred drug as well. "Who could blame him?"

"He could have done just fine, he had the pedigree and peerage. He had his share of conquests—Marie Antoinette herself was even rumored to have had a short affair with him—" one of them piped up.

"We don't know that that's true," the Duke corrected. "What we do know is that through his family he had come to know a woman named Charlotte Corday, who may not have been a complete royalist but didn't believe Louis should have been killed, and who fell in love with our Prince."

"So, what?" Brody asked, bored.

"So," the man said, mocking him, spite in his voice. "After secretly aiding those who led the march on the chateau, which sent the royal family fleeing, our Prince then convinced Charlotte to murder one of the architects of the revolution, thus working the other side of the equation. Just to keep the strife going. Do you understand?" he asked flatly. I did. I understood. I wished I could talk to Lance now, or at least look at him, I was sure he was putting this together too. Charlotte Corday had killed a politician or journalist, what was his name? Jean-Paul….Marat, yes. He was a populist and radical, I think he had called for the murder of the royal family. I was foggy on the details but this one bit had stuck out in that way things do when they don't quite fit: how often, in those times, did you really hear of women murdering political figures?

"Whoa. That's freaking brilliant," Brody said.

"Indeed," said the Duke.

"So he wasn't on either side?" Brody went on.

"He was in favor of chaos and destruction, he fed on it, and continues to. As we all do, don't we," the Duke laughed and the table joined in. Just as quickly he snuffed it out. "So onward, now to the planning of more of it," he sounded annoyed. "Kip, please."

"Right, so, as I was saying…" I peeked again. He was flipping through pieces of black paper written with red ink—at least, I hoped it was ink. "So the Prince is deciding who will be with him on the Tower. I think it's gonna be us, so that'll be the prime battle location, not to mention a great view of what's happening everywhere else." I heard chairs shifting and poked my head up once more. A map of Paris was now projected on the table. "We'll have the more disposable demons—"

"I believe the word you're looking for is *expendable*," the Duke corrected.

"Right. We'll be sending them all throughout the city. Landmarks, subways, the river, we've got enough of 'em to generally flood the place. The greatest locations will be taken on a basis of who's most important."

"Seniority," the Duke said, studying the grand ring on his pinky finger before looking up at Kip again. I ducked.

"The goal will be to kill the angels, steal as many souls as possible, and kill the rest. We claim this city, gain that foothold and then move on from there."

"The angels will have their work cut out for them."

"But how is it to begin?" the Duke prompted. "Have you told them?"

"Oh! Right! Some of us will be at the chateau. The Prince is inviting a bunch of world leaders, business leaders, the most influential to Versailles."

"In perfect Metamorphosi fashion," the Duke explained. "He's planning an event to incorporate their adolescent offspring. In hopes of winning some of the most powerful souls all at once."

"Will they come?" It was Jimmy.

"Of course," Kip laughed.

"It will have all the markings of something not to be missed by a certain set," the Duke said. "In the meantime though, we need to continue adding to our forces, increasing our numbers. We need bodies as well. Despite Martin's failings, we did gain some tonight. The lowest caste will be bringing the bodies up on the appointed date to begin."

"Is that still prudent?" asked one of the old guard.

"It's what the Prince wants," the Duke said.

"We're launching this thing with a bang," Kip said, a nervous twinge to his voice, as though realizing that he didn't quite have control of this gathering. "We're setting the tone. We wanna say, 'Listen up, things are about to change.'"

"Well put," the Duke said.

"And the angels? We bring them to us?" asked another. There was no time to respond. A manic knocking rattled the door and before anyone could answer, it burst open.

Silence. And then, the Duke: "How kind of you to make time for us in your busy schedule, *Monsieur*."

I had to look: Trevor stood in the doorway, his face frozen, unblinking. He looked as though he had just awakened from a coma. He stared blankly at the table.

"They're here. Angels," he panted. "They were with the prisoners."

The whole table stood, barking questions.

"Did you capture them?"

"Where are they?"

"Who?"

"I couldn't see them that well. But I think it was her. The one the Prince is after. And the one we lost." Trevor's words gave me chills, hearing him refer to us this way.

"How did they get here?"

"Where is our angel?"

"She's gone. They did something to me," he put his hand to his head, leaning against the doorframe.

"You're worthless," Kip said. "They can't have gotten far."

"They must've gotten in through the catacombs. My guess is the portal in the tunnels near the Cimetière du Montparnasse, that's closest to where the festivities occurred."

"Then they'll be looking for a way out through there as well, let's go!" one said, looking to Kip as though for permission.

"Kip and I will inform the Prince," the Duke said, staying behind for a moment. "The rest of you are dismissed to go find them and report back. We'll reconvene shortly." The group took off en masse, whipping past Trevor. He dropped to his knees, as though this had been enough to exhaust him. He slumped onto the floor and they simply stepped over him.

If I had been breathing, I would have done so in relief: I was sure they wouldn't guess we had come in through the well.

Kip looked dejected.

"These things happen," the Duke said.

"They don't respect me."

"They will learn…" he said as they left the room together. He continued soothing Kip until they were out of earshot. We waited many long minutes before we crept down from our perch. As Trevor lay, still out cold, we ran back down those steps.

"There was a portal along that tunnel, just past where you found me," Drew said. "That's where they're going." We could hear many footsteps, like hooves, in the distance and voices barking orders.

"We saw the one in the fork that we passed before we got to you," I said.

"I don't know that one, I only know the one they were talking about that goes to that cemetery. It's one of the routes they take to bring down some of the bodies. I came through that one. But maybe you saw the one that links to Père-Lachaise or something? I actually don't really care where it goes as long as it's out of here."

"Yeah. I've had enough of this place too," Lance said.

"Agreed. Let's do it. In this case, an unknown evil is better than a known evil," I said as we ran.

We retraced our steps back to the central pentagram and then on toward that place where the path had split. Just as we reached it, we heard a pair of demons careening around the corner in the distance. We threw ourselves into that portal and it swept us in its spinning fury.

It spit us out, dizzy and drained, slamming our bodies against a marble checkerboard floor in a darkened entrance-way with vaulted ceilings far above us. I turned my head and looked straight down the nave of a place I recognized from pictures: Notre Dame Cathedral. I couldn't quite move yet, every inch of my body ached.

"Of course," Lance said as soon as his eyes opened, his voice a low groan. He faced the grand west side door. His fingertips ran over the grooves of its ornate design. "The guy who designed this made a deal with the devil," he said, as though to himself. "To do this."

"What? Who?" I croaked, rolling onto my side to pull myself up. An organ piped in the background nearly drowning us out. "That sounds familiar, actually. He had no inspiration, right?" I said, recalling a bit of dark history I had read.

"Where are we?" Drew asked. Then she turned her head to face me and saw the full view of the cathedral's interior. "Ohhhh."

"Yeah, so when the door went up, it didn't open at first."

"So they've got a stake in this place," Drew said, struggling to get up.

"Exactly. It makes sense they'll want to take it back."

We pulled open the mammoth doors—not something the average tourist might be able to do, but thankfully not a problem for us. The morning sun streamed in and I had never been so happy to see it. We had gotten lucky. Tremendously lucky.

We let ourselves out, passing a group of sightseers with their guidebooks open, murmuring as we exited.

"I thought it didn't open until 8, how did *they* get in?" a sixty-something woman in a large-brimmed hat asked her husband in an accusatory tone.

"I don't know, that's what the guide says, dear," he sighed, pointing. "See? Eight."

23

Just One More Thing
I Have To Do

Connor had been waiting in the field for us when we arrived. He made it seem as though it were a coincidence and he had just been walking to the other end of the complex. But Dante said he had been worried—they all had—and that Connor had been out there hourly, wandering as though lost. Connor's face had fallen when Dante told them how we had all been separated in the catacombs. He had asked Dante the same questions again and again and then he had finally dismissed the group and instructed those in the Illumination Chamber to keep careful watch, even dispatching a pair of angels to patrol the streets near the catacombs. Dante and Max had insisted on going back to search too. They had fled the party, following a group up through another manhole not far from the Montparnasse Cemetery, while Emma, River and Tom had escaped with Gavin and his crew up through the museum exit. News reports in Paris spoke of debris left behind after a nighttime gathering and signs of a fire. The museum would be closed for repairs. There were missing persons reports, too.

We told Connor all we had learned at the meeting and he listened with a stern expression on his face. From his look I expected him to find fault somewhere in our actions. But when he commended us for the choices we made and for managing both to gain the information we had and to rescue Drew, I decided he must just be inwardly wrestling with something that he wouldn't share. He said the Administration would be appreciative of our work and, as usual, he added depth to what we told him, and helped make sense of it for us.

"We don't know why people do the things they do. We don't know why greed and thirst for power bloom in some like a cancer until it becomes them, defines them, and destroys them," he had said thoughtfully, transfixed. "We do know that it's taken hundreds of years for the Prince to build his army. He has been training demons more powerful than any we have known, and he will be fighting too. But remember, he's weakened. And he's never tried to mount anything on this scale. The world of angels is one of turnover and regeneration. He never considered our exis- tence such a tremendous threat, and had done well extinguishing some of us through the years. Until now. Good work, guys." He stood up, as though in respect, as he dismissed us from his office.

Lance held the door for me but before ducking out, I had one more bit of business. It had been nagging at me, at the back of my mind through all of these recent challenges. "I've just got one more thing I have to do. But I'll be back soon, not a big deal," I said in a tone that said I wasn't asking for permission.

He understood. "You know, even with the breach, you've earned your wings from your efforts with Lucian," he said, sur- prising me.

"Thanks. But I wouldn't feel right turning my back on some- one out there looking for some help, you know?"

"Of course. Well, you know the rules: send word when you go and we'll start the clock and keep an eye out for you. Pick up the materials you'll need from Dante's lab, if the facilitator has anything for you it'll be there too. Get a portal assignment. And watch it, OK? We need all of you guys."

Lance and I filed out but Connor called Drew back. As I turned to pull the door shut behind us, I caught a glimpse of Connor leaning in to kiss her forehead.

━━◈━━

Preparations made, I wasted no time in going. "You're all that's keeping the rest of us from getting our wings so, for purely selfish reasons, make this fast, OK?" Lance said, walking me to the portal as though he were dropping me off after a date. I could tell from the tension in his voice and the way he looked at his feet, and pushed those glasses up on his nose, that he was trying to mask his concern.

"Got it," I smiled. "I promise not to hold things up too much. At least it's in our 'hood." I shrugged.

"Should I worry you're going to run away and become a can-can dancer?"

"Yes, that's a definite danger," I laughed. "I'll be the next La Goulue, you know, kicking off people's hats and guzzling all their Champagne."

"Well, that worked out well for her. Toulouse-Lautrec certainly appreciated it." This was pure us, calming nerves with our trivia one-upmanship. I loved this about us.

"Even so, if I become part of the show at the Moulin Rouge then you'll know something has gone very wrong."

"We'll watch out for that." With that and a kiss, he sent me on my way.

━━◈━━

When I landed in that familiar spot in Père-Lachaise, night had fallen, and the air was warm and sweet. I made my way to the metro and back to our neighborhood in the village of

Montmartre. It was beginning to feel like a place I knew, a home away from home, but then I reminded myself that I was entirely alone this time. There would be no one waiting at our apartment on Rue des Martyrs. No group to set out to our favorite bustling café with, to face our chairs toward the street and watch the evening pass as we spoke in code about the challenges that lay ahead. Everyone was tucked away at the other end of that portal above, so far from here.

I walked to the famous windmill, sneaking a glance at my phone, combing through my target's file as I dodged couples strolling the sidewalks. Her name was Léa. Church bells chimed the hour in the distance. The timing ought to be just right. She should be taking the stage.

A few blocks away, I ducked into one of the markets lining the main thoroughfare just as it was closing up. Bouquets of vibrant red and pink blooms blossomed from the front window. I bought a dozen roses and a small card. I scribbled a note.

When I turned the corner, the red windmill's golden lights glittered in the sky. A familiar bicycle, hers from that first day, sat chained to a lamppost out front. I arrived as the show was in progress, jaunty music drifted out into the lobby, signaling a party in full swing behind the theater doors. I flashed the ticket I had found among the items gathered by Dante and the facilitators and slipped inside. It felt like stepping into a circus. Music swirled, sweeping me up as I found my way to one of the red-tableclothed cabaret tables. A delicate lamp cast a dim rosy glow from its matching shade. On stage, a riot of colorful plumes paraded by on the headdresses of barely clothed dancers. Feathers burst like fireworks atop their heads as they pranced, danced, and kicked with glee in little more than sparkly heels and sparkly unmentionables. Their strong, slim legs cut through the air like long, golden scissors. I had never seen anything like this, beauty flaunted so outrageously. I had never been to Las Vegas, but it seemed that this production would have been just as at home there, so over the top in its spectacle. If Dante were here he would surely have said that I could learn something from them.

A tank of water rolled out onto the stage, a handful of plump, meaty snakes slithering inside, large enough and long enough that they looked like wiggling tree branches even from this far away. A dancer emerged from the wings, preening in her uniform, a crystal-and-sequin swimsuit barely covering her. She circled the tank like a predator then launched herself, diving in. Her body kicked, mermaid-like as she swam among the snakes, weaving through them in time to the music, tangling with them, wearing them as though they were as harmless as feather boas, all the while flashing a blinding smile, having the time of her life. She finished her routine by shooting up from the water, perching on the side of the tank in a one-armed handstand, snakes woven around her arms, neck and torso in a way that looked like they should have killed her. But she grinned winningly and the crowd rose to their feet in applause. I jumped up too, but for a different reason. As I focused on her, balanced there, her shapely figure transformed into a beastly one. Her decaying soul on full display only to me. She was one of them. The audience cheered, hoisting Champagne glasses filled from the bottles chilling on their tables.

No sooner had the aquarium been carted off—that creature still posed atop it—than she returned. This time she was dry, makeup perfect, and leading nearly two dozen girls all wearing red, white and blue ruffled skirts. I recognized the music. Of course. This is what they had all come to see. The snake woman—the demon among them—took a place at the center of the group and they lifted their skirts to reveal sequined matching bloomers. They began their famous kicks: stretching so high and free it seemed their endless legs weren't even attached to their bodies, as though they might just fling a limb clear above their shoulders and into the air. The trademark pep of the can-can music picked up and the kicks sped along with its tempo, the women's skirts whipping so fast from side to side, fanning up and down you could almost hear them snap like they were part of the percussion section.

One of the girls broke out now and I sat up in my seat to watch; this was the one I had come to see. I might not have noticed her before this moment—if her image hadn't have been shifting back and forth in that pulsing way I was getting used to, toggling between someone beautiful and something horrific. The kick line, like a graceful, overgrown centipede, moved back to give her some space. Even the snake charmer stepped aside. Léa, threw herself, high-heels and all, tumbling across the stage, turning back-handsprings so fast in her full skirt she looked like a spinning wheel. She stopped for a moment in the center of the stage to kick for a few beats, then flung herself down the middle of the stage in another series of quick flips. Just a few steps from the edge, she pushed off, propelling herself through the air in a final backward somersault toward the audience. The trick gave me chills, not for its athletic prowess but for what might be behind it: the demonic force seemed already at work. Was I too late? Time was so crucial to these soul captures. It took only a blink of an eye to become trapped by the under-world, only a breath to lose the chance to change someone's course. She landed on the table directly in front of the stage. As she did, she stumbled just a moment, her right foot turning out, perhaps twisting that ankle. But she caught herself, never once losing that smile, her arms in the air, triumphant. I smiled too now: in that misstep, there was hope. That was human. The dancers all struck this pose. I noticed that the snake charmer now twirled upside down above the stage, grasping what looked to be a long silk scarf suspended from the ceiling. The music crescendoed to its booming finish and the lights went dark. The audience rose to their feet again, applauding as the lights came back up and the dancers took their bows.

I didn't wait for the curtain call. Instead, I slipped out of the theater, pulling a headset from my bag and adjusting it, playing the part of the stagehand—like she had once been, according to my file. I had a few other accoutrements inside, disguises if necessary, but I left them there, my gut telling me to take the chance. I found my way back to the locked, unmarked door into the backstage area. With one sharp smack against the door, I got it open and crept through, flowers in hand.

I was swept instantly into the oncoming traffic of the long-limbed girls and their tall and handsome men surging off stage in their costumes, beaming and bubbling at another fine per-formance. Other headset-outfitted staff weaved around them, speaking into the microphone pieces. There was too much com-motion, there were too many bodies, to pay me any mind, so I followed the pack, letting them lead the way to their dressing rooms. We passed mirror-lined spaces with long, shared vanity tables and rooms housing racks full of grand costumes, some even hanging from the ceiling. Many of the dancers peeled off. I trailed behind those remaining: the snake charmer, Léa, a small orbit of the most beautiful men and women of the troupe, and another tall and lean young man, who looked like he could have been a dancer but instead wore crisp black pants, a black t-shirt and a tailored blazer. He had kissed many of the girls as they rushed off stage and now he transformed before my eyes turning into a demon. The group flocked to a door with a star marked "Dominique," all disappearing inside except for Léa. She said something in French, sweetly, most likely along the lines of, "I'll be right there," then she let herself into the room next door with her name scribbled on a piece of paper, as though the room had been a recent prize.

I waited for both doors to close again and then I rapped on Léa's. I practiced my French in my head until she called out for me to enter. As I did, I secretly locked the door behind me. She sat before a mirror, unpinning her dark hair. She looked even younger here than she had on the stage. Under all the makeup and the perfectly coiled hair wound back in a bun, she was still that pretty girl I had seen on the bike. She looked at me in the mirror, expectant.

"*Bonsoir, Mademoiselle.* These arrived for you," I said in French, my accent not so bad, surprisingly. I handed her the flowers. "Lovely performance tonight, you're very talented." She looked at me with a questioning smile as she took the flowers, digging into the blooms with delicate fingers to pull out the card.

"*Merci,*" she said, opening the envelope. I had thought a lot over these past few days about how I was going to do this, whether I should say anything or just do what needed to be done and trust that if she really was repentant and I was skilled enough, all would go smoothly and quietly. All the angels had different methods, and we were given carte blanche to carry out our missions however we deemed necessary. It had all sounded a certain way in my head; it had made sense. But now standing in this room, I was beginning to feel like some sort of hit man. What I had to do was, on the surface, a menacing sort of action. I *was* an assassin, but I would be killing a part of her that she wanted extinguished to preserve the human part of her. When Lance had done this in the catacombs, it had been amid such chaos: a party roaring, people getting jostled, darkness all around, so many distractions. But here with the bright white lightbulbs framing the mirror and our reflections staring back at us, there was nowhere to hide. *Don't overthink*, I had once told myself in a message on my phone. *Trust your instincts.* I reached into my pocket for Dante's antidote-laden spear. It was maroon, and looked like some sort of spiked root the length of a number two pencil. As she read the note, I stood at the ready. I wanted her to read it first. It said, in French:

"Dearest Léa, You will get there on your own and it will be sweeter. Trust in yourself, give yourself time, and you will reach your dreams. You do not need them or anything they have promised you, you are right to want to walk away from them. Watching always, Your Guardian Angel."

She glanced up now, with angry eyes.

"Who are these from?" she asked, in English, as though wanting to be sure nothing was lost in translation.

"Someone who understands and who cares," I said. I was going to go on but she looked at herself in the mirror, studying herself like it was someone else sitting across from her. She wiped at her eyes preemptively, as though warning them not to tear.

"I'm going to be the snake girl," she said still in English, her accent thick. She looked at herself in the mirror, in a trance. "I've already been practicing. And I can almost do it. They said Dominique is going to be leaving soon. It's a secret." I knew what this meant: when the agreement is made, the wishes granted, it was only for a short span of time and then the person who had pledged their soul to the Prince in exchange for those wishes would be taken to the underworld. "And then I'll get to take over her role. They said that I would be able to do things even she can't. They just needed something from me in return." Her voice was leaden. "And now you bring me this," she shook the card, her eyes spearing mine in the mirror. "Is this some kind of joke?" Her image during this exchange had remained steady, flickering only once or twice.

"It's not a joke. You don't need them," I said gently, gauging whether she would believe me or just kick me out of the dressing room. "You can do this on your own. I know that you were in the chorus before this. You worked your way up from a stagehand by yourself. You can go the rest of the way on your own too. It seems like a harder path now, but it's so much better than taking this shortcut."

"Before this, when I was offered….the role," she shook her head at this euphemism for the soul agreement. "I was stopped one day on the street by a girl warning me about something dangerous and evil coming for me. I had thought she was just a beggar or someone trying to steal something, you know this happens. But she didn't seem harmful and I kept thinking about her. And wondering if I had made a mistake." She looked at my reflection now. "She looked like you."

A knock rattled the door. "Léa! We're going, c'mon!" came the man's bright voice, in French. It was the director I'd seen. The door shook, he was trying to open it.

I was about to lose my window of opportunity. "It *was* me," I said, making sure to keep her eyes focused on me as I readied that spear. "And you're getting a second chance."

I plunged the spear into the fleshiest part of her back I could find. And at once I understood the mechanics of this process: It felt as though something had grabbed the spear from inside, wanting to wrestle me for control of her. Her image transformed into that horrific creature, her eyes fiery. She unleashed a scream. The door shook again. "Léa?!" the man called.

I pulled to defeat this thing, this diseased part of her, closing my eyes to focus on splitting her soul and snuffing the evil one out. The spear pulled away from my hands now, and I opened my eyes for a flash to see it liquefying and being absorbed into her skin, healing that puncture wound. She was frozen still in the form of a creature of the underworld, the portrait of a rotting soul. I closed my eyes again, holding my hands out toward her and I immediately felt myself lifting her even though I wasn't touching her. I felt that evil part of her rising out. If I opened my eyes now, I was sure I would see a light beam connecting to her body floating in the air.

I doubled over, the exertion wiping me out for a moment. She fell to the ground, sweating, her makeup running, but she was breathing and her image was steady now. I pulled that small strip of paper from my pocket and held it against the inside of her wrist. It dissolved into her skin, leaving no visible mark, but I knew what would appear if the demons looked. "You'll be OK. You'll be recovering for a few days. You'll return and continue practicing and you will be able to do all you could before, and your soul will be with you. Be strong with them, but you have your wings and should be safe."

She nodded. The door rattled again, and I ran for the window, leaping out into the warm summer night just as the door to her room opened. As I scaled the side of the building up to the roof, I heard people rushing to her aid. They would just assume she had collapsed from exhaustion, had some kind of seizure. But she would begin to pull away from them, and when the demons looked at her wrist they would see the mark glowing: angel wings only they could see.

I pulled myself onto the lit panels of the windmill, pushed off from one and propelled myself onto a nearby rooftop, and another and another, staying in the shadows of the darkest streets, making my way back to Père-Lachaise and the portal, my test completed.

PART THREE

24

Your Initiation is Complete

We had been to a number of rituals in our short time as angels-in-training, all of a dark variety, and none intended for us. We had crashed induction ceremonies for freshly recruited demons in Chicago. We had witnessed the gruesome transformation rites for an angel who had fallen to the underworld in New Orleans. We had managed to ambush the sacrifice at Père-Lachaise. But we weren't accustomed to being the center of attention at one of these affairs, and we certainly didn't know how to behave at a gathering that was actually meant to be joyous. I had returned from my test, walking up through that warm, breezy field feeling at peace, as if my entire being understood what had been accomplished and my body was ready for new skin. I had gone straight to Connor's office and been greeted with a proud handshake, and been informed that the Initiation would take place that day. This was what we all had been working toward since our first challenge. What I had been working toward since that first day at the Lexington Hotel.

Now, as we lined up prepared to begin the ceremony, I felt the way I had always expected I would have felt at graduation. I registered an internal shift, a moving on to a new phase in my life. The very word—initiation—wrapped its arms and wings around me, as though ushering me into this new chapter, a new beginning. I had gained admittance to the angel realm and all that went with it. I was included, I was part of something and embarking on this with these seven friends, who had all already risked their lives for me as I had for them. I felt welcomed even if I still had much to learn and to understand, and so much work still to do.

"So, I think angels need to have more parties, am I right?" Dante said, slapping Max on the arm, as we all stood outside the door to a room unfamiliar to us, awaiting the cue to enter. This part, this waiting *did* feel like graduation. Except this time, Lance stood beside me.

"Definitely," Lance said. "When was the last time we were at a party?"

"Well, actually—" I was about to say the catacombs, Mardi Gras, prom at the Lex.

"I mean, without demons in attendance," he cut me off, pulling me in, his arms around my waist. I felt the back of his shirt with its two slits cut at the shoulder blades. We had all been instructed to wear something that exposed the scars on our backs or to cut whatever we chose to wear. Dante had pretended to be irked as we got ready, joking, "This is really going to mess with my wardrobe." But we were all grateful to have made it this far. I looked at him now, talking to Max, smiling. Lance grabbed my hand, giving it a squeeze and kissing me. Connor opened the doors and we stepped in. The room was all gold and silver, sparkling. One entire wall made of windows looking out onto the field. A walkway floated from the doorway leading to a platform, which also floated. Below, all of our fellow angels had gathered, summoned not just from their work stations, but from cities across the planet. For us. They each had their own glowing halos above their heads. But most shocking of all: on their backs they wore the grandest, most brilliant white wings, as perfect as if chiseled from marble. They looked like they were seated, but they were actually floating, their legs folded and their wings making the smallest movements keeping them all aloft, like treading water, except that it seemed to require no effort for them. Their collective fanning generated the gentlest of breezes. They wore serene expressions and soft welcoming smiles as they gazed up at us. Even after all I had seen these past two years, to look out onto a sea of beautiful winged creatures tested my mind's ability to process its environment.

"Wow, so everyone got the memo on wearing the wings," I whispered. Dante smiled.

"Anyone else kind of feeling like their mind is blown?" Tom asked. Emma raised her hand.

"Everyone is so frigging happy here all the time," River said.

"I wonder what kind of wind power they can generate with those," Lance said, as though to himself, awed.

"I'm pretty glad I lived to see this. Thanks guys," Drew said, looking out. "I mean, not to be heavy or anything, but you know." Emma shook Drew's arm lovingly.

Henry motioned for everyone in the audience to stand. They unfolded their legs, their feet at once touching the ground soundlessly and then, just as smoothly each angel raised up several feet in the air and bowed to him.

"We have many glorious days doing what we do: when we guide someone through a particularly dark wood; when we save a soul; when we pull someone back from the brink of the underworld. And today is one of those days. Today I give you a new class of angels. These are the strongest we have ever known and I hope each of you takes great pride in this group because, as you are well aware, each of you helped bring them here. Kindly stand if you helped identify the souls that became these angels..." A group of angels stood and rose upward. "And if you helped locate where they fell to earth...." More began to float. "And if you helped identify the guides to assist them in their new homes." Still more joined them. I thought of Mariette in New Orleans. "And if you helped Connor in his efforts to train them." A final group stood. Everyone was now on his or her feet. Henry turned to face us. "In case any of you ever feel alone…" he said smiling. "Don't." He laughed. "We are all invested in you."

We looked out at them. Without thinking, just acting on a deep need to offer some sign of appreciation, I bowed my head, nodding once at them all with my hand to my heart, took to one knee, then stood up again. The others on the platform with me followed my lead and Henry smiled at the gesture. With warm eyes, looking touched, he nodded back. "And we have brought you here now with great hope for the help you can give us, to make us better at what we do. We have already seen such remarkable gains since you've joined us. With your superior powers, we have made our first successful journeys through time. This is something that could revolutionize what we do, allow those whom we couldn't reach in time to have the second chance they deserve.

"We will need you now more than ever. Dark days are upon us, bright ones," he continued gravely, looking out at the group, then turned to us. My mind shot to what I had seen on my travels: staring into my own dying eyes, my broken wings behind me. *This is not what I would like to be thinking about right now*, I scolded myself. This is why they looked so proud—we were part of them; they had helped bring us here. They had given us these abilities and now they hoped we would lead them all against what lay ahead. I hoped we wouldn't let them down.

"As you know, a revolution is coming. The underworld has waited hundreds of years to try to stake its claim to the world above them—to destroy us, to impose their destruction and chaos on the mortal realm. The Prince has been in power a great, great long while and feels that he can not be defeated, and understandably so. In the coming weeks, we will face grave challenges, but we can rise above. Trust that we can rise above. We have all made sacrifices to be here. We have left loved ones behind. We have changed the course of our own lives, putting aside our wants and needs to guide others. It is painful at times, but noble always. We have come to accept the battles of life or death that are our daily lives. In some cases, we have given our lives in our ongoing quest to aid others. As always our souls grieve for those we have lost. We pray to not lose any more. You are our future and are capable of greatness." He bowed his head to us.

"So let's grant some wings," he smiled. "Today is a day for joy. That's an official edict." The room laughed, a lightness restored to the air.

The rest happened silently. He waved us over one by one. We each faced the gathered angels and bowed as he floated above us. He placed his hands on our backs, those spots on our shoulder blades where we each had three slashes, three scars, as though giving the wings permission. With that, they shot out like switchblades. There is, of course, no way to prepare for something like this: I had never had the sense of anything lurking beneath those scars. Sure, they had burned to signal danger—the presence of demons—but only at this very moment did it feel as if something had been retracted beneath there. For just that second, it was the briefest sensation of an arm finding its way through the sleeve of a sweater, and then there they were. Like Emma and Drew, I wore a sundress with thin straps, no need to make room for the wings and so they pushed out into the air, unfettered, as easily as if they were extensions of my shoulder blades. I looked back and my eyes struggled to make sense of what they saw: blinding white wings fanned around me, as tall as I was. It was like a huge bird was sitting just over my shoulder. How could this be me? "Go on, give 'em a try," the man whispered. Instead of consciously debating how to isolate what muscles might control these new appendages, I just instinctively knew how to do it. My shoulder blades and back fluttered, making tiny movements I hadn't realized they knew how to do, generating a sweeping motion.

When it was Lance's turn next, I saw him go through the same thought process—awe at the sensation of having something so grand now part of us, then confusion and finally surprise as he figured out how to wield them. Once we had all received our wings, we stood on that platform gazing out. "Your initiation is now complete. Congratulations," Henry said to us then looked out to the group. "I give you your new angels." At once the formality slipped away. They all rose up, nearly as high as the platform and cheered, their wings fluttering joyously. Music filled the air. We all smiled at each other, taking deep breaths, administering hugs.

"You wear those well," I said to Lance.

"You, too," he said, sweeping me up and planting a kiss on my lips.

The entire group now pushed forward to greet us. One by one, we met each of them, many stopping to tell us the role they had played in our evolution.

<hr />

When we had greeted every last one of them and they had all returned to their work, business resuming once more and the Administration filtering out, Connor stayed behind with us. He gestured for us to have a seat on that floating platform. We did, gently, frequently looking over our shoulders to be sure our wings were in place. I wasn't entirely confident about how to retract them yet, and no one else had attempted it either.

"The fun is over, right?" Dante asked, his legs dangling over the edge of the platform.

Connor laughed. "Well, I wouldn't say that but…" he sighed, as though giving up even trying to make a joke. "Yeah, kinda. I just mean that now that you're initiated, you have work. First, of course, you have to get accustomed to these things."

"There's no, like, user's manual?" Dante said.

"Not quite. You can, of course, practice here, any time you like. I expect to see you out in the field there and in the gym. But I also know that you've been away longer than you might have planned and unlike the rest of us up here, who have our covers worked out and don't have anyone waiting up for us, so to speak, you still have to tend to life back at home." He paced in front of us, in full drill sergeant mode now, except that he hovered above the ground, walking on air even though his wings were no longer out. I wanted to know how he was doing this. "Here's what I need you to do immediately: establish a temporary cover with your loved ones that will allow you to be away for periods of time because we're going to need you here a lot. Now it may take some time. Do what you need to do, we understand. But know that at the first sign of demon activity, we're calling you back."

"What do you—" River started, but Connor just kept going, ignoring her.

"While you're home, you can still practice flying. In fact, you need to. Just be sure to work only at night and in deserted areas. We'll go over the mechanics of how this works but it's largely mind-controlled unless you're really going for speed, in which case—" I was still stuck on the very first directive about going home, when Emma interrupted, raising her hand.

"Wait, wait," she called out, not intending to be ignored. "This might sound stupid, but does that mean we can't, like, tell our parents what's going on?"

"What are we supposed to do about college?" Max asked.

"How long until we come back here, and how much time will we spend there?" Tom asked.

"We're not going back," I said, a revelation, everything setting in. "I mean, not in any real sort of way." Connor looked at me with the tense, regretful eyes of someone who doesn't want to tell you that you've lost a loved one.

"Listen, guys," he put his hands up to silence us. "You have to let me lay it all out. You always did want to get ahead of me, didn't you?" He shook his head in a loving way. "In case you haven't noticed, your lives have changed," he said slowly, with the proper reverence. "We've got a revolution to prepare for and you each have work you'll be doing here. Those things on your backs? They mean you're important and you're needed, but you're needed here. You don't belong…there… anymore," he said this last part gently. "For all sorts of reasons. You are physically so strong now that you'll actually have to put effort into *not* using your full force, in appearing normal when you're there. That will drive you crazy, trust me. It drives me nuts when I'm there and I'm not even as strong as you all. Another thing: you aren't going to age. And at some point people are going to start to notice. I could go on. But I'd rather talk about the solutions."

I studied my hands, picking at my fingers nervously as my mind raced to wrap itself around these new truths. I was used to not fitting in, but this was an entirely different scale.

"What many of us do is we consent to let the Facilitators concoct something to account for our disappearance during the next Metamorphosi Day—because as you've learned, there is always some sort of accident or 'natural disaster,'" he said it as though those words had quotation marks around them, "that accompanies the events of those days."

It was as if each new statement was received like a punch to the gut. Deep down, I suspected all of this, of course I did.

But to have it spelled out so rigidly. I hadn't expected such a swift severing of our old lives from our new ones.

"What if we need to slip away a little more gradually from our lives?" I asked. I couldn't bear to think of Joan having to face something like this.

"Go home, Haven. Take a deep breath, all of you. Learn to fly, and I need to see you back here for a check-in in two weeks. Check your phones. If I need you sooner, I'll let you know." He clapped his hands twice, as though punctuating a shift in our discussion. "Now on your feet. We're gonna go through the basics, we'll hit the field, and then you all are going home."

25

Please Fasten Your Seatbelts

We could have taken a portal to the greater Chicago area, of course, but we couldn't quite come up with a plausible way to explain arriving home on our own with no luggage after several weeks in Europe. So instead, we returned to Paris, to our Montmartre flat, to pack what was there and then catch an old-fashioned flight back home, booked by our resident facilitator, Drew. We found three cars idling outside O'Hare Airport containing three very anxious mothers. Lance's hadn't seen him since December when we had left for New Orleans—he would be lucky if she ever let him leave home again. It had been among our greatest accomplishments that the emails we had sent on his behalf before rescuing him hadn't set off her radar for trouble.

Joan had the most attuned Doppler for danger though, and was the toughest of the three, which is why I came prepared. I was armed with anecdotes of our supposed travels and with souvenirs too. The trip back to Paris had at least given me a chance to do the shopping I hadn't had time for between intelligence-gathering trips to the underworld, demon-hunting missions and initiation ceremonies.

On the way home I regaled her with tales of what little we had actually seen of Paris and fictitious adventures from

London, Scotland and Prague. Pulling an all-nighter, I had printed out some online guides before we left and used the flight to study. I waited until we got home to present her with her gifts, just as she was getting that look and starting down an unfortunate path:

"So then Lance flew straight to Europe? He couldn't bother to come home and see his mother first?" She said it innocently enough, chopping vegetables for a salad as a homemade lasagna warmed in the oven, the cozy scent filling the room. I stopped in the middle of setting the table.

"I have something for you!" I said in an overly peppy tone, ignoring her as I ducked into the living room to rifle through my bag.

"And how is that Lex doing? He was so lovely," she called out to me. I located the three small shopping bags.

"*Les cadeaux!*" I said, holding them out.

She stopped chopping. "For me?" she asked, her face lighting up.

"*Mais bien sûr!* Of course, go ahead," I shook them at her. She wiped her hands on her ruffled "Kiss the Cook" apron. I took her place, slicing carrots and tomatoes as she sat down at the table.

"Well, you really shouldn't have…but merci beaucoup!" She opened them each, squealing as she dug through tissue paper to find the treasures: a scarf like the one Dante had gotten for me, which she wound around her neck immediately ("Oooh la-la!" she gushed), a tin of hot chocolate from that tearoom we visited the first day, and two boxes of puffy, delicate macarons in an array of pastels. "One for you and one for the ladies at the hospital," I said.

"Oh, don't you just think of everything? Thank you, sweetie!" she said, unwrapping one of the boxes to sample a treat. "I can't wait for you to come in and tell them everything, they've been asking all about your trip and…" She went on and I breathed a quiet sigh of relief as our conversation shifted back into more neutral territory.

Even though we weren't jet-lagged, the three of us waited a night before beginning what we called our flight training. I gave up on sleeping. Connor hadn't been kidding about needing to dumb down our powers here. I noticed it the moment I stepped out of the car when we arrived home. I swung the door shut, using what felt like no force at all, and it sounded as though I had slammed it. The front of the parked car moved nearly a foot, leaving it at an odd angle on our driveway. Joan, already at the front door, had turned around at the jarring BANG: "Haven!" she said, it was the tone she used on the rare occasions when I slammed doors on purpose, which only happened when I was angry. She looked at me confused.

"Oops, sorry, I didn't mean to…" I couldn't even come up with an excuse. I just smiled sweetly. "Sorry!"

The pulsing energy kept me awake all that night, looking for an outlet, bursting from me, my muscles demanding to be used. I unpacked. I cleaned my room. I re-read the books I had brought to Paris. I did push-ups. I felt like a prisoner in a jail cell. I knew that Joan would hear the creak of the stairs if I left my room. Her eyes would flip open if she heard the TV on downstairs, like I had tripped a hidden wire somewhere alerting her. It would be a red flag that something wasn't right, she would wonder and she would ask questions and it would be a *conversation*. So I hid out.

At dawn I went running in the already warm, dewy morning air, the sun painting the sky shades of pink. I called Lance and Dante on the way. Neither of them had slept either. I circled around to pick them up: "Gotta be back this afternoon. My mom says we need to catch up, which is code for 'what have you really been doing all these months?'" Lance said by way of greeting, shaking his head. "Super weird to be back, right?" Dante asked as he joined up with us. "It's freaking me out. My mom asked me to open a jar of pickles last night and I shattered it, like, without trying."

Together we raced each other past our old high school, then backtracked all the way to Lake Shore Drive, where rush hour traffic was just beginning to fly by, horns honking and cars zipping along. Onward we went to the edge of Chicago before turning around and coming back through Northwestern's campus. I picked up my pace, getting ahead of them now without intending to. An involuntary response to being back at this place I hadn't seen since my visit to find Lucian. It gave me chills to pass that otherwise idyllic patch of shady trees where I had landed, their branches now full and lush in the summer sun. Or to run this path now where I had followed Lucian up to the buses that would take him into the city to be wooed by Aurelia. It was too much. I led us back toward home.

Our strength still buzzing, with no sign of depleting much as we tried for those hours, we decided to take a break.

<hr />

When night finally fell, Lance appeared at my front door. It had been his idea to charm Joan, of course. He brought a small plate of cookies his mom had made to celebrate his return. Joan loved Lance but had been wary of him ever since he hadn't returned with us from New Orleans. She seemed to assume that he had somehow hurt me, that there was something I wasn't telling her, and so she had nearly written him off. She was right that there was plenty I wasn't telling her, of course, she just never could have guessed how wrong she was. But when she opened the door to find him there, with his glasses and his shy smile and his plate of cookies, she thawed instantly.

"Why, Lance, I almost forgot what you looked like!" She greeted him with a hug. I peeked out from the kitchen, where I was tying my shoes and otherwise trying to look occupied to give them a moment. "How *are* you? And what have we here?"

"Hi, Ms. Terra," he said, pushing his glasses up. "My mom made so many of these for me, I thought you might like some. They're chocolate-peanut-butter chip. I'm not sure if you like that kind of—"

She cut him off, "That is just so thoughtful of you, thank you so much. Come, come," she said, taking the plate and ushering him in, her arm around his back. "She must be so happy to have you home. You're quite the traveler, aren't you?"

"I know, it's good to be back," he smiled. She sat beside him on the couch, chatting now and nibbling on a cookie. I watched and then grabbed two bottles of water from the fridge and joined them.

"Oh, Haven, Lance was just telling me all about rebuilding New Orleans after the storm, what a time he had," she shook her head. "That must have been such grueling work."

"It was tough but that place was a mess. I just couldn't leave it that way," he said. I could hear that twinge of guilt in his voice, both for the lie and because I know that he wished it had been true. He really could have stayed there and worked. We all might have stayed longer if we hadn't been otherwise consumed with his rescue.

"You two getting all reacquainted?" I interrupted.

"Look at these delicious cookies," Joan said. "Tell your mother thank you. So good to see you, Lance," she twinkled, thoroughly won over. "Where are you two off to?"

"Ice cream, then over to Dante's," I said, hoping she wouldn't wait up. This could take a while.

We swung by Dante's house on the way and then headed to the lakefront together, making our way past the running path where we had been earlier right down to the beach. The night sky shimmered an electric navy blue, starry and clear like a crystal-studded tapestry. The air grew stickier the closer we got to the water and I wondered what it would feel like to be up above this, to feel the breeze coming off of the lake from there. The blood hummed through my veins, my arms and legs anxious to fling my body skyward and try to soar.

Connor had taken us through the basics, the checklist of what we needed to know, the way a flight attendant went over the safety instructions before takeoff. Then he had watched us practice in the field for a short time. He leaned against the side of the building, arms folded quietly studying us, letting us figure it out for ourselves. I had managed to get airborne with little trouble, launching myself straight up, much higher than any of the others and I had stayed that way for several minutes. But I hadn't been as skilled at any kind of lateral motion.

Finally, he nodded his head when he had seen enough: "A solid start, you all will have it in no time," he said. And that had been it. He had led us back inside and to the portals. Perhaps this was how it would be now. We weren't in training any longer; we would need to pick up new tricks quickly and on our own.

Our location was perfect, dark and desolate enough, no one to see us.

"So I know we need to be able to do this without a running start, but I say, get up there however we can, stay up as long as we can, go as fast as we can," Dante said.

"Test our limits, I like it," I nodded. "Wings or no wings?" It was a legitimate question: Connor had informed us that we would actually be able to do plenty of flying without our wings. They were merely an extra throttle, they kicked things up. With them we could go even faster and higher.

"Go big or go home," Lance said, smiling.

"Wings it is," I said.

Unlike with birds, flying for us was supposed to be more mind-control than even biology or physics, channeling the principles of levitation into something more explosive and powerful.

"Fasten your seatbelts and be sure your seat is in its upright position," Dante said, with a shrug that said, let's go for it.

"Please stow your tray tables and—" I didn't get to finish. Dante started running toward the water and launched himself into the air, just before his feet would have gotten wet. His wings fanned out, reflecting the creamy moonlight as he dipped and dived through the sky. He looked so graceful, as though dancing or swimming, so at peace. For a moment I forgot that theoretically this was something I could do too, and that I should be doing it right now. Lance snapped me out of it, squeezing my arm.

"Let's show him how it's done," he smiled. "See you up there." He took off running too.

"I'll race you," I called out as he jumped up, wings reaching out toward the sky. I took only three leaps and then pushed off from the ground, shooting up like a rocket, higher than either of the two. I didn't push my wings out until I was already up and hovering at least thirty feet. It was true, I could feel it now: there was more power in me than I had even used and all without the wings themselves. I found that encouraging. At the back of my mind that image of me in the future still lurked, though I had tucked it as deep as I could. But I shook it out now, as I looked along the river toward Chicago in the distance. From here I could see so many lights twinkling. The Ferris wheel of Navy Pier illuminated. The water shimmering as it caught the light of the moon. I breathed in the pure air, letting it fill my lungs and clear my mind. I focused on cutting through the sky toward that Ferris wheel. It should have required more work and effort to be floating up here, but it was canceled out by the pure wild rush of it all. It was the weightlessness of being in a pool mixed with the otherworldly freedom of being surrounded by air. The headiness was so all-consuming, I forgot where I was, I tuned out Lance and Dante as they chased each other. I needed to soak this all in, the euphoria and the peace. With a flick of my shoulder blades, as through shrugging off a jacket, I set my wings free. I felt them unfurl, catching the air and snapping at it, hungry to slice through it. They shot me higher as though they were in control, like a race car built for speed that can't help but hit 100 miles per hour with just a tap of the accelerator.

"Haven Terra, you show off, come down from there this instant, young lady," Dante called up to me. I hadn't realized how high I had climbed; I was so taken with the view and the sensation. It reminded me of something, this thrill and this rush, but I couldn't quite place it. I floated down, and focused on lateral motion while angling my arm and wing just a few millimeters. My body took off, straight past them.

"Whoa, you should have that engine checked," Dante joked. "Betcha can't catch us!" he said as he zipped past me. Lance shrugged and whooshed past us too. We played a game of tag, laughing as though we were kids playing in a schoolyard.

It was after midnight when it finally occurred to us to head home. We could have stayed out there all night—it seemed that the more I flew, the more strength and energy and power I had, even though it should have been just the opposite. I knew the others felt the same way, I could see in the way they pushed to fly higher and faster, in their smiles and glowing eyes, I felt it in their spirit. But we also knew we couldn't get away with getting home too late. We floated down, landing on surprisingly soft feet, ordering our wings to retract and shocking ourselves when they obeyed.

We walked Dante back first, taking the long way through the center of town where the shops had closed for the evening. We needed to slow ourselves down before getting home.

"I kinda thought this would be harder, you know?" Dante said as we stopped in front of his house at last, lights off inside.

"Yeah, it seems too easy, like we're picking it up too fast and there's gotta be a catch," Lance said, pushing his glasses up as though working it out. I imagined him going through all the calculations, the mechanics of flight, how it was even possible for us to be doing this. He was right though. And then something hit me.

"Maybe the catch was that it was really hard to get here," I said, shrugging. "How many times did we almost get killed trying to get here? Maybe that's the point. You have to go through so much but then once you do, you finally make it to somewhere that makes it worth it. You finally have earned the chance to have something feel easy."

They were quiet for a few long seconds.

"Yeah, and maybe, you know, it feels easy by comparison too," Lance said thoughtfully.

"Anything would be a cakewalk after nearly being burned at the stake," Dante said, gesturing to Lance.

"Or escaping hell," I offered.

"Or traveling through those portals. I mean, people complain about taking off their shoes and stuff when they go through airports. Try a portal, you know?" Dante laughed. He waved goodnight and promised to meet us in a few hours for our morning run. "And please can we run to that bakery on Clark for some croissants or something? I really miss those and I know technically we don't need to eat much these days but I miss classy Parisian carbs."

"*Mais bien sûr*," I smiled.

"I missed all the fun," Lance said.

"Goodnight, you cheap-thrill-seeking adrenaline junkies," Dante called out, letting himself inside.

"In my book that's a compliment," I said.

"That's how I meant it," he said, closing up as we walked on.

"You know what it felt like today?" Lance asked, kicking a rock as we made our way along the quiet, tree-lined streets of slumbering houses, only an occasional car passing by. "It felt like the toxins, like the night when we were tagged in New Orleans. A little shot of that, you know?"

He was right, that was the feeling I couldn't place. "Yeah. I mean, this was better. But yeah."

"Definitely better," he said. We slowed our pace as we neared his house, mine was just a few streets beyond it.

That wooden glider creaked in the breeze, beckoning to us. The light near the door shone dimly, as though about to burn out. Inside the curtains were drawn, pure empty darkness behind them.

"I'm shocked," Lance said, peeking in the black window. I pointed to the far window upstairs where a soft light glowed. "Yeah, that seems more like it," he laughed. He took a step away to continue on, intending to walk me home, but I pulled his arm back.

"Joan will definitely be up," I shook my head. "And I don't feel like going home yet."

"Good," he smiled. Instead we crept up the porch steps to the swing where we had spent so much time the summer before, its peeling white paint so comforting.

I sat with my back against the arm of the swing, my legs over his lap. "I walked by here every day when we got back after New Orleans," I said, after listening to the sweet night-time silence for several long minutes, almost not realizing I was speaking out loud. I picked absentmindedly at a thin line of paint, pulling it up into a curl, then brushing it off. "Like I expected you to be here," I shook my head, not meaning to sound dark, especially after a night like this. I looked in his eyes, golden flecks dancing in those light brown irises. I let myself drown in them and felt a calm wash over me and slow my pulse. I breathed him in. This was the first moment we had had like this in so long. No one barging in to send us on some kind of far-flung mission. No one to fight; no one to save. A moment without life and death consequences, a moment to breathe. I could feel my guard let down, I let myself melt into the corner of the swing and into the crook of his arm.

"I'm glad you didn't forget about me," he smiled a slow smile, trying to be light but a serious current beneath.

"Likewise," I said quietly, into his eyes. I took his glasses off gently, folding them up and hanging them on the neck of his tee shirt. That scar beneath his eye: I ran my index finger along it softly, feeling the deep groove. My mind returned to that day when he had come into the gallery at the Lexington and asked me to erase it from the picture I had taken of him. Before we really knew each other. But I knew at that moment that he was like me and I started to fall in love with him then, without even realizing it at the time.

I kissed that scar now, then found his soft lips. He lunged, kissing me back, leaning into me, his hand in my hair. I forgot that we were outside, on a sleepy street, not a soul around.

It was with great effort that I eventually pulled myself away, setting back out into the peaceful night and home to find Joan asleep on the sofa, the lights and TV still on.

⋯⋯◈⋯⋯

We flew every night. In three nights, we had it down. We had the control, and we could go great distances without our wings at all. We had gotten quick and skilled at shooting them out and retracting them, as though we'd had them all our lives. We were pros.

We would fly over the lake, clear out to the city and to that Ferris wheel, careful to go only after Navy Pier had closed for the night to avoid detection. We would do laps, with and without our wings. The difference was breathtaking though: with our wings, it took just a few minutes. The speed was intoxicating, the wind roared through us. We would cut each other off, veer off changing course with no warning, all under the guise of practicing our agility but really, it was just to feel the spike and surge that came with wielding this new power of ours. The thrill showed no signs of wearing off. You felt invincible up there, it was delicious and freeing. I was grateful for Lance and Dante though—it would have been terribly lonely without them. It would be a strange feeling to be up there knowing there was no chance of running into another soul, no one to help if something did go wrong. Having each other let us be daring and take risks and push ourselves, we would be there to catch each other. We flew low enough to avoid planes, high enough to avoid eyes and always landed back where we started, on the empty lakefront taking the same path home. Lance walked me home every night after a few precious minutes on the porch. And every night, I found Joan asleep on the sofa, waiting.

26

Is That Where You Were?

We had settled into a fine routine, relatively normal even. We spent our morning and nighttime training, and I'd spend the afternoons at the hospital while Dante and Lance worked in town. We had nearly two weeks of calm, I knew it couldn't last and checked my phone constantly waiting for Connor to summon us back, even though I had made little progress on tying things up at home as he had directed us to do. I wasn't the only one though. In my correspondence with the others I learned they, too, were trying to make sense of being at home and yet not quite feeling at home anymore. The date for Northwestern's orientation week was fast approaching, but I continued to ignore it and to change the subject when Joan mentioned a shopping trip to get ready for school. The best I could do was float changes to my master plan: maybe I didn't want to be pre-med after all. Maybe I should live at home; it's just a few blocks. Joan tried to laugh it off, making jokes about how she had brainwashed me, convincing me to stay home or that now I was going to turn into one of those party girls I always scoffed at.

It was a Sunday when news of the massacre broke. I had just returned from our morning jog and hadn't bothered to look at my phone while we were out or I would have seen it.

It was nearly lunchtime, Joan had taken the day off from work and had tuned in expecting to find her usual medical talk show on her favorite news network when a story in the hourly round-up rang out. Joan watched the TV screen, washing dishes while I dried them. My mind had been elsewhere: Lance, our nighttime walks, the fleeting moments that we had before saying goodnight. Joan shook her head, handing me a dish and shaking out her sudsy hands: "What has happened to this world?" The chyron read: "Massacre in Paris: Bodies Found in City Park." I dropped the plate I was drying and left it to turn up the TV.

"Haven!" she yelled. "What am I going to tell Nurse Sanders? She needs twelve plates for the party, not eleven." She bent down to pick up the jagged pieces of floral china.

I grabbed my phone from the mail table, scanning for head- lines and peeked at the other one inside the pocket of my hoodie.

"The people of Paris are waking to a gruesome sight in the center of the city," the newscaster reported. "We have to warn you, these images are upsetting. Nearly one hundred bodies were found at the Place des Innocents in Paris this morning."

"Is that anywhere near where you were?" Joan asked, coming in to watch. She hovered by the TV beside me.

"We were there," I said, clipped, not wanting miss a word as I pulled up a story on my phone.

That familiar gathering place—Place des Innocents, which had in pre-revolution times been a communal burial site, a dumping ground for bodies, had become one again, overnight. Silently, with none of the violence or gunshots or turmoil that usually accompanies a scene of mass casualties. It seemed there were no witnesses. But tellingly, another mess had been left in the catacombs. Bottles shattered and left behind, bags, purses, cigarettes, trash, iPods attached to portable speakers, a laptop or two. The cataphiles would never have done such a thing; that just wasn't their style.

"Just steps from the Louvre and Notre Dame among other famed tourist sites in the city's first arrondissement—" the anchor went on.

"I wouldn't say steps. What's the cause of death? What happened? Are there survivors?" I talked at the screen, but it gave me no answers.

"…Recovery efforts are underway to identify the dead. So far, police have few leads. Autopsies will be performed, but early word says there have been no identifiable signs of cause of death. And no witnesses have come forward. In recent days, images of pentagrams had been found painted on landmarks throughout the city. Those were thought to be cases of vandalism or attributed to what many believe may be an increase in gang-related activity, but police have no suspects. So early risers finding a shocking sight there, we'll be keeping you up to date as news comes in. And now—"

The newscaster moved on to a story about Greece's economy. Joan returned to the kitchen, saying something about how nowhere is safe these days, but I wasn't listening.

My fingers tapped out a text to our group, everyone at once: *Check the news. Paris massacre. We're going back.* Drew wrote back first: *"On it."* My next message, to Gavin: *"Hey. You OK??"* The seconds were endless. Joan was talking to me but I was just staring at my phone, willing it to buzz with a message. The dread crept in blackening my heart, a familiar feeling that I had not kept close enough watch. And then the phone vibrated and a box popped up. *"Thanks Rosetta. All OK here. Heeded your warning—haven't been partying so much since saw you. Much gratitude."*

"Stay safe. We're coming back ASAP."

My other phone buzzed in my pocket and I peeked in: Connor. *"Need you all back."*

"Haven!" Joan barked at me, from back in the kitchen. She slammed the soapy sponge against the counter in frustration.

I jumped. It dripped suds onto the floor. The newscaster read the death toll again. Ninety-nine.

"Sorry, yes, no, what?" I had no idea what she had said. My mind was too busy racing. We were leaving.

"If you answer me the first time I ask then I won't keep asking you. Why are you not listening?" She was frustrated because she was concerned, but I couldn't focus.

"Was that the question? Why am I not listening?"

"No!" she barked again, shaking her head. "Were you careful when you were there? I feel like you aren't bothered enough by the troubles in these cities you like to go gallivanting in—"

"Gallivanting? Seriously?" I shot back, taking offense, even though I couldn't blame her for not knowing just how heavy my work was in these places that looked like vacation locales.

"I see this all day long at the hospital—you used to, too— remember? I think you feel invincible. And let me tell you my dear, you most certainly are not."

"Got it, thanks Joan," I had meant just to end the conversation but my words came out more bitter than I had intended and I instantly felt bad.

"I don't know why you can't just promise me that you'll be smart about things."

"I am."

"I don't believe you."

I threw my arms up. There was no winning this.

"I'm just worried. I know I've always been worried, but as you grow up I find myself worrying more instead of less and I'm not sure what to do with that."

"You have to trust me," I said, picking up the pieces of the broken plate. Luckily it had shattered into just a few large chunks.

"I know. Promise me that I can trust you."

"You can," I said, still exasperated.

My phone rang, "La Vie en Rose." "Lance," I said, holding it up. He had set the ringtone as a joke a few nights ago during one of our late night walks as he had kidded again that we had been living "La Vie en Rose" while he was languishing in the underworld. I reminded him that I was the one who had literally thrown myself into the fire to save him, and he rewarded me with a kiss not unlike the one I'd earned at Père-Lachaise.

"Go ahead, take it," she sighed, in that way that said we weren't finished, that this was just an intermission.

"You sure?" We hadn't been getting along as well as we used to, she and I, these past two years. That's what secrets will do to you. You start getting so worried about letting on that you stop saying anything at all, and it poisons you. She just nodded.

"Thanks," I said, picking up on the last ring.

"Hey," I said, letting myself outside.

"Connor wants us back," he said.

"Yeah, I heard." We started walking toward each other, still on the phone until we met up a few blocks later. "What shocks me is that they didn't keep them as recruits. What does that mean?"

"To me it means they've got a surplus, they could afford to spare some," he said.

"That's what I was afraid you'd say. And no witnesses?"

"They probably killed them or captured them, right?" he asked, confirming what I had thought too.

We walked into the main drag near campus, jostling past groups of high school students taking over the town for the university's summer studies program. They were called Cherubs, and they were heading into their senior year of high school. I had always wanted to go and would have applied last year if I hadn't been so occupied battling demons at the Lex when applications were due. It had been a wonder I had managed to apply to colleges at all. And now we would be going right back into it all. I was ready in many ways—I could fly, I trusted that I could make it through what lay ahead, and I felt in limbo here—but there was one real sticking point that nagged at me now as it had ever since this had begun. I could battle demons and escape the underworld, but I had no idea how to navigate leaving parts of my old life, my old self, behind.

We turned the corner and found Dante setting a tray of pains au chocolat in the front window. He smiled instantly and then read our expressions and knew.

<hr />

By the time night fell, we had heard from everyone. Connor's latest message told us to take a portal up to him as soon as possible. *"There's something else: Lucian's body has been recovered."* I stopped reading for a moment, needing to fully absorb what that meant. The revolution was nearing. The body was finding its way back to the living. *"In Père-Lachaise outside the tomb where he was killed. The wings are on his wrist. There was an invitation pinned to him. It's just what you overheard: a party at Versailles. October. We're burying him there for the time being."* The connections fired in my mind: all he needed was for me to survive through that October day. Something else occurred to me: his body had likely been in one of the cells near Drew.

We had stayed at the bakery through Dante's shift, talking in code at times when we were all alone and his boss, a jolly woman who adored him and made the best cupcakes in town, was in the back. Lance and I kept scanning news stories and found that someone had dropped dead at a café on Rue Sainte-Honoré that afternoon. Another body washed up on the banks of the Seine near Notre Dame in the evening. We needed to be there but we couldn't risk taking the portal before nightfall.

"So, like, when are we coming back here, do you think?" Dante had whispered as he closed the place up, walking back with us. Lance and I just looked at each other, neither of us answering. "How are we going to explain it this time? I don't want my mom to think I keep running off to eat cheese and drink wine."

"And buy scarves," I said, thinking.

"Thanks for that, by the way," Lance said to Dante. "My mom loved it. I think she knows I didn't pick it out though."

"Band-aid," I said firmly, not having a real solution.

"What?" Dante asked.

"We'll put a band-aid on this." I had thought if we could just make it the few weeks until school started then it would be so much easier to sneak away, but it didn't look like that would happen now. It had been a long shot. I knew it. This was pure denial at work. "We go up tonight. Come back as soon as we can. Tell them we're visiting friends from the trip before school starts. In, I don't know, Ann Arbor? Or something. Any plausible, relatively close college town accessible by train."

"Works for me," Lance said. "We can say it's a really early train. We'll meet at 5 am. Go up just before sunrise. Good?"

When I got home, Joan was making dinner, singing along in the kitchen to one of the music channels on TV. I smelled something buttery and cheesy toasting.

"Bon jour, sweetie," she called out from the kitchen, her apron on and a spatula in her hands.

"Hi," I said, unsure. When I left she had not been very happy with me, I hadn't expected to return to this. "I brought some pastries from Dante's shop."

"Perfect! Or, what would that be? *Parfait?*"

"Yeah," I laughed.

"Because we're having croque monsieurs!" She pulled open the oven to give me a peek at the cheese sandwiches toasting directly on the rack.

"Wow, those look really good. Thanks."

"I haven't made them in ages and ages, and I thought we need to start having fun. You got some mail from school," she smiled, proudly. "It looks like it's about moving in. I didn't open it, but I know it's soon. So only fun times until then!" she declared.

"OK, great," I smiled, picking at the shredded gruyère on the counter. She pulled out plates and silverware and I pulled out placemats, setting them on the table. "So speaking of … fun. Our friend Max, you know, from New Orleans, is going to Michigan and invited us to come hang out before school starts." I hopped up on the counter, nibbling nervously on more cheese. She crossed her arms and cocked her head to the side, waiting for it. I felt the atmosphere turn. "So, if it's cool, Lance and Dante and I were just gonna grab a train in the morning." I tried to make it sound like no big deal. Her pursed lips formed a straight, tight line.

"Haven," she said, taking a deep breath and closing her eyes. "I am really trying here." She clenched her fists. "But you. Are. Pushing. Me." She spoke slowly, an effort to keep it all in. I wasn't surprised. When you have a kid who has never been rebellious and then has a couple of years like I had, it's a lot to take.

"It'll just be for a few days," I said, keeping my voice light, hoping to defuse the tension.

"Why can't you just stay in one place for a few days?"

"If I were actually going away to school, then I would be… going, like, soon, really far," I shot back. I wasn't good at fighting with her and I didn't want to so it came out poorly.

"I know that. It's not about that," she said, she put her arms on either side of the sink, still trying to remain composed. "I just don't know who this person is!" Her voice came out loud, accusatory.

"Who?"

"YOU! I don't know who you are anymore! I am trying to understand whatever's been going on with you but it's too much now. It's just too much."

"What? Why?" I played dumb; it was the easiest thing to do. I still believed we weren't actually going to have this fight. We had been on the verge of hashing this all out since last year. Since the Lex. We had deferred it, the way people do with college when they have other things going on requiring their full attention. For me, that was angelhood. But you are only allowed to defer for so long and our time was up. I felt a panic begin to vibrate in my veins, my mind searching out which lies to pursue.

"It was one thing when you took that internship in Chicago and then left for New Orleans, but each time you come back *changed*. And I know you're growing up, but this is different. And this last time, these idiotic emails you sent me…I just don't know what's going on."

"I'm…finding myself. You know, people go to Europe, they find themselves," I said, trying.

She put up her hands, rolling her eyes at me. "You were always excited about college, about medicine, about graduating, and I just don't see any of that joy or any interest in anything. You're out all night, don't think I don't know that. And I don't even want to think about what you're doing. I know you're almost 18, you can do what you want, but I just feel like you're hiding something from me." She paused for only a moment. I hadn't formulated a response yet and she began again.

"Look, I came of age in the 60s, Haven, so don't talk to me about finding yourself. I've seen people on every kind of drug imaginable and I'm not about to let that happen to you." I had to stop for a moment.

"You think I'm on drugs," I said, shaking my head, pushing off from the counter. She grabbed my arm, shaking me.

"For God's sake, you were in the country where Jim Morrison is buried. The Doors? You probably don't know them. At any rate, he died at 27, Haven. TWENTY-seven. That probably seems old to you, but it's not. He was young and handsome and—"

"I saw his grave," I said under my breath.

"Of course you did, on one of your adventures doing God knows what with God knows who."

"I'm not on drugs—" I said but she cut me off before I could defend myself any further.

"That's exactly what someone on drugs would say," she said, pointing with the spatula. "You've been hiding from me for the past two years and I've been patient and kept watch and tried to give you space but I'm not going to lose you." There was something new in her eyes, in her voice—a desperation. It was what people must see when their loved ones are about to have them committed. A feeling that the person speaking to them is trying to reach out across such a grand expanse of time and space and understanding to pull back someone balancing on the edge of a cliff. I had never expected to be spoken to in this way. There was a finality in her tone, as though she had reached the end of her frayed emotional rope.

"I just don't know you anymore and I fear it's because you've gotten into something bad. I like to think my instincts aren't so off. Though I wish they were in this case. I found you on the side of Lake Shore Drive and the only thing that has lessened that horror in all these years is the fact that you have seemed to grow into a well-adjusted, happy, healthy young woman. But I am worried," she revved up again, her voice growing louder and more angry. "As worried as I have ever been—more worried than when the hotel burned to the ground or New Orleans flooded or Lance didn't come home. I am worried you have gotten yourself into *something*, and that you are in some kind of trouble you won't tell me about. So there, I've said it. I'm not going to apologize for caring." She was shouting now.

A beeping sounded from the ceiling. I had been so stunned silent by her shouting I had failed to notice the smoke filling the kitchen. "Oh!" she shook her head, another thing going wrong. She grabbed a pot holder but I reached in front of her turning off the oven. Then I flung open the door, angry at every-thing—the noise, the smoke, this conversation—and reached in, pulling them out with my bare hands.

"HAVEN! Stop!" she tugged at my shirt manically to pull me away. "What are you DOING? You're going to burn your-self. Stop!"

I shook my head. I wasn't so much angry at her as at the secrets I had to carry. And I was angry because she deserved to know, didn't she? I thought I'd been protecting her by not telling her, but it hadn't worked, she had worried anyway. And I was angry because I couldn't afford to have this on my mind knowing what we would be heading into. It was all too much and I felt the energy bubbling up, pushing against my skin, needing to get out.

"You are RECKLESS! I don't understand what you're doing!" she shouted.

I felt myself snapping. I gave up, I didn't care what Connor said. The pressure had been too much, just as the power con-tained within me had been too much. I needed to get into the air, I needed that outlet.

"You want to see what I've been doing?" I stormed past her. "Follow me and watch me ruin a perfectly good shirt," I muttered, throwing the front door open and stomping out in the night.

"What are you talking about? You say these things that don't make any sense," she called after me. All the way through town, she followed me past the sweet, mild-mannered high school Cherubs lining the tables on the sidewalks outside restaurants, drinking their coffee and laughing and talking, and onward to the lakefront, to that spot. She trailed behind me the whole way, calling out to me for those first few blocks. "Where are you going?" she cried. "Stop, Haven!" And then she gave up and just followed.

When we reached the lake, she shouted again, "Please don't jump in, don't make me go in after you." Her shouting scared away the few people who were walking along the beach.

"I'm not jumping in," I said. There is never a good time to share certain things. This was one of those things. And the time had come. "This is where I come every night with Dante and Lance. And this is what I do." I jumped up, just one leap into the air, and up I went. My wings cut through the back of my t-shirt with a slicing whoosh, but I didn't mind. They shot me up fast, up into a hazy sky of dim, obscured stars, and it was as perfect and glorious as if it had been cloudless and clear. To be up there, embraced by the air, cleared my head, and brought me to my senses again. I caught my breath. I whipped around as though doing a lap in a pool, cleansed and centered, and then let myself float back down until I landed in front of her. Her jaw dropped, but no words came out of her mouth.

"This is what I've been doing. This is the only thing I'm on. Air," I shrugged. "But I guess it's what's been messing me up. Flying comes with a lot of baggage." I felt the tears welling up, relief at no longer having to keep it from her, at getting to explain myself and what had been going on for the past two years.

She reached out to touch my wings with tentative fingers, as though to pet a zoo animal.

"Can I put these away?" I asked, avoiding her eyes, fidgeting.

"These are your scars…" she said. "They turned into this."

"Yeah, kind of. Yeah."

"All those years looking for tops that covered them up," she shook her head in a daze. "This is beautiful." She threw her arms around me in one of her bear hugs, and I pulled my wings in, wiping away my tears.

"Tell me, Haven. Please tell me everything," she said, still embracing me. I heard the catch in her voice and knew her eyes had welled up too. "And then I will tell you that it will be OK, because it will." She may have been trying to convince herself as much as me, but it didn't matter. It was what I needed to hear, and in that one moment I wondered why I hadn't told her sooner.

27

I Call It The New Normal

She kept her arm around me during the whole walk home, as though protecting me from the world.

"Well, I always knew you were special, didn't I?" she said, smiling as she squeezed my shoulder. "See, I know what I'm talking about, don't I?" She seemed to sense that I needed to gather myself before launching into an explanation and unlocking these many secrets I had tucked away. She didn't press me. She waited until we got home and then she salvaged what was left of the croque monsieurs—"Some of these aren't so bad," she said, cutting off the edible bits. "And then some of them have nearly disintegrated." She held up an entirely blackened sandwich and dropped it straight in the trash, wiping her hands. "We'll keep a better eye this time," she winked, as she put the fresh ones she had whipped up into the oven. I had returned to my spot on the counter, slouching as I sat nibbling cheese again. We were getting a second take at this scene, and it had to go better this time around.

She kept our talk light until the food was ready: "You certainly did find a lovely spot for your practice sessions. It must be a stunning view from there. The city lights in the distance, so nice." This, of course, is what made her such a good nurse. I had watched her at work so many times, taking blood from a squeamish patient or bandaging up someone in pain, and she would keep talking, distract them and put them at ease. Right now, she was stitching me up and healing me. She pulled the sandwiches out, this time a perfect golden brown, the cheese gooey and oozing. She poured us tall frosty glasses of soda—"Do you want a float?" she asked, like I was a kid. "No, it's OK," I said. She gave me a skeptical look and I changed my mind. She dunked a scoop of vanilla ice cream in each of our glasses and added straws. I set them on the table as she placed the sandwiches on plates, one in each hand. She flicked her head toward the living room. We curled up on opposite ends of the sofa with our dinners. It was after 10 pm by now.

"What's the verdict? You're the expert," she said with her mouth full, winking again.

"*Très bien, merci*," I smiled. They were perfect, rivaling any I'd had in Paris. The company probably helped too.

"Feeling better yet?" she asked. She meant was I feeling ready to talk. I put down my sandwich and nodded.

"I didn't want to worry you—" I started.

"Well, that was your real mistake," she smiled. "Worry me, please. I'm good at being worried. But let me also say that I'm just very grateful it wasn't drugs."

I smiled, "You're welcome."

"Ha-ha!" She could laugh about that now, and she did, taking another bite.

I took a deep breath. "So, you're going to have to suspend your disbelief a little for this. Like when you read those romance novels you like."

"Consider my disbelief officially suspended. Promise," she held up her hand as though taking an oath.

"I don't think it's something you can understand. I can't even really understand it, but I thought I was just this normal girl—"

"No," she wagged her finger. "I always knew you were special. I thought maybe curing cancer special or first female president special. But I just didn't quite know how special, did I?" she asked, rhetorically.

"You can call it special, I guess I just call it the new normal."

"Go on, tell me everything from the beginning."

"This started at the Lexington Hotel. There was a lot of... shady stuff going on there and that's where we found out what we were—"

"We?" she asked. "So, Dante. And wonderful Lance?" I was glad that Lance was wonderful again. I nodded. She nodded back, soaking it in. "And what about that handsome Lex person?"

I sighed and shook my head. "That's a really long story."

She waved her hand as though trying to erase those last queries. "Never mind, I'll save my questions. You just go on, sweetie, take your time. We've got all night and there's nowhere I'd rather be. Please let me hear it all."

"So, the hotel..." I started again and it poured out of me. All of the horrors of the Lexington, the soul stealing, the fire, then the stabbings and attacks of New Orleans, the storms, Lance's capture and finally Paris and what had really gone on there. She listened to my adventures as though I were telling her about a comic book I had read or a wild movie I had seen. From time to time she would shake her head, smiling, or she would gasp or say in her perfectly Joan way, "Oh, good gracious!" as I told her of another twist or turn. When I finished at last, I felt my shoulders ease. The weight I'd carried for so long was gone, the albatross lifted. She looked at me with tears in her eyes, perfectly still, curled up on the sofa, the remnants of dinner on the coffee table.

"I don't even know what to say, Haven," she said finally. "All this time, these are the things you were doing." She shook her head, smiling to herself. "Well, no wonder you didn't want to tell me. I was already worried about you. I gave you such a hard time about things, didn't I?" I just smiled. "And to think, I had *no idea*." She put her hands to her cheeks. "So what do we do now? Here, come here," she held out her arms for a hug and I scooted over from my side of the couch. "But what *do* we do with you now?" Then, putting together the pieces, she answered her own question: "You're not really going to Ann Arbor, are you?"

I shook my head, guiltily.

"Can I ask where you're going?"

"Back to the angels and then Paris again."

"Well, now that I know how important this is to the world, I certainly can't keep you from going, can I?" She thought for a moment and then, as though reading my mind: "Are you scared, ever? Of all these things you do now?"

That wasn't a question I wanted to answer, I didn't have the luxury of being scared anymore. I had too much responsibility. "Well, I'm freakishly strong, which is helpful. And you know, I'm a soul-illuminator," I had explained this to her too. "And I passed those three tests, which weren't easy, so I've got some skills." I stopped myself and sighed. "But, yeah, you know, a little bit. I'm kind of a little bit terrified."

"Well, that's because you're smart and smart people know what they're up against. Idiots don't and that's their problem. And I know you may feel a certain way right now. But sometimes you just need to let yourself crumble a little bit before embarking on a journey that requires you to be your strongest. It's a way for our bodies to re-up." I turned that all over in my mind. I had tried to keep rock solid for so long, to not let myself buckle beneath all that had happened. But in order to go on, to face what was coming, I needed to let the levee break as it had today. I needed to get out the emotion in order to steel myself again.

"Maybe you're right," I said.

"Oh, I know I am," she said, patting my shoulder. "I'm just so disappointed that I missed the ceremony. This initiation, I sure would have liked a picture of that." I had to smile.

"Yeah, sorry. No pictures. But, if you wanted to come this morning, without the camera maybe...."

We stayed up into the wee hours and when we were too tired to talk anymore, we simply curled up and dozed off watching TV, like we were at a slumber party. I hadn't slept much and didn't need it like I used to, but there was something comforting about it here. I managed to send a text just before closing my eyes. I needed to give Dante and Lance fair warning.

"Change of plans: Joan's coming to our send-off this morning. Feel free to invite your parental units. I gave up and gave in, sorry." My phone rang immediately. "Um, hi," Lance said. "Curious about your text. I couldn't tell if it was a weird joke or..."

Dante came right out with it though: "I think a WTF is in order: so, WTF, Hav?!" He wasn't angry though, he was laughing. "I'm totally telling Ruthie now," he said of his mom. "Mom!" he yelled, still on the phone. "Wake up!"

⟫⟩◈⟨⟪

At a quarter to five in the morning, the three of us said our goodbyes and gave our hugs and leapt skyward as all three of our moms, and Lance's dad too, looked on, mouths agape. The moms all pulled their souvenir scarves around their shoulders in the cool early morning breeze, waving until we disappeared above.

⟫⟩◈⟨⟪

"So, let me get this straight," I said to Connor as we gathered in the library with the entire group of angels from the Illumination

Chamber, lab and workshop. An image of the engraved invitation that had been pinned to Lucian was now projected on the wall. "We're being *invited* to the revolution?"

"It looks that way," he said.

"How very civilized," Dante said in a formal accent.

"I don't know whether to be honored or to be offended: they think they can win even without any element of surprise?" It made me angry, the cockiness of it all. But it was good to be fired up, that was ammunition I could use.

<hr />

We quickly fell into a routine. We were on a rotation. At any given time, six of us were "on the ground" as they called it, based in Montmartre, and two above, recharging. I logged time in the Illumination Chamber flagging targets for all the angels to investigate and then joined the group in Paris to work. Our days were spent looking for trouble and our nights were spent thwarting it.

The authorities had closed the catacombs following the massacre and even reinforced the manhole covers with an extra layer of locks, so there would be no getting down there. Or at least, not for most people. We did go, with the help of Dante, who doused one of the covers with a serum allowing us to take advantage of its magnetic properties and lift it off with our hands. But once there, we found all the entrances to the underworld blocked, all the portals sealed off. Quite simply, nothing led anywhere. Even the well had dried. Lance and I had gone so far as to leap down into that empty, narrow pit only to hit its rocky bottom and be forced to fly back up. It all made us feel as though we were going crazy, but this was just how the demons operated, their goal being to hide out before reappearing to cause mass casualties. The trip hadn't been entirely fruitless though: we had found one endangered soul still locked up in a cell just steps from the well-trodden paths of the catacombs museum. Like an animal left for dead, he crouched low in the corner, staring at us, unsure as we worked to free him, dazed and dirty in a torn white t-shirt. "I don't know where I am or why I'm here," he mumbled over and over. We took him to the nearest hospital.

Pentagrams now dotted the city—spray painted on streets and sidewalks, etched into buildings—but we had our own answer to them. Dante and his lab concocted a lesser, temporary version of the wing tattoo we gave out during our tests. The original one was meant only for those whose souls were already decaying; it could kill a pure human. But this new version could protect against what toxins we knew existed, like a vaccine. We left piles of them in cafes, metro stations and shops, beside stacks of the free weekly newspapers. Before long, we even began seeing them on bodies—living, breathing ones—throughout the city. They were designed to remain visible until a week following that October date, no matter how someone might try to scrub them from their skin before then.

We slapped them on the endangered souls we came across too. There were so many souls calling out to me every day now, it was overwhelming. I could turn a corner and walk headlong into a wall of endangered souls, some flickering so intensely that I knew they might be announced as another missing person on the news within 24 hours if we didn't do something. Every night now there were stories of people disappearing with no trace, "*Les Perdus*," on the local news. The Lost. So many every day, and yet no bodies turning up anywhere since the massacre. I had identified more endangered souls than we had angels to tend to them, and there was a backlog. I had flagged some demons too, now that I was able to clearly see them. Paris was overrun.

Just as my illumination powers had become sharper, the others found themselves receiving clearer readings from their scars. Based on their wanderings, the researchers sent us maps of areas with highly concentrated demon activity. We combed those neighborhoods, though we were hunted too. We were out in the open more than ever.

If you were in Paris at that time, you might have brushed up against one of us reaching for a book in the cramped charming quarters of Shakespeare and Company, the book shop where Dante and I once saved the soul of a repentant young woman playing the piano in its upstairs hideaway. We left a stack of tattoos beside the free postcards near the bulletin board on our way back down the staircase. Or you might have been sitting beside us at the sidewalk café across the street from Notre Dame when, while scanning for targets, we found a handsome tourist asking a demon for directions. We left Max to pay our bill as Dante, Lance, Tom, River and I abruptly left, following the pair weaving through those narrow streets of the Left Bank until they ducked into the open doorway of an apartment building. We shadowed ourselves as soon as we reached the house, maimed the demon, and helped the man escape.

You might have even been an endangered soul yourself and not known that a stranger had smacked you, quick and pain-less—like a mosquito—with a wing-shaped antidote to protect you from the toxin about to attack your system. .

We were everywhere and nowhere: spotting targets, chasing them down, shadowing ourselves and then doing what needed to be done to free our prey. We did the work of saints with the skills of assassins. We had managed to be quick and obscured our faces and bodies enough to avoid getting caught. Most of the attacks occurred at night or at least dusk, which allowed us some shadowing opportunities. But night fell so late that those hours could be packed and relentless with soul saves. The demons began traveling in larger packs too. And since we were perceived as stronger and more intimidating as a group, we also stayed close together.

The impending revolution made us cling to each other even more than ever. Dante had outfitted our Montmartre home with what he called "demon traps," which amounted to a mixture of oils and powders—not unlike the gris gris bags of New Orleans—that literally sealed the space off from intruders. We continued to use it as our home base and war room, posting maps along the walls of the living room, and gathering there in between our soul-saving sprees.

Waiting for our evening adventures to start frayed our nerves, and we each found our own ways of dealing with it. One evening I was in the bedroom scrolling through the file on my phone that mapped our marching orders for the night, plotting where we would be looking for endangered souls, when Emma appeared in the doorway holding up a copy of French Cosmopolitan.

"I know you're totally busy and it's a totally terrible time, but do you ever just need to take your mind off stuff?" she asked, shaking the magazine. I had promised her, of course, and she had a point. "Even just like a page or two?"

"Sure," I smiled. "I'm sick of looking at this thing anyway." I put the phone away.

She lay on the bed flipping through. "You know Jackson?"

"Cute facilitator guy?" I asked.

She nodded. "I think there may be something there," she cooed. "We kind of had a *moment* at Initiation."

"Go, Emma," I said.

"I know, right? I mean, it was just a look or whatever, but you know." She flipped through the magazine. "OK! Oooh, this one looks good!" She opened up to an article illustrated with a photo of a guy in boxer shorts and a girl wearing his button-down shirt and little else.

"Wow, OK then. Let's see," I scanned the title. "*Faites qu'il vous désire.*" "Make Him Desire You."

"Perfect!" she said, she lay on her stomach, feet crossed in the air, her chin propped on her hands, listening intently. "Go, go!"

"OK, here we go, I'm gonna kind of paraphrase: 'We have all had this happen, you see him across the room and want him to notice you. But how?'" I read slowly. "*Le désir naît d'une atmosphère d'excitation et de mystère.* Desire is born of excitement and mystery. It is part beauty and part attitude...." I read the entire article as Emma nodded, mentally taking notes. When I reached the end, having done a pretty decent job reading—and after learning the secret seemed to be a combination of being aloof and gorgeous and wild—she applauded.

"That. Was. Awesome," she said.

"This is basically what I learned at my first internship," I shook my head, tossing the magazine on the bed. "The demons have it figured out."

"Can we read more tomorrow?"

<hr />

On the days when I was in the angel realm on Connor-mandated recharging sessions, I divided my time between the Illumination Chamber and meetings with Sophie and Peter of the research team. They were blond twins—the only twins among the angels—and long, lean and graceful, with matching wide smiles and infectious laughs. We met in a room adjacent to the gym, in what would have been called a music room if this were a proper estate. A white grand piano sat alongside a harp, with a small patch of white parquet flooring for dancing, and that view of the field encompassing one entire wall.

"So is it a requisite that everyone learn to play this thing here?" I asked, strumming the harp.

"Luckily, no," Peter laughed. Sophie sat down at the piano, fingers fluttering over the keys playing a classical piece on fast-forward at a much quicker tempo than it should have been.

"Whoa! I can't dance that fast. I can't really dance at all."

"Just warming up, don't worry," Sophie smiled.

"OK, ready?" Peter looked in my eyes, nodding as he counted. "One, two, three—"

"So you're sure this will be the dance?" I interrupted before we even started.

"Our studies suggest that this was the most popular dance in his day. I think we can count on it."

"He's a fan of tradition. Who would've guessed?"

He counted again, "One-two-three, ONE-two-three…" I started too soon and stepped on his foot. "Wait one more measure."

Sophie watched over the piano as she played. "Lance was in here the other day and you know he's picking this up pret-ty fast," she taunted with a smile. "You don't really want him to lead, do you?"

"You guys aren't kidding, you really did do your homework, didn't you?" I joked, as Peter bowed to me and I bowed back, and we twirled around each other on the floor.

"My sources tell me you guys both have a competitive streak, especially with each other, which I love," she said, glancing up from her playing. "So you've gotta show him up."

"Sophie's competitive too, in case you can't tell," Peter said as we spun to face each other. The music sped up faster and faster. "And she thinks Baroque music is too slow," he laughed.

28

We'll Be Hunting—And Hunted—Here

A week later, as the other angels carried out the work we had left, the eight of us all boarded a train out to Versailles, traveling just as the tourists would and getting swept up in a mess of them making the pilgrimage to this palace of such splendor. We turned the corner from the station and there it sat, stretched before us and set behind glorious golden gates. They gleamed in the morning sunlight, celestial emblems of the sun king bursting forth from the ornate ironwork. I felt as I had before entering the Lexington Hotel all that time ago—the sense that this grand place was going to signal a change in my life as soon as I crossed its threshold.

Drew handed us each our printed tickets and waved us past the groups to a small ramp: "Trust me, you do NOT want to get stuck in those lines," she said.

"Not bad for what was once just a hunting lodge," Lance said, taking it all in, the sweeping panorama from the courtyard, before we stepped inside.

"Little known fact: this guy is a great hunter," Tom said, pointing to himself.

"A pretty good demon hunter too," River said.

"Oh. We'll be hunting here," Dante said, fussing with his audio guide. Lance took it from him and got it working.

"And hunted," whispered Max.

"Always hunted." Drew looked over her shoulder as we stepped into a crowded room with a dollhouse-sized replica of the estate.

Dante paged through my guidebook, repeating after the audio guide piping in his ear, "OK, original hunting lodge for Louis the fourteenth—"

"*Quatorze*," Emma said. "*Quatorze*." She said again, pleased with herself.

"Wow, Emma, your French is getting really good," River deadpanned, kidding.

"Thanks," Emma said, sincerely. "Before Haven's help, the only thing I could say was, *voulez-vous coucher avec—*"

"Thank you, Emma, *merci* for the credit. I'm glad we've expanded your vocabulary beyond phrases heard in disco music."

We took our time, trekking through the grand estate, marveling at its opulence from the marble to the gilded ceilings to the artwork. We stopped to gaze out at the gardens from Marie Antoinette's bedchamber. "I have an idea, remind me later," Emma whispered, eyes dancing around the room with its romantic floral wall coverings and gilded fleur-de-lis along the molding.

"Is it about decorating?" I joked, then it occurred to me. "Or, Jackson?"

"All that, too," she laughed. "But something else."

When we turned the corner, proceeding through the war room, we understood the reason for the bottlenecking. I had seen plenty of pictures of the Hall of Mirrors, but to stand there at one end of it now and see it stretched before us so lavishly, I felt transported to another era, to the Prince's time here, I supposed. Sixteen grand mirrors studded one wall, each opposite a matching window arcade with views of the sprawling, expertly manicured gardens. The space rolled on forever, all marble, gold, and dotted with statues every few steps.

"So, it'll be here," I said to myself, and to my reflection in one of the mirrors. Lance stood behind me, gazing at the ceiling, his furrowed brow telling me that he must be calculating how far apart each of the grand mirrors must be to be set equidistant from one another in this great space. But he had heard me.

"Yes," he said quietly, sure and serious. "It will be here."

We all walked through slowly and silently, committing every inch of the place to memory, every bit that could be useful to us. We snapped pictures, we noted the distance to the ground below from those windows and also the distance up to the roof. We roamed around on our own, in our own worlds. I wondered if, like me, my friends were all trying to envision how it might look that night in the coming days when we would return. The heft of that date sunk like a stone in the river of my heart.

When we finally left that space and had wound back around through all of the private apartments of the king and queen, and the various entertaining spaces and hallways and sitting rooms, we cut across the courtyard and into the gardens. The sun shone high in the afternoon sky, familiar music greeting us, majestic and celebratory—yes, I could place it now. I looked at Lance and he nodded. This was the music for the dance we were learning.

"They know their stuff," Lance said, stopping before a fountain spraying water into the air in time to the tune.

Dante and Max had split off from us and returned now bearing plastic cups of orange juice. "How amazing is this?" Dante said, passing them out. "Fresh-squeezed orange juice? I mean, amazing," he pointed to a dainty little umbrella-covered cart. "They're from the orangerie here. Delish."

Hedges at least 20 feet high lined both sides of a central path with entry points to mazes whose twists and turns I had seen from the windows. So many places to get lost, to hide, to escape if necessary. We committed it all to memory, strolling for more than an hour as the music played on, sipping our drinks, trying to imagine how to thwart the kind of destruction that would soon be coming to this beautiful place.

——⬦——

We stayed until just before closing time, leaving just shy of the crowds and managing to have a train car to ourselves. Even so we sat in benched seats closely facing each other and spoke in low voices. The walls of the train bore artists' renderings of the palace we had just seen.

"So, this is just kind of a personal preference," Emma started, filing her nails. "But I don't feel like going through the portal in formal wear and, like, heels."

"You've got a point," River said. "Not that I plan to wear heels, but you know."

"Dude, let's just primp at the apartment," Dante said. "Like it's prom."

"And rent a limo?" I joked.

"No, we'll fly, of course," Dante said.

"Shadow and fly?" Drew asked.

"Not bad," I said, thinking.

"Not to sound like my priorities are off," Dante went on. "But it's a fact that we're going to have to find time to do some shopping."

"Yes," Emma nodded, emphatic. "Yes."

"I nominate you, Dan," I said. I let them talk. And whispered to Lance: "We need to find out exactly what the numbers are: how many are going to Versailles. How many throughout Paris. Everything."

Tom leaned in to listen. River had her ear buds in, looking out the window. "We should all be there," he gestured in the direction we had just come from. "That's where the action is, right? The Prince will be there," he whispered. River looked over and took out one earphone.

"I want to be there," she said.

"We'll all be there—some inside, some outside," Lance said, getting excited now. This is what he loved, strategizing. "They'll be set up throughout the city, so we need to get the corps fanned out, but the Prince will be here and I'm sure many of his closest advisers. If we can contain them here, then that will keep casualties at a minimum."

"We know so many of the power players. We need to find them that night. We won't be safe until they're all accounted for," I offered, thinking of Aurelia, Beckett, Kip, that tier that had personal grudges.

———

We would spend a lot of time strategizing the next two weeks. Dante and Emma took control of the wardrobe for Versailles, freeing the rest of us to continue our soul saving missions. We kept ourselves busy. There was certainly plenty to do, but I knew by now that there was really no way to keep yourself from focusing on a date circled in blood on your calendar. A day that could be your last. It has a way of making you take stock. As it neared, the usual dread lowered over me like a shroud.

Connor had informed us that the portals closed the day before a Metamorphosi Day, a celestial event we had never needed to be concerned with. The demons would need to be below by sundown or risk losing their powers. Now it made sense why they had always seemed to disappear right before those battles. For us, though, the portals didn't close until sunrise, which meant a night with no threat of attack or of being hunted or having to chase down demons trying to capture souls and bodies in the eleventh hour before the revolution. The freedom of these few hours was almost more than we could comprehend. We had asked Connor to explain it twice before it really set in. We weren't accustomed to living even a few hours without the threat of encountering death in some form.

A week before the revolution though, it was still business as usual. I was passing the time between afternoon and evening rounds at the Montmartre apartment—fully transformed into a war room—printing an updated map from the computer on the delicate desk in the bedroom, when the machine jammed. I gave it a shake and in the process knocked over the stack of books piled up next to it. I supposed it was my fault, they were mostly mine—guidebooks, French magazines, a French-English dictionary, novels—but the desk was too small. I restacked the books and as I did, I noticed a yellow sticky note poking out from *The Time Machine*.

"*Please read if I'm not here to tell you in person,*" it read, scrawled in that familiar handwriting that I knew even without the "*L.*" that followed. My heart stopped, as though I'd seen a ghost: I suppose I had. I opened it up and found an inscription on the title page, dated June 21. "*Dear H—If only we had met at a different time. With love and gratitude for all you've done for me, and with confidence in all that lies ahead for you. Yours always, L.*"

I traced the letters with my finger, reading it again. I closed it back up, holding it for a moment. There was so much riding on this. I had to make it through, it wasn't just about me. There had to be life after that date.

"Hey, Drew?" I called out, placing the book back on the desk and ducking out into the living room. She popped out of the kitchen. "Wondered if you could help me with something?"

———◦◇◦———

"So it kind of occurred to me," Lance started, the sun just beginning its ascent on a mild autumn morning. We walked ahead of the pack back toward Rue des Martyrs after another night spent running around the city in search of souls. We let the others walk along the street and we cut through the park behind the Abbesses metro to leave more of the angel wing antidotes on the love wall: an art installation of tiles painted with the words "I Love You" written in hundreds of languages. We had found that if we taped a stack of them up there, they were gone in a day. So we kept them coming. Lance pulled a small roll of tape from his pocket as I held up a row of the tattoos. "We've never really had a date," he said as he taped. "I mean, have we?"

I leaned against the wall, thinking. "Actually I don't know." I had to smile. "I mean, not to get caught up in semantics and all, but what's a date, right?"

"I know, I wondered that too," he smiled, leaning against the wall now. Neither of us had done much in the way of dating before we'd met each other. And since our meeting coincided with us discovering we were angels and being forced to battle Aurelia and her enclave, we hadn't quite had anything that resembled a traditional relationship.

"Maybe something that doesn't involve running from or toward anyone or anything actively trying to kill us?" I proposed.

He laughed, "Yeah, that seems to qualify. I don't think we've had that, right?"

"Yeah, no, not so much." We started walking. The group was a block ahead of us. I slowed our pace.

"And now that I think about it, that's kind of a tall order, so I can't really promise that right now," he said, shaking his head.

"What with a revolution coming up and all," I finished his thought.

"Exactly," he laughed again, almost nervous. "But, I mean, we're in Paris," he put his arms in the air. This fact was still kind of stunning to us, second only to the angel realm in shock value. "And…." He paused long enough for me to understand what he wanted to say without saying it: that this was more dangerous than anything we had faced before. This really could be the end. He just shook his head, setting down another path: "…and I just think we…we should do something, without all these guys, much as we love 'em. What do you think?" he asked with his hands in his pockets.

"I'm in," I smiled. "Absolutely, I'm in."

The gold flecks sparkled in his brown eyes, a sunbeam catching them right as we turned onto our street: "So, what do we do?" he laughed, ruffling the hair at the back of his head. We stopped at the top of the street; we could see straight down the hill.

"I have no idea," I laughed back. We had been inseparable— his time in hell notwithstanding—ever since we began at the Lexington. But this idea of planning was so foreign. "What do people do?" It was actually an honest question.

"I guess they go to dinner and stuff," he shrugged.

"OK, so we'll eat something, somewhere, and then we'll go do something somewhere? I'll brainstorm and you brainstorm." This was how we handled demon events, so it was fitting that this was how we would tackle a date night.

29

So This is What a Date Looks Like

By the eve of the revolution, we were all so on edge we were grateful to have all made plans to distract ourselves. Those hours were so precious between the closing of the portal to the underworld and our own, we couldn't *not* take advantage of them and the fleeting chance to center ourselves, catch our breath, *and live* before whatever was to come. A sense of finality hung heavy in the house that day and followed us through our work in the city, but by evening it had given way to something more hopeful like clouds parting to reveal the sun: the shared feeling that tonight was rare and could be the last of its kind so we needed to soak it in and make it count. We all buzzed around the apartment, while music played, setting a festive mood as we got dressed. Dante, River and I crowded into the bedroom, Drew controlling the music on the laptop and Emma flipping through her magazines and offering styling tips. After the rest of us went out, she and Drew planned to head up to the portal. I could only imagine it was with hopes of logging extra time with certain fellow angels.

Dante had forced me into one of the boutiques down the street and found me something for tonight: a black cap-sleeve mini-dress that flared at the waist. It was simple but special: when I put it on, it felt perfect even though I didn't quite look like me. I looked like the person I wanted to be. Dante insisted I get shoes too: "Please, Hav, these ankle booties are dying to go home with you," he had said, clicking them together. "You'll thank me."

Outside the window, dusk shaded the cloudy sky, the air still warm for October. I opened the bedroom door just as Lance was about to knock.

"Hey, hi, wow," I said, awkward. He wore new jeans and a new button down and I wondered if Dante had earned a consulting credit there too.

"Wow, OK, so this is what a date looks like, got it," he said. "We should be doing this more often." He kissed me quick. "That is definitely not what one would wear on a demon-hunting mission."

"Thanks, yeah, that's what we were going for. Not demon appropriate. Dante helped." My sentences came out a little jagged. "And you too—not typical demon battling attire."

Though we had been through so much together and spent every day together, I felt butterflies. Tonight I felt like we were different versions of ourselves—non-angel, less force-of-nature physically-powerful versions. We were more like the people we were when we had just started at the Lexington. Tonight would be an alternate universe.

<hr>

He led us out into the street. In one hand he held a small bag from a nearby cafe.

"So I've got ideas. Do you have ideas?" he asked.

"Oh, I've got ideas," I smiled.

"Good. Me first," he said, heading up toward the hill. I stumbled on the curb. I had fought demons wearing heels but for some reason, I felt particularly clumsy on the cobble-stones tonight. He grabbed my arm. "Though I may have to rethink this," he joked as we reached the steps up to the Sacré-Coeur. It was late enough that the crowds had all gone home. It shone, bright and white perched on the hilltop. "Thought we'd start here."

"Nice. I'll meet you up there," I smiled and took off running up the steps, no problem now. Maybe I just needed to be dis-tracted. Perhaps I had been walking too slowly before.

"Hey," he called after me, with a laugh. I waited for him at the top of the steps, but he was only a few seconds behind me. "What are you waiting for? We're going up there," he pointed toward the dome of the church.

He ran ahead, looking back over his shoulder at me and then leapt up into the air, as though we were out for just another one of our flight sessions at the lakefront. Up he soared, gliding winglessly into the night sky. I jumped, feeling the air embrace me and I shot upward. I swooped so close to the building, weav-ing around it, I almost scraped my hands against it. I couldn't resist though, I had climbed here but hadn't flown here, I could appreciate it more this way. I flew past the open room-like space at the very top, buzzing by where Lance was busy laying out the items in the bag he had brought.

"Hey!" he called as I zipped past. I flew straight up to the very top, above that space and hovered for a moment gazing at the city below as the lights twinkled and the tower burned so bright in the distance, looking back at us. Then I shot back down and in through the pillars lining the spot where Lance was.

"It sure beats having to take all those stairs inside, right?" he laughed.

"It sure does. How high is it again?" I climbed up to stand between the pillars, looking out at the city, a breeze in my hair and billowing my dress.

"I think around 217 feet, give or take," he said easily. "It looks nicer when we aren't running around it or scaling it, doesn't it?" he smiled. It was true. It felt so much more peaceful now, on a night like this.

"I love it. Good pick," I said gazing out. I looked at him and he held up a hand to guide me as I hopped back down.

"I thought we should go somewhere not everyone can, and I didn't want to see another soul—"

"Yeah, literally," I laughed.

"Right," he shook his head, smiling. "And I also didn't feel like sharing you with anyone, angel or devil or whatever." He said it shyly, sweetly, looking away.

"Good answer," I smiled. "And likewise." In the center of the space, he had set out a blanket with a softly glowing candle burning at the center, brie sandwiches from the boulangerie we loved, and two bottles of fizzy orange sodas. "This is beautiful, all our favorites," I took a seat and motioned for him to sit down too.

"I almost did wine, should I have done wine?" he asked nervously. "I just thought, I know we're probably going to be flying a lot tonight and you know, drunk flying really is not something I want to try the night before a revolution. And then…"

"No, it's perfect, it's us," I smiled. "*This* is us."

"Yeah, I thought so too," he said relieved. He held up his bottle. "Then to our sort of first real date—" he said, and added, joking: "And to hoping it goes well. Because I think I'd like to see you again."

"Yeah, this could be the start of something," I laughed.

Us being us, we didn't sit still for long. We picked up our sandwiches and hopped up on the ledge between the pillars, letting our legs dangle over the edge, to watch the city, ranking the places we would like to go to if we were just touring.

"Well, I was always curious about the catacombs, but they were kinda ruined for me," he laughed shaking his head.

"Yeah, wow, we sure took a wrong turn there," I smiled. "Don't go in the well, people. It's behind bars for a reason."

We tried to guess where each of us planned for our next stops tonight.

"Pressure's on, this was a good one," I said.

"I know, good luck," he joked.

We even practiced our dance steps for the first time together, giggling and tripping over each other's feet as we bowed and turned and twirled. "OK, I'm not the best, I admit, but you're terrible," Lance laughed, turning around me. "They told me you were bad, but wow. Thank God I'm not actually going to be your partner."

"You're mean and jealous," I joked, curtsying. "And anyway, I'm totally dumbing down my skills right now so you don't feel inadequate." He shook his head.

Finally we packed up our things, deciding to leave the candle and the blanket at the door of the church, in case they could be of use to someone. "My turn," I said, leaping into the air as he followed.

We touched down in the shadow of the Louvre, managing to find a deserted spot for a quick, quiet landing not far from the river. There were a number of bridges nearby but I needed to find one in particular. In the distance, I saw a pedestrian walkway, where couples strolled hand in hand as the lamplight reflected off of what looked to be ornaments hung along a metal framework. "That's it," I pointed. "C'mon."

"Where does it lead to?" he asked.

"It doesn't matter," I smiled.

We stepped onto the Pont des Arts bridge overlooking the Seine, boats passing underneath, and slowed our pace. Both sides of the bridge were covered with padlocks: large and small, an array of colors, some painted elaborately, all bearing initials or names, some even engraved, and each one looped into the metal fencing lining the walkway. I felt inside the pocket of my dress, patting what lay in there.

"So, this is the Pont des Arts bridge," I said, turning that piece of metal over and over inside my pocket. Lance crouched down to get a closer look at the locks, reading their names, studying them. "And there are all these locks here and, you know, people put their names on them and all, and apparently you're supposed to sort of lock your…" I realized I didn't want to say *love*. It hadn't occurred to me until right now that this whole thing might have been just too much. I backpedaled. "So, anyway, you know you can, like, put your names on a lock and lock it on here," I explained again, fidgeting, my nerves on full display. But he stood up, nodding at me in understanding.

"So, it seems we're gonna need a lock then," he said, in a way that told me this was OK after all. I pulled the brass padlock from my pocket and dangled it from my fingers, shy. "Well, then, now we just need a marker or something." I turned it over and he smiled again, taking it from my hand to look more closely. On the other side I had drawn the intertwined L and H of the Lexington Hotel, which we had once adopted as our own monogram, and in tiny letters across the bottom, I had written our first names. He looked at me. "I love…this. This is amazing," he said. "And you did a really good job, actually."

"I know, right? Thanks. I messed up on the first one and had to buy another," I shook my head, I was rambling, relieved that this was going all right.

"So let's lock it down," he said, looking around. I knelt down, searching for the perfect spot, but he touched my shoulder. "I don't know, I'm thinking maybe it should be up high," he said pointing to the ornate streetlight beside us. "It can look out over the other ones, keep an eye on them."

"I like that," I said. He offered it to me, but I nodded at him. "Go for it," I said. There were others walking on the bridge, and he looked from side to side. Satisfied we weren't being watched, he leapt up, holding onto the lamppost, so it would appear to anyone else as though he had climbed. With one hand he looped the padlock, attaching it. It caught the light and shone a bright gold.

"Oh," I said, almost forgetting. I reached in my slim pocket again to pull out two tiny keys. He jumped back down to me and took one of the keys, leaning against the railing. On one side of us sat Notre Dame, grand and imposing, and on the other side the Eiffel Tower poked up into the sky in the distance. "We have to toss these in the water now. To make it official or whatever," I said, as I wound up to throw. But he grabbed my hand.

"No, wait," he blurted, surprising me.

"What do you mean?" I asked, worry nagging at me. "You don't want to be locked up with me?"

"Of course I do. I want to be locked up with you, in all this madness, forever. I love you, Haven." The words were so shocking to my ears, I felt like I lost hearing for a moment. I had to shake my head to snap out of it. "I've loved you from the first day I met you at the Lex, when we didn't know what we were in for—"

"...when we were just two total outcasts hanging out in the hotel library trading books and stumping each other with trivia questions," I cut him off, not meaning to but caught up in it all. I turned to face him, leaning with my back against the railing, watching the golden flecks sparkle in his eyes. "I love you too. I can't imagine going through this crazy, terrifying world—"

"—or underworld—" he cut me off, joking, as he leaned down to look in my eyes, arms on the railing on either side of me.

"—or underworld or angel world or wherever with anyone else." He leaned in to kiss me. I put my arms around his neck, still holding the keys. His lips still on mine, he took my hand and claimed the keys. He pulled back just a moment.

"I think we should keep these," he said, holding them in his palm. "—not to ever unlock them, but just to remind us of where we've been. I want to have this with me tomorrow, through whatever the hell is going to happen." I took one of the keys from him.

"You have all the best ideas, don't you?"

"I do, and it's my turn now," he said. "We're going that way—" he pointed in the direction of the Eiffel Tower.

<hr />

We walked along the path overlooking the river. As we wandered, I slipped the tiny key onto my angel wing necklace. "Nice," Lance smiled. He looped his onto the leather string around his wrist with the fleur-de-lis from New Orleans. We cut through the sprawling green gardens of the Tuileries, and found a stage set up and a band playing before a crowd seated on the lawn. The lyrics were French but the music was just what Lance listened to, anthemic and guitar-heavy. I thought we might be stopping here, but he kept pressing onward, holding my hand to keep me close as the band wrapped up and the crowd dispersed. I saw the lights ahead and I wondered if he and I had actually had the same idea. A carnival stretched out before us, a strip of game booths, food carts, and rides. The lights were flickering out one by one though, closing up for the night. The main attraction lay at the end: a Ferris wheel, lights still on, but grinding to a halt, having given its last ride.

"We're not going to the Ferris wheel are we?" I asked. He stopped walking.

"Yeah, why? I mean, we were," he looked ahead as the lights went out panel by panel. "Sorry, it got late I guess."

"No, I mean, that was my next idea too," I said, smiling.

"Well, then, in that case, let's go anyway," he shrugged. We hung back behind one of the game booths until the ride operator left for the night, then crept out once we were alone. We stared it down. Even without its lights, it was so grand and yet felt like home: like a piece of Navy Pier and our own history transported here.

"C'mon, I'll race you to the top," I said. "But no flying." Even with no one in the immediate vicinity, we were still dangerously close to the street, which was lined with hotels looking out. Climbing would be easier explained if we got noticed. I launched myself up, leaping to hold on to the lowest of the enclosed compartments, then swinging and jumping up along the giant spokes of the wheel. In seconds I reached the top, just as Lance did. We crouched up there looking down into that car. He nodded, gesturing inside and I shrugged, why not. We slid open the door and swung down into the car, feet first, then closed the door to seal ourselves in. We took seats on opposite benches and looked out the side window.

"This is familiar," I said. It was just like that day we'd taken a break from distributing poisoned chocolates throughout Chicago on Aurelia's behalf to visit Navy Pier. "I mean, except for this thing staring at us." I gestured to the window, leaning forward to see the tower, now so close that its light cast a soft glow inside our car.

"My first Ferris wheel ride," he said softly, as though remembering. "That's why I wanted to come here."

"Me too," I said. Eyes locked on his, I moved to sit beside him. "I think the view is better on this side." My gaze shifted to the window for only a moment and then to him again.

"It is now," he said, looking at me. In a flash, his lips were on mine, fast and feverish and the geometry of our bodies, their angles, had entirely shifted: my arm around his neck, his arm snaked around my waist sliding me down on the bench, my hand in his hair, his lips on my neck. I breathed him in and that freshly laundered cotton scent that I loved, that was him.

All thinking and overthinking was suspended. My brain was a film reel at its end, turning and turning in the machine before a blank, bright screen. I didn't know how things were happening, only that they were and at a velocity too fast to process: I had undone a shirt button or two but then my hand had pulled both of his shirts over his head and away. Likewise, the zipper at the back of my dress seemed to have been lowered because I could feel the vinyl bench against my skin. My mind started to catch up, the rebooting process beginning, the *thinking*. And then just as quick, all activity stopped. His lips pulled away mere centimeters, but enough to signal a change.

"Wait a second," he whispered, surprising me. I felt like we had been underwater. I had forgotten what voices sounded like. He inched up to lean on his arm; I propped myself up on my elbows. We were so twisted and entwined, I couldn't even begin to unwind our limbs.

"I thought that was supposed to be my line," I whispered, lightly, but trying to mask my nerves and confusion. The guy wasn't supposed to say that, from what I had heard of these things and read in Emma's French magazines.

He smiled. "No, I know," he spoke slowly, looking out at the city, only briefly setting his gaze on me. "I kind of have a history of telling you things that are not the coolest thing for a guy to be saying. And I can't believe I'm saying this right now. But, we're smart people and I think we should be…practical," he said with regret heavy in his voice. We were nothing if not practical. That was how we had always operated, for better or worse, forever weighing the options and making sensible decisions. Behaving that way was not normal for people our age, shipping off to colleges to begin life on their own. But we had never been normal.

"You think we shouldn't do this now," I finished his thought.

He looked at me now, brow furrowed. "I know, I can't believe I'm talking about, like, *pragmatism*, now. That's really not very sexy at all," he said, rolling his eyes at himself. "I don't think other people are like this."

"Well, I don't see any other people here," I whispered. "And besides we're not like other people anyway, which I think is a good thing. And, also, I happen to find pragmatism very sexy."

"I'm glad to hear that," he said, not sounding convinced.

"And…I was, like, a nanosecond away from saying the same thing," I admitted. Now he looked at me, his face brightening though still unsure.

"Seriously?" he seemed relieved.

I nodded. "Yeah. I was trying to be practical too."

"I mean," he went on, thinking aloud. "On one hand, life is short—" he started.

"Possibly much shorter for us," I added.

"—Despite being immortal."

"We could be the shortest-lived immortals ever. In the history of immortality."

"So you know, I get that. It's crazy because it's like I'm talking myself out of doing something I want to do," he said, trying to make sense of it.

"You do?" I asked, just to clarify.

He nodded.

"Good," I said, glad it wasn't something about me.

"Good?"

"Yeah," I looked away. "In theory, you know."

"Right, exactly," he said, so we were in agreement at least. "However…" he started.

"However," I said, and took a chance: "This is kind of an intense time, with tomorrow and all. For instance, the city may be destroyed and we may be killed and I don't know about you but I maybe need something to kind of live for, you know?"

"Yes," he said, like it was a revelation. "Exactly."

"Like, I don't know, athletes before a big game or whatever," I offered. That made sense to me. To be honest, even if what faced us had been something less than death and destruction, but just finals or the SATs or something, this would probably still be too much.

"Right, like it might help to have some kind of extra incentive to get through tomorrow," he said. "I mean, if we don't make it through tomorrow," his voice softened, as though sorry to have said that out loud. "Then it'll seem like a stupid waste of time tonight to not be…spending it…that way."

"Yeah. But it could be sort of a distraction, what with a possible apocalypse brewing and needing to go into battle and all," I said. "We sort of need to focus."

"I'm pretty sure that if I do what I want to do tonight, I'm not gonna be in the mood to fight a revolution tomorrow," he smiled. "I'm gonna just want to stay here, even with the world ending around me. You know?"

"Yeah, actually, I do," I said. "So…we'll revisit after the impending apocalypse?"

"Deal," he said, readjusting so he was sitting upright. "In the meantime, come here." He held out his arms. I curled up against his warm chest and closed my eyes, lulled by the steady beat of his heart. There we stayed until the alarm on my clock charm buzzed for us to head skyward to the portal just before sun up.

30

The Beginning of the End

We made it through the portal with plenty of time to spare and quickly reconvened with the others, trading carefully edited notes on our evenings as we were all ushered into the library for a final meeting before taking to our assigned locations. The Administration took their places, Connor and Jackson reviewing what we knew of the demons' plans. Elodie updated us on the weaponry we'd each be carrying—various poisonous spikes and stars, antidotes, powders to help extinguish demon fire, those wing markings formulated to protect mortals, as well as a new, highly potent variety to banish demons to the underworld. Henry sent us off simply: "Be strong and fearless, as you all are. I will see you soon. The world will be grateful for your service, as am I." He was as serious as I had ever seen him, almost dejected, which stung me as it always did when someone so usually hopeful, like Dante, darkened. I mentioned it to Connor on our way to wait for the reopening of the portals.

"Yeah, he gets bummed out at Metamorphosi time," Connor said in a soft, reverent tone. "He wants to fight but he can't leave here. He was injured in a battle with the Prince years ago and he's too brittle to make it through the portal now. It's sort of like a curse."

"Does that mean that it could be reversed?"

He didn't answer, as if it was a tangent not worth exploring right now. He looked at me and said: "Just go on and do me proud. I'll see you on the battlefield." He nodded and was swept into the mass exodus whipping through the portals.

———◆———

It was nightfall when we returned, and between the recharging and that adrenaline drip I had come to expect on nights like this, I almost couldn't control the power shooting from me. I was a powder keg. I hoped that all of this kinetic energy, when put to use, would amount to enough force to destroy all that would be in my path. We shot through the air to our home base in Montmartre and dressed briskly, silently, like firefighters gearing up with the alarm sounding. In minutes we were ready. We wore formal black tie attire with the attitude one reserved for donning army fatigues. Dante and Max had found a gold beaded dress with spaghetti straps for me, the idea being to command attention, distract from the soul-stealing efforts. My arrival would likely signal the start of the horror. My gold-beaded heels matched but had been created in Lance's workshop, where they had been reinforced to withstand all manner of physical activity and pack a punch of their own. Beneath the dress I wore items constructed by Dante's lab: "I call it Devlar," he had said. "It's like Kevlar, but way better, because I made it and it guards against a whole lot more than bullets." The girls wore long dresses in different shades, with the same uniform beneath. The men had tuxes, also treated for demon battle. But, despite our finery, we didn't compliment each other or gush in any way. It just wasn't that kind of night.

———◆———

We soared, high over the city and shadowing so we would appear only as dark birds in the night sky should anyone bother to look up. When we arrived at Versailles, we landed within the twists of the garden maze. Several of our fellow angels were already stationed there, watching, waiting, ready. Baroque music played and the fountains danced, lights trained on them giving a serene glow to the sprawling gardens. We walked up the steps, candles lighting the entire way to the Hall of Mirrors.

"Fire hazard," Lance whispered as we walked.

"Something tells me there'll be a lot of fire hazards tonight," I said, scanning every inch of the hallway, taking everything in, preparing. We reached the entryway and heard the same music from outside, this time fuller and with a background soundtrack of buzzing conversation.

"They always have known how to throw a party," Dante whispered. The entire space was covered in candles: they were perched on every windowsill and every sculpture and chandelier, the only light coming from their glow, which was reflected in those many mirrors. White-gloved waiters flitted around bearing trays of crystal Champagne flutes or canapés. A string quintet sawed spiritedly at their polished instruments in the corner. The crowd had already gathered, hundreds of people milling about. I recognized many faces from news headlines. They were titans of the international business world, some were world leaders, several wore military uniforms, and a large percentage had brought along their poised and well-attired teenage sons and daughters. This had been the goal after all, adding to the demon population and extinguishing the old guard here all at once. Everyone, every single body flickered before my eyes with that strobe effect again, that constant transition between human and rotting beast. The only exceptions were the eight of us, the other angels mingling under the radar in the room, and a few lucky souls who already bore those winged markings poking out on a back here or an arm there despite concealing makeup that had been applied atop of them. Then there were those creatures glowing in the blood red of the underworld: demons. There were scores of them, evenly distributed throughout the room, some as guests, some as wait staff, some as musicians, all beautiful on the surface with a lethal spark behind their eyes. I had to take a moment to sort it all out and make sense of this blinding scene.

The ping of silver on crystal filled the room. The music stopping for a moment. The candles, somehow, all seemed to dim at once. After all of our splitting up and circulating, Lance and I now stood near the entrance to the room beside a window to keep an eye on any arrivals or departures outside. I noticed the same reflection appear in each of the mirrors: it was that of the Prince. We expected a speech of some sort, a welcoming, but there was none. Only a deep voice calling out: "Your distinguished host."

The Prince strode in. The room stayed silent, watching and admiring. He wore a tuxedo, his hair slicked back and a smirk on his face, his eyes scanning the room as he walked. He took a deep, cleansing breath as though savoring this, all of these people here for him. This is what he had waited so long for, and this home and this city were his at last. The Duke trailed him, Kip beside him—he still had not fully healed from New Orleans, one side of his face pocked as if from a severe burn—and I spied Clio, Sabine and Raphaella. I wondered where the others were right now and traded glances with Lance. As they walked, a space cleared around them until they took places standing in the center of the room, the men lined up facing the women. The crowd stepped back to give them ample space and the deep voice called out again: "Those wishing to partake in the courtly dance are invited." The music began again as they stood there, other pairs lining up: dates; fathers and

daughters; mothers and sons. The lines stretched out at least a dozen duos facing each other. Lance and I took our place at the far end of the group. Ready. At last those six in the center began, and the rest of us joined in. Lance and I bowed to each other and carried out the steps better than we ever had before, turning around those beside us, each making our way through the line toward our intended targets: he would go after Clio, and I was to take the Prince. Within a few repetitions of the routine, we had reached the central sextet. Sabine and I locked eyes, trading death stares. She, too, I could see now, still bore the evidence of our tussle in New Orleans: burns along her face, artfully obscured with makeup. I swooped in front of another girl my age, cutting her off, in order to twirl directly in front of the Prince. He smiled the cruel, hard grin of someone with a dark, violent secret to tell.

"So nice of you to join us," he said, staring me down as we turned linking arms, his so fiercely hot.

"It seems everyone wants to dance with the devil these days," I said coldly. "We're going to have to do something about that. If you'd like to let these kind people go, I'd be happy to destroy you without an audience."

He ignored me. "I'll be taking them with me. But I was waiting for you." He could have killed everyone so quickly, instantly without breaking a sweat, but that wasn't the point for him. He had a fantasy he wanted to live out. He had waited for this, planned for it, and he wanted to relish it. That is what gave his chilling brand of evil its dark depth, and that would be our saving grace and our opportunity to stop it. The baroque music transformed into something I recognized now, something more current. Lance would know it, something made eerie and haunting by the strings. I looked for him now.

"So you waited. Well, aren't you well-mannered for a psychopath," I said. I had to wait to be struck first. That was how this worked, that was when our powers were their strongest. I felt every inch of me on guard.

He smiled and laughed as we turned. I cut off the next girl who was supposed to link arms with him. "A psychopath, is that all?" he whispered in that voice, honey-soaked. "You don't give me enough credit." We twirled once more. "I was so enjoying this, but it appears you need me to show you all that I can really do. Very well," he said it all with a bored sigh. I noticed the Duke had dropped out of sight. I spotted Lance pinning him to the wall in the back.

The Prince stopped short now, everyone still dancing around us, and he began to raise his arms toward the mirrors. I rammed my elbow fast into his chest—which felt as though it were made of steel. He grabbed my arm, spinning me around as though dancing again. With my other hand I grabbed one of Dante's spikes from my hair, where it had been acting as a barrette. I slammed it into his neck as I twirled around him. He threw me aside, ripping it out of his skin easily but the dancing stopped. The music didn't, it only quieted, a red glow now emanating from the entire devilish string quintet.

"*Excusez-moi*," the Prince said. "Welcome to the beginning of the end, or perhaps the end of the beginning. *Amusez-vous bien*," he announced calmly to the puzzled group, with a grand bow. At once, the strings crescendoed, wailing.

With one sweep of his arms he brought the mirrors crashing down, punctuating the music. BOOM.

The entire room scattered, women slipping in their heels, men clumsy and stumbling as they hurried away. The candles flamed higher and higher, as though a dial had been turned up. They danced, trying to leap from their wicks onto anything in their path. Clio hurled herself at me, knocking me down, as the fire caught onto the walls, the sculptures, engulfing things you didn't expect to burn so swiftly. Still more flames crept in from the adjacent room, the war room we had arrived through, effectively blocking that exit.

I heard the rumble and felt the subtle quaking underfoot only seconds before it happened; there was no time to herd everyone away. The center of the floor gave way swallowing everyone, everything down, down, down like a sinkhole. The fire slithered, wanting to return to the underworld, hungry. Our fellow angels followed those who had fallen, swooping down to catch them and return them to solid ground. I threw Clio off of me, ramming a pointed star into her shoulder, just in time to see Sabine attacking River. I flew to her aid.

"This is the worst kind of reunion," I said as I pried Sabine off of River.

"Tell me about it," River said, delivering a kick to Sabine's gut.

"Didn't wanna see you either, but watching you die will make it worth it," Sabine answered, so confident even as I threw her across the room into a wall.

The room now a conflagration, guests scurried to break windows, trying to climb down to the garden as the hole in the floor deepened and spread. I caught sight of hazy crimson spots outside, like red fireflies, and knew demons awaited the fleeing masses. I hoped the angels there could intervene. As I kicked at Sabine, I caught a glimpse of the Prince on the other side of the room, still standing at the edge of the pit. He stared in for a moment, as he sipped Champagne, gleeful and at peace as the music carried, the strings section clearly instructed to keep playing at any cost. He leapt over to one of the broken windows and with one hand he plucked away a man trying to escape and threw him effortlessly into the pit. Then he jumped out the window himself. The upper echelon all stopped fighting and fled along with him, out into the night like rabid dogs hunting down prey. We followed them to the window. As I ran, I stripped off my dress. The others did too, leaving us in tank tops and slim knee-length cargo pants all made of that thick, leather-like material Dante's lab had constructed. We couldn't let the Prince and his most powerful get away. I flung myself out the window and then up instead of down, flying over the grounds where more of our kind were sparring for souls. Fire spit out of the fountains now and the once vibrant green of the grass and gardens charred before our eyes into a deathly gray, dying. A crash echoed behind us shaking the ground and heat radiated out at us. We stopped midair to look back.

The palace was engulfed in flames reaching far up into the sky. The pit to the underworld had swallowed the entire center of the compound and worked its way out to the edges.

Tom had flown ahead of us, hovering over the maze of high hedges, where that same deathly gray was withering them. He and the other guys had shed their tuxedo finery to reveal t-shirts of the same lab-constructed material as our clothes. "They went through here," he shouted as we cut across the air to him. He pointed down to another fire-spewing fountain.

"Portal," I said.

"There's gotta be another way," Tom said.

"They're not done," I said. "There's no way they're done."

"It's just a shortcut," Lance said. They couldn't fly as we could, but they had plenty of portals to get where they needed to go. He had to be right.

"Back to the city," I directed.

⁂

As soon as we neared central Paris, we saw it. A blackout had fallen over the city, all light extinguished, all power gone. It should have been in complete darkness, but the fires lit it up. Buildings burned, flaring up in pockets surrounding the greatest landmarks. Elsewhere in patches of red haze we could make out people being dragged into the street by demons and attacked for their souls while angels, many of whom we recognized and many with the wings sprouting on their backs, fought against them. They would herd those they could save, carting them to the Sainte-Chappelle—a church that could serve as our small fortress—for safekeeping. Dante and his team had worked throughout the week to seal off all known portals. He had started with Notre Dame, where we had even stationed angels to keep watch, and the various cemeteries. But now smoke seemed to rise even from Sainte-Chappelle, and Dante and Max veered off to investigate.

Demons climbed out of every manhole, like sewer rats, catching anyone who wasn't one of their own and killing or converting them. The latter was a quick enough process: the terrified humans were simply restrained and stabbed with the toxin and then, within minutes, the demons had a new member. But what fun was it to have so many devils and not enough people to kill? So a great number were murdered on the spot—the act bonding them and giving the demons a newfound strength. Everywhere we looked was a new kind of horror bearing the trademarks of torture of an earlier time. Outside city hall, a guillotine with a blade of fire had been set up, where demons had already disposed of those whose souls they didn't care to seize. They rolled the heads to one side of the lawn, and discarded the bodies on the other. In the Tuileries, a mortal was being drawn and quartered. But instead of four horses, a quartet of demon brutes held a captive by his four limbs, running and pulling in opposite directions until he was in pieces.

In each of these acts of unspeakable violence, our fellow angels arrived, circling and swooping in just as we reached the scene, but we were so vastly outnumbered. For each angel thwarting one of these attacks, five demons would pounce.

One by one our group split up to aid those on the ground. But Lance and I continued onward. The only hope was to cut off the head of the snake: find the Prince. Destroying him meant crippling everyone else. We looped back to the Eiffel Tower, black and foreboding. In the firelight we saw several figures scaling it, leaping fast, easily swinging to the top. As soon as they reached that pinnacle, the top of the tower started glowing red.

"They're there," I said as we flew ahead.

"It looked like there were at least three, maybe more."

"Probably more."

"We don't know what they can do, but we've got our own arsenal and we have the power of flight," he said, rehashing the strategy we had worked out. "Keep moving and take your shots. He's weakened. Our best chance is to wear him down. My guess is he's only got a few big moves and he'll run out of steam." As he spoke he soared faster, and I matched his pace. The faster we flew, the faster I wanted to fly. I felt the adrenaline begin its welcome drip into my bloodstream.

"You've always been surprisingly good at a pep talk. But I never knew you to be such an optimist."

"Easy, we're getting through this," he said, his voice firm. "Got to." As we neared the tower, we could see the four of them there: the Prince, the Duke, Kip and Brody. They looked out onto the burning city, as though preparing for their next move. We flew low and came up from below them, flying around the side of their lookout perch. There we found Trevor. He shouted the minute he saw us, "Prince! Look who—" Lance just sped up, flying right at him, crashing through the protective caging of that upper level of the tower and twisting to kick him in the head, knocking him out. We expected him to get up and we hovered, poised for it, but that was it. Lance marked him with the wings, and his grotesque body withered, banished below again.

But the Prince and his crew had heard him. Kip and the Duke came running now, along with at least half a dozen enlisted in their army, none of whom we recognized but all with fire burning in their eyes, flaming spears in their hands. We dodged and kicked, throwing Dante's stars when we had the chance and managing to hold them off sufficiently enough to slap those wings on them, until only the Duke and Kip remained. Just as the four of us were about to pounce on each other, the Prince appeared.

"Am I really going to have to do this myself?" he asked, perfectly calm but in a tone that sent shivers. He had his arms behind his back as he strolled out from his lookout in front. "You've made things difficult for me. So it's high time I make things difficult for you."

With that he held his arms out and shot a wall of fire at us. It was so powerful the fierce heat emanating from it seemed enough to melt our skin, overcome our mental faculties, and push us off the viewing deck. We tried to run from it but it chased us to the railing and we went over, no choice, freefalling a moment until we regained our strength. We shot back up only to find the fire waiting for us: it had crept up to hang in the air, on the clouds.

The sky was on fire.

We flew into it before realizing and singed our wings, the sharp burn searing them, sending us falling down to the ground again. Two other bodies followed: Kip and Brody. They pushed us further back with fire in their hands. Lance sprung to his feet, tripping Kip and kicking him with such force he hurtled straight back several yards away to smack against one of the tower's steel legs. I pegged Brody in the chest with one of the poison-laden stars. He fell to the ground and struggled to pull it out as two low-flying angels appeared over his shoulder: River and Tom.

"They've got Emma," she shouted to be heard over the roar of the fire. "But they're looking for *you*. It's Aurelia." Kip was rousing in the distance. "Connor and Jackson went in with Drew, but we got separated."

"Go," Lance said, watching. "I got this and I'll be there when I'm done. We'll come back for the Prince together." He strode off toward Kip, as he did, he pulled a street sign up from the ground with one hand, then took another in the other hand and walked over, strong and tall, as Kip leapt up on his feet. From the air though, I could see the stream of demons rushing toward the tower and to Lance and Tom. Tom stayed behind while I zoomed away, following River.

31

Ladies' Night at the Louvre

River led the way as we flew low to avoid the fire above us, the flames hovering in the sky, suspended there, trying to lick us as we jetted by. Below us the city lay ravaged—a war raging, screams piercing the air, demons running wild, bodies scattered on the ground. My great hope was that Dante and Max were rounding up the living and keeping them safe. We reached the courtyard of the Louvre and I understood. The space had been transformed into a contained battlefield. More bodies lay on the ground as demons, glowing red with their diseased souls on full display to me, charged at our compatriots with bayonets of fire, shooting them like javelins. The angels flew and dodged, retaliating with the weapons from the arsenal we each carried and using levitation to hurl other objects at them—streetlights, signs, trash receptacles—and finally, projecting those blinding laser-like beams to spear them back. If the demons took enough jabs they could be weakened, and banished again.

"Do you know where they are?" I asked River, scanning the scene as we approached it from above, not sure where to begin in this melee. Some demons spotted us and launched fire bolts at us; we swerved to avoid them.

"I think I know where they want *you*," River said, pointing ahead. I had been so focused looking down I hadn't yet noticed it.

On the sparkling glass pyramid at the center of the Louvre courtyard, my name—"HAVEN"—was scrawled in blood. A fire seemed to be burning underground in the space beneath the pyramid, its light illuminating the glass where smoke was trapped. The fountain surrounding it looked like it had been filled not with water but with something darker and thicker, stagnant. I had seen something like this once before in the underworld: a pond of blood.

River went on: "I fought off as many as I could but they pinned me down. They seemed to be dragging her in there." She pointed to the pyramid, well below us now as we flew to hover up near the top of the Louvre itself. I spotted quiet Jackson, in warrior regalia now, he hovered just above a pack of devils near the fountain, spinning in the air, so fast he generated a wind that blew them back into the bloody water, against the building, mowing down others in their path. He finished with a bolt of light like a shock. I made mental notes on this display as River went on. "They brought some mortals in there too. I saw Connor here, it looked like he was headed that way. We're stronger than most of them but there are just so many." She shook her head. "I just felt like we needed more help here, I had to find you."

"Glad you did. Let's go," I said, launching out from our perch toward that pyramid again.

"Should we go through up here?" River asked, proposing crashing through the glass.

"No. I don't like that it's filled with smoke, we can't see where we're going. There's got to be a reason. Let's do this the old-fashioned way," I motioned down around the other side to the bank of glass doors, smoke still obscuring our view, guarded by demon sentries, their arms folded as chaos swirled around them. They looked calm, at peace, as though they were simply bouncers guarding the doors to another nightspot, like the Vault of the Lexington. There were three of them at this entrance. We floated up at the top of the pyramid, the glass so hot to the touch we couldn't lean against it. With just a nod at each other, we swept down, crashing onto the men and knocking them out, smashing their bodies through the glass doors to give us an opening. Smoke rushed out at us. In no time those fighting would discover this and come after us, so we slipped into the building, taking advantage of the cover and on guard for an attack.

We found ourselves at the top of the spiral staircase. An elevated platform, like a cylinder rose up from the floor below and as it did, we found Emma laying there. Smoke swirling around us, we reached to pull her out fast. Just as we did, a fiery blade shot down from the top of the pyramid, burning through the platform. If we had come in through the glass, we would have flown directly into that weapon—I was sure that had been the hope.

"Emma!" I shouted into her limp body, as we knelt over her. I checked her chest to see if she was breathing, then felt her pulse and detected only a faint beat. Just above her heart I found a deep burn glowing red like a hot coal. I touched it with my palm to pump her heart but it seared my skin. "Emma. No. C'mon." I tried again. I wouldn't allow this, I wouldn't accept it. Emma was strong. This wasn't possible. River was stunned silent.

"Can you fly with her?" I asked. She nodded manically. "Take her to Dante and Max. If anyone can do something, they can."

The smoke filtered out and I heard footsteps. I braced myself. Through the haze I saw the wings. It was Connor, leading a group of angels, Drew among them. All beaten, all bloodied, but alive.

"It's clear down here," he said, a handful of angels at his back. "We're going back out there and—" he stopped midsentence. Drew ran ahead to us.

Through the doorway, I saw demons charging our way now. "Cover River," I told them.

The smoke dissipated and I looked up to see Aurelia poised like a jungle cat, staring down. The fire cast a glow and I could see she hadn't entirely healed from our battle in Chicago. She still wore her diseased soul on the outside, her face marred around the eyes, though her hair was still lustrous, her lips still curled in that smirk she did so well. I charged up through the pyramid, shattering the glass all around me, raining it down onto the battle scene below, overcome with the need to destroy her again and for good. For Emma. Outside was deafening after having been away from it: the roaring and crackling fire; the sirens piercing the air; the screams and the yelling. A soundtrack of chaos and hysteria. In the distance I could see that Ferris wheel come untethered and start to roll.

Aurelia leapt away, skittering across the battlefield clear to the other side of the courtyard as I soared over it determined to get to her. She landed on a railing outside a strip with tables bearing half-eaten meals, chairs knocked over, a scene from which people had fled. I walked back through the outdoor tables and inside, my footsteps now clicking against the black lacquered floor. It was entirely dark, the haze from the fiery pyramid not carrying this far. Silence swallowing us.

Candlelight flicked up somewhere in the back. My eyes went to it: the flame was attached to Aurelia's finger. She walked closer. She opened her hand and a fire sphere hovered there, lighting her pock-riddled face. Her still luminous hair glowed golden.

"And how is your friend?" she cooed. I didn't speak, I just stood there watching, waiting for the right moment. "I just wanted to get your attention. So busy these days, you don't even have time for an old colleague. No matter. It's so fitting I should meet you here, my young protégée," she went on, in that raspy voice of hers. It gave me chills, transporting me to another time before I had known what was ahead for me. I clenched my fists. Ready. "Remember when you ran my gallery? You were such a gifted photographer."

"I didn't come here to reminisce, Aurelia," I said flatly. My mind shot back to Chicago, to the battle when I had come so close to not making it through. I was a different girl now.

"Oh, no? Well, then, why *are* you here?" She leaned against a table, the way she always used to sit on her desk at the Lexington, asking her smooth, slow, venom-laced questions to make you nervous.

"You know why," I said, managing to match her calm.

"Ah, yes. Of course. This sweet angel has come to kill me," she smiled. "Someone has to go. What a shame. And in a place of such beauty," she said with that mocking tsk-tsk. "You never seemed to understand that we could be so much stronger together. You and I. Oh, the Prince has always had his favorites," she flitted her hand and rolled her eyes. "One foolish boy after another, thinking they were going to become all-powerful. This Kip person or Beckett or your dear Lucian. But we are so much more than all of them. They underestimate us, to their detriment. Aren't we sisters in the battle against the men in our worlds?" she asked.

"I don't think so. And unless you're looking to join *my* ranks, this conversation is over," I said.

"You could have had such a beautiful life with *us*…" She hissed on the word "us" to be sure I heard correctly. She held her hands out to either side, another fire sphere forming in her other hand. Behind her now, a trio of figures stepped forward from the shadows: Sabine, Clio, and Raphaella. The women who had haunted me, tormented me, tried to destroy me. They smiled vicious smiles.

"So it looks like it's ladies' night at the Louvre," I said.

"I'm afraid *your* night is ending. A pity," Aurelia said. "You could've had a beautiful life," she repeated. "But at least now you'll have a beautiful death."

With that she launched her spheres at me, their flames crisscrossing as they pursued me. I dodged them as Sabine and Raphaella charged at me.

"Say hi to Lance for me," Sabine said. But that was all I needed to hear. I held out my arms, levitating two of the tables between us and hurling them with such force I managed to pin her and Raphaella against the far wall. Clio leapt up behind me but I flew away, soaring up to the ceiling and, from there, sending a barrage of debris shooting at them: light fixtures and chairs and plates and dinner knives. They pelted me with fire but I grabbed a tall lamp and wielded it like a sword, deflecting the bolts and sending them shooting back their way. I kept aloft, landing on the floor only long enough to kick them across the room, then leaping up again into the shadows. Aurelia, angered and frustrated, sent a fire spear at me, nicking my leg, and I went down. I understood now—there was something new in these bolts, stronger than we had encountered before. They lodged in you and threatened to burn you from the inside out. I couldn't imagine what it would have been like if I had not had the barrier of that material from Dante's lab to mitigate its effects. As it was, I had lost most of the feeling in my left leg. I had a tingling sensation there, though, and that gave me hope that I would be able to move soon. The four of them descended on me. Still on the ground, I reached into my tool-belt outfitted with antidotes and flung those stars at each of them in rapid fire before they reached me. Sabine and Raphaella dropped instantly. If I could just get to them with the wings, they would be banished. It would take more to stop Clio and Aurelia, though. They both froze for a moment, gasping, to tend to their injuries as I gathered my strength. "Look at those two.

Lightweights," Clio cackled at the fallen demons as she patted the spot on her arm I had hit. Aurelia just shook her limbs out and shot another fire bolt at me, which I deflected with a beam of my own. Clio stepped into the crossfire, yanking my top to pull me the rest of the way up to my feet. "C'mon Aurelia, hiding over there behind all that firepower," she looked over just a moment then spoke directly into my face. "Let's get our hands dirty, it's more fun that way."

As soon as she said it, she let go of me and fell to the ground, smoke coming from her body and her skin turning to ash.

I stumbled a moment but caught myself, my leg steady again. I whipped my head around. Aurelia stood there, a smile on her lips.

"She always bothered me, so cavalier," she said slowly, pleased. "I don't enjoy being told what to do. I've been wanting to do that for quite some time."

I didn't move. This is what made them so different from us: they would kill each other without a thought during a battle even if it meant no longer outnumbering their opponent. I cautioned myself to keep my guard up. I knew she would turn on me again. My fingers readied themselves, set to pull a spear sheathed in my thigh pocket.

She stepped closer, the blaze from the courtyard lighting her face, competing with that red glow that surrounded her. "I certainly wasn't about to let *her* kill you," she said in the kind of voice that could lull a person to sleep. "I have at least earned that much." She threw out her arm, unleashing another bolt, and I flew up above it and flung the spear. I heard footsteps running through the adjacent room. The spear wedged itself in her shoulder and she cried out in pain, arching her back against the sting. But still she remained on her feet, holding out both arms and turning in a circle, lighting the whole room with vicious, poisonous fire. I swooped down to tackle her, trying to stop her.

But I felt it immediately. The air entering my lungs was deadly, heavy. The air outside had helped dissipate its effects as it burned the city, but here there was no escape. I dropped to my knees, my vision hazy. Aurelia grabbed a fistful of my hair, the hair she had once cut off in my sleep during my stay at the Lexington. That memory flooded back, along with all she had done to me, to people I loved. She placed a burning index finger to my neck. The room crackled and spit around us. She was going to slit my throat with fire. "Did they tell you what happens if you're killed by one of us on this day? Your soul doesn't come with us, you know. It dies. It withers like the delicate, weak thing that it truly is. What a terrible waste. You could have been so much more." I knew she meant I could have been so much more with *them*. But the words burned inside me, infuriating me. I shored up my strength, let myself appear to go limp for a moment so she eased her grip and then in one sharp movement I grabbed both of her hands, leapt onto my feet and flipped her in front of me. I swung and threw her into the flame. Her body jumped, the flames kicking it around before charring it, but she righted herself again. Her body was entirely on fire as she walked slowly toward me. Now I saw that the fire had roused Sabine and Raphaella too. Before I realized it they each had slithered over and grabbed my legs to hold me, hoping I would go down in flames. I tried to take flight with them attached, hoping to kick them off, but I couldn't. My muscles went slack. I had precious few minutes. I twisted, shooting what laser power I had left. Raphaella let go, dropping again. I looked behind me and Drew rushed through the doorway. She shot another spear at Sabine.

"I never liked you, Sabine," Drew said in her strongest voice. "And I like everyone." I slapped angel wings on their wrists, banishing them for good.

"Thanks, nice timing," I shouted over the fight. Seeing her gave me a jolt. I sprung up to my feet again as Aurelia closed in.

"I owed you one," she said quickly, then threw one of the pellets at her to lessen the fire and let me get close enough to slash at Aurelia with all the light power I could muster. With two sharp swipes across her chest and torso, I felt her soul shear from her body. I separated the two, focusing all my efforts on levitating it free as Drew beamed a final star at her. The flames crept closer toward our circle. Aurelia's body dropped. It instantly reduced to ash, but unlike that time in the Lexington, today there would be no regeneration. Her soul turned from a grotesque hazy blur to a ghost of her attractive former self to a more reserved looking version. This must have been the Aurelia who had first been recruited. Then it too turned to ash. I fell again.

"C'mon!" Drew said, pulling my arm. "Outside." She tugged and got me to my feet and helped drag me, one arm over her shoulder, back out into the battle raging in the courtyard. But now the red glow had diminished. Our side seemed to be holding the others off, knocking them out. We stopped in the shadows of a doorway, catching our breath just out of sight from the battlefield. Sirens rang, those tortured screams continued and the temperature had risen since I had been inside.

"I would've come sooner, we got attacked, but things have eased up now," she explained, looking around the corner onto the courtyard.

"Thanks. Seriously," I gasped.

"Glad to help."

"Emma?" I asked.

"River took her. They got out but that's all I know."

A few breaths of cleaner air and I began to feel better physically but in the pit of my stomach my fear grew: I hoped I had enough fight left in me to do what needed to be done. I still had a Prince to destroy. In the distance I noticed now the entire Eiffel Tower glowing red. He was still there; I was sure of it.

32

At Last, You're Mine

We flew low, intending to head toward the tower but didn't make it very far: the Sainte-Chappelle with its stained glass and centuries old stone had been reduced to rubble, smoke rising from it but fires no longer burning. It, too, had become a battleground. But while the building had not stood up against what had been leveled at it, I took hope in the many red-hued bodies lying lifeless on the ground as mortals ran and angels swooped in the air. Our brethren hovered, directing the fleeing masses, which had been seeking safe haven inside. Some of our kind helped pull those still trapped, while others fought the remaining demons that had infiltrated, striking them down and banishing them as swiftly as possible.

"Where will they take them now?" Drew asked, horrified as we flew nearer. I could make out Dante and Max from this distance and breathed a sigh of relief that, despite the madness, they had things as much under control as anyone could. I wanted to help. I wanted to be everywhere, but I knew I couldn't. The burning sky had begun to rain hot embers. They left burn marks dotting our wings, a sharp pain registering in our shoulders. I just flew faster to cool them.

"I don't know, they may have to—," I started, but was distracted. I looked back at the tower again. I wondered where Lance was.

"Go," Drew said. "I'll help here and then we'll come to you."

I nodded, "Thanks," I said. "Watch yourself." I swooped away, surging back toward the tower.

⊷◆⊶

As I neared it, flying close enough to the Seine to see the many tour boats left abandoned on the banks, I found that the battles had become more centralized. The masses had crowded from the side streets onto the park surrounding the tower. Typically a place of rectangular-pruned trees, peaceful symmetry, and lush greenery, now it had all gone gray, just like the gardens of Versailles. It was a war zone. The skies were crowded with angels directing those sharp beams down at their predators. I dodged fire bolts shooting up from below as I flew, and rose up higher to escape the demons leaping many feet in the air as they attempted to grab hold of our arms and legs and tug us down.

That blinding red glow at the tower's spike-like top assured me that the Prince must still be there gazing down on the bloodshed with pride. I didn't dare go after him without some backup. The hardest fought battles would be those closest to the tower, that's where I would find Lance. I flew on, weaving between angels and demons, so fast their crossfire didn't have time to hit me. I slowed enough as I neared to take in the red lights now adorning the tower. Demons hung along the top half of the steel frame, ready to stop us. Some angels had made it onto the second viewing platform but had been thwarted from going higher. Some tried to climb rather than fly, need-ing the leverage they got from holding onto the tower to keep them from being dragged down by the demons clinging to them. Everywhere I looked, demons tried to pry angels from the ornate latticework, wounding them to make flying diffi-cult, trying to gain any advantage. I rocketed upward, my wings pushing me higher. Only a few angels hung on at the very top. The air filled with a charred scent and a thick haze hung beneath the sky. I pulled my wings in for a moment, my instincts telling me I might need to hide. It was dark enough that I could shadow myself. Under the smoke screen, I found them now: Lance and Tom. I could understand why few had made it up here: if I hadn't had the ability to see the sinister glow of their many attackers, nearly a dozen of them, it would have been complete darkness. Lance and Tom were fighting in the dark. In the glow, I saw Lance hovering, paralyzed as five demons hung from him. He tried to fly upward against them and managed to kick two from his legs. The demons sunk through the haze, gone. Tom held onto a rung of steel with one hand, throwing punches at demons perched above him and below. One had trapped Tom's hand beneath his fiery paw: it was Brody. I flew snuggly around the steel structure just below Lance and Tom, and tucked myself behind one of the beams. Even amid their struggles, I heard something behind me, breathing. I looked over my shoulder: several yards away clutching beams, a trio of glowing bodies waited, whispering. I felt a breeze, heard that telltale flap and looked to see another winged creature. It was the angel from Lance's workshop, Owen. No sooner had he appeared than the trio descended on him. Before I could get to him, they snapped his wings so they hung limply, then dropped him, watching him fall, disappearing into the darkness as he plummeted to the ground. This must be what they did, they waited for angels to show up and they attacked instantly, a coordinated assault. I had to act.

I crept up a few feet and threw off one of Tom's attackers, a demon clutching one wing. I swiped at him with a light beam, forcing him to let go. Tom, his vigor renewed, threw a punch at another demon hanging from his arm, and was then down to just one grasping at his leg. I pulled him off now, throwing him against the tower, hoping to knock him out. Meanwhile, his legs now free, Lance had the strength to redirect his body in the air. He shifted, holding each demon an arm's length away and flew full force into the tower, ramming them against it. He let go and they slid down, pummeling to the ground below. The trio of demons standing watch leapt out from the shadows, fire in their hands. One landed on my back with a thud. I felt the full weight of a hot mass much larger than me. He tugged, wrestling me, trying to pull me down, and I fell several feet before refocusing and steadying myself. He was forcing me to fight against him to remain aloft. His arms wrapped my neck in a chokehold. Reminding myself demons couldn't fly, I stopped fighting for a moment. He loosened his grip as we fell another several feet, and then like a switchblade, I shot out my wings. They fanned, fast and full, knocking him right off of me with a thump. He grunted at the impact and went tumbling down.

I flew up and nearly into Lance, free of demons and on his way to me.

"Nice," he said, as we flew back up to Tom.

"Yeah, these things are pretty good as flyswatters," I said.

Tom delivered the final kicks to the chests of the two remaining demons, flipping himself backward as he sent them smashing into the side of the tower. We watched them fall.

"I think we're good here," Tom said, looking around should anyone else emerge hell-bent on killing us. "Time for the main event?"

This time we knew what to watch for. We flew to the upper viewing deck, through that break in the metal barrier and landed without any interference, having apparently taken out all the demons on watch. We walked cautiously around to the side that would overlook the battlefield. This high up we occupied an odd space between the sky and that hazy layer that we had just come up from. We could feel the heat from above, licking us and spitting its embers, but we could see with no trouble. With each step, I expected something, someone to pounce. My muscles twitched, ready to respond. Each second it didn't happen, a larger dread settled into the pit of my stomach.

Until, at last, we turned the corner onto the three of them.

The Prince and the Duke stood with their backs to us, watching the battlefield below through a vast area cleared of the haze, proving that the smokescreen itself was a strategically constructed weapon. The battle raged so far in the distance it was impossible to make out individual figures, only masses of red hues or white wings. All security impediments, those pesky enclosures to keep a tourist from going over, had been removed. Kip turned to face us now, leaning against the modest guardrail, his arms folded. He didn't need to say a word. The Prince, still looking out, his back to us, spoke into the air:

"Lovely isn't it," he said in that hypnotic voice then breathed in deeply, as though tasting the burning heat and the chaos below. "They are destroying each other so exquisitely, just as I dreamed. All that could make this image more pleasing…" he said, as he slowly turned around, his face glowing red, his eyes crimson and hungry for blood, while the Duke, on his other side, smirked, "…would be to add two dying angels." I noticed he said "two" and not "three," but I had no time to fully process his words. The moment he said it, the Duke and Kip shot out like attack dogs on Tom and Lance. They knocked them over, the two pairs landing clear on the other end of the platform, sparring on the ground and then in the air. I took a step to run toward them and was instantly stopped. A wall of fire blazed up separating me from them. I tried to fly around it and it bent to keep me away. The wall advanced now, forcing me to back up until I was just a body's length away from the Prince. I whipped around to face him. He hadn't moved an inch.

"I'm afraid it's just us now," he said, so still. I steeled myself.

"I find it interesting that you're afraid," I said in my steadiest voice, clenching my fists, sweat covering my skin.

"Ahh, clever," he smiled. "You always were a smart one. That was why we tried to give you so many opportunities to make the smart choice." He moved from his perch now. For each step he took, I took an opposing one. We were slowly circling each other.

"Joining you?"

"Certainly that's better than dying," he grinned.

"I think there are other options."

"That's precious," he cooed. He lunged at me, catlike, and grabbed a fistful of my hair, pushing me back over the railing with a switchblade of fire now at my neck. My hands flew up to try to push the blade away but his rock solid arm wouldn't budge. "You may have a false sense of your power here, my pet," he said, his voice perfectly calm. The fire of the blade sizzled the thin layer of skin at my neck. I didn't fight yet. I sensed he wouldn't kill me until he had had the joy of telling me how much thought had been put into my ultimate demise. I focused away, refusing to look at him until I knew my eyes showed no fear. "I can only imagine that if you have made it to me then you have made it past Aurelia, Clio, and their ilk. And past those associates of yours from New Orleans who joined our fold, and the others placed in your path. Because they had all been charged with destroying you and informed that their failure to do so would result in their own death. At my hands," he spoke carefully, savoring these words. "But they are all nothing really. So allow me to rephrase. What I should have said is: 'At last, you're mine.'"

"Yeah, I don't think so," I said simply, trying to mask what a struggle it was to speak while contorted in his grip. My scalp screamed, his hot claw felt welded onto it. "And all this talk is really boring me." I began gathering my strength. "I'm sorry that you've underestimated me. *Again*. Allow *me* to rephrase:

tonight won't end well for you." With that I curled my legs up fast and pushed off of his body, away from the blade poised at my neck, and flipped us both over the edge of the railing. He didn't let go of me but he was startled enough to drop the blade. He was so heavy as he clutched me though. I snapped my wings out again. He kicked me in the stomach, with such force he propelled himself all the way back to the platform, taking a seat atop the guardrail. It sent me flying many yards back, doubled over. I felt as though my ribs had detached like puzzle pieces. I caught my breath and flew back to him as strong as I could.

"You may wish to reevaluate," he said when I was close enough, a new bite to his tone. He smoothed his hair. "After this." The moment the words crossed his lips, he leapt up onto his feet on the slim railing. Arms outstretched, he roared at me as his hands turned as red as the sky. A torrent of fire shot from them like water from a burst pipe. It swept me up, pushing me, my wings on fire, my whole body burning. The power knocked me over again and again, my body spinning as I hurtled through the air. I couldn't even steady myself enough to see where I was. My skin could withstand a certain level before succumbing to fire, but I worried I was reaching my limit.

When I thought I couldn't take anymore, the heat began to lessen just enough. I hoped it meant I had traveled far enough from the Prince that he couldn't sustain that amount of fire-power over such a great distance. Unable to move, I opened my eyes. Below the Seine glowed, reflecting the sky. I tried to angle my wings, but couldn't feel them. I used every ounce of strength to break free from the fire pushing me across the sky. I jerked my body, like a car swerving to change direction with no warning, and I dove, as though I was a meteor crashing to earth.

I heard myself plunge into the waters of the Seine but it took a moment to feel it, even as the warm water surrounded my body sinking it deeper, trying to heal it. My skin still felt aflame, the way a bad sunburn will continue to sting even against the cool sheets of your bed after a day at the beach. I wasn't sure I was breathing. I felt myself floating, the water licking my wounds trying to soothe me. The river rippled in my ears. I thought of Lance's words. The Prince was weakened; he didn't have the stamina to keep up this kind of attack. If I could outlast him, I would have a chance at destroying him. Not just banishing him so that I'd only have to face him again, but *destroying* him. I fluttered my legs, trying to kick my way back up to the surface. My skin felt tight, like it had been pulled over the frame of a drum and would make a hollow sound if struck. But I kicked and kicked again and slowly began to move.

My head poked up and I choked to take in air. The night tasted of char and death. So much burning and so much extinguished. I turned onto my back to float for a moment but felt myself tugged downward instead, my wings dragging me. I tried to retract them but I couldn't feel them. Hauling the lifeless weights on my back, I swam to the water's edge, hoisting myself up on the stony banks. Laying there against the warm, wet ground, I felt my well of strength run dry. It was all I could do to hold myself still enough to keep from rolling right back in the water. I heard footsteps behind me and then felt the wind rush as something crossed in the air overhead.

A face lowered itself level with mine. The Prince.

"Still alive, are we? How disappointing," he said with that taunting smile. I couldn't quite move yet. The toxins embedded in that intense fire had dulled my reflexes, slowed my wilted body. All I could do was stare into the face of this monster. His hair had become uncharacteristically mussed, his complexion sallow. There was something newly weathered about his overall appearance and aura. I wanted to believe that those exertions had been taxing on him. "Except that it means I get to find more interesting ways to destroy you."

He took a deep breath, gazing above, peaceful. "Come, let's step away from the water, I'll help you," he said kindly. Then he wound up and the crisp, shiny leather of his shoes connected with my stomach, as though delivering a swift, game winning penalty kick. I felt every organ dislodge as I was sent airborne. There wasn't far to go, so I slammed into the wall of the embankment. My wings smashed against it, the tiny bones cracking like long matches snapped underfoot. My head smacked against the ground. I couldn't see anything, but I felt another blow to my chest.

I felt my soul slipping from me, dying. I tried to catch it but it fell through my fingers. In its place, I found a black curtain being drawn over me. Everything grew dim, the world fading away. I had always heard you were supposed to see a light as you're dying, but this was pure, suffocating darkness. It gripped me, squeezing out the last bits of air. I felt everything slow, my system grinding to a halt. The Prince was talking to me, but I couldn't make out the words even though he seemed very near, the heat from his body invading the space above me.

"Aurelia always said you were your own worst enemy," he started, so close. If I could open my eyes I was sure he would be crouching above me. "That despite your supposed angel strengths, you would always have that very mortal uncertainty, questioning yourself, not quite believing. I doubted her. She was wrong about plenty, look at what happened to *her*," he said this like it was a punchline. His tone was perfectly upbeat, making him all the more deranged. "But, it appears she was right about this. Because there you are, the great hope of your kind. And here I am. And it's clear who will win. You are as hopeless. Worthless. Powerless…" he leaned over me, brushing a strand of hair—matted down by my own blood—from my face. "…as that first day I saw you. There was such promise. You didn't understand your strength then and don't now."

His words echoed as though he were repeating them on a loop: Hopeless, worthless, powerless. I hated that this creature whom I despised somehow knew me so well, knew how to hurt me most efficiently. He was calling out my greatest fears. I feared falling short. I thought of those I would let down, those I loved, who I had to be sure were safe, who I prayed were doing better than I was right now. But the Prince knew all of this too.

"If only you had joined us, the body count would have been much better for you: your Lucian would still be with us. Such a shame, the harm you caused him. And you could have brought along those friends of yours who are surely being destroyed as we speak. Lance and the one Etan is presently killing." I now understood the scene I had witnessed outside Sainte-Chappelle: Dante's first love, the demon Etan, had come back to battle him. I couldn't lose them, I wouldn't. And I thought of those far away from here too—like Joan—who I worried would become targets if this creature before me was allowed to defeat us tonight. Defeat, itself, was just a euphemism for death. This needed to end. Now. I heard footsteps, the Prince pacing before me. He stepped on my broken wings and I heard them crunch in a way that bones should not. The pain sent a sharp jolt through my body. He grabbed the wing pendant at my neck, tugging to rip my necklace off and lifting my whole body along with it. When he threw me back down against the hard earth, it knocked the wind out of me. My lungs and my heart struggled to pump. He kicked me again, like a single beat of a snare drum. It could have been a final death knell, I felt so broken, but instead it jarred my body alive again. My eyes sprung open. I still couldn't see but I felt the air on them. This must be what I had glimpsed of myself in the future. But I hadn't stuck around to see if I actually did die. So there was hope, wasn't there? I heard the jingle of the necklace and its charms being tossed beside me. Slowly I heard the sirens again and the roar of the fire. Until at last I could make out his figure, he still stood there by the water, breathing in that victory he seemed so sure was his. Chaos swirling, this beautiful city—his beautiful city—being torn apart, I could see smoke still rising from Sainte-Chappelle in the distance. A few more breaths and I might have the energy to stand…if I wanted to. I needed to wait until I was sure I could do what needed to be done. I would have only one shot.

"The question remains, how best to dispose of you?" he asked walking toward me again, leaning down once more. "By hand? By blade? What will you enjoy the least?" I heard a snapping whoosh of that fiery switchblade. Summoning my strength, I spun on the ground to kick the blade from his hand. It landed, as I had intended, in the river. It didn't extinguish immediately but burned in a contained ring like a tiny chain of islands. Shock clouded his face and gave me a moment to prepare. I closed my eyes, focusing every ounce of my being on catching that diseased soul. I would need to pull it from its body, leaving that soul homeless and dead. Unlike the other souls I had levitated before, this one was solid, firmly entrenched. I would have to wear him down in order to pry it loose. I opened my eyes again.

"This is just another way we couldn't be more different," I started. He spun around at the sound of my voice, frozen as he took in the sight of me standing there, my broken wings trailing behind me. "You start celebrating a win before the clock has run out." I charged at him, then leapt in the air, shooting a light beam. It swiped his chest, paralyzing his body for a moment. I tried to fly up above him, but I couldn't do it. My wounded wings were too heavy. The best I could do was snap another sharp, solid kick at him, knocking him into the water to buy myself a few fleeting seconds to catch my breath.

He burst up, erupting out of the river at least fifteen feet in the air, raining water down on me as he did and shooting lethal firebolts. I dodged, bobbing and weaving, bloodying knees that had already worn through that protective fabric. He leapt, landing atop the railing of the closest bridge. The Pont des Arts, covered in locks, the one I had visited with Lance. I spotted the remnants of a burned tour boat in the distance. I held my arms out toward it, for extra leverage, and willed it to rise, guiding the huge chunks of metal and wood and shooting them at him. The barrage surrounded him, knocking him off the bridge and back into the water. This time he propelled himself up by shooting flames from his hands into the water but rose quickly ten feet up only to have the fire go out, plummeting him down again. *Yes, he is losing strength*, I thought. The possibility itself gave me a jolt. I ran along the bank toward him and beamed one of those poison-tipped stars at him just as he emerged. It connected with his shoulder and he grunted, holding his hands out to the water. A spark ignited a fire around him. It expanded into a circular blazing platform that he rose up to stand on now and continued to creep out into the water. We couldn't have the sky *and* the river on fire. I knelt, skimming fire antidotes along the water like stones, one after another. The water fizzed and the fire sparked and went out with each hit. Something hit my back, burning it like a hot raindrop. I looked over my shoulder: and found a tiny fire drop there. Another landed beside it. I patted them out. The sky was beginning to rain fire. Time was running out.

From the center of that circle, the Prince looked upward, arms aloft as though conducting an orchestra above. He was telling this violent sky to rain. A new ferocity rose in my blood. I set a fierce gaze on the river, swept my arms, and at once the water level pulled down to build a wave like a wall before the Prince. I sent it crashing upon him, then directed it to recede quickly enough to not flow into the city itself. The fiery circle burned black now, the Prince sunk beneath it. I had a few moments. I leapt, dragging my broken wings behind me, and landed on the spot he had occupied on the bridge. I stared down into the black charred water. And found blood-red glowing eyes staring back at me. I held my arms out toward the lethal being and closed my eyes. With all that was left in me I used my soul to pull apart this diseased one. In my mind, the Prince faded into a vile, rotting, beastly creature. It was made of lead and steel, this soul, and it tried to pull me down. I felt myself leaning forward now, like I might fall into the water. My foot slipped and I had to reach down to steady myself on the railing, crouching. My eyes opened too: the river had begun to ripple.

A rush of water exploded and he shot up from below. I saw it all as a flash: Gasping, roaring a guttural roar, his body—the grotesque one in my mind—jerked and whipped as though in the throes of an excruciating pain. As he cried out, his muscles ripped through his neck, the skin dripping from his body, his eyes melting. That red glow still surrounded him. The wind swirled, threatening to knock me down, but I held on, focusing on this creature. As long as that red haze was not extinguished, the soul was still not extracted. But the wind made it hard to hold on: It flipped me, I grabbed onto the railing but my hands were ripped away. My body soared skyward but then stopped. Below me, that beast thrashed. I focused again and now I saw what I had back in New Orleans when we had all first tried to extract diseased souls: a glowing beam tethering my body to the Prince, the white light creeping over him, pulling out his soul. That force is what had propelled me up. This was working. In another minute I might have him, if I could just hang on. I felt a dial spinning inside, about to overload, signaling that my body couldn't maintain this intensity much longer. I descended a few feet in the air, my muscles going limp. Below the Prince sputtered, still alive, trying to grab the bridge and save himself. The red glow around him dimmed. I fell several more feet, my power waning. His upper body flailed above the water. I slipped down again hovering just over the river's surface, my arms still outstretched, my light still pulling at him.

He grabbed my foot. Fire drops began to fall more rapidly now, landing with a sting on my arm and leg, my cheek, and my scalp. The burns would only get worse. Holding my palm out toward him, I blasted one final beam. That red haze separated from his body, like an eerie glowing hologram of the handsome illusion he had been. It flared up into a flame and then went out, shattering the air like a gunshot. At once his decaying body burst up to float atop the water. It sizzled like it was on a skillet. Still hovering, I reached down to slap the wings onto the bony, gnarled hand that had clasped my foot. His body was dead; his soul was dead. I didn't need to do it, but the second I did, his deterioration accelerated. His body convulsed like it was being kicked. It hissed and disintegrated, becoming a film in the water and then nothing. Gone. The fire drops let up too. I looked into the sky to find it darkening again, that canopy of fire dimming, the smoke dissipating, the night returning. Dust sprinkled down, coating my skin: ash from the sky, then pebbles and charred rocks. My body flew up once more, involuntarily, like a balloon released into the sky and then, my energy fully drained, I smacked back down against the earth just as fast, entirely spent.

I landed on my broken wings. They cushioned my body, fanning out protectively around me to bear the brunt of the impact, which still sent a sharp stinging through me. The night had grown quiet though, I no longer heard the screams or the sirens or the battle raging. I rolled to my side: Notre Dame stared back at me in the distance. The stained glass of its rose window now a shattered jagged jaw. In its place I saw the silhouette of an angel. I knew it was Lance, keeping watch over those inside, and also looking for me. I needed to get there, if I could.

33

I Can't Help But Notice We're Still Alive

I pulled myself up, struggling to get on to my feet. If they were still there, I would go to them. We needed to return to the portal before it closed—I needed to get there to heal. There was no form of medicine available here that would possibly repair me. One slow foot in front of the other, I walked, my broken wings scraping the ground. Before my eyes, the color began to come back up on the world. All that had been gray and wilted returning to its natural state. Even in the dark of night, I could see a rich, fullness rushing back. The grass of the Tuileries was greening again, the Seine losing its murky viscosity. The streets here near the Louvre were almost deserted. But then there were still the bodies. So many littered my path: grotesque figures with dead souls; mortals who had not made it; and some of my brethren, battered but most still alive. I stopped before my fellow winged soldiers, helping them to walk on with me. Those who could fly transported wounded mortals to the church. We found pockets of survivors clustered together, hiding out in dark alleys and huddled inside storefronts with broken windows, even up on balconies overlooking empty streets. The buildings we passed housed the silent hundreds, tucked away inside hoping to be spared what had been raging outside their doors. We aided those we found along the way, administering some of Dante's antidotes, taking as many wounded with us as we could and vowing to send help for the others. When I came across a demon, I checked to be sure it carried a wing marking and would be banished before I trekked on.

I encountered only one demon still breathing, perilously near Notre Dame. The group that had arrived with me on foot went ahead inside. I lingered though, catching sight of a figure slumped against the towering statue of Charlemagne in front of the grand west facade. I checked the time: it was five minutes to midnight now. The demon leaned up on bare stark white elbow bones, the skin gone, and looked at me with two eyes hanging from their tethered cords. The skin of his face appeared ripped off in large patches, a gruesome quilt.

"I could kill you now," he said in a low croak as I stood above him. "But I would rather wait and leave you wondering when I'll next strike. I *will* come for you, and make you pay for what you've done to us all."

Without a word, I slashed at him with the last dull spark of light I could muster. He fell to the ground again and I slapped the wings onto the melting skin of his wrist. "Or maybe," he went on, struggling to speak. "I should thank you for eliminating the competition. I am the new king," he gasped as he fluttered now, back to the beautiful version that I had come to know in Chicago.

"Beckett," I whispered as though to myself, my weak body chilled. I tried to focus my gaze and power to sever that deadly soul, but I just couldn't grab hold of it. It was too firmly rooted in him and I was too worn. All I could hope was to maim him enough that he may be permanently weakened or at least take some time to rehabilitate. As Connor had warned, it would be impossible to destroy them all, there were just too many of

INITIATE

them. But we had thwarted their revolution tonight. We had saved lives and we had claimed many of their own. They would need to rebuild before they could try something of this magnitude again. In some of the city's greatest landmarks, angels stood watch over mortals, over endangered souls. And still more angels had defeated demons, preventing them from killing on a grander scale, or recruiting more for their evil cause. I had banished Beckett once before, in the tunnels of Chicago, when I was far less powerful. I would just have to hope my efforts tonight would keep him at bay for a good long time. I managed one last light-beam-slash sharp across his chest and through his heart. As I did, a cry tore out of me from the effort. As my legs gave way and my body crumpled to the ground. His form turned to dust instantly, but my body was spent. As the last trickle of adrenaline evaporated, I now felt the wall of pain hit me full force. Everything I had faced—the bolts that had been shot so repeatedly at me, the fire that had singed my skin, the kicks and blows I had endured—all now registered. It was as though now that the Prince was safely destroyed and the remaining devils tucked away below, my body could finally allow itself to *feel* after a night of self-imposed stoicism and utter numbness. I heard the clomp of footsteps running, but didn't last to see whose they were.

That was my final complete memory of that night.

It felt just like initiation, except that I was alone up there on that floating platform. And we were in the field this time, surrounded by flowers in bloom that I had never seen before: enormous bulbs in fuchsia and plum and canary. Everyone had assembled. This time though, they had all been beaten and bruised and had only just healed again—physically, at least. If they were anything like me, they must have still carried the emotional battle scars with them below the surface of the skin that would never fully fade. Which is why it didn't feel right, my being *here* and them being there. It wasn't as though I had done this entirely by myself. Without my brethren keeping the rest of the demons occupied far away from me, I never would have been able to square off against the Prince and defeat him. Without them, I never would have even made it back through the portal but would have been left to die beside that statue, and the rotted dust that had been Beckett.

My compatriots comprised the first row of the gathered masses. Everyone had returned—everyone who had made it. There were some gaps in the sea of levitating winged creatures below though. Like missed stitches in a tapestry, these holes were all I saw when I looked out, this empty space where some of our own had not come home. Emma among them. I hadn't even had the opportunity to process her loss, let alone to properly mourn. I had never forgotten how she had appeared at my door, reaching out to me when Lance had been taken. She was one of the few female friends I had ever really had. And where Drew was the sweet one I could count on and River the tough one whose sparring kept me sharp, Emma, whether she knew it or not, had occupied the role of an older, wiser sister. From her I had learned how to navigate not the demon or angel worlds, but relationships in the real world—which can be just as foreign. I would replay those events forever to see what I could have done differently to have saved her, hoping to heal that hole in my heart. It was all a sick, sad blur for now.

The last 72 hours had been another kind of void. I still wasn't quite sure how I had managed to get back here. I knew only what I had been told. That those who had walked to Notre Dame came out looking for me with Lance. Then he had found me and carried me inside, my broken wings crumpled against his chest. Dante and Max had turned the cavernous cathedral into both a triage center for the injured and a safe house for those seeking shelter from the soul-hunting demons. Sections had been cordoned off for those who had not made it: in one of these, on a pew behind the choir and before lit candles, Emma had lain. She had succumbed to the lethal fire of the demons, burning from the inside out until only a charred mass remained. The angels had been unable to revive her.

Angels had stood watch over all entry points, including the portals that Dante had sealed, and fanned out around the perimeter, attacking any demons threatening to close in. Dante himself had gone out to battle Etan, shooting those poison-tipped stars while deflecting his firepower. Max had delivered the deathblow, though, banishing Etan below and earning a kiss from Dante. Lance had arrived at Notre Dame only minutes before me, expecting that I would already be there. He had managed to extract the lethal souls of the Duke and Kip. Tom had been injured and Lance, who was also worn from their battle, had dragged his friend back to the cathedral on shaky legs.

Max and Dante had taken to City Hall, searching for any survivors they could aid before leaving. They had returned with only five minutes to spare, just as screeching emergency vehicles arrived to aid the wounded. Certain flashes of memories had returned, like the sound of Lance's voice forcing an upbeat tone to soothe me when he found me: "We've been waiting for you, what took you so long?" And Dante too: "Not enough drama tonight, Hav? You had to cut it down to the wire like this? You've turned into such a renegade. I kinda like it." I remember a roll call, taken to a soundtrack of rushing wind, which must have been when we had gathered at the spire atop the cathedral: "Drew went with Connor's crew and the ones left at the Louvre," Max had said. And River's voice to Lance about me: "I can get Tom, take her." I remember the comfort of Lance's soft t-shirt against my cheek and his arms cradling me so tight as though my body had folded up into itself. The portal registered only as a swirl of pain and light and upheaval.

When I awakened after so many hours, I was back in my room, in the angel realm. Alone. I felt for my wings with my hands, like someone patting their pockets for a missing wallet. They had vanished entirely. Slowly I tried to raise myself up. No sooner had I sat up in bed and managed to get my feet on the ground than Lance and Connor poked their heads in the door.

"Well look who's up," Lance said, his smile as bright as the light of the portal that night. My arm was still swung over my shoulder, scratching my back, searching for signs of healing, or at least something.

"Don't worry about those," Connor said, noticing. "How d'ya feel?"

"Kind of like I crashed my new car on the way back from getting my license," I said. I patted my back where my wings should have been. "Are these, like, going to be OK?"

"You're getting an upgrade," he said, smiling conspiratorially at Lance. I just looked at them, confused.

Henry took his place at the center of the platform, arms raised to silence the group. "It is with great pride that I welcome you today to a first: a ceremony that we have never had the joy of witnessing, at least not as long as I have been here. And that's a pretty long time, I must say." They all laughed. "One of our own has done the unimaginable. Only in our wildest dreams did we believe this might be possible. When we built this breed of angel, we weren't entirely sure whether they would meet our expectations. And they have exceeded them. All of you have," he looked at the row of my friends, my closest friends in this or any world. "But…" he looked out at the larger group again. "I hesitate to give ourselves too much credit, my winged ones," he said it with a smile that brought more light laughter from the crowd. He turned to me now, speaking directly to me as though it were just the two of us.

"It is the responsibility of anyone with great gifts to push himself—or herself—in order to reach his or her greatest potential, to put in the work, to sacrifice. The gifts we bestowed upon you, Haven, would have been virtually useless without your determination to develop them. It is important that you understand that. It's important that everyone understands that." In the audience, I saw many nodding their heads in agreement. Again, as I had during the initiation, I bowed toward them and they returned the gesture this time, Henry among them. "Though I know you, and I know that you feel this distinction should be shared, it is yours alone. You destroyed the Prince, and for that we are eternally grateful. We're not naïve enough to believe that evil is gone from the world, from the universe. We know that the demons will rebuild, but it will take time and we will be there to battle them back again. But we are safer now and we will be stronger than ever before with you among us, our illuminator." He bowed his head to me, which surprised me and I answered it, bowing back.

"Your wings were broken in this endeavor but they have healed and with your fearless slaying of the Prince—" he said this slowly and carefully enough that my mind had time to turn it over, weighing each word. I had done this. It seemed unfathomable that the path through Chicago and New Orleans and Paris had led me here, had shaped me, pushed me to evolve into someone bolder than I ever would have imagined. You never quite know who might be locked away inside you. I was aware more than ever now of these dual personas coexisting within me. There was, most definitely, an intense other identity that had been born, and I slipped into it—my emotional armor—to carry out these angel acts. It wasn't the sort of personality you could inhabit every minute of every day. You wouldn't want it to be; it was too much, too singularly focused. But it was the part of me that could take control and take no prisoners. I was grateful to have grown into this person.

"For your unrelenting courage, you earn our highest honor." He floated above me. "I hereby bestow onto you, Haven Terra, the gilded wings." I knelt, bowing my head and when he touched my back, my wings fanned out around me. Golden and resplendent, they didn't feel like they could possibly be mine. I leapt, involuntarily, my wings making one grand sweep carrying me upward into the space above him. My mind flashed to that angelic creature I had viewed on my visit to the Louvre: not the Jeune Martyre but the Winged Victory. I hovered for a moment, my wings leading me, commanding me to take this moment and the crowd rose up too, cheering. *For me.* I lowered myself, glancing back at my wings for a quick second and shaking my head. The group seemed to notice and chuckled warmly, and then they rushed the platform to greet me. Lance jetted out ahead of them all, pulling me to him, to kiss me. "You wear those well," he whispered into my ear. Then he hung back, allowing the others to float around me, shaking my hand, offering kind words, pats on the back, hugs. Music struck up. There was a celebratory buzz in the air, a warmth embracing us all. Lance took a Champagne glass from a table where they had been stacked in a tower formation and tossed its contents into the air. But before his drink could rain down, he stretched his hand out and the many drops became bits of light twinkling like metallic confetti. Dante did it too, and then Max and River and then others. Some angels began to dance, and then more joined them until it seemed everyone was dancing. I watched them from a perch by those vibrant hedges where we had first arrived. The scene was as free-spirited as any of the demon rituals, but so much better.

Of course I knew it wouldn't feel this way all the time. There would be another Metamorphosi Day. There would be newborn angels pitted against fresh demons. There would be more battles. Our lives were not ours to live as we pleased; they would be built on sacrifice. But they were noble. Connor had told me that. He patted my back now with a smile as he walked past me, his other arm around Drew. In a few private moments walking outside before the ceremony, he had reminded me that my survival meant that Lucian had been returned to his previous life. "He won't remember anything that happened after that night that he first pledged his soul to Aurelia. He won't remember meeting you at the hotel. And he absolutely won't remember the second chance you gave him when you traveled back. But he *will* have that marking on his wrist," he had explained.

"He just won't know where it came from," I added.

"Right," he said. "But, all of that said, since he won't know you, you are welcome to watch over him from the periphery as long as you don't speak to him or establish any kind of relationship with him, no matter how casual. Keep your distance. But we're allowed to check in on the folks we've pulled out of harm's way."

"Kind of like a doctor checking on a patient?"

"Kind of. You can observe, you just can't engage. Anyone who's been given that marking won't remember us, which helps." He had said I was welcome to look in on him as soon as the portal opened, that I was likely to find him back at his school. Civilians had already been hearing stories of those who had disappeared over the past few weeks—"*Les Perdus*"—returning to their homes with no idea where they had been. This would happen to Lucian, he would return, confused, and eventually

AIMEE AGRESTI

be absorbed back into daily life, no clue of all he had experienced as this other identity. He would be John, the shy student with great dreams.

I hadn't realized how my mind had wandered until Dante interrupted my thoughts, elbowing me as he sidled up beside me, a drink in hand.

"Check *those* out!" he said. "Gold is totally your color."

"Thanks. I'm not sure, but, you know, no returns, no exchanges."

"Don'tcha hate that?" he laughed, then nodded toward the party unfolding. It certainly wasn't any mild garden party. "Sure beats the Ring of Fire, right?" Music seemed to be coming from the trees. A light show overtook the sky, rivaling the atmosphere of any of the nightclubs we had found our way into over these past couple of years. The spirit was just raucous enough. We shook our heads at his reference to that VIP space within the Lexington's club. "I was skeptical about angels' collective ability to have fun. But these guys are letting their hair down."

"Work hard, play hard, right?"

"I mean, did you *see* the blond twins breakdancing?"

"Is that what was going on? I was worried it was some sort of delayed time-release demon toxin at work. And I mean that as a compliment."

"Yeah, no, lemme tell you there's no antidote for what was going on on that dance floor. I told 'em to teach you some moves."

"Never know when something like 'the worm' could come in handy," I laughed. "Maybe on the next trip through those narrow tunnels to the catacombs."

"That's what I'm talkin' about!" he joked. But I knew the banter was cover, I could feel it. From the way he looked down at his glass, I could see the shift coming. "So…" he started. "You guys are going back down when the portals open?"

"That's the plan," I shrugged. I knew I would need to be up here, that my office would be that Illumination Chamber and that people depended on me. But I also knew that the demon portals would be closed at least until the winter solstice, and probably much longer. They had been wounded, weakened and banished below and all of that would not be overcome for years and possibly generations. "We're gonna rebuild Paris for a little while, maybe get some college credit for it, you know, while the guardian work is slow. And then pick that back up, up here and all, when things start heating up again." It was all so vastly different from what I had thought I would be doing, if I had been asked this question two years earlier. And yet, I knew with all my soul that this is what I was meant to do. I also knew what Dante was going to say. "But maybe I should be asking *you* that question," I said it with a smile, knocking my shoulder against his, letting him know it was OK.

"Hav," he started, a nervous edge to his voice. "You know, you did an amazing thing: you freed Henry when you killed the Prince. He can go back now; the curse is lifted, he can work in the field again. He wants to do that, for a little while at least. And they, the Administration, asked me if I wanted to…kinda like…take his place for a bit. I guess it doesn't have to be the most physically powerful one here, just someone who can kind of motivate everyone. And it won't be forever, just a little while. So, anyway, I'm thinking about staying here when the portals open. I'm excited but sad to be away from you and Lance and all and I hope you don't…"

"Hey," I stopped him, with a smile. "Who do you think nominated you for the job?"

Dante brightened at this. "Seriously?"

"Of course. But it's not like they hadn't already thought of it—you're perfect. It's so Dante." It was true. Connor and I had spoken of this on our walk too. He had said I was welcome to fill the role but added, "I've always gotten the feeling you wouldn't be content to stay in one place too long. There's a surprising restlessness to you, it's what makes you so good at what you do for us here. You like to be on the ground, in the fight. It's where you belong." It was not a way I ever would have thought to describe myself. But Connor had always seen me first as my angel self. That version was far more fearless than the me that engaged with the mortal world, the me that had trouble matching a dress with the right pair of shoes or knowing what a date night was supposed to look like. But he was right; I did want to be everywhere, not just in that Illumination Chamber. "You're unlike any angel we've ever had here, so I guess we'll have to let you craft how you do your job," Connor had said. I asked if that was like choosing my own independent study major and he had laughed. And when I told him, without a doubt, it should be Dante to fill that role, he said he couldn't agree more.

"Thanks, Hav," Dante kissed me on the cheek. "And, you know, we'll be back together in no time. You're gonna have to be up here plenty. I guess it'll just be like if we went to different colleges or something and saw each other at breaks. No biggie." He said it almost convincingly. I wouldn't let myself think of what those months away from Dante might be like. I would miss him desperately, but I knew the time apart would make no difference really. A best friend occupies a special place in your heart. They're always with you even when they're miles— or worlds—away.

"Right, no sweat," I agreed. "And Max?" I asked, nodding toward him dancing in the distance, one eye on Dante.

"Yeah, he's staying up here."

"Good thing. Someone needs to make sure you don't get into too much trouble, even among angels."

"We're angels but we're not saints," he joked, repeating that quote from Connor that we loved.

"Amen to that," I laughed.

"Speaking of, if you'll excuse me, I see a devilishly handsome angel in need of a dance partner." As he said it though, he looked over my shoulder for a moment.

"Get outta here already." I pushed him in Max's direction.

Dante looked above my head and smiled, "She's all yours," he said with a wave.

I gazed up and found Lance, sitting atop those high hedges. He nodded back at Dante then floated down.

"It's tough to be a wallflower with these," he said, nodding to his wings. "But with those"—he jerked his chin towards mine—"forget it." I shook my head, embarrassed. He had pulled his wings back in now, I noticed most of the others had done the same. I did too. "For the record," he whispered in my ear. "I think those are pretty badass." He said it sweetly, giving a line reading from an old script of ours and I had to smile. He had said that to me before, about my scars, back when I had first shown them to him at the Lexington, before we really knew each other. We had been through so much since then.

"Thanks, yours too." I answered just as I had back then, so he knew I remembered.

"Thank you," he said, his warm brown eyes glowing.

"So, I can't help but notice we're still alive," I said and watched the recognition flash in his eyes this time. He had said this to me in the alley behind the burning Lexington after the prom.

"We are, aren't we?" he laughed. "So, are we even yet?"

"Oh, you and me? The ongoing life-saving toll?"

"Yeah, that."

"Thanks, by the way."

"No problem."

"And, yeah, I think we may be even. I mean, until next time."

"Because there will probably be a next time."

"Because there will probably be a next time," I repeated. "Though hopefully not for a while.

"Well, if we've got more of this ahead of us then I'm going to need you there," he answered, recalling another promise we had made. "And," he reached in his pocket. "I thought we had decided not to throw these away." He held out his hand. In his open palm lay my necklace, which the Prince had torn from me. The brass key charm shone brightly alongside the angel wing, the fleur-de-lis and the tiny clock on a repaired gold chain. It felt like so much history, this artifact. He swept my hair to one side to fasten it around my neck. "So imagine my surprise when I found this on my way to Notre Dame."

"You know I didn't throw—"

"Of course, I know," he cut me off, serious, and I could see the worry in his eyes. We had come so very close to losing each other so many times.

"How did you....?"

"It was just blinding, it caught the light from the fire. I was flying, fast as I could after that battle, trying to find you, and I spotted this instead. And, I just..." He shook his head; he didn't have to go on. "I tried to see it as something hopeful, but I didn't know."

"We'll look out for each other," I said, simply, echoing the promise we had made at the start of everything. This was our shorthand, leaning on these words we had told each other back before we had any idea what trials we would face together. Before we knew what we would mean to each other. The sentiments had never been truer, and yet they also couldn't begin to convey the depth of feeling between us. Watching his eyes, I saw everything I felt reflected back at me. We understood: we were each other's guardian angels and so much more. His hand still at my neck, where he had fastened the chain with those charms, he pulled me in to kiss me.

In the distance, the celebration beat on and a calm washed over me, the warmth that comes with a true sense of belonging. That group was my family; they had been with me as I had become this version of myself. This was a home, and in this place I had purpose. The music pulsed in my veins and the lights cast their muted glow above us, flickering in time with my heartbeat. For once, I wasn't thinking ahead. I breathed in Lance and the sweet flower-perfumed air, soaked in the peace and joy of this day and this place and this moment. We had fought hard-won battles to get here; we had made sacrifices; we were alive and embarking on a new life. In my mind, I slowed the sweeping hands of the clock to savor it all.

Epilogue

It was while awaiting the portal's reopening that the idea came to me. With the Administration's blessing, I recorded these experiences in the hope they would be useful to future angels-in-training like you. It is my understanding that these three volumes will be made available to you when you first learn of your identity. I hope you find all you need to guide you to your own initiation one day. You have great challenges ahead through the battles and tests of Metamorphosi, but none that you can't handle.

To be an angel, I understand now, is to accept that you do not fit in anywhere else. It is a difficult life but a rewarding one. The highs are intoxicating and the lows are defeating. My journey wasn't a perfect one. None are. But I learned from my missteps and I hope you may as well. I've also shared those personal relationships most dear to me because I would not have been the same without them. I credit them with my survival.

Since the events of this account, Lance and I have gone on to aid the Great Reconstruction of Paris, as it was called, and we still haunt Montmartre. We feel at home there. We spend a good deal of time in the angel realm searching for signs of demons and preparing for the next Metamorphosi. Some have begun to resurface but it has taken many years. The demons we have hunted we destroyed easily, and they have posed little threat to the new angels who have emerged. During times of relative peace, we have even been so bold as to send for our beloved parents, allowing them to visit us here in Montmartre. We keep in touch as best we can, with encrypted messages that would be unreadable to anyone but their intended audience. But we guard our families fiercely, which means we can't allow ourselves to keep as close as we would like. I miss Joan. But I cherish what time I do have with her. And though they have all been advised to keep their transmissions to us short and spare, Joan writes long, meandering notes almost daily. And I love her for it.

I am often asked what became of Lucian. Did I check in on him after his return to life? Yes, I did. And I continue to do so. It's been a few years now and yet that's all it has taken for him to grow into the person he wanted to be and had sold his soul to become. Like a doctor attached to a patient whose life she saved, I visit him every January on the anniversary of my first day at the Lexington. He has graduated from college—he transferred to Northwestern, in fact—and lives in Chicago. I've watched him get his first job; I've watched him find a home and friends and even fall in love. I will watch him grow older and wiser and more successful, as I remain seventeen, which is something I still can't entirely grasp. But he is my greatest achievement, living a life of his own creation now. It gives me comfort to see him; it inspires me. But there is still the slightest pang there too, I admit. I've stood across an L platform watching him breathe in the cold air of a winter evening, waiting for that Ravenswood line to take him home. On a good day, I might catch a glimpse of those wings on his wrist, or he might offer the kind smile one gives a stranger. And then I wonder if there might be some memory of me locked deep in his subconscious, the kind of thing that pushes through in a dream. But that's when I take my leave, as silently and stealthily as I arrived, causing no ripples in his life. I will usually just go on ahead to visit Joan, who I do miss, and then soar onward back up above where I'm grateful to be among those who understand me and who have their own souls to watch over with a similar bittersweet satisfaction.

The best advice I have for you is that which was given to me by Connor and intended for our guardian angel assignments, but I always kept in mind for myself too: no one knows what life holds in store for us, the best we can do is keep our eyes and hearts open and our souls strong. Be ready for anything, including greatness. The most seemingly unremarkable day just may be the one that changes your life and sets you on that path toward who you're meant to be—and when you find yourself on that journey, don't just deign to be led to your destiny—fly boldly toward it.

The End

Acknowledgments

Many, many, many thanks to....

My fantastic publishers around the world.

The truly amazing Stéphanie Abou, friend and agent extraordinaire. You are the very best. (And an extra *merci* for correcting all of my French!)

The fabulous Stephanie Land.

The incredible Richard Ford.

My encouraging pals: you all know who you are and I adore you! With an extra shout-out to Jami Bjellos, Sasha Issenberg, Jenny Laws, Albert Lee, the Louisiana gang, Jessica and Andres Lucas, Ryan Lynch, Kevin O'Leary, Jennifer O'Neill, Marta Pozzan, Poornima Ravishankar, Cara Lynn Shultz, Anna Siri, Kate Stroup, Jennie Teitelbaum, Kate Zeller, Eric Andersson and my pals at *Us Weekly*.

My loving family: awesome parents Bill and Risa and sis Karen (my beloved first reader, you rock!), and super supportive in-laws Steve, Ilene, Lauren, David, Gabrielle and Jill.

My three favorite guys: Brian, Sawyer and Hardy—the best characters a girl could ever hope to be around!

And, finally, an enormous thank you to *you*, dear reader, for following Haven's adventures through these three books. I hope you've enjoyed her journey as much as I've enjoyed writing it and I hope we'll meet again in the pages of another book!

A Bonus Short Story!

Turn the page to find out what happened to Lance—in his own words!—after he was captured and imprisoned in the underworld at the end of *Infatuate*....

LANCE'S INFERNO

A GILDED WINGS STORY

AIMEE AGRESTI

"Abandon all hope, ye who enter here."

THE INFERNO by Dante Alighieri

I am on fire. That is the only explanation.

The flames wrap around me. Tighter. Blistering my skin. But it's more than that. A vortex. Pulling me with its searing grip through this tunnel, a space that does not want me. It wants to shear my skin from me. I am not falling. That would be passive. This is violent, active.

Where is Haven? Is she here? Is she safe or…no, won't even think it. Where are the others? WHERE AM I?

An electric zap flays me, every nerve stinging. Skin—liquefying. In seconds there may be nothing left. There is a screeching all around me like microphone feedback. Soundtrack of madness. Then it stops.

Fight. NOW. You are stronger than this. My lungs rip from my chest, straining to produce sound. None comes.

Am I dying? How would I know?

I hear nothing. See nothing. Black. Then shades of blood. Fresh crimson, sticky maroon.

Search your mind: fight with science, fact, logic, numbers. This is your arsenal.

Numbers breed calm. Calm breeds escape. Math, science: your saviors.

There is this: Human flesh is destroyed at 162 degrees Fahrenheit. Mine is not purely human still, is it? I am angel.

Wingless, for now, but angel. *Believe in that*, I force myself. Imagine angel skin hardening into armor, cells changing. My heart beats outside my body, uncaged.

YOU NEED A REASON TO LIVE. My mind fastens on her. Grips her image. *Haven.* Kissing her in the rain. Minutes ago. I had thought that *that* would have been the end of it tonight. The battle won, for now. The two of us alive. Together. Not this, not whatever this is. I let that scene, the two of us, play on a loop as I burn. Is she…alive? I need to believe she is.

Where are they, Haven and the others? Maybe it is not them, it is me:

I am gone.

They are on Royal Street still. New Orleans—with that storm raging. Mardi Gras. The city destroyed by devil and nature. A day made for mass killing and destruction. So many gathered to celebrate while the underworld assembled for chaos. Our second test for wings. We had almost made it through the night, battling those creatures unleashed in the crowd, saving so many souls. We fought for our own souls too, and Haven and I had *survived. Again.* We were seconds from their underworld portal closing, from peace, when we all converged. The Prince hooked his demon arm around my neck, clamped his hand like fire on my bicep and there was that flash, like a lightbulb exploding when turned on. Then this fierce ache as I began to hurtle.

I am dying.

NO. Logic, science, calm. FIGHT.

I should be numb by now. But I still feel pain. Yes. In pain there is hope. Sound trickles into the silence. That high-pitched static again. Still cannot see. Haven. Rain. My hands in her hair, pulling her to me. My heart flares: Does she know? I have to survive long enough to tell her.

Haven has to know. She has to know not just how surely, madly, I love her but this: I did not lead the Prince blindly to her. She can't think that. I kept him away as long as I could. I thought the clock would run out as we arrived on Royal Street. *It SHOULD have run out.* This should not have happened.

Did she see the look I gave her when I said *Lucian* had found me? I knew it wasn't really him. I knew it was the Prince. That he had traveled from the underworld, shapeshifting into the form of an ally in order to break us apart. But there was no time to explain. I thought the Prince would have dematerialized by then, he should have been gone at midnight. It makes no sense. This is the science of their realm, the nature of their world. Science, I trust—even a dark science that governs a world I don't understand.

Are there no consequences for breaking these rules in their world? Why do they exist if—

Moving faster now. I am a comet, trailing fire—it comes off of me in streaks.

Fire slices through me again. The blaze crackling within me. A pressure collects inside my heart, my chest, my head, crushing the living parts of me.

My body slams into hot stone. My bones smack against it.

I am too broken to move. It is still cooler on my skin than wherever I have just been.

Another discovery: *I am breathing.* And feeling. That hand, still gripping my arm, eases. A guttural groan beside me, a wounded beast. My body begins to cool, sweat pouring from me as steam. The fire extinguishing from within—for now. Before I take a second breath, the creature yanks me to my feet. The haze lifts and the world turns on again.

But it's different.

A cavern of darkness: stone and low-burning fire. There is no mistaking it. I am here, in the underworld, realm of demons. Flickering torches line cave-like walls. My legs struggle to keep up, my vision still unclear. Can't tell if my glasses are still on my face. Who is dragging me down this corridor? Focus my eyes. He is taller, more solid than me. Older.

The Prince.

A voice I don't recognize calls from the distance, "A pris-oner—victory!" The Prince is too fast, careening and unsteady. We stumble, colliding with a pair of men—no, they couldn't be much older than me, boys—in black uniforms, soldiers in a dark army. The tall one with ruddy cheeks is still talking:

"Sir! Shall we wait for the rest or assist—"

The Prince smacks him across the face and storms away, tripping as he pulls me along.

We reach a clearing, fire raging above us, suspended like a cloud formation. The Prince stumbles, taking me down with him. We hit the rocky ground hard.

He roars, grabbing his chest, as though having a heart attack. Do these creatures *have* hearts? I'm pinned beneath him, cheek against the hot stone walkway. Urgent footsteps echo. I try to shake him off, want to run. No time. Black military boots stop before my eyes. Someone jerks me up to my feet, nearly pulling my arm from its socket.

The Prince growls—pure sick rage. He punches the ground hard enough to dent the stone. I feel a chill, even here.

"Careful, sire," the man says, sounding bored, as the Prince stands again. "Perhaps you should have taken a less turbulent passage back here. I would say we should go directly to the war room but I fear you need rest. I have never seen you quite so...*diminished*."

The Prince smooths his hair, grips my bicep, burning me again. But even in this half-light I can see his skin is wan, sweaty.

"I must remind you to consider the tone you take with me, Duke," the Prince says grinning, as sinister as I've ever seen. His eyes shift just behind the Duke: the torches lining the corridor flare. Flames balloon to encompass nearly the entire passageway, almost licking us where we stand. The fire singes the back of the Duke's head. He straightens up, grimaces just a moment.

"Of course, sir," the Duke bows. At once the fire retreats. "Then might I suggest you and I do retire to the war room and Trevor take your prize into his custody?" A uniformed figure steps forward from the shadows, standing at attention. He is a stranger to me but would've fit in among the demons of the Lexington Hotel. Slick and soulless.

"Indeed," the Prince sighs. He snaps his gaze to my wrists— fiery handcuffs encircle them—and then my feet—flaming shackles appear.

The screams wake me. They are ragged and pained. I am sweating, woozy. I last remember being shoved into this cell, a space like a pocket within an igneous boulder. Flaming bars seal me inside—it's nearly a curtain of fire. The heat overwhelms this confined space.

More screams, rasped and raw: a girl's voice. I know it. I would know it anywhere. It brings me to my feet, strength I didn't know I had. Involuntary.

Haven. Where is she? The fiery bars dull, fusing into a line on the ground and burning down a dark corridor in the direction of her voice. I follow, passing other cells, some with wailing prisoners inside. With each step my handcuffs and ankle shackles fade until they are gone.

A piercing shriek. My body jerks to run, but can't. I drag my limp legs, feeling drugged.

"*Lance...Lance...Lance...*" It comes as a desperate whisper, a quiet chant. My body finds strength, messy limbs shooting toward a dim light at the end of this passage. As I grow closer I hear water, sheets of rain. I stumble out of the tunnel and the shock stops me: I am on Royal Street again. The French Quarter of New Orleans, just outside our apartment. Mardi Gras night. It's the night of our second test for angel wings. Haven stands in the distance. I try to run but my legs are still too heavy. Not far from Haven, something shoots out from the shadows: a silhouette taking aim at her. It strikes her. She collapses. It happens so fast. I try to yell, but have no voice. The demons disappear. Haven lies in the wet street, skirt and shirt clinging to her, rain pouring down on her. A spike pokes out from her heart: the poisoned weapon of the demons. *Isn't this what* almost *happened? But it didn't lodge in her heart, she fought it, she was OK. I got to her sooner then. She was alive. I kissed her lips. My fingertips remember her smooth, wet skin, the pulse beating at her neck.* But now, I gather her listless body in my arms. Her eyes are open, but they don't see me. They are dead, like her. The rain pools around us, thick and sticky. I pinch my fingers, they are tacky with her blood. The scream tears out of me, I clutch her body against my chest. I was too late—but how? Even as I hold her, I am being pulled away. I feel my body being ripped from this scene, as it was when the Prince took me.

I slam against rocky ground, my body weak. It's black again. I see nothing.

The screams wake me. They are ragged and pained. I am sweating, woozy. I last remember being shoved into this cell. Flaming bars seal me inside. Screams again, a girl's voice: I would know it anywhere: Haven.

I follow the fiery path to Royal Street. Haven is struck, she drops to the street. Dead. I am too late.

The screams wake me. They are ragged and pained. I am sweating, woozy. Flaming bars seal me inside my cell. I last remember a sick feeling of loss and failure but I don't know why. Screams again, a girl's voice. I would know it anywhere: Haven.

I follow the fiery path to Royal Street. Haven dying in the street. I am too late.

The screams wake me again. With a dull rock I make a hatch mark in the ground beside me. Counting. This is the fifteenth time I have done this. I don't know what will happen next but I understand that this has happened before. My mind is sorting itself out. A fog is lifting, however slowly. Haven screams my name, I go to her. I am too late.

The screams wake me again. With a rock I make a hatch mark in the ground beside me. Counting. This is the twenty-first time I have done this. Haven cries out my name. But my body remains still. My mind says, *Wait. Think.* I take a deep breath.

Clouds fade and an idea smacks me: *I have done this before.* The screams are Haven's, but I have done this *twenty times* before. I don't think these creatures want me to know I've done this before. That is the torture of it; that is what destroys a person.

I am in a fever dream. Endless and looping. Some part of this is not real. Memories flood me now: I will follow this path and somehow be on Royal Street again. I will go to her, and be too late. Again. I remember now. She can't keep dying. Either she died once and I keep rewatching it. Or...maybe.... there is a better answer.

I follow that fiery path, with my eyes truly open, for the first time. My brain not muddled. My pace picks up, I am able to run. I'm not as strong as I should be, but I'm not paralyzed. I will get to her this time. I will grab her away from that spear. I'll let it hit me instead. If I'm still too slow, I will find my voice, I will yell. She can elude them, she's done it before. She can probably do this all without me. Why was she so helpless? *This is not the Haven I know.*

I reach this warped version of Royal Street.

Wait. *This is NOT the Haven I know.* Haven would fight back.

This is someone trying to torture and trick me. Make me give up, stop wanting to live. I stare her down.

"SABINE!" I shout into the storm, calling out Haven's nemesis, the demon charged with destroying her on Mardi Gras night. "SABINE! Only a coward hides behind the face of a hero."

At once it all stops. The rain. The thunder. The fire. I look up and I don't see the dark sky, I see faces in the clouds—not poetry, there are *faces* up there. *People.* I'm being watched. We are in a theater and I am *the show.* My suffering. This is what goes on here. They watch like this is a gladiator arena and I am the one being mauled by tigers. The Prince is seated above me in this colosseum. His face glows red, shock in his eyes. Silence. Hundreds of sets of eyes, but silence. I turn around to see them all, to take it in. It's not enough for them to have captured me or for them to win. They need this spectacle too.

"Can he SEE us? Why can he SEE us?" The Prince barks, bolting up from his throne.

"He's powerful, willful," the Duke, standing beside him, responds in that bored tone. "I warned you of this, sire." Do they not know that I can *hear* them?

The Prince whips past him, knocking into the Duke's shoulder. The force sends the less powerful demon stumbling back a few steps. The Prince heads for a doorway.

I can feel his rage, electric in my veins. *No. Wait.* This rage is my own: I am seething. I won't let them think they can defeat us. I can't stop myself.

"If you want to kill me, come do it yourself!" I shout up at him. It is not smart. But I don't care. Gasps from the surrounding audience, this must not be how this usually goes. Good. The Prince stops with a shudder, like he's been stabbed in the back. He turns. I yell again: "WHERE IS SHE?"

He stares down with deadly eyes that tell me he wants to kill me. My boiling blood won't cool. "TELL ME NOW!" I roar at him, I am now the animal in this gladiator match.

My body lunges, throwing itself onto the smooth black stones of the arena wall. I scale it with strong, fast limbs until I'm standing at the top, just before the front row of spectators. They run from me.

"Go on and fight me!" I hold out my arms, daring him. "Doesn't even matter what happens to me in this battle. You're not gonna win the war. She's too smart for you."

He doesn't say a word, only raises his open palm in my direction. That microphone-feedback screech assaults me again. And pain. A bolt to my chest like lightning.

I see Haven. In the rain. I'm kissing her. Again.

Then I see nothing.

***

I am back on the Ferris wheel at Navy Pier. You are sitting across from me, gazing into the sky. I want to kiss you but I can't. I have, already, during that blackout at the hotel, opening night. But I am sure you didn't know it was me. Maybe I should be flattered that you thought it had been Lucian. That you wouldn't have expected that from me. But now I'm in this strange no man's land: you don't know that we had this…electricity… between us in the darkness, that it was ME. *And I sure as hell can't tell you that right now. So I don't speak because I don't know what to say. If I try to combine words into sentences, I will likely come up with a variation of: "I am inexplicably in love with you." Love. Not something I remotely understand. Not logical at all. I don't know you that well, really. But I know you better, already, than I've ever known anyone. You showed me your scars and you accept mine. Literally, the physical ones. And figuratively too. You are a true friend, and you are kind, taking me here. And I love you for that.*

But I can't say any of this. So I watch the clouds, the dull lake the color of cold. And when you're not looking at me, I am looking at you and wondering how this happened. And how I can keep feeling this way. And how I might kiss you again someday.

Screams awaken me.

"Witching hour," the voice is not Trevor's. "The other prisoners." He steps into the glow cast by the flaming bars. I brace myself, want to stand, but can't. Too weak. I lay on the hot stone floor of my cell. The boy is wearing that same military uniform and looks my age, like he could've sat next to me in AP Euro. But weathered. Dark circles ring his hollow eyes; his black hair is greasy, wild. The boy reaches out his arm as his eyes fix on the fiery shackles around my wrists and ankles. The restraints slowly fade until they're gone. "Sorry, I'm not so good at that," he says. "I'm new." I flex my wrists, stretch my ankles. My body is made of lead.

He extends his arm through the fiery bars: he wants to shake my hand. "It's an honor. I'm Victor," he whispers. "And I need to get out of here too. Help me, and I can help you."

It doesn't make sense. He is too kind for this place. My reflex is not to trust, but my gut tells me he's genuine. I might shake his hand. If I could.

"Can't move," my voice sounds like something dragged through gravel.

"Of course," he pulls back, looks apologetic. "Your powers will return. I'll give you weaker shackles. You'll be better soon, just don't let them know." He whispers, quick and efficient. Eyes shifting like he could get caught any minute.

I have no strength and two vital questions, so I struggle, finding the air to push them out:

"Why didn't he kill me?" I groan.

"You're too valuable. You're bait." A surge in my veins: my dead heart charging up again. He's saved me some trouble, answering my second question before I ask. I am grateful. He must have seen this.

"Yes, bait for her. She's alive. He wanted to take her that night but he failed. He will use you to get her now and then he'll kill you both."

She's alive. I have no use for the rest of what he said. Except: "When?"

"Only his circle knows, but soon. I will tell you everything I can find out. But I need to escape. I've made mistakes but I need to try again. At life, you know? I've hurt people. I've let people down. I left someone behind." He is quiet for a moment. I can see him thinking, as though he is somewhere in the past. "I've let the demons take my soul and my mind. I sold myself for, for….for so little. I need to start over." He doesn't have to say anything more. I've seen enough of how this world works, I understand. "Promise to help?"

"How?" It aches to speak, my ribs feel shattered. I don't know why he would think I could be useful to him in this state.

"It will be chaos, when it starts. I'll be in the group guarding you. But I'll turn on them and fight against them all, if you'll take me with you when you escape."

He has an awful lot of confidence in me. Still, it costs me nothing to give him that same hope. I nod.

"Thank you," he says, exhaling as though in relief.

Over the next many days a series of soldiers come and go, Victor among them. It seems almost hourly, this rotation of monsters. Some taunt me, others spit fire at me, Trevor shoots actual bolts at me as he cackles. I lay motionless, silent, acting withered and defeated.

But I'm not.

My shackles are mostly for show, I can move with them. They aren't siphoning off my strength as before. When I'm alone, I train. At first the most basic exercises are impossible: situps, pushups. But soon I can run up the side of my cell and flip backward on to my feet. I am strong again. My mind too: always, I think of Haven. Of that night at the botanical garden. Or the night the lights went out at the Lexington Hotel and I found her in the dark. Or when we watched the hotel burn from the alley after prom, our clothes in tatters, her hair scented by her tangerine shampoo and the charred building. Or that night in the rain. I think of her eyes, the way she looks at me when we have survived another of these scrapes.

I will never again let her wonder how I feel for her. I will make sure she knows. If I ever get out.

Victor hasn't spoken since that first day. He diverts his eyes as though he's being monitored. But on this day, he looks at me as he passes and whispers an unfamiliar word: "*Xoxocotlan.*" And then, "*Mexico. Two weeks.*"

I don't know what that means but my mind works at it. In another few days, he speaks again.

"*Merry. Romania.*"

Then: "*Zentralfriedhof. Vienna.*" The first part is central in
German. Central something. And for some reason I can picture these words, I've seen them. Where? Somewhere behind
plastic. With mom. Yes: On the back of her old Beethoven
CDs at home. She played classical music at the orphanage, she
always said she believed it was soothing to the kids. She had
read somewhere that it made babies smarter or something. She
joked that that's why I turned out the way I did, she played it
from the moment I showed up there. Made me take piano les-
sons too. I didn't mind, music is math. She was always reading
those child psychology books while she listened. She loved us
all. I was lucky, wasn't I? The photo was of Beethoven's grave.
This is a cemetery. We are going to a cemetery. For some reason,
this knowledge is reassuring. It begins to feel real, a fight is
coming but now I will be ready.

Days later Victor looks nervous. Speaks again.
"None of those were right. I'm sorry. It's tomorrow." He
freezes. Eyes darting. I hear it too: Footsteps echoing in the
corridor. He backs away from me like I'm poisonous and then
he is gone.

The next day, a dozen of them come in. Trevor leads them
and with an open palm, as though catching a ball, he extin-
guishes the bars of my cell. He tugs me to my feet and Victor
steps forward to hold my other arm. The others create a barrier
around us as they march me to that landing with the fire suspended above. So many are walking, a mass exodus. They stop
for us to join the procession. There is chatter among them and
Victor whispers, barely moving his lips:
"Père-Lachaise. Paris." These places were all cemeteries, of
course. "*Now.*" But he chokes on "now," his eyes bulging, and

pitches forward onto me. I try to catch him, but my shackles pull tighter than they've been in weeks. He hits the ground. A fiery bolt, shaped like a dagger, wedged between his shoulder blades.

"Oh, Victor," Trevor shakes his head, smirking. "Such potential." My stomach drops. This is an introduction to the horror that awaits me. I hadn't expected anything from Victor, barely knew him, but he was an ally where I have none. I am unmoored. Alone. Again.

The Duke pats Trevor on the back, then signals the group to make way. "Fine work. Let's not get cocky now. More to be done." A hush falls and the mass kneels, bowing their heads. The Prince takes his place at the front of the group. I am the only one standing, shackles flaming. He stops before me.

"You are being led to your death," he says with a wide grin, delicious hatred. "And to her death as well. Onward."

The group rises, chanting in a language I don't know. Their own language. As one they march with burning purpose. To Père-Lachaise cemetery in Paris. To destroy my angels, my friends. My Haven. I understand now.

I am swept along, fiery shackles infecting me, weakening me. But I will get there, to Père-Lachaise. I will fight. And I will reach Haven before they do. I have to. I trudge on, dreaming of a new beginning for us....